The Gamester

The Gamester

G.K. COLLIER

St. Martin's Press
New York

THE GAMESTER. Copyright © 1994 by G. K. Collier. All rights reserved. Printed in the United States of America. No part of this book may be used or reproduced in any manner whatsoever without written permission except in the case of brief quotations embodied in critical articles or reviews. For information, address St. Martin's Press, 175 Fifth Avenue, New York, N.Y. 10010.

Library of Congress Cataloging-in-Publication Data

Collier, G. K.
The gamester / G.K. Collier.
p.   cm.
ISBN 0-312-11277-7
1. Gamblers—England—Fiction.   2. Man-woman relationships—England—Fiction.   I. Title.
PR6053.042368G36   1994
813'.54—dc20   94-18213   CIP

First published in Great Britain by Robert Hale Limited.

First U.S. Edition: October 1994
10 9 8 7 6 5 4 3 2 1

To my beloved family
and to the treasured memory of a very dear aunt
Gladys Annie Vernon
who so enjoyed reading a Romance

One

It was almost dawn when they brought their captive into the prison on the outskirts of the city and handed him over to the turnkey. He was led away through a maze of narrow passages with walls of stone, inches thick, which rang the echoes of their footsteps as they marched inexorably onwards. The air was chill and fetid, no breath of the fresh, new day penetrated into these noisome warrens, no shaft of sunlight pierced this indelible gloom. Only the flickering flame of the gaoler's lantern brought grotesquely capering shadows out of the darkness behind them, to creep furtively in their wake. Once or twice the deep silence was broken by eery cries and soft moans as of some poor wretches in troubled and tormented sleep. The prisoner shivered involuntarily.

Now they were descending a flight of steps and ahead of them loomed a low-arched doorway. He was obliged to duck his head before passing through it to enter a vaulted, torch-lit chamber in which stood a large, iron-barred cell containing some thirty or forty men. The stench was sickening and pulling a white silk handkerchief from his coat-sleeve, he held it to his nose, the chains on his wrists jangling dismally.

"*Lasciate ogni speranza voi ch'entrate,*" he muttered beneath his breath. The gaoler unlocked the door with one of the great keys hanging from the belt about his vast girth and, jerking his head, indicated that the prisoner should enter.

The gentleman, for so indeed he appeared to be judging from his attire, responded with a slight, mocking bow and stepped into the cell. He looked about him calm-eyed, for all the world as if he had just entered the finest salon in Rome.

Behind him, the door clanged to and the key rattled in the lock.

'Thank you, my good man,' he called after the retreating figure of the gaoler. 'The accommodation is not precisely to my taste, I must confess. I should have preferred a private room myself, however I am not one to complain and shall make the best of your notion of hospitality.' Then to himself, 'Ah! I think I perceive a sitting-room.'

Carefully he picked his way over the sleeping bodies on the straw-strewn floor, until he reached a place spacious enough for his requirements and eased himself into a sitting position with his back against the damp wall.

Sighing resignedly, he tilted his hat over his eyes, crossed his long, booted legs, folded his hands restfully on his stomach and composed himself for sleep. After some little while he gradually began to drift into a doze but was soon roused again when the man lying beside him fell into a sudden paroxysm, his whole body racked with the violence of the seizure.

The gentleman leapt to his feet and quickly made his way towards the bowl of water that he had noticed in a corner of the cell. A wooden scoop lay beside it and he swiftly filled it and brought it to the sick man. Gently he lifted him up until the drooping head rested against his broad shoulder and then he put the ladle to the man's pallid lips.

Gratefully, his fellow prisoner sipped the water and lay back in the gentleman's arms, his breathing harsh and ragged. When eventually he recovered enough to speak, he thanked his companion in English.

'Save your breath, my friend,' the gentleman replied. 'There is little enough that I can do for you in this devil's pit. Rest easy now, you will feel better in a few moments.'

'You ... you are an Englishman!' the poor fellow gasped breathlessly, the dull eyes flying to his comforter's face.

'I prefer to think of myself as a cosmopolitan. How come you to be here in Italy and in such extremity?'

'My story is a long one and I have not the breath to tell it to you now. It is five years and more since I was last in England and I fear that this foul dungeon will prove my last resting place. As you see, my health is quite broken down and even were I not lying here so helpless, I doubt that I should ever be able to survive the journey home.'

His voice was wistful and he lapsed into silence for a while. Then he raised his eyes again and continued, 'My name is Richard Colton and I am a lawyer by profession. You see me languishing here for the want of fifty pounds, although it might as well be a thousand for all the hope I have of ever possessing such a sum. But you, sir, you look to be a gentleman of means, I think. What is your misfortune that brings you to such a place as this?'

'Oh, I am here at the whim of a perverse fate. The cards were stacked against me tonight and though misfortune did indeed bring me hither, it is Madam Luck shall escort me hence, I'll wager. She and I are seldom parted for long!'

'You speak like a gamester, sir,' Colton commented with a wan smile.

'We are all gamesters, my friend, as long as we have breath. Each of us has a hand to play; it is all a question of skill, good judgement and a quantity of luck in this hazardous game of life,' he smiled gaily. 'And life has taught me a trick or two, I own. I find I am an adept at calculating the odds and summing up an opponent's hand. My discards are seldom reckless and I have learnt never to register a disappointment. Allow me to introduce myself, James Farenden *à votre service, m'sieur*.'

Mr Colton lifted a feeble hand and it was immediately taken in a firm grasp. 'I am delighted to make your acquaintance, Mr Farenden. It is a long while since I had the pleasure of conversing in my native tongue. When were you last in England? Tell me what news you have.'

'Alas, I cannot oblige you, Mr Colton, for I cannot recall ever being in England.'

'But you speak English faultlessly!' cried Mr Colton in great surprise. 'And you have an English name.'

'What's in a name? Actually I was born in Paris and as for my tongue, it clacks as nimbly in French, Spanish and Italian. I might also engage to entertain you in passable German and even a little Russian or Portuguese.'

'Indeed? You seem a very resourceful gentleman.

Perhaps you may soon win your freedom from this cell; your friends will not desert you I am sure. When you do accomplish your release, you ought to go to England and if you do, remember me and visit the south lands. Go to Sussex and walk upon the Downs. I tell you in all truth that you have never breathed air as sweet as the air of the English countryside when it mingles with the scent of the sea.'

He ceased speaking and Farenden guessed that his thoughts were far away, hovering over the distant fields and woodlands of his beloved homeland.

'Courage, Mr Colton! We shall both win free of this prison and you may yourself return to your own country.'

The old man gave a croak of laughter. 'There speaks the optimism of youth. Oh, that I had a little of your young blood flowing through my veins! I do believe then that I still might hope.'

'Ah, but Mr Colton, you have forgot, I think, that you are still in this game. Do not throw your hand in just yet, I think the odds are about to fall in our favour. Listen! Do you hear voices?'

He jumped up and, leaping over the sleeping forms crowding the floor, reached the door of the cell just as the gaoler reappeared, closely followed by an elegantly dressed gentleman.

'Justin! I thought I recognized your Oxford accent mutilating the poetic music of mine host's native tongue. I must say you have it pruned to a nicety, for once a delight to my ears. You are a capital fellow to have managed the thing so neatly.'

'*Buongiorno*, James, *mio amico*. My sincere apologies for leaving you kicking your heels in this loathsome hole for so long but I had the devil of a time trying to make these imbeciles understand their own language. Now what are you laughing at? I am amazed that you can find anything humorous about this vile situation,' he complained, waving a scented handkerchief to his aristocratic nostrils.

'My amusement is the result of a lively imagination coupled with a knowledge of your linguistic abilities. I take it that despite your obvious deficiencies in that area of your education, I am about to be granted my freedom?'

'Yes you are, it is the least I could do for you under the circumstances. Now, would you save me any further mental anguish and instruct this portly Charon to bring you up out of this malodorous Hades without further delay?'

'*Si, certo*. But first, do you still have the money that you won last night?'

'Yes, I have most of it. I had to give this fat fellow some to grease his palm; he was intent on keeping you for a few more days otherwise. Why? You need not give him more, I have already been most generous.'

'I want to bring a friend with me, he is dissatisfied with the accommodation here and I wish to pay his shot. Give me your purse and I will arrange matters with our greedy landlord.'

Thus it was that after months of hopeless captivity, Mr Colton found himself a free man and all in the twinkling of an eye. Thanks to his erstwhile fellow prisoner, he was soon being led along the dark, twisting passages towards the daylight and the golden glory of an early September morning.

The light was so intense after the gloom of the prison, that it hurt his eyes and he was almost blinded. His two companions sat him on a low wall nearby, in the shade of a cypress tree. As his sight gradually grew accustomed to the brightness of the day, he began to look about him in awed wonder and took a deep breath of the fresh morning air.

'Oh, sirs,' he whispered brokenly, 'I can never thank you enough for what you have done for me this day. May God bless you both for your kindness to a man who thought himself without a friend in this land. I can scarcely believe it even yet.' He passed a shaking hand over his eyes as he spoke. 'I am not dreaming am I? So many times I have imagined such a moment as this but always I awoke and found it was not reality, only the phantoms of a fevered mind.'

'No, you are not dreaming,' replied Farenden reassuringly. 'Come, lean on me and I will take you to the carriage. You are coming to my lodgings until you are well enough to travel and then, if you wish it, you shall sail back to England.'

The old man bent his head to hide his tears of inexpressible joy, his heart too full to speak.

Gently, his two new-found friends lifted him up and bore him off. Soon, he was leaving the prison buildings far behind as they sped away toward the city.

A short while later and the chaise swung into a pretty, little square surrounded by tall, graceful houses. Each floor had its own wrought-iron balcony and long, shuttered doors, some of which were flung open; the chatter of voices and a peal of carefree laughter floated down to them as they stepped out on to the cobbled street.

Then a snatch of song from a beautiful tenor voice caused Mr Colton to look up in the direction of the glorious sound and he suddenly noticed that the sky was a clear and startling blue. He stood spellbound, gazing heavenwards until Farenden took his arm and steered him towards a short flight of steps. 'These are my lodgings, Mr Colton. I hope you will oblige me by making them your own for as long as you deem necessary. Fortunately, my rooms are situated on the lower floors. Shall we go in?'

Between them they helped him into the house and settled him in a seat by an open window. It overlooked a small courtyard with a marble fountain at its centre which sent glittering strands of crystal beads high into the air. The tinkling music of the water charmed his ear as he hungrily feasted upon the colourful scene before him.

Here there were more balconies, each decorated with pots of flowers in bright shades of red, pink, orange and yellow. The colours smote his weakened sight fiercely but he could not look away. It was all too wonderful after the months of darkness and drab misery.

Mr Farenden brought him a glass of wine and he sipped it delicately; the rosy liquid glowed in the light of the day and, as he swallowed it down, a warm feeling spread through his thin frame and began to soothe and comfort him as if it were some magic elixir he had been handed.

'Now I know that I really am alive,' he smiled up at the younger man, his eyesight growing clearer.

For the first time he was able to study Farenden's face closely as the light from the open door fell full upon him. It was an arresting face, lean and swarthy of complexion.

Hair, eyebrows and lashes were black as a raven's wing. The eyes, dark and luminous, seemed to hold a great deal of intelligence as they coolly returned his regard unwaveringly. His handsome features were marred by a long, thin scar that ran from his left temple and across his high cheekbone. It looked as if a dagger or sword had laid open that side of his face at some time and the scar was white against the sun-browned skin.

Mr Colton's eyes narrowed into a quick frown.

Noticing the old man's reaction, Farenden fingered the mark and gave a rueful smile.

'It is not my best feature, is it? Madam Luck is a fickle mistress and this is a memento of a time when she bestowed her favours on another.'

'I am sorry, you must forgive me for staring; it was very rude of me. It is only that I thought I knew you but I daresay it is just my mind playing strange tricks on me. For a fleeting moment I felt that we had met somewhere before .... No, the memory eludes me. I have mistook you for another no doubt.'

'I say,' broke in Farenden's companion, 'I don't suppose you have ever fallen foul of sea pirates, have you, Mr Colton? Because if so, that would account for your natural error. He does have a rather buccaneering appearance, do you not agree? I have often remarked it myself. All he lacks is a gold ear-ring and the kerchief about his brows and there you have it, as bloodthirsty a villain as you could wish!'

'I often said that you were wasted in a political career, Justin, you would have been a proficient in the art of the Gothic novel. Please make allowances for my young friend, Mr Colton, imagination must serve to colour an otherwise dull existence. Permit me to make you the rather dubious acquaintance of Lord Justin Trevingham. You need not be impressed with the title by the by, it is not of any historic interest being but lately acquired by the family.'

Lord Trevingham merely grinned appreciatively at this sally and held out his hand to acknowledge the introduction.

He was a tall, slim gentleman with a kind, open face and

an engaging smile. The merry, blue eyes twinkled down at Mr Colton. 'No, please don't stand up, sir, I beg of you. James, you may eschew the deference due my exalted position but allow me to inform you that it at least served to expedite matters this morning. The *commissario* of the prison recognized in my noble mien all that betokened my obvious gentility. Superior conduct in the face of adversity, loftiness of intellect, tastefulness of dress, gracefulness of speech....' Here, a sudden explosion of mirth from Farenden, prevented his continuing in this strain and despite a worthy endeavour to maintain a haughty expression, his lips began to quiver and he collapsed into undignified laughter. Mr Colton gazed from one to the other in lively amusement, their infectious good humour seeping into his heart and the horror of the last few months began to flee like darkness at the break of day.

When their laughter had finally subsided, Farenden crossed the room to open a scroll-topped escritoire. He called over his shoulder to his lordship, 'I suppose, amongst your other qualities, the *commissario* recognized a generous nature? I know these petty officials, always ready to pluck a pigeon. Here, take this purse, it should cover my expenses.'

'No really, James,' expostulated Lord Trevingham, flushing darkly. 'You insult me. If it had not been for you I should not only have my pockets to let but very likely have been bled into the bargain. Please allow me to render you this trifling service for friendship's sake.'

'Very well, if you will have it so but don't fly up into the boughs, there's a good fellow. No insult was intended, I assure you. It is just that I always like to pay my own debts.'

'On the contrary, it is I who am indebted to you, you must know that I was completely at the mercy of those Captain Sharps. What a flat you must think me. I am quite cast down to think how easily I was gulled.'

'Don't be so hard on yourself. It would have taken an astute pair of eyes to rumble their game.'

'But you did,' Trevingham observed gloomily.

'You forget my profession, Justin. I am wholly familiar with such practices. Experience is a notable tutor and I have been taught by many such. Now come, will you breakfast with us? I confess I am ravenous.'

His lordship having eagerly assented, Farenden called for his manservant.

'*Mario! Vieni qui, presto!*'

'*Si, signore, cosa vuole?*' Mario appeared as if by magic at his master's summons. He was immediately given orders to prepare a substantial breakfast.

'*È il dottore, Mario, per favore. Il* Signore Colton *é malato.*'

'*Si, certo, signore. Me ne occupo io subito.*'

Thus it was that Mr Colton, the most wretched of creatures but a few hours since, found himself nourished, doctored, bathed and ensconced in a comfortable bed. His bodily needs so assiduously attended to, he very soon fell into a deep slumber and did not waken until the following afternoon.

Rising much refreshed and feeling a good deal stronger, he found clean linen and a suit of clothes laid out for him on a nearby chair. He dressed carefully and having arrayed himself in his new finery, went to the mirror to admire his modish garb.

He was shocked to see his appearance so altered. A thin, gaunt face looked back at him with its prison pallor, the cheeks sunken, the eyes hollow and dark-ringed. His frame, once of a sturdy build, was now emaciated and could only be described as skeletal. Long, lank hair hung about his shoulders in wispy elflocks, as white as the beard that adorned his jowls.

'Dear God! My closest friends would not know me! I hardly recognize myself! Here is no matter for admiration; I will betake myself downstairs and henceforth avoid every looking-glass as may come in my way.'

Having delivered himself of this monologue, he went in search of his host. The general factotum, Mario, met him as he slowly made his way down the staircase and greeted him politely.

'*Buon pomeriggio*, Signore Colton. You sleepa good, yes? Signore Farenden 'e go out for a leetle. 'E coma back for ze dinner. You want that I bringa you somethin'? *Mangiare?* Yes?' he enquired in his quaint, broken English.

'*Grazie*, Mario. Some *caffe, per favore.*'

'*Si, si,* I bringa. Please to sit.' He opened the door into the room overlooking the courtyard and left the guest to sit in solitary state. Presently settled in a deep-cushioned armchair, his coffee and a tray of delectables at his elbow, Mr Colton sat back to enjoy a quiet read. He had found a leather-bound copy of *Lives of the Poets* among the books on the shelves. His choice had been somewhat limited owing to the discovery that nearly all the tomes he had selected were in foreign languages, mostly French. Unfortunately, his knowledge of that particular tongue and indeed many others at his disposal, was insufficient to allow of his being able to apprise himself of their contents.

Eventually he even cast Johnson aside, the lack of eyeglasses proving an insuperable obstacle to his deriving any enjoyment from the exercise. It was a sultry afternoon, still and quiet save for the distant murmur of voices from the neighbouring apartments and the occasional rumbling of carriage wheels in the cobbled square outside. He gazed with pleasure upon the brilliant blooms in their terracotta pots and idly watched the honey bees at work amongst the fragrant petals. The incessant hum of the tiny wings gradually lulled him into a gentle doze and for a while he slept, until the sound of whispered voices intruded into his drifting consciousness. Assuming that his host had at last returned to the house, Mr Colton arose from his chair and went to the door to announce his presence.

As he opened it and glanced out into the hall, he saw Mario deep in converse with a stranger garbed in a long, black cloak, top-boots and a bicorne hat, pulled low over his eyes.

They both glanced up at the sound of the door opening.

'*Mon Dieu! Qui est là?!*' exclaimed the stranger, frowning in apparent annoyance.

'*N'avez pas peur, m'sieur, c'est un ami de* Signore Farenden. *Il ne nous comprends pas, je vous assure.*'

The unknown caller appeared not to wish to be introduced, for he swiftly turned his back upon Mr Colton and hurried below stairs to the basement area. '*Un momento, scusi, signore.*' Mario executed a rapid bow and hastened after the stranger.

Mr Colton, much puzzled by this odd behaviour, merely shrugged and returned to the comfort of his armchair where he soon resumed his interrupted siesta. When he was next awakened, it was early evening and this time the voice that had brought him from his slumbers was loud and cheerful as his lordship called out a greeting to announce his arrival.

'Good evening, Lord Trevingham, I am afraid you find me alone at present. Mr Farenden is still from home, I understand.'

'Good evening, sir. How are you feeling today?' his lordship enquired solicitously.

'I am much recovered, my lord, thank you, although to my chagrin I find I am as weak as a kitten and have slept like an infant the entire day.'

'Then please resume your seat, sir. Don't stand on ceremony with me, I pray. I wonder what is keeping James from his dinner? He engaged me to dine at eight of the clock and it wants but half an hour to the appointed time. I hope he won't be too late, I'm so hungry I could eat an ox!'

'I envy you your constitution, my lord,' smiled Mr Colton in answer. 'You are to be congratulated.'

Lord Trevingham gave a boyish grin. 'Ain't I though? My Uncle George thinks I have the digestive system of a bovine and sometimes even I think that he may be right. Oh, I do wish James would hurry back, I hope he has not got himself embroiled in any more set-tos, I don't think my spirits could support another conversation with that *commissario*.'

Mr Colton looked alarmed. 'You don't really suppose that anything of that nature could have occurred?'

'From what James tells me, he is quite *au fait* with such occurrences. Yester-morn was not his first experience of incarceration. But no, even he I feel, would be hard pressed to have himself arrested on two nights in the same week.'

'I confess myself much amazed by the events that brought me here. How such a thing came to pass I still do not comprehend.'

'Then let me explain it to you while we await our host. It is a stirring tale enough, though not much to my credit, alas. Two nights ago, I accompanied James to a gaming hell. You know the sort of thing. No, I can see you don't, well, never mind, let me just mention that there were some respectable gentlemen there. Unfortunately I was green enough not to know the difference and accepted an invitation to play faro with a group of officers. At first I seemed to be on a lucky streak and won several of my bets. I should have guessed that the bank seldom loses and as the night wore on, I found myself badly dipped. James had finished his game and came to watch our play. I had just thrown down my last rouleaus in disgust at my ill-fortune, when he suddenly leaned across the table and seized the arm of the fellow holding the bank. As he did so, some cards fell from the man's sleeve and fluttered on to the floor. Then all hell broke loose, or so it seemed to me and I found myself with a sword at my throat. Now, I can acquit myself tolerably well with a pistol if necessary but I am not known for my swordsmanship and was somewhat at a disadvantage. Things were looking extremely ugly for me as you may imagine, when suddenly the table was overturned and my antagonist fell back momentarily. That was James entering the fray with an excess of zeal which I could only wonder at. He laid out one of the officers with a regular hay-maker and snatching up the fallen rogue's sword, leapt upon the other two with apparently joyous enthusiasm. In a very short space of time he had ousted them completely with an elegant series of feints, lunges and ripostes such as I have never witnessed even at Angelo's. It quite took my breath away I can tell you, although it seemed that James was hardly even winded. He has a wrist of steel and the agility of a cat, its nine lives too, I shouldn't wonder. It appears that he once made a living as a fencing-master or so he informs me. There seems to be no end to his accomplishments. Then the soldiery arrived and James was arrested, much to my horror but it only seemed to amuse him; he has a very whimsical nature you will discover. Anyway, there ensued a heated argument which appeared to include everybody present and all babbling away at the top of their voices so that I was unable to make myself understood, even had I been heeded which I most certainly was not.

James was hauled off and I was obliged to follow on his heels as best I could; the rest you know.'

'Good gracious!' exclaimed Mr Colton, his eyes wide with astonishment. 'Is Mr Farenden a duellist? I did wonder when I saw that terrible scar on his face.'

'He may have been. Or just a careless instructor?' grinned his lordship wickedly. 'I confess I am curious to know whether that particular story is true.'

'Why? Do you doubt it?' asked Mr Colton in surprise.

'Perhaps. I really don't know. You see, James and I have been acquainted for only three months and our first meeting was rather peculiar. Let me explain. My uncle is attached to the office of Foreign Affairs in London and I am his secretary. Now that Bonaparte is safely marooned on Elba and Pope Pius returned to Rome, Uncle George thought it would complete my education to travel abroad. He himself made the Grand Tour in his youth and thinks that I too would profit by it. He has old friends here in Rome and I am making my stay with one of them. One evening, I accompanied this gentleman to a reception where I was introduced to an Italian Count. Some card tables had been set up and I engaged to play a few rubbers of piquet with him. Such was his skill, that in a very short space of time he had fleeced me of a small fortune. However, to make amends, he cordially invited me to sup with him and I, being at pains to show that I bore him no ill-will, accepted the olive branch.

'We supped in lavish style and he entertained me royally. During the course of the evening, I had been hard put to it to converse intelligently owing to my execrable Italian. Imagine my astonishment therefore, when half-way through our supper, the Count suddenly informed me that we ought to dispense with the formalities as my pronunciations were seriously affecting his digestion. It was not the remark that astounded me for I had already observed that my host was apparently struggling to conceal some secret mirth. The source of his amusement had hitherto remained a mystery to me but as he now addressed me in perfect English and told me that his name was James Farenden, the matter became resolved. At first I was inclined to anger, suspecting him of entertaining himself at my expense but he begged my pardon so beseechingly that I soon forgave him. Indeed, he proved so very droll that I could not long refrain from laughing myself. He really is the most complete hand and excellent company. You will discover that he is extremely well informed on any number of subjects, owing I daresay to his having travelled a great deal.

'He then confessed that his title was assumed and admitted quite frankly that he uses it only to gain an *entrée* into the higher social circles in order to make the best of his professional skills! You must know that he makes his living at the gaming tables; he is not at all ashamed to disclose it. In fact I have it on his own authority that he changes his name and rank as any other man might select what garments he will wear. One cannot help but admire his *sang-froid*. He tells me, without turning so much as a hair, that he is completely unprincipled and that I should place no credence on anything I hear of him. But I am certain he is a gentleman and he lives in some style as you see. One cannot help liking him; he has great charm and has proved a most amiable companion and of course, I owe him my life.'

'Indeed, my lord, I am in like case. But I am at a loss to understand such singular behaviour. From what you have just told me, one might conclude that he is something of a mountebank yet, having received nothing but kindness from his hands, I cannot believe it to be so.' Mr Colton shook his head slowly in deep perplexity.

'Well, shall we suppose him to be something of an enigma?' offered his lordship helpfully.

At that very moment they heard the gentleman himself returning and he stepped briskly into the room without staying to doff his hat and cloak.

'Good evening, James, we were just speaking of you,' Trevingham hailed him heartily.

'Then I am sorry to have interrupted so interesting a topic,' he replied with his ready smile. 'My apologies, gentlemen, I was unavoidably detained on a matter of business. I have instructed Mario to serve dinner immediately. Allow me but a few minutes to put off my dirt and I shall be with you again directly. Mr Colton, I am

The Gamester 21

delighted to see that you are able to dine with us this evening but you must take care not to over-exert yourself, you know.'

'Oh, indeed I have not had the least exertion, save only that necessary to dress myself and descend the stairs,' he hastily assured him.

'Well, we mean to see that the doctor's orders are obeyed to the letter, so prepare yourself for an enforced rest while you recover your strength,' he warned sternly but the words were robbed of all semblance of admonishment by the disarming smile that accompanied them.

Later, after having consumed a superb dinner, the gentlemen sat back to enjoy a bottle of port.

'So, Mr Colton, you are familiar with the particulars of our adventures it seems. Perhaps, if you have no objection, you might tell us a little of your own story?' Farenden poured out another glass of wine for his guests as he spoke.

'Certainly I will, as simply as I can. To begin with I must remind you that I am a lawyer, a partner in a firm of solicitors in London and it is in connection with that office that I left for India five years ago. I was several months in Calcutta transacting my business and, at its successful conclusion, I set sail again for England in the spring of 1811. The captain had orders to call upon the British garrison in Sicily and this duty he duly performed. Unhappily, our vessel was then overtaken by a violent storm and we were blown off course and foundered somewhere north of Naples. By an act of Divine mercy, I was brought safely to shore half-drowned but otherwise without much hurt. It so befell me that I was discovered in my extremity by two fishermen who bore me away with them to a nearby village. I was kindly used by these honest folk but I could not long remain a burden on them for their condition was such that they had little enough to keep themselves alive. As soon as I was able to travel, I took my leave of them and made my way along the coast, hoping that by some means I might contrive to reach Sicily and take ship again for England. I had not been but three days on my journey when hunger made me reckless and I sought succour in a small town. I was in a sorry state and spoke precious little Italian. I could neither understand nor be understood and was treated with suspicious hostility. Not entirely surprising I suppose.' His lips twitched into a slight smile at the remembrance. 'Judging it best to suffer the pangs of hunger rather than arouse any further speculation, I continued to follow the road because it afforded easier travel than the trackless fields and I was anxious to conserve my strength. Within an hour or two of my leaving the town, I heard the sound of horses and turning my head beheld a troop of soldiers galloping furiously towards me. I was quickly overtaken and being unable to answer their questions and having neither papers nor money, I found myself placed under arrest and taken into French custody. My captors accused me of being an English spy and I was sent to the prison where you found me, to await my trial. Of course, I was never brought to answer the charges made against me and when news eventually came to us that Bonaparte had abdicated, I had hoped to have obtained my release. The gaoler informed me that I could be set free only upon the payment of fifty pieces of gold which naturally I had no means of acquiring. So there I would have remained were it not for the kindly providence that sent me two such generous benefactors. And now my tale is at an end and so too, I must admit, is my strength. If you will excuse me, I am feeling rather tired and with your permission would like to retire. Please do forgive me.'

'Of course, you must get your rest. I should not have detained you for so long. Thank you for acquainting us with the details of your unhappy plight. I am truly sorry to hear of all your sufferings and am glad that we have been instrumental in ending them. May I wish you good fortune from now on, Mr Colton and a happy return to your own country?' said Farenden helping him from his chair.

'I am very much obliged to you, dear sir. That shall be my sole object now, to regain my health and strength so that I might the sooner be home again.' They bade each other goodnight and Mr Colton left the younger men to broach a second bottle together.

'Poor fellow,' remarked Trevingham feelingly as he

replenished their glasses. 'He has certainly had his share of sorrow. Those damned Frenchmen have a lot to answer for!'

'*C'est la guerre*, my friend. Let us drink to Mr Colton's safe return and a peaceful future for all of us.' He raised his glass and they saluted each other. 'Now come, let us enjoy a hand or two of piquet and you shall try and win back that two hundred guineas I had of you yesternight.'

'By all means!' cried his lordship enthusiastically. 'I feel lucky tonight.'

This emotion proved entirely unreliable and Trevingham presently threw down his cards in disgust.

'Why do I continue to delude myself that I can win even one rubber?'

Before his partner could offer an explanation as to the cause of this phenomenon, they were distracted by a soft tap at the door and Mario entered.

'*Signore, c'è qualcuno alla porta.*'

'*Chi è?*'

'*È il* Signore Lacroix.'

'Ah, *molto bene, Mario. Mi aspetti.*'

Farenden arose from the card table. 'My regrets, Justin, it seems I am called away on business. Do pray excuse me for leaving you without the chance to redeem yourself. Perhaps another time?'

'Oh, as to that, I've not the least hope of doing so and you know it! But I shall keep trying I daresay. Well, I'll leave you to your business, though it's a rum business that calls a man from his home at this hour of the night. However it's none of mine so I bid you farewell. Good night, James.'

Mario hurried to bring him his hat and cane and he sauntered cheerfully off to seek his bed.

Two

A few minutes after Lord Trevingham had departed, Farenden slipped quietly out of the house with his late-night visitor. They entered a closed carriage which was awaiting them in the square and soon they were heading out of the city. It was a beautiful night, still and silent under a velvet sky spangled with a myriad glittering stars. The waxing moon shed a soft, refulgent glow over the sleeping countryside as they left the last of the houses far behind.

The carriage, which had been bowling along at a good pace for about an hour or so, presently turned into a rutted track and the driver was obliged to pull in his horses a little. His passengers were now subjected to a great deal of discomfort as they jolted and rattled towards an old house set well back from the road. It was a squat building with dirty, white stonework and shuttered windows that showed no light within. The place seemed utterly deserted and as they drew to a halt outside no one came to greet them.

Farenden descended swiftly, closely followed by his companion and, stepping boldly to the dark, forbidding entrance, gave three quick taps on the weathered panels. He paused a second or two and then knocked twice again but this time slowly and deliberately.

There followed a lengthy silence but he did not repeat his summons, merely waited with down-bent head as if listening intently. After some minutes there came the soft scraping of wood and the door opened a chink. Then a hoarse whisper sounded and Farenden replied with a quietly spoken word. At his answer, the gap widened enough for him to slip through while Lacroix remained on watch outside. Meantime, the coachman had driven his vehicle to the rear of the building out of sight of the road.

Without another word exchanged, Farenden shut fast the door and followed the bright beam of the lantern, held aloft by the man who had admitted him to the house.

He was led to a sparsely furnished room where he found a gentleman awaiting him, seated at a large table of unpolished wood which was strewn with papers. A heavy pistol lay close to his right hand and on his left stood a single branch of candles that threw a pool of light in front of him. The rest of the room was draped in shadow.

Farenden strode forward into the light. '*Salutations*, Monsieur Arnaud. *Vous travaillez très tard, non?*'

The man arose and held out his hand in greeting. '*Bienvenu*, Monsieur Gérard. *Il est trois heures du matin seulement. La nuit est jeune encore. Asseyez-vous, s'il vous plaît.*'

He indicated a chair beside the table.

'*Merci.*' Farenden turned, apparently unconcerned by the style of address and handed his hat and cloak to the manservant, then he seated himself.

'*Comment ça va?*' enquired Monsieur Arnaud resuming his place at the table. '*Et l'Anglais?*'

Farenden leant back in his chair, a faint smile curving his lips.

'*Ça va bien. J'étais sûr de réussir. Il est un jeune homme très confiant. Nous sommes les plus grands camarades.*'

'*C'est bon à entendre*,' the Frenchman replied with a quick nod. '*Mais premierement* ... Jacques! *Deux verres et un bouteille de vin, vitement!*' he called to his servant. Then turning back to Farenden he said, '*Et maintenant, je pense que nous parlerons en anglais.*'

'*Oui, certainment. Vous êtes très prudent.*'

'I have learnt perforce, that it is the wisest course. I could wish you might follow my example, Gérard. Dupois informs me that you have a stranger staying with you. An Englishman. Evidently he overheard some private conversation. Dupois was not well pleased.'

'He need not have concerned himself in my affairs. Mr Colton is no threat to us. He does not speak French and besides, he is an old and very sick man who has spent the last few years locked away from the world.'

'Even so, one cannot be too careful. You are always so impetuous, my friend. I merely caution you to be a little more circumspect. That incident the other night, it could have ended most inconveniently for us. You ought not to have taken such risks, there is still much at stake.'

'I could not well avoid it,' replied Farenden with a quick frown. 'It appears that we are not the only people interested in our young friend. I was forced to bring matters to a head in order to safeguard our own interests. His well-being is paramount to my plans.'

'You think they meant to kill him then?' interposed Arnaud incredulously.

'I dared not take that chance. They intended to force a quarrel on him. He's a young hothead and you know what these Englishmen are like: sticklers for fair play. He would soon have realized their duplicity and been quick to face them with it. I had to spoil their game for them. I shall be relieved when he is safely on his way home. He is too free with his opinions as are all his countrymen. These secret societies are unknown in England; he cannot be aware of the dangers they impose, although I have tried to put him on his guard.'

Arnaud gave him an amused look. 'Somehow I had not envisaged you in the role of *"le petit père"*.'

'*Mon Dieu!* I should hope not!' exclaimed Farenden aghast. 'He is but eight years younger than myself.'

'Ah! But what a vast gap in experience, eh, *mon ami?* He has been reared in a feathered nest, safe and secure whilst you ...'

'Oh, I never had a nest, feathered or otherwise,' interjected Farenden carelessly, his long fingers idly twirling the stem of his glass as he lounged at ease, one arm draped over the back of the chair. 'I would describe myself as *"un coucou"*,' he added with a wry smile.

Arnaud, contemplating the darkly handsome face opposite him, tried to trace some sign of emotion to lend colour to the words so lightly spoken. Gérard was a strange man. They had worked together on several occasions over the last few years but he had never once spoken of his private life. However, his past was no secret to his employers: they had made it their business to find out all they could about his background.

From the moment Arnaud had set eyes on him in Madrid, he had recognized his possible potential as a useful member of their select group. Gérard had killed two of their men and wounded six others that day. It was not merely his mastery of the sword that had impressed him; Arnaud saw also a man with sublime audacity and a courage that sprang from a *joie de vivre*. This, together with his ability to slip fluently from the Spanish into the French tongue, had induced the commanding officer to stay his execution while Arnaud made discreet enquiries. Eventually he had received the information that the young man they held imprisoned was the natural son of an impecunious Frenchman named Gérard, who spent his days wandering across Europe indulging in vices of every kind but most especially that of gaming.

During the Revolution, he had taken the boy out of France and placed him in the care of the brothers at an abbey near Toledo where he had become one of their pupils. His lively intelligence had been carefully nurtured and his cleverness had made him well remembered among his teachers who were delighted with his scholastic attainments. After some years his father had removed him to Lisbon and it was not entirely surprising to learn that he had soon followed the same profession as his degenerate parent but with rather more success. In the early part of the new century, they had returned to Paris where the young Gérard supplemented their income by acting as an interpreter at the Emperor's court by day and gambling by night. He began to add to their fortunes by creating several new identities for himself. His silver-tongued eloquence made it simple for him to pass himself off as a man of means and he invented impressive titles which enabled him to move in exalted circles.

He had either grown bored with Paris or decided that his masquerading might soon be discovered. Whatever the reason he had resumed his travels, continuing to use a string of aliases which made it impossible for Arnaud's agents to follow his history any further. When he had been captured in Spain, he had been taking part in the Madrid uprising of 1808.

Arnaud had been pleased with the results of these investigations and lost no time in recruiting Gérard for the cause. It had not been difficult to persuade such a man to join them. It was merely a choice between death or freedom with the offer of generous rewards if he chose to serve the Emperor.

Arnaud mentally congratulated himself. He had read his man well and Gérard had become his most useful agent. No frontier proved an obstacle to him; he moved about the Continent as easily as he moved from one language to another. He never lost his head, no matter what the situation, and always acted his part with such a degree of confidence that it precluded all suspicion. Gérard was the perfect spy and with his help and others like him, the Tricolour would be raised again in France!

'Do you never grow weary of this gypsy life you lead?' Arnaud asked curiously.

'On the contrary, I would soon tire of any other,' he said with certainty.

'Well, for my part I am glad to hear it. And so to our business – what news have you?'

'Then let us continue to speak of matters ornithological. The eagle begins to stretch out his wings, he feels his strength returning.'

Monsieur Arnaud leaned eagerly forward across the table, his gaze intent and alert. 'Is it possible, do you think?'

'I think it likely that our bird may try to fly soon. He observes the storm clouds gathering over France and but waits for the wind that will bear him away to old haunts.'

Arnaud gave a long, drawn-out hiss of breath between his teeth. 'So! It is only a question of time, you believe? I need not ask you if your sources are reliable?'

'It is known that even Campbell himself has grown increasingly uneasy of late. The Emperor has been constantly complaining that the promised pension has not been paid; you know how vociferous he can be when he feels himself slighted.'

'He will not bear the delay with patience,' replied Arnaud, a humorous quirk to his lips.

'Quite so,' agreed Gérard, sipping his wine and watching the other's face attentively.

'We must be in readiness. I could wish that you might have remained here a little longer. When do you leave for England?' enquired Arnaud.

'Within the month. I still have some business to attend to here. But what of you? Do you remain in Italy?'

'No, I too have my orders. I am needed in Vienna. But you and I must remain in contact through Dupois.'

'Very well, though I would prefer that you chose another. Dupois seems to have taken me in dislike and we are seldom two minutes together without quarrelling.'

'He is the only one I can send: his English is as good as yours. I think he is jealous of your success. You play this game so well, he is envious. You see, Gérard, you are a man to whom success comes easily. Too easily perhaps, for you never appear to be conscious of it and to some this is tantamount to arrogance. Dupois sees you excel at all you undertake to do. Rich rewards fall into the palm of your hand, while they always seem to elude his grasp. Whether it be the sword, the pistol, the cards or the women,' he added with a short laugh. 'Always you win. I recognized that cleverness in you from the very first, it is why your life was spared.'

'Ah!' interrupted Gérard, carefully setting down his glass. 'I was not clever enough to avoid capture, was I?'

'No,' replied Arnaud leaning back in his chair and surveying his companion from beneath hooded lids. 'But you would have done – if you had not been betrayed.'

There was a short silence, while Gérard seemed to be studying his glass and without raising his eyes, said in a cold, even voice, 'And may I enquire as to the name of our betrayer?'

'It hardly matters now,' replied Arnaud dismissively. 'When he had outworn his usefulness, Murat had him shot. Our commander, you see, believed that if a man betrayed his friends, then he could not be depended upon to keep faith with his enemies.'

'The Emperor's brother-in-law is living proof of the truth of that!' scoffed Gérard contemptuously.

'I cannot argue with you,' agreed Arnaud quietly, 'but the fact of the matter is that we cannot afford to harbour any grudges. The Emperor needs him if he is ever to regain power. We must woo him to our purposes. All disagreements must be forgotten, including those which exist between you and Dupois. They must not be permitted to interfere with your duty to the Emperor. Personal feelings must be set aside for the good of the cause. The Emperor will thank you for it.'

'It is not the Emperor's gratitude I would earn but his gold. As you of all people must be well aware. But why do you risk your neck, Arnaud? For your beloved France?'

'The Emperor is France!' replied Arnaud, his eyes glittering fanatically. *'Vive L'Empereur! Vive* Napoleon!'

'France will always be France,' remarked Farenden deliberately. 'But will Napoleon again be her emperor? However, I shall continue to do his bidding, never fear. Now do you have my papers ready?'

Arnaud searched among the articles littered on his desk and picked up a small pile of documents. 'Here you are. You will find everything in order as usual. This is your passport. I have left out the name – I will leave that for you to decide.'

'I shall think of something appropriate, no doubt,' smiled Farenden, concealing them inside his coat. 'I have had some practice in the art. Now as to the other matter that has concerned us lately, I am quite certain that our crafty innkeeper is playing a double game. He has been in contact with Eugène in Bavaria and yet he also intends to send an emissary to Vienna. That is why the Englishman was sent here, to arrange a secret meeting for him with one of Castlereagh's people. I may be able to learn more of this scheme in London. Perhaps you also can investigate when you arrive in Austria?'

'Perhaps,' Monsieur Arnaud responded, thoughtfully stroking his clean-shaven chin. 'Let us see how the game progresses. It might be easier for you to discover their schemes; they will not be so suspicious in their own country. In Vienna they will be on the alert for our agents.'

'That is true. Trevingham may be of further use to us there. You, meanwhile, will need to watch the discards very carefully,' warned Farenden, eyeing him keenly. 'They may well prove our undoing. As for me, I must remember that our man betrayed his emperor before and may well do so again.... But come,' he added encouragingly, 'Let us drink to our success in this as in all our other ventures. *Santé*, Monsieur Arnaud, *et bonne chance!*'

So saying, he lifted his glass and drained it to the last dreg; then setting it down again upon the table he held out his hand. '*Au revoir*, we shall meet again when all our plans are satisfactorily accomplished.'

'Amen to that,' Monsieur Arnaud answered fervently and shook his hand heartily. '*Au 'voir*, Gérard, *et bonne chance aussi!*'

A few minutes later, Farenden was once again in the carriage and speeding back to the city through the early morning mists.

Two days after this nocturnal expedition, he received a visit from Lord Trevingham who called to apprise him of the news that he was returning to England.

'I have my uncle's instructions to take ship immediately. He is to go to Vienna in Castlereagh's entourage and I am needed to attend to affairs in London while Uncle is absent. I have left my valet to oversee my packing and am come but to bid you goodbye.'

'No, no, I do not like your English word. It is too final and should therefore be used advisedly. Let us rather say *au revoir* for we shall certainly meet again, my friend. Meanwhile, I wish you a safe journey. I could wish that our friendship had been of longer duration and sincerely hope that we may resume it again in the near future.'

'I wish it too,' Trevingham answered with great warmth. 'You may be assured of my receiving you with unaffected pleasure and the best of welcomes should you ever come to London and here's my hand on it!'

'Thank you, Justin. You do me too much honour.' He gripped his lordship's hand, pricked by the slightest twinge of conscience at his own rather questionable conduct in the face of such genuine feeling.

However, once Trevingham had departed, his sense of guilt soon ceased to trouble him. One could not afford to be squeamish in this business but must remain cool and detached from every emotion. That way there was little likelihood of making a fatal error of judgement. He had always followed this golden rule and it had served him well.

Lord Trevingham, with no inkling at all that his erstwhile companion would be following close on his heels, regretted to find himself obliged to forsake so congenial a friend. Nevertheless, he was now homeward bound and his thoughts turned in eager anticipation towards the happiness of reunion awaiting him in London.

When his heavily mud-splashed post-chaise finally drew up outside an elegant establishment in Albemarle Street, he had barely time to step down from the vehicle before being almost bowled over by the enthusiastic welcome of his eldest sister.

He returned her warm embrace laughingly, crying for mercy. 'My dearest Constance, at least allow me to draw breath! There, that's better,' he gasped as she quickly released him. 'What strange new custom is this in merry old England that desires a man must be half-strangled upon returning to his own house?'

'Oh, it is not new, the women of England have long been overwhelmed with that desire! Ever since the Crusades, I should imagine,' she replied instantly, her eyes sparkling with joy. 'Oh! It is good to have you home again, Jus!'

'And it is wonderful to be back, I assure you,' he answered, hugging her. 'Now we must go into the house before this dreary English weather chills you to the bone.'

He took her arm and hurried her up the short flight of steps and into the welcoming light and warmth that spilled through the open door.

'Good evening, my lord. May I say how happy we all are to see you safely returned?' greeted his butler with a deep bow.

'Thank you, Basset, I hope I find you well?' enquired his lordship, handing over his curly-brimmed beaver while two footmen assisted him from his beautifully tailored redingote.

'Indeed, my lord, excellent well. Her ladyship awaits you in the drawing-room.'

'Yes, do hurry, Justin, Mama is longing to see you,' urged Constance, seizing his hand and dragging him across the hall and up a sweeping staircase to the first floor.

'Here he is, Mama!' she cried exultantly.

'Justin! My darling boy! Come! Kiss your mama at once!' demanded her ladyship with a squeak of excitement. Her errant son was at her side in a few, quick strides, hardly before she had time to rise from her chair. He kissed her soundly and then held her at arm's length.

'Let me look at you! You seem a little pale, have these sisters of mine been fagging you to death?'

'Certainly not! We live very quietly, you know,' she twinkled up at him. 'And I daresay you think I look pale only because you are grown so prodigious brown! Now, come and sit beside me and tell me everything you have been doing. What is it like in Rome? Is it as beautiful as you imagined?'

'Every bit as beautiful and more besides. You would have adored it, Connie, all those ancient monuments and such like. I thought of you as soon as I saw them,' he enthused, looking across at his sister.

She threw him a droll look. 'How should you not? I am in my dotage after all.'

'That's not what I meant as you very well know,' he grinned appreciatively. 'You are only my elder by two years and I don't consider myself ancient history yet! Oh! but how I wish you could have seen it, truly. Such glorious architecture! The entire city is a work of art. At least Bonaparte could not remove that to France.'

'Is it very much despoiled of its treasures, Justin?' his sister enquired sadly.

'I'm afraid so. Is it not infamous?'

'Indeed it is and what is worse, that despicable creature has not even been compelled to give up any of his plunder. It is a disgrace that he has been treated so leniently.'

'Well, as to that, Connie dear, there are many people who would agree with you,' he replied. 'My uncle told me that the Regent himself thinks so.'

Just then, the sound of hurrying feet drew his attention to the door and suddenly upon the threshold appeared a vision of loveliness dressed in a modish walking-dress and fur-trimmed pelisse. A fetching bonnet framed a little, heart-shaped face that at the moment was pink with excitement. She paused only briefly and then with a girlish squeal of delight and all unmindful of her finery, sped across the room and fell upon her brother's neck.

'Oh, Justin! You're here at last! We have missed you dreadfully, have we not, Mama? But how dared you arrive while I was from home? It is too bad of you, really. Oh, why did I promise Julia that I would accompany her to the park this afternoon?'

'Because you cannot resist the temptation to show off your plumage, you minx! Though I must say you look a regular dasher in that elegant creation you're wearing.'

She twirled around before him that he might the better admire her fashionable attire.

'You look as neat as ninepence, Sophy,' he assured her smilingly, inspecting her from feather-trimmed bonnet to her dainty feet clad in orange jean half-boots.

'It is all the crack, you know, is it not, Connie?' She turned to her sister for confirmation.

'Oh, bang up to the mark!' concurred Constance readily. 'Now, do but go and put off your bonnet and pelisse and we can all have some tea and a delightful coze. Justin can then tell us about his adventures without having to repeat himself.'

'Oh, yes, that's a splendid notion! I shall be back directly. Don't begin without me, Justin, will you?' she implored him.

'Don't worry, *bambina*, you won't miss a single exciting moment of it. Away with you and be sure not to keep us waiting!' he called after her as she raced eagerly out of the room. 'Little hoyden,' he said, fondly gazing after her.

As soon as the tea things had been brought in, they all sat round the fire, listening avidly to everything he had to tell them of his voyage and experiences in that most romantic of capitals.

When he began to regale them with the fascinating details of his first meeting with the mysterious Count and their subsequent amazing adventures, he judiciously gave a somewhat expurgated version wishing only to excite and not alarm the ladies.

Sophy's clear, blue eyes were round with astonishment as she listened open-mouthed to the description of that horrendous prison.

'Oh! It is just like one of Mrs Radcliffe's novels!' she gasped rapturously.

'Well, I suppose *The Italian* inevitably springs to mind,' Constance agreed, smiling at her young sister's excited countenance. 'This Count of yours sounds sufficiently dark and villainous by your colourful description, Justin.'

'I did not mean you to think him villainous. He isn't at all, you know. In fact he is perfectly charming. It is just his misfortune that he looks rather sinister. That scar on his face, you see. He is quite aware of it himself, although he seems to think it more a cause for amusement than a matter of regret. You would like him I think, Connie, he is vastly knowledgeable and converses easily and sensibly. He certainly appears to be very well read. You would have derived a great deal of pleasure from discoursing with him, I'm sure. And yet he does not take himself at all seriously. He gives the impression that life is just a game to him and I never knew when he was just funning or in earnest.'

'I'm not at all sure that I should have liked him,' she replied disapprovingly. 'He doesn't sound at all the thing. Indeed, I imagine he might he considered a bit of a loose fish, as you would say, Justin.'

'Connie!' cried her mother in shocked accents. 'Please refrain from using that vulgar language! It is not at all becoming in a young lady of breeding.'

'Well it is exactly what Justin would say and anyway, Mama, I am seven and twenty and long past my first blush. Though not my last, I hope,' she added with a twinkle in her eyes. 'So don't fear that I will embarrass you with such cant in public, for I hope I know better than that how to behave. Besides, how can I help knowing these quaint phrases when I have a brother who associates with felons and card-sharps and the like society?'

'Well, for my part I find it all perfectly thrilling,' Sophy interrupted with a rapt expression on her lovely face. 'How I wish I could have travelled with you, Justin, I should have enjoyed it above all things. 'Tis monstrous dull in London these days and I long for some new excitement. What a great pity it is that you did not bring the Count with you to London. I should have adored to meet him.'

'Never mind, Sophy, I think it very likely that you will

soon have someone else to practise your arts upon. Besides, I thought Dilly was making calf-eyes at you last season?'

'What a horrid expression,' she answered crossly. 'I'm sure I never saw him looking the least bit calf-like. He is far too young anyway.'

'Calves usually are, you know,' he commented sagely. 'And I wasn't aware that you were dangling after a Methuselah.'

The blue eyes flashed indignantly. 'Of course I am not! It's just that Dilly is so ... so immature.'

'Ah! I see! Well, you are bound to think so, I suppose,' he remarked, exchanging amused glances with Constance. 'After all, a girl embarking upon her second season is not exactly just out of the school-room. I expect your tastes are rather more refined now and Dilly has not much to recommend him, has he?'

'Oh no,' broke in Constance. 'Of what possible advantage to a woman is a handsome face, a pretty fortune and a sweet temperament? A man ought to have at least some attractions if he aspires to a young lady's hand.'

'Stop teasing Sophy you two,' admonished their mama who had been listening with fond amusement to the banter of her offspring. 'Now we must all go and dress for dinner, it is growing late.'

Justin jumped up and offered her his arm. 'Then come, my lady. I shall escort you to your room,' he said nobly.

'Thank you, my dear,' she accepted, graciously curtseying and they made their way upstairs, the two girls following behind them.

When Justin came down again some while later, he discovered his uncle awaiting him.

'Uncle George! What a pleasant surprise! I had not looked to see you until tomorrow.' He strode eagerly forward and shook hands heartily.

'Your dear mama kindly invited this crabby old bachelor to dinner this evening, being the benevolent lady that she is. How are you, my boy? How was your journey home?'

'I am very well, sir. I cannot thank you enough for arranging everything for me. I would not have missed it for worlds.'

'I am delighted to hear you say so, Nevvy. Perhaps you could call in at the office tomorrow morning at eleven o'clock and we will discuss the politics of your sojourn. Meanwhile, here's your mother looking as radiant as ever.' He went forward to meet her and kissed the proffered cheek.

'Flatterer!' she accused him playfully.

'By no means, Amelia. You look in high bloom,' he insisted gallantly.

'You are much too kind a brother, George. Save your compliments for my girls. They are more deserving of them.'

'Uncle George is right, Mama, you do look beautiful,' Justin confirmed. 'What an elegant gown you are wearing. It is most becoming.'

Lady Trevingham laughed delightedly. 'Have a care now or you will turn my head with your pretty speeches.'

She did indeed look very handsome in a lavender silk evening dress styled 'à la Turque' and on her head she wore a turban of silver tiffany. She was quite tall with a fair complexion and deep-blue eyes and although in her early fifties, she looked much younger. Her figure was still slender and her skin soft and almost as perfect as that of her two daughters who were just at that moment entering the room.

Sophy, as soon as she clapped eyes on her maternal uncle, flew into his arms and kissed him thoroughly.

'Well, well, puss. I hope you don't greet all your mama's gentlemen guests in that fashion? She would never have the house to herself,' he chuckled, highly delighted at being received so affectionately.

'Ah! But there is not another gentleman in all London as handsome as you, dear Nuncs!' his youngest niece informed him gaily. 'Is it not so, Connie?' She turned to her sister who had followed a little more sedately in her wake.

'Indeed and none so welcome either. Good evening, Uncle George.' Constance kissed his freshly shaven cheek and slipped her arm through his. 'We hear you are going abroad again soon. Vienna this time, is it not?'

'Yes, that is so. Castlereagh is rather wary of the

Austrians and has his own people at the embassy. I have been given the task of supervizing the security arrangements.'

'And how long will you be away this time, George?' enquired Lady Trevingham.

'That is uncertain, my dear. I cannot say. Perhaps I may be home again for the Christmas festivities.'

'I hear it is very festive in Vienna,' continued Constance. 'The Emperor has spared no expense to entertain the members of the congress. You will no doubt be invited to attend a great many parties, grand balls and galas and will not wish to leave.'

'How exciting!' cried Sophy. 'Oh, I wish that you could take me with you, Uncle dear! How vexing it is that the gentlemen always seem to have all the fun while we ladies must stay home and sew samplers!'

'Have you not heard, Sophy, that Talleyrand has taken his young niece to act as his hostess?' Constance asked mischievously. 'The Comtesse de Perigord is said to be very beautiful. Perhaps you may meet her, Uncle?'

'Well, if she is a beauty, I do not suppose that a grey-haired, old dullard like me will even be noticed. She will be surrounded by every young buck in the vicinity.'

'I envy her the opportunity,' sighed Sophy. 'Are you sure you would not change your mind, Uncle George? If Prince Talleyrand has taken his niece, it must be thought quite unexceptional. I'm convinced that I would make an excellent hostess if you cared to throw any grand parties.'

'I daresay you would, my pretty, but you see, I am not going to be hosting any parties, grand or otherwise. My visit is to be a very discreet affair. I shall not be attending any of the great social occasions, in fact I doubt whether I shall see much more of Vienna than the embassy building. You see what a dull dog your uncle is?' he asked ruefully.

'Oh, in that case I should not enjoy it at all,' conceded Sophy, greatly disappointed.

'Never mind, dearest,' Lady Trevingham said consolingly. 'We shall have a grand ball at Christmas when we all go down to Chailey and you shall help me with the arrangements if you wish it.'

'May I, Mama? Thank you! I shall begin drawing up a

list of guests immediately!' cried her delighted daughter, clapping her hands with glee.

'Would you mind very much if we went in to dinner first?' pleaded Justin in affected anguish. 'I declare I am almost faint with hunger.'

As Basset came at that very moment to announce that dinner was being served, the subject was abandoned for the time being.

The following day, Lord Trevingham went to his uncle's office as promised. He arrived at the appointed hour looking extremely *de rigueur* in an exquisitely tailored coat of olive-green, immaculate biscuit-coloured pantaloons and highly polished Hessian boots.

He found his uncle sitting at a massive, walnut desk placed in front of two long windows that overlooked the busy street below.

Lord George Kemsley was occupied with his paperwork but he glanced up as his nephew entered the room.

'Punctual as ever, I see, Justin? Come in and sit down, I won't keep you above a minute or two. I have some urgent papers to sign.'

Trevingham settled his tall frame in the chair his uncle had indicated with a flourish of the quill pen he held; then he laid his hat and cane on a corner of the great desk and waited for his uncle to finish writing. He watched with mild interest as sheet after sheet of thick paper received Lord Kemsley's distinctive signature.

At last he had finished and with a deep sigh, he threw down the pen. 'Damned bureaucracy,' he muttered beneath his breath. 'I shall be fortunate if I manage to leave this desk never mind the country!'

Then, relaxing his broad shoulders, he sat back in his chair and fixed Trevingham with his bright-blue eyes, deep-set beneath shaggy, grey eyebrows.

'Well now, Justin, how did you find my old friend Signore Cavalli?' he asked.

'He is in good health and sends his kind regards and hopes that you and he might meet again one day soon.'

'Indeed, indeed and I hope we may. I should like to see him and talk of the exploits of our youth. Ah, what happy days they were, in a more gentle age.' He paused briefly before continuing in a matter-of-fact tone, 'But what of his opinions? I am anxious to know what they might be.'

Trevingham drew his chair a little closer and placing his elbow on the desk, leant toward his uncle. 'Bendinck has undoubtedly caused some unrest with his call for an independent constitutional state. That business in Milan in the spring was possibly a result of his proclaimed views. Cavalli thinks that his remarks may have lit a long fuse but the situation at the moment appears to be settled in favour of the Bourbons. As for the north, the liberals have very little support as yet; he cannot see that changing for the forseeable future.'

'Then that confirms what I have been hearing from other sources,' Lord Kemsley remarked approvingly. 'Now what of your meeting with the Neopolitan emissary?'

Justin sighed heavily. 'Well, I had some difficulty in arranging that but I did manage to see him eventually. I put forward the suggestion that if adequate compensation could be made to the Bourbons, Castlereagh would be prepared to support the Austrian agreement with Murat in order to establish a lasting peace in Europe.'

'And what did he say to that?' questioned Kemsley leaning back again in his seat and fixing his bright eyes keenly upon his nephew's face.

'He said that he would of course lay the matter before King Joachim but that he could offer no assurance as to his majesty's acquiescing in such an arrangement. He pointed out that the king is in a very strong position, his troops command half of Italy and he reminds us that by the terms of the agreement made last January, the king's claim to the throne of Naples has Metternich's full support and therefore they have no need of further bargaining.'

'Yes, damn him,' muttered Kemsley. 'That's the stumbling block!'

'I'm afraid that Bendinck's remarks at Piedmont have considerably undermined our credibility. Murat will not readily accept Castlereagh's assurance that he does not want a nationalistic Italy.'

After some while without speaking, Kemsley suddenly pushed back his chair saying, 'Come, let us go to lunch before I am given any more urgent papers to sign.' He walked around the desk and linked arms with his nephew. 'And while we eat you can tell me more about the interesting people you met in Rome. Connie was telling me some fantastic tale which sounded as if you had been roasting your sisters somewhat.'

'Very well. But you can be sure that I will tell you the true story, you would not credit it else.'

Three

One morning, about a sennight after her brother's departure, Lady Trevingham was alone in her private sitting-room writing a letter to her sister Lady Mary Dawlish. Her daughters were making a visit to friends and her son had gone to his office to attend to some correspondence. She had barely put pen to paper, when Basset tapped gently on the door.

'Excuse me for disturbing you, my lady, but there is a gentleman called to see Lord Trevingham. I have informed him that his lordship is from home this morning for a short while but he insists on waiting. Unfortunately the gentleman is a stranger to me but he has asked me to bring you his card.'

Lady Trevingham looked rather surprised, Basset was usually perfectly able to deal with such matters himself.

'He really is quite a persistent gentleman,' he said with a note of apology in his voice.

She took the card from the salver and glanced at the inscription. 'Count Fabricati,' she read aloud.

'Yes, my lady, a foreigner,' announced Basset as if that explained everything.

'I see. Well, show him into the blue saloon and tell him I shall be down directly.'

'Very good, my lady.' Basset bowed and withdrew, much relieved that the matter was now out of his hands. It was one thing to be able to depress the pretensions of an unknown caller who spoke the King's English but quite another to evict from the doorstep a top-lofty gentleman who apparently understood nothing that was said to him. All the usual ploys available to an experienced butler were entirely wasted upon this impassive stranger who seemed to converse only in gibberish.

A few minutes later, Lady Trevingham entered the blue saloon to find the gentleman awaiting her. He was standing in front of the marble fireplace gazing at a portrait of her three children, likenesses taken when they were all quite young.

He turned at the sound of her approach and she knew instantly who he was; there was no need for further enquiry.

'I was just admiring this charming portrait. A Lawrence, is it not? Quite exquisite.'

She smiled and held out her hand. 'So you are an art-lover too? Good morning, Count Fabricati, what a pleasant surprise, I have been looking forward to making your acquaintance. You were most kind to my son when he was in Italy and I am glad to have the opportunity to thank you in person.'

'*Buongiorno*, Lady Trevingham, *come sta?*' He took her hand and kissed her slim fingers, at the same time giving her a keen glance from beneath thick lashes.

'Please be seated. My son will not be long, I think. I shall ring for some refreshment while we are waiting. You and I can enjoy a little conversation – in English, of course,' she added with emphasis and a sparkling look.

'But of course,' he assured her, giving a slight shrug of his broad shoulders which struck her as an oddly continental trait.

'Good, I can see we understand one another very well. We shall now get on famously,' smiled her ladyship, tugging the bell-pull.

He grinned appreciatively. 'I never doubted that, my lady. I count myself indeed fortunate to have obtained your approval on so short an acquaintance.'

'Oh, as to that, sir, you come to me highly recommended as I am sure you must be aware.'

He acknowledged the truth of her statement with a gracious bow, saying, 'Then allow me to assure you that I am extremely grateful for your warm reception of me.'

'Thank you, sir,' she replied with a slight inclination of the head.

She sat down in a winged armchair and invited him to be

seated also. He settled himself in a chair opposite to her just as Basset answered the summons of the bell.

'Some claret for the Count, Basset, and a glass of ratafia for myself.'

'At once, your ladyship,' he said bowing and then bestowed a look of ill-concealed suspicion upon the strange visitor before he went out of the room again.

'Would you care to move your chair a little closer to the fire, Count? I daresay you are unused to such inclement weather.'

'I am perfectly comfortable, thank you, your ladyship. I have already become acclimatized during a stormy crossing of the English Channel not long since.'

'I do not envy you that!' she answered with a shudder. 'I endured such a voyage in 1802 and have never forgotten it!'

'*Mal de mer?*' he enquired sympathetically.

She nodded. 'It must be said that I am not a good sailor, although I do enjoy travelling. Of course, it has not been possible to visit the Continent in recent years but I have not entirely forgotten its pleasures. I did so like Paris.' She sighed gently. 'Such a fashionable city. The Empress Josephine introduced such style. Those beautiful classical gowns! Ah! those receptions in Paris were so very elegant. I was sorry that we had to leave after such a short while. But there, I did not mean to begin reminiscing. Please forgive me.'

She broke off as Basset entered with the tray and served the refreshments. The Count tasted the wine and pronounced it to be an excellent vintage.

'I congratulate you upon your cellar, Lady Trevingham, this claret is quite exceptional.'

'Thank you, sir. My late husband had it laid down, you know. He prided himself upon it.'

'With good reason, my lady. He was undoubtedly a man of great taste.' The Count raised his glass in a salute to her and there was no mistaking the look of admiration in those dark, compelling eyes.

Her ladyship, who had been a reigning beauty in her youth, found that she was not as yet immune to masculine charms and could still enjoy a compliment paid her by a handsome young gentleman, especially one with such a devastating smile. Basset, whose indignant gaze was not lost upon the visitor, took himself off to his pantry muttering animadversions under his breath against persons who resorted to base trickery to gain their own ends.

'I suppose you have been in Paris, Count?' her ladyship enquired politely in an endeavour to restore her equilibrium.

'Yes indeed. Oddly enough, you and I must have been there at about the same time,' he said casually but giving her a sidelong glance.

'Really? I wonder that we never met? My husband and I went there to pay a visit to my brother. He was on diplomatic business and invited us to join him for a few months. We attended several receptions; perhaps you may have been at some of them?'

'I certainly recall being present at several. Most particularly one that was held in March '03,' he said meaningfully.

'Oh, were you there?' she asked interestedly. 'It must have been perfectly dreadful. Charles and I did not attend on that occasion but George did, I think. How Whitworth managed to get himself into such a deplorable public argument, I cannot imagine.'

'It was a clash of temperaments. The fiery outbursts of the volcanic Corsican versus the icy reserve of the glacial Englishman, with such elements as these war was inevitable.'

'Yes, my husband insisted upon our sailing home immediately and the opportunity to return has not come again since. But perhaps now that the war is ended, I shall get my wish and see Paris once more.'

'Well, do not plan your journey yet awhile, Lady Trevingham,' he advised warningly.

'Oh? Why should I not do so?' she enquired curiously.

'Because you would have to endure a most unpleasant Channel crossing,' he explained glibly. 'You would do well to wait for the warmer months. A winter voyage ought to be avoided at all costs; it would be a most uncomfortable journey for a lady of your sensibilities.'

Lady Trevingham eyed him suspiciously. She had the distinct impression that he was prevaricating and that there was some other reason for his advising her against travelling. However, she did not pursue the matter and instead decided to change the subject.

'And what other cities besides Paris have you visited, Count?' she asked.

'Quite a few I suppose. Madrid, Lisbon, Vienna, Zurich, Venice, Naples and of course, Rome.'

'Goodness gracious, so many? What an odd sort of life you must lead to be sure. Are you now settled in Rome, sir?'

'I never settle anywhere permanently,' he replied carelessly.

'But have you nowhere that you can call home?!' she exclaimed incredulously.

'Not in the sense that you use the word. Home to me is wherever I happen to be.'

'Then you have no family?'

'No, I have none,' he answered in a cold, unemotional voice.

'How very sad,' murmured Lady Trevingham, her glance lifting involuntarily upwards to rest upon the portrait of her own family.

'Naturally you would think so,' he remarked, noting the direction of her gaze. 'But please don't waste your sympathy on me, I am not in need of it or deserving either. I am well content with my lot I assure you. Having no family ties gives one absolute freedom. I always am able to do whatever I want and go wherever I choose, without having to consider anyone else's wishes or feelings. Am I not rather to be envied than pitied?'

'Then there is no one to care what becomes of you?' she responded in a softer voice.

'I perceive that you are determined to make me an object of your compassion, my lady. It is ever a woman's way. But I shall prove a sad disappointment to you if you persist in regarding me in that light. Pray believe me when I tell you that emotions of a sentimental nature are completely unknown to me, as you may soon discover for yourself. I give you fair warning,' he concluded in all sincerity.

Looking at his dark, uncompromising features, she could well believe it but a mother's heart beat in her breast and his harsh words made her pity him all the more.

They were interrupted at this juncture by the sudden arrival of the master of the house. He came bursting into the room without ceremony and in great excitement.

'Good grief, it is you, James! I thought poor old Basset had gone off his head, babbling about foreigners in disguise invading the premises. Well, this is famous news indeed! You here in England! I never thought it remotely possible. How long do you make your stay?'

He gripped his friend's hand and shook it heartily, beaming all the while.

'You promised me a warm welcome, I remember and I see you meant it,' smiled the Count observing the young man's enthusiasm.

'I shall leave you two alone now,' interjected Lady Trevingham tactfully. 'I daresay you have a great deal to say to one another and I have a letter to finish. Perhaps you would care to join us for lunch, Count Fabricati?'

'I should be delighted, madame,' he accepted gratefully and courteously escorted her to the door to hold it open for her.

When she had gone, he turned back to resume his place by the fireside and Trevingham threw himself into the chair vacated by his mother.

'What's this I hear? Count Fabricati? Is that how I am to address you while you are in London?' he queried with a comical expression on his face.

'Yes, that is correct. It is almost a complete fabrication, is it not?' he said humorously, leaning back in his seat and stretching his long legs to the fire.

Trevingham could not help laughing at the man's audacity. 'You really are quite extraordinary, you know, James,' he managed to say at last.

'I am obliged to you, Justin. I think. Was it meant as a compliment? Well, no matter, the adjective thus applied is perhaps rather apt.'

'But this is London, my friend. It will not be so easy to

establish your credit here. People are bound to ask a lot of awkward questions and matters could become rather, well, complicated,' he finished lamely.

'Don't let it trouble you, I never do. People are the same the world over; they will believe the evidence of their eyes. You will soon see that I am right.'

Trevingham still looked doubtful, he could envisage several difficulties.

The Count studied his countenance thoughtfully. 'Would it make you feel any easier if I were to tell you that the title is quite legitimate?'

'What? Are you saying that you really are a Count?' exclaimed Trevingham in utter astonishment. 'Or is this another of your Canterbury tales?'

'Not at all,' he replied, completely unoffended by the accusation.

'But I thought you told me it was assumed?'

'The name was, the title not so. It was conferred upon me by King Ferdinand himself – for services rendered, you understand,' he added enigmatically.

'You are serious this time?'

'Perfectly. Be easy, Justin, you will not be compromising your integrity, I assure you,' he said lightly.

'Very well then. I must say it does make me feel a little less apprehensive,' conceded his lordship, rather relieved. 'Now tell me, where are you putting up? I should be glad if you would come and stay with us while you are fixed in London.'

'That is most kind of you, Justin. But I have already taken a house in Brook Street.'

'Have you, by Jove? Then you do mean to make a long stay?'

'Perhaps. My plans are not settled precisely but I hope to remain here for three or four months.'

'When did you arrive in Town? And what made you leave Italy? I had no notion of your coming away when I took my leave of you. What decided you?'

'Mr Colton. He was anxious to be on his way home and I could not persuade him to delay his journey any longer. I thought it best that I accompanied him on so arduous a voyage. He was still very weak but his spirit is such that I need not have entertained any qualms about his well-being. I left him at Lewes ten days ago, safe in the bosom of his family once more. They were overjoyed to see him as you may imagine and not wishing to intrude at such a moment I came away immediately. Now here I am and eager to acquaint myself with your great capital. Tell me, what do you do here for amusement?'

'Oh, any number of things. Fencing at Angelo's, sparring lessons at Jackson's, shooting at Manton's. If you've an interest in the Fancy there's Cribb's Parlour. And cock-fighting, racing and gaming of all kinds, any number of opportunities for the betting man to lose his blunt. And you must be seen at Almack's. It is a most exclusive club and although it's pretty dull most evenings, once you are accepted there you will find it opens many other doors into London society. If you wish to ride, you may have the choice of any suitable mount in our stables.'

'Thank you, you are very generous but I have already paid a visit to Tattersall's a few days ago and yesterday rode over to Long Acre to cast my eye over a carriage or two.'

'You did, did you?' commented Trevingham in amazement. 'You certainly have not wasted your time I must say.'

'I mean to enjoy myself, naturally,' smiled the Count. 'And from what you tell me, there are any number of ways in which a man may fulfil that ambition.'

'Well, I shall begin by putting your name up at one or two of the clubs and I shall introduce you to a set of excellent fellows, friends of mine who will, I am sure, engage to assist us in committing all kinds of folly. Speaking of which,' his lordship continued with a rueful smile, 'I have to confess to having behaved a little foolishly myself.'

He arose from his chair and walking to the fireplace, leaned an arm along the mantelshelf and gazed broodingly into the flames. After a few seconds of silent contemplation, he turned back to face the Count.

'The thing is, James, I told my family about that incident in Rome, the night we got involved in that brawl. Only I wasn't exactly truthful about what occurred. Oh, I am perfectly aware that I ought not to have mentioned it at all but you know how it is! My sisters are forever reading romances, well, Sophy is anyway, and I suppose I thought it would do no harm to indulge their imaginations with a tale of danger, dungeons and the like sort of nonsense. I had no idea at the time that you had any intention of coming to London or I should never have done so. However, I let my tongue run away with me and I invented a fine adventure in which you figured as a rather, shall we say colourful? character and I was the hero who rescued you from your dreadful fate. I did not dare reveal what really happened because my mother would be scandalized to learn that I frequented gaming hells and if she heard that I had been in a sword fight, she would be absolutely horrified.'

'I see,' said the Count much amused. 'Well, you need not fear my denouncing you. After all, it isn't so very far from the truth, is it? As far as I am concerned you may retain your heroic image. I am quite happy to play the villain; it suits me well, you have said so yourself on several occasions.'

'Oh, I did not say that you were a villain precisely but I did give the impression that you were something of a reprobate. In fact, my sister Constance said that you sounded a bit of a loose fish,' grinned Trevingham with a quick glance at his friend's expression to note his reaction to this piece of information.

The Count was at that moment reaching for his wineglass and this remark made him pause in the act of lifting it to his lips. He raised his eyebrows in feigned surprise saying, 'What an interesting vocabulary your sister has to be sure.'

'Yes, she is considered to be something of a blue-stocking. A very clever woman in fact. Remarkably astute too,' he added, his eyes alight with merriment.

'Indeed?' commented the Count dryly.

'Oh yes. Mama thinks that is the reason why she has never married.'

'I should think it has less to do with the hue of her hosiery and more to do with her colourful language,' observed his friend deprecatingly.

'Oh, Connie's no bread-and-butter miss. She never cuts up stiff. A very sensible sort and pluck to the backbone. She's got me out of some sad scrapes, I can tell you,' declared his lordship proudly.

'How ... er ... edifying,' murmured the Count with a faint smile curling his lips. 'She seems a perfect paragon of womanhood.'

'I daresay you think these but the ravings of an over-fond brother but wait till you get to know her. You will see that I don't exaggerate.'

'Oh, I am certain she really is quite Amazonian but what of your younger sister? She looks to be a very sweet girl.'

'Ah, Sophy,' sighed Trevingham eyeing the angelic-looking child in the portrait. 'She's the beauty of the family and an absolute stunner. They are both gone out this morning but you'll meet them soon enough. Now let us go and see what cook has prepared for lunch, I'm famished!'

'Then let us to it, my lord, and perhaps tonight we shall feast on the pleasures of London. I hear that her tables are well laden.'

'That is true but I warn you that those who sit at them have enormous appetites. There's many a fortune has been swallowed up overnight.'

'Thank you for putting me on my guard but you need not fear, I do not mean to bite off more than I can chew.'

'Very well, James. You know what you are about I daresay. And from what I have learnt of you, I think you have the stomach for it!' laughed Trevingham, throwing open the door.

'Never doubt it! I have dined at almost every table in Europe and grown fat upon the fare,' said the Count following him out of the room.

Later that day, when the gentlemen had departed, Lady Trevingham heard her daughters returning. They came laughing and chattering into the room having spent an enjoyable morning with their friends visiting Bullock's Museum in Piccadilly, which contained many thousands of exhibits including divers reptiles, birds, animals and insects besides various works of art and ancient artefacts.

'Oh, Mama! We have had a splendid time. The Egyptian Hall is fascinating! We were not able to see the half of it!

Was it not marvellous, Connie? We saw the dearest little monkeys and Georgiana nearly fainted at sight of the snakes!' exclaimed Sophy delightedly, her eyes and cheeks glowing prettily with excitement. 'They looked so fearsome!'

'Well I hope you don't mean to tell me that you now have a notion to buy such a creature, a monkey that is, not a snake, of course. Lady Caroline kept one as a pet in her house and I remember it was forever breaking the ornaments and spilling food over the furniture,' her mother replied with a grimace. 'Horrid little beast.'

'No, of course I have not any such thought but that is not to say I wouldn't very much like to own one,' she added with a regretful sigh.

'I'm sorry we have left you alone all morning, Mama,' broke in Constance. 'We had not intended on staying away so long but we were invited to lunch with Georgiana and her cousins and I thought you would not object. I know you had some letters to write today and I expect you were glad to be rid of us,' she explained, smoothing her crumpled gown as she took a seat by her mother.

'Oh, I haven't spent the morning alone, my dears. I have had a most interesting time myself, entertaining a gentleman, you know!' she said with a roguish twinkle in her eyes.

'Indeed?' smiled Constance, sensing that the gentleman caller must have been somewhat unusual for her mother seemed to be big with news. 'And who might this unknown cavalier be, pray?'

'Well, he was not my cavalier unfortunately, Connie. Though if I were nearer in age to you, my dear, I might have used all my womanly arts to have made him so. He was quite out of the ordinary way. He called to see Justin but as he was from home earlier today, I endeavoured to entertain the gentleman until his return.'

'And are you going to tell us his name?' Sophy enquired, her curiosity aroused by the gleam in her mama's blue eyes.

'It was Count Fabricati!' she announced grandly and sat back to watch the effect of this revelation on her daughters' faces.

Sophy looked puzzled and Connie merely raised her brows in surprise. 'Count Fabricati,' she repeated slowly and then as realization dawned, she sat upright in her chair. 'Not the Italian?' she gasped incredulously.

'The very same, my dears, and in appearance exactly as Justin described him to us. He had not exaggerated either, he really does look rather piratical. In fact I felt a little afraid of him at first but he is quite charming when one becomes better acquainted with him.'

'Oh, will we see him?' cried Sophy in thrilling accents. 'Is he still here?'

'No, they are gone out now but I should think it likely that you will meet him soon. Justin tells me that he has taken a house in Brook Street and means to be in London for some while.'

'And is he very handsome?' enquired Sophy, who had not yet learnt to judge a man other than by his appearance.

'I thought him so but I daresay you might not. He is several years older than you, my sweet.'

'I do not give a fig for that,' she pouted prettily. 'I am tired of silly, young men.'

'But what did you think of his character, Mama?' questioned Constance anxiously. 'Did he seem gentlemanly in his behaviour? Justin is such a trusting creature, his own manners are so frank and open that I am afraid of his being taken in by an unscrupulous person.'

'Then you may calm yourself. The Count is very much a gentleman. He is a man of good breeding and excellent address. I thought him remarkably self-possessed and he has the oddest way of looking at one as though he could read one's thoughts.' She paused reflectively. 'It really was most disconcerting.'

'And what of that scar on his face?' queried Sophy, much intrigued by her mother's description of the visitor. 'Is it very hideous?'

'No, of course not! I thought it made him look rather heroic and lent him a kind of strange fascination.'

'Oh, I wish I had been here! I would dearly like to have seen him,' Sophy complained in disappointment.

'I would have thought that you had seen enough

exhibits for one day,' Connie interrupted playfully. 'I wonder which will prove to be the most sinister – an Italian pirate or a Mexican serpent? We shall have to wait and see!'

They had not long to wait, for that very afternoon as they drove in the park at the hour of the fashionable promenade, they saw their brother strolling towards them with a group of his friends. As soon as he saw them he hailed their carriage and the barouche drew up beside him.

They all exchanged greetings and then Trevingham drew the Count forward in order to perform the necessary introduction, for he was the only gentleman in the party with whom they were as yet unacquainted.

'Connie, Sophy, I would like to make known to you a good friend of mine from Rome, who is staying in London for a while. This is Count Fabricati of whom you have already heard me speak. Count, these are my sisters, the Honourable Miss Constance Trevingham and the Honourable Sophia Trevingham.'

The Count doffed his high-crowned hat and swept them an elegant bow. 'Good afternoon, ladies, your brother has spoken so eloquently of you both that I almost feel as if I know you already and am therefore more than happy to be able to make your acquaintance at last.'

'Thank you, sir. It is kind of you to say so,' responded Constance, politely bowing her head in acknowledgement.

'Good afternoon, sir,' Sophy said, peeping shyly at him from beneath demurely lowered lashes. 'We have been very much looking forward to meeting you also. We were so disappointed to have been from home when you called this morning, were we not, Connie?'

'I expect we shall have several opportunities to meet the Count now that he is fixed in Town,' Constance answered coolly, thinking that her sister had spoken a little too effusively. She determined to let this stranger know from the first that she had no intention of being quite so easily charmed. She still thought him a decidedly shameless character from all that her brother had told them.

'I shall anticipate with pleasure each one of them, Miss Trevingham,' replied the Count smoothly as he replaced his hat firmly on his dark head and met her challenging gaze with complete equanimity.

'Will you take us up with you as far as the Stanhope Gate?' Justin asked them and having received Sophy's immediate agreement, he turned to the other two gentlemen.

'We will meet tonight then, as arranged. At ten of the clock. Dilly, I shall call in at Mount Street for you on my way there.'

Lord John Dillcott did not reply at first, his attention being still fixed in contemplation of Miss Sophia's exquisite countenance.

'Dilly! Are you listening? Or are you day-dreaming again?' demanded his friend in exasperation.

'Oh, I am sorry, Justin, I was ... er ... just thinking,' he apologized, tearing his eyes reluctantly away from the fascinating face of the young lady of his dreams.

'You ought not to set yourself so difficult a task, Dilly, you will find it is seldom worth all that effort,' advised the other gentleman, Sir Francis Brascombe. 'Now come, I think I see Alvanley ahead of us and I want a word or two with him. Until tonight, gentlemen,' he added with a flourish of his beaver hat and bidding adieu to the ladies, they walked away.

Trevingham and the Count climbed up into the barouche and his lordship gave the coachman the office. As they proceeded along the carriage-way, he began to point out to the Count various sights and persons of interest, ably assisted by his younger sister. The elder made use of the momentary distractions by surreptitiously studying the newcomer.

He was smartly attired in a single-breasted jacket fastened with three gold buttons. The fine cloth of a shade of dark blue, seemed moulded to his broad shoulders which apparently had no need of buckram wadding to enhance them. He wore his shirt collar fashionably high but without bordering on the ridiculous and his white muslin cravat was neatly and intricately tied. She calculated him to be some six feet in height, about the same stature as her brother. His long, muscular legs were encased in close-fitting pantaloons tucked into gleaming

Hessian boots, the tops of which were decorated with a small, gold tassel. From all this finery which she could see was of the very first stare, she opined that he was a man of some means. His taste in dress was refined and that at least met with her approval, the garments being exquisitely tailored but displaying none of the extraordinary affectations adopted by some members of the dandy set. The only jewellery he wore was a single fob at his waist and a plain sapphire and diamond pin in his cravat.

When she was sure that she was unobserved, she fell to studying his rather swarthy features. She guessed him to be somewhere in his early thirties. His brow was broad and high beneath the thick, raven hair which though close-cropped still strove to curl and as yet showed no touch of grey. The eyebrows were straight and very black above well-opened, dark eyes. His profile was Grecian in its perfection, the nose straight, the lips finely chiselled and the cheekbones high and well defined. The scar on the left side of his face did not after all render his appearance sinister but seemed to add to his undoubted masculine attractions. It somehow made his looks all the more arresting and she could well understand her mother's reactions to him. There was something else too, that was less easy to define. A certain aura that the man had, as of some latent power that was more than mere physical strength which he indubitably also possessed. It lay in his air of dispassionate composure, a complete self-confidence which set him apart from other men of her acquaintance. It was as if he cared for nothing and no one.

No wonder Justin had described him in such piratical terms, he certainly was cast in that mould but it was not the bold image of his face that impressed this upon her. Rather it was this last, strange sensation that remained with her long after he had departed and left her feeling distinctly uneasy.

Four

If Constance felt certain reservations about her brother's new companion, Sophia definitely did not. She declared him to be the personification of all her romantic dreams and endowed him with every heroic attribute that an active imagination could supply. For days after meeting him she talked of little else but the Count and what he said and did and how he looked, until she almost drove Constance to distraction. Justin found her infatuation highly amusing and teased his little sister unmercifully.

'There's no use in setting your cap at the Count, Sophy. He is not like to fall victim to a girl scarce nineteen. You would do better to cast your lures for a younger man. Poor old Dilly for instance. He dotes on you, you know.'

Sophy's blue eyes flashed fire. 'You know very well that I am doing nothing of the kind! Just because I happen to admire a man doesn't mean that I wish to marry him. And as for Lord Dillcott, I am not the least interested in his feelings. Besides, before he met me he was enamoured of Maria Westerly and a man who can fall in and out of love so quickly is not to be relied upon,' she added contemptuously.

'Neither is a man who by his own confession has no wish to lead a settled life,' warned Constance, looking up from her reading as their conversation broke into her concentration.

'He may wish to do so one day,' retorted Sophy, stung by her sister's disapproving words. 'When he meets the right woman.'

'And you think you might be that woman, I suppose,' laughed Justin. 'Well, you had better not be choosing your bride-clothes yet. James is a wily bird and has escaped the net so far. I would lay odds that he means to continue to do so.'

'I am no Diana,' Sophy replied coldly. 'You speak as if I were deliberately trying to entrap him. Other women may have to resort to such means but let me assure you that I have never found it necessary. Now if you have no objection I should like to change the subject.'

'I for one would welcome the change,' sighed Constance, throwing aside her book. 'It has become quite tedious.' She yawned and stretched her cramped limbs for she had been curled up on the sofa most of the afternoon. 'What a dismal day it has been; we shall have to have the candles lit early, I think. Do you go with us to Lady Holland's ball tonight, Justin?'

'I might take a look-in around eleven o'clock perhaps. It depends upon the other fellows – we are all dining at Brascombe's tonight before going on to Brooks's,' he answered non-committally. 'Does Mama go with you?'

'Yes, she is looking forward to it. That is why she has been resting all afternoon. I think I will go and see if she is awake.'

She swung her feet to the floor and stood up but instead of leaving the room immediately, she paused a moment and looked at her brother frowningly. 'Is the Count accompanying you this evening?' she asked suddenly.

'And what is your interest in the Count?' he replied in astonishment. 'I thought you did not want to hear any more about him?'

'Is he going to Brooks's with you?' she insisted, ignoring his question.

'Of course. Why should he not?' enquired Justin curiously. 'He is a member there after all.'

'Did he ask you to put up his name?'

'What does it signify whether he did or not? What is so odd about his being a member of a few clubs? I don't perfectly comprehend why you should be so concerned about the matter,' he said a little impatiently.

'My concern is only for you, believe me,' Constance assured him quietly. She put a hand on his arm and looked up into his face with an anxious expression in her eyes. 'You really don't know a great deal about his circumstances, do you, Jus? Is it wise to trust a man whose fortunes are entirely dependent upon the turn of a card?'

'I know he must sound a pretty havey-cavey sort of fellow to you, Connie, but he truly isn't such a loose screw as you imagine him to be. I wish I had never told you that tale, I ought not to have done so. Please forget it, will you?' he pleaded, a guilty flush colouring his fair skin.

'Is he not a gamester then?' she asked in surprise.

'Yes, he is,' he admitted reluctantly. 'But he is completely trustworthy; you need have no qualms on that score. He's just got a bit of an odd kick in his gallop, that's all. Likes to be mysterious, I suppose, but there's no harm in that. And he's a good man in a fight. Plenty of bottom; I would trust him with my life.'

'Well,' replied Constance, unconvinced by these credentials, 'I hope you never have to put that belief to the test. I just wish that you might tell me something a little more respectable about him. I don't like mysteries myself. I much prefer known facts. Will you at least promise me that you will be careful that you don't get yourself into any awkward scrapes?'

'What possible trouble do you think I might fall into?' he laughed, highly amused. 'I declare you are becoming as clucky as a mother hen!'

'Perhaps it is because I can sense that there is a fox about,' she answered pithily as she went out of the room.

Lady Trevingham was with her maid when Constance tapped at the door and asked if she were awake.

'Come in, my love,' she called out at the sound of her daughter's voice. 'I am just trying to decide which gown to wear tonight. Which do you think will be the most becoming, the purple silk or the sapphire satin? I suppose at my age it does not really matter,' she sighed, holding one of the dresses up against herself and glancing in the cheval glass. 'A woman with two grown-up daughters ought to cease concerning herself with her own appearance. After all, who will notice what I wear when I shall have two such beautiful, young ladies with me?'

'If it's reassurance you require, Mama, you need only look in your mirror,' laughed Constance. 'You know very well that you and Sophy are the only beauties in this family. I never could hold a candle to either of you but do not think that it irks me to know it,' she continued gaily, before her mother could utter a protest. 'Because Papa always said I had a great deal of common sense which he assured me was far more becoming in a woman. At least he thought it so and he is the only man whose good opinion I have ever cared for, except perhaps for dear Uncle George.'

'Yes, I know, dear,' replied her mother giving her a searching look. 'But I can't help wishing that you might have spent less time studying and a little more time enjoying yourself. It does not do for a girl to appear bookish. When a man is choosing a wife he does not consider cleverness an asset. I was used to tell your father so but he would have it otherwise. He was so proud of you. Even when you were quite a little girl, he would introduce you to people saying, "She's the clever one". I think it would have been better if he had not encouraged you to concentrate entirely upon your education. You never seemed to have much fun when you were Sophy's age. I could rarely prise you away from your books. Perhaps if I had tried harder.' She paused and sighed heavily. 'I feel I ought to have done so for your own sake. You might have been a wife and mother by now.'

'Oh, Mama, don't let us become embroiled in useless speculations,' broke in Constance cheerfully. 'I never had the slightest desire to be any man's wife. I am perfectly contented as I am – truly. I am leading a life of my own choosing and that is what pleases me most.'

'How strange. Count Fabricati said something of the sort when I first met him,' mused Lady Trevingham. 'I suppose I'll never understand you young people, for I did not value my independence so highly when I was a girl. In fact I longed to be married.'

'Yes, I know. You were a bride at eighteen were you not? Which reminds me,' she went on slowly, 'I wanted to speak to you about Sophy.'

'What about Sophy?' enquired her mama distractedly as she threw aside the satin and took up the purple gown.

'Well, you must have noticed that she is somewhat enamoured of this Italian Count. She speaks of nothing else lately. I am beginning to feel concerned that the matter is becoming too serious with her.'

'Oh, is that all that is worrying you? You need not be apprehensive about her. A girl of her age often fancies herself in love with an older man. I was madly in love with a friend of my papa's when I was only seventeen and he was not half so handsome as Count Fabricati. It is natural that she should have formed an attachment, he is after all a very romantic figure. You must have remarked upon it yourself, Connie. Even you cannot be completely blind to his attractions. He has only to walk into a room and every woman present is aware of it. Do you know what the ladies are saying about him?'

'No I do not,' Constance retorted uninterestedly.

'They think he is exactly like the Corsair. And, what is more, I quite agree! I could not help noticing it myself when I first set eyes on him. Don't you think so too?'

'I can't say that I have noticed any resemblance,' replied Constance, not quite truthfully. 'Besides, everyone knows that Conrad is a thinly disguised George Byron.'

Lady Trevingham shook her head despairingly. 'Oh, Connie, my poor girl, you are your father's daughter. But you cannot surely be so prosaic as you pretend, I will not believe it. I do not speak of Conrad's soul, that is wholly Byronic I should think but the Count has all the appearance of a Corsair.'

'Well, I am not of a romantic inclination, Mama, but Sophy is and I beg you will try to curb her enthusiasm in that direction. I would not like to see her hurt.'

'You are too serious, Constance, which I am certain Sophy is not. Besides, I am sure that an experienced man of the world like the Count can easily find ways of dealing kindly with love-sick young girls just out of the school-room.'

'I hope you are right, Mama,' sighed Miss Trevingham abandoning the conversation as a lost cause and going from the room. 'Wear the blue satin, Mama,' she advised as she opened the door. 'You are far too young to be wearing purple.'

'Oh, do you really think so?' Lady Trevingham asked doubtfully, holding up both gowns and looking from one to the other.

'Most definitely. Indeed, I think it would better become me to wear purple. Between you and Sophy, I feel positively ancient!'

However that might be, by the time they had attired themselves for the ball that evening, all three ladies looked very elegant.

Sophy wore a long robe of gossamer net over a celestial-blue satin slip and her bright, golden curls were entwined with tiny pink rosebuds. Lady Trevingham looked stately in the sapphire satin gown with a spangled scarf draped over her elbows and a diamond aigrette in her hair.

Even Constance, when she eventually appeared downstairs, had obviously taken great pains to look her best. Although she did not claim to have her sister's angelic beauty, she was none the less an attractive woman with regular features and honey-coloured hair which tonight she wore in dishevelled curls threaded through with green satin ribbons. The low, square-cut neckline of her deep-emerald silk gown displayed a generous bosom and the new, shorter length of skirt revealed a well-turned ankle. She was of average height, slender and with a good figure.

'Well, my children, you do me great credit,' beamed her ladyship, looking fondly at her daughters. 'I think you are not like to be without partners tonight. Shall we go?'

They put on their thick velvet mantles and stepped out to the waiting carriage. Soon they were wending their way through the busy traffic of Piccadilly, the streets brightly lit by the new gas lamps. When they neared Kensington, the press of carriages grew steadily thicker and they were some while before their coachman pulled up at the entrance to a magnificent Jacobean house. Two footmen in splendid livery came forward to open the carriage door and let down the steps. Then the ladies were handed out and found themselves standing on a long red carpet which had been laid down the flight of steps that led from the main portico.

Inside, all the spacious apartments were ablaze with lights. The swirling music of the stringed orchestra vied with the noisy clamour of many voices all speaking at once. As they climbed up the broad staircase where Lord and Lady Holland were waiting to greet their guests, Sophy turned to her sister and whispered loudly in her ear.

'Look, Connie! That is Lady Anne Rossmore ahead of us. I do hope Justin does come tonight, he will be sure to want to ask her to dance.'

'Much good will it do him,' replied Constance flatly. 'Our poor brother could never hope to be accepted by her family. Nothing less than a duke will do for them.'

'I am sure she likes him though,' mused Sophy. 'Whenever they are together in the same room, her eyes are often turned in his direction. I feel quite sorry for the poor girl. She does not seem to enjoy herself very much. Her guardians seldom allow her out of their sight and that Kirby woman who is, I suppose, her duenna, watches over her like a hawk.'

By this time they had reached the entrance to the ballroom and were being announced by the master of ceremonies. Lady Holland came forward to greet them, saying in her forthright way, 'Good evening, Amelia. How you continue to look so young at your age, I cannot conjecture but if you are to carry it off you ought not to have brought your girls with you. Good evening, my dears,' she went on in her rather loud voice. 'I'm afraid you will find it a dreadful squeeze as usual tonight but I know you won't mind that. Oh, excuse me, there is Mr Rogers.' She wandered off to greet her next guest and the three ladies went on into the ballroom.

The musicians were on a raised dais at one end of the room and at the other, supper tables had been set out in the room immediately adjoining. Rows of chairs had been placed along the walls for those not wishing to dance and here sat the dowagers, the older gentlemen and those unfortunate young ladies who had not as yet managed to fill their dance cards.

There were some three hundred persons present and the Trevingham ladies found themselves in constant danger of being uncomfortably jostled by the surging throngs.

'Oh, look!' cried Lady Trevingham, striving to make

herself heard above the din, 'there is Mrs Chessle waving to us. Let us go and speak to her for I think we shall be crushed to death if we stand here any longer.'

'Good evening, Amelia,' called out Mrs Chessle as they slowly negotiated their way around a group of people deep in conversation. 'See, I have secured some chairs for you. Come and sit by me, do.'

'Thank you, Dorothea, so good of you,' replied Lady Trevingham accepting the invitation gratefully and sinking down upon a fragile-looking piece of furniture her old friend had conveniently placed for her. 'Oh dear, what a squeeze!' she exclaimed and began to fan herself briskly with an ivory-handled fan of painted silk.

'Yes indeed. Lady Holland is justly famous for her entertainments. She is a marvellous hostess. One always meets such interesting people at her gatherings.'

'I wish she were not so outspoken though,' said Lady Trevingham. 'She is forever putting one to the blush! But tell me, where is your Georgiana? Is she dancing?'

'Yes she is,' replied Mrs Chessle proudly. 'We had scarce sat down when Mr Phillips carried her off. Oh, there is Mr Fanshawe coming across to us. I think I may hazard a guess as to who has commanded his interest,' she declared archly, glancing in Sophy's direction.

A young gentleman in a bottle-green coat and an exquisitely embroidered waistcoat came and stood before them. The points of his shirt collar were so high that he had great difficulty in turning his head to address her. He bowed stiffly and politely and enquired whether Miss Sophia might oblige him with her hand for the set that was then forming.

Sophy accepted gladly for she loved to dance and Mr Fanshawe was recognized as being an accomplished dancing partner. She went off happily with him, pleased that she would not have to remain a mere spectator and aware that she had triumphed over the other young damsels who watched their progress with envious eyes.

Constance, who cared not a whit whether she danced or no, sat down beside her mother and contented herself with observing the colourful pageant that moved around the room. She was absorbed in this interesting spectacle when a voice close by roused her from her reverie and she looked up with a startled expression on her face.

'Oh, Colonel Dyson, what a pleasant surprise. I did not look to see you here tonight, I know you are not wholly enamoured of these grand affairs.'

'Good evening, Miss Trevingham,' he said, his cool, grey eyes smiling down at her. He took her proffered hand in his own steady grasp and raised her slim, white fingers to his lips. 'I do generally dislike such gatherings but now that I find you here tonight, it seems that I am well rewarded for having put myself to the trouble of attending. May I sit down?'

'Please do, sir,' Constance invited him warmly as he drew forward another chair. Lady Trevingham and Mrs Chessle exchanged greetings with him and he sat down next to them.

Lady Trevingham was particularly delighted that he had come for she knew that Constance liked him and enjoyed his company. That he admired her daughter she knew very well but whether he entertained any stronger feelings for her she could not yet ascertain.

As to Connie's heart being touched, it was impossible to judge. If she felt any special regard, she did not show it. Her manners were always calm and reserved and she showed none of the usual agitations attributable to a woman in love. However, they made a handsome couple and a fond mother could not be blamed for at least hoping that her eldest daughter might yet find a husband, especially one so amiable as Colonel Dyson.

Her thoughts were interrupted by Mrs Chessle's putting a question to her and so she was obliged to give all her attention to that good-natured lady, whose rather florid countenance was growing redder by reason of the great heat in the room.

'Would you care to take a turn about the terrace?' she asked kindly, concerned by her friend's obvious discomfort.

'Well, perhaps for a minute or two,' she agreed readily. 'You will not mind if we leave you for a while?' she enquired of Constance.

'Not at all. I shall do very well now that I have Colonel

Dyson for company. Do you go and get some fresh air.'

'Thank you, my dear, we shall not be long,' assured Mrs Chessle and the two ladies moved away.

'I am glad to have the opportunity of speaking to you again, Miss Trevingham. It is some while since last we met, is it not?' said the Colonel reseating himself and turning towards her.

'Not since Lady Jersey's *soirée* as a matter of fact,' replied Constance returning his smile. 'You see what a good memory I have?'

'Then it was on September 20th that I last had the very great pleasure of your company. There, I also have not forgotten the occasion,' he responded in a low voice and fixed her with a speaking look.

She felt flattered that he had remembered the exact date and then mentally scolded herself for presuming that she had been the cause of his having done so. After all, there could be a dozen reasons why he should have noted it so particularly. She blushed slightly at her foolishness and plied her fan to cover her confusion.

'I understand your brother is now returned from Rome? Did he enjoy his sojourn there?' he went on, giving no indication that he had observed her heightened colour.

She was grateful that he had introduced a topic which would allow her time to recover her composure. Why was it that she behaved so ridiculously when he looked at her in that singular way?

'Oh, he enjoyed it immensely! He had plenty of opportunities to explore the city and has visited all the historic sights. There are so many buildings of great antiquity that are breathtakingly beautiful. He visited the famous Colosseum which he tells me is awe-inspiring and his descriptions had me in ecstasies. How I wish that I might one day see it all for myself. I should take my sketch book and my water colours and immerse myself in the joys of attempting to capture some of that magnificent grandeur on paper.'

'I am sure that those skilful fingers of yours and that perceptive eye would accomplish the task with ease. I was given the pleasure of admiring your work when I attended your mother's musical evening. You are a gifted artist, Miss Trevingham.'

'It is kind of you, sir, but I do not think I merit such very great praise,' replied Constance frankly.

'It is like you to say so. However, in this instance your modesty is misplaced. You are a very talented and intelligent young lady. In fact, I can honestly say that you are the only woman of my acquaintance who does not bore me to distraction. You are in all respects an exceptional person,' he finished, his eyes still holding her gaze.

She met his look consideringly. He spoke with such feeling in his voice that she wondered if he were trying to fix his interest with her. There was nothing flirtatious in his manner that she could detect, which seemed to imply that he was in all seriousness. Was it possible that he might indeed have formed a deeper feeling for her? Or was his partiality more that of a friend who shared similar tastes and interests?

'I am grateful for your good opinion, Colonel,' she replied lightly, not wishing to reveal the trend of her thoughts for fear she was mistaken in him. 'I only hope that I may never give you cause to revise them.'

'There is not the remotest possibility of my ever rescinding my views on that particular subject,' he reassured her warmly.

There was no mistaking his fervour as he uttered these words and she began seriously to suspect that he might indeed be growing enamoured of her. At this interesting juncture, their tête-à-tête was interrupted by Sophy's coming to press them into making up the next set.

Having yielded to her persuasions, they took their places beside Sophy and another of her gallant swains. The movement of the dance made further conversation difficult and Constance had ample opportunity to assemble her thoughts.

She indulged her imagination in speculating on the possibility of the Colonel's making her an offer. How would she receive such overtures? He was certainly an attractive man, intelligent and with pleasing manners and she liked him very much. She admired his military bearing and his easy and friendly disposition. It was this that had first recommended him to her notice when they had met at a Burlington House dinner party and on subsequent occasions during that long summer of celebrations for the visiting allied sovereigns. Since Wellington's victories had brought peace once again to the nation, the Colonel had found himself back in London and attached to the War Office, a position in which he appeared to have very little to do but attend numerous social functions.

'Now I suppose I must practise the art of cut and thrust with repartee, since my sword is no longer needed. A fact, I must confess, that I find somewhat irksome,' he had confided to her on one occasion.

She watched him as he went down the dance, noting how well the scarlet and gold tunic became him. His person was neat and precise to a pin, his light-brown hair brushed carefully to achieve a windswept look that suited his rather Roman features. He was of a stalwart build and of medium height which brought his expressive, grey eyes almost on a level with her own. They settled on her now with a tender concern in their cool depths.

'Why so silent?' he remarked softly. 'I wonder what occupies your thoughts? I hope nothing is troubling you, you looked so serious.'

'Oh, I was merely wool-gathering. Pay no attention to me,' she responded lightly.

'You ask the impossible. Your very presence commands it and I am your most obedient servant,' he replied earnestly.

She felt her heart skip a beat at the intensity of his gaze and knew not how to reply. Thankfully, the dance steps led her away from him again and she was spared the necessity of doing so. Her pulses continued to flutter for some minutes afterwards and she took herself mentally to task, feeling vexed by her weakness. Really! She was behaving like a love-sick schoolgirl instead of a reasonable woman of seven and twenty who ought to know better how to receive a compliment from an admirer.

When the dance ended, the Colonel offered her his arm and asked her if she would allow him to take her in to supper. She agreed willingly, not averse to resuming their conversation and hoping to restore her self-respect by behaving a little more sensibly.

As they moved towards the supper-room, she suddenly

espied Justin who had at that very moment entered the ballroom and was looking all about him.

'Oh, there is my brother. Let us go and speak to him,' she said pointing in his direction with her fan.

'Of course. I should like to have a word or two with him about his news from Italy. Perhaps we may persuade him to join us?'

They threaded their way through the crowds to gain his side and Constance called out to him as they approached.

'Justin! I am surprised to see you here. I thought you would not wish to leave your friends after all.'

'Oh, Connie, I was just looking for you. Good evening, Colonel Dyson,' he said with a quick nod and the Colonel bowed politely.

'Good evening, Trevingham. I trust I find you well? We were about to ask you if you would care to accompany us to the supper-room.'

'Well, I have not long since dispatched a substantial dinner,' he admitted hesitantly, 'but I daresay I might manage to swallow a bite or two.'

'I am certain you will,' Constance replied laughingly. 'You must know, Colonel, that my brother's appetite is quite remarkable.'

'At least my family think so for they mention it several times a day,' retorted Justin.

'As often as he takes sustenance, in fact,' she responded gaily. 'Now come, let us hurry for I see Mama and Sophy have already gone in.'

They continued on their way and joined the others who were just sitting down.

'Justin!' cried Sophy in delight, 'how long have you been here?'

'I have but this moment arrived. I know it is late but I had to change my clothes. Are you enjoying yourself, little one?'

'Immensely! I have not been without a partner all evening,' she announced proudly. 'But tell me, where is the Count? Did he not come with you?'

'No, he and Brascombe and the others have gone on a spree. I attended because Dilly was so insistent that we come. Have you seen him yet? He is supposed to meet me here.'

'No, I haven't,' replied Sophy carelessly. She would have much preferred to have discovered that he had brought the Count with him. 'I wish you might have prevailed upon Count Fabricati to have accompanied you instead.'

'And who is this Count that Miss Sophia is so eager to meet?' enquired the Colonel in a low voice as he drew his chair closer to Constance's side.

'You have not met him then? He is an Italian gentleman, a friend of Justin's. They met in Rome and he has recently come on a visit to London.'

'Indeed? No, I have not yet had the felicity of meeting him. But I should be most interested to do so. Do you find him as agreeable as your sister obviously does?'

'I reserve my judgement on the matter. He is agreeable, certainly, but most well-looking men can make themselves appear so – especially to women.'

'I perceive then, that such an advantage does not recommend itself to your more discerning eye?'

'I hope that I have at least learned to form my opinions on a sounder basis than mere physical attractions. I am certain that when my sister has as many years in her dish as I now have, she also will have gained a little wisdom in assessing the characters of such people as may come in her way.'

At that moment, Lord Dillcott came hastening towards their party, having already searched the ballroom for them.

He hurriedly bid them all good evening and asked if he might join them. He placed his chair as near to Sophy as he dared and sat himself down. He had taken great pains with his appearance knowing that she would be present and this had made him late in arriving. His guinea-gold curls were carefully pomaded and brushed *à la Titus* and he wore a snug-fitting tail-coat and immaculate, white satin knee-breeches. He fixed his pale-blue eyes on Sophy's face with dog-like devotion.

'There is to be waltzing after supper, Miss Sophia, I wondered if I might beg the very great honour of being permitted to stand up with you for one of the dances?'

'Well, it is very kind of you to ask me, Lord Dillcott, but you are rather late you know and I think my card is quite full,' she replied, slipping the ribbon from her wrist and casting her eyes along the list of signatures.

He looked so crestfallen that she immediately relented saying a little more kindly, 'Perhaps you may be able to dance with me at the end of the evening.'

He was inordinately pleased at such condescension and thanked her profusely. Constance hid a smile behind her fan, much amused at her sister's grand manner as she deigned to grant him his wish. If only this young lord would not wear his heart on his sleeve, she was certain that Sophy would soon begin to value his sincere regard.

After supper, during which the Colonel had asked Lord Trevingham a great many questions about his visit to Italy, they returned to the ballroom and reached the doorway at the very moment another party had risen to quit their table. Justin, who had been slightly ahead of the others stood politely by to allow these guests to pass out of the room. As he did so his glance fell upon the young woman who had almost collided with him. Constance, walking immediately behind him, saw the expression on his face alter as the colour crept into his cheeks and his blue eyes widened.

'Lady Anne!' he exclaimed in wonderment and executed a hasty bow. 'I had no idea that you were in Town. I had heard that you were gone to Hartsmere.'

'Good evening, Lord Trevingham,' she replied blushing as deeply as he. 'I came back to Grosvenor Square but yesterday. I am here with my aunt and uncle. You have recently returned from Italy, have you not?'

'Yes, that is so.'

'I wish you might call on us when you have time and tell us about the wonderful things you have seen on your travels,' she said shyly.

'I should be delighted to do so,' he answered eagerly. 'Perhaps tomorrow morning? Or would that not be convenient?' he added.

'We shall be at home on Thursday morning. Perhaps you could call then?' she suggested, her voice tentative.

'Most certainly,' he began, his eyes shining.

Before he could say anything else, the young lady's companion, a hatchet-faced woman in a lace cap and a black silk gown, seized the girl's arm.

'Come, my lady, we are crowding the doorway. It is time we went. It will soon be dawn and your uncle will be wishing to leave.'

'Oh, very well, Mrs Kirby,' she sighed. 'Goodbye, Lord Trevingham,' she smiled, casting him a last, glowing look from her huge, dark eyes as she was hurried away.

Justin stood gazing after her as if spellbound until Constance recalled his attention to the fact that he was impeding their progress.

'I had no notion that she was here,' he murmured in his sister's ear. 'If I had had the least inkling that she would be gracing this house with her presence, I would have given Brascombe the go-by and spent the entire evening laying siege to the fortress.'

'Then you would have sacrificed a good dinner for nothing,' answered Constance with asperity and then in a softer tone she added, 'You must know that her people will never look with kindness upon your suit, Justin. They are stiff and proud and determined that she shall be wed to the highest bidder. That family has always set great store by wealth and lands and you may be sure that they will never permit her to bestow her hand on any man who does not bring money and estates to join with hers.'

'I know,' he sighed despairingly as they moved on, 'but a man can dream can't he?'

'That is all it can ever be, Justin, a dream of happiness. She can never be your wife. It would be better for you if you did not call on her,' she advised him gently. 'I can see that your pursuing such a dream will only end in unhappiness and pain for you both. She might return your regard, indeed I think perhaps she does, but she would never go against her guardians' express wishes. She is too much under their influence.'

'I would free her from it, if I could,' he groaned bitterly. 'It is intolerable that they should hold such sway over her.'

'Her chains are golden ones, Justin, the heaviest and most difficult to break. I doubt that she would have the strength to do so even if she desired it.'

'Don't you think I know that?' he said bleakly. 'In this world she is beyond my reach but I must and will see her.'

Five

Lord Trevingham did not achieve his goal for, having presented himself in Grosvenor Square on the appointed morning, he was politely but firmly informed that her ladyship was indisposed. There was nothing more to be done but take himself off disconsolately, stopping only once on the corner of Brook Street to take a last, lingering look towards the grand mansion wherein lay concealed from his avid sight, the woman upon whom he had set his heart.

Being in the vicinity of Count Fabricati's chosen dwelling place, he betook himself to his door and knocked loudly.

Almost immediately his summary tattoo was answered by a little, dark-à-vised man who, having apprised himself of the visitor's name, invited him to step up to his master's dressing-room.

Trevingham went with heavy tread up the staircase, following slowly behind the servant who ascended to the upper floors with the speed and agility of a monkey. Before his lordship had even reached the door, he heard the Count's voice call out, '*Qui est ce?*'

'*C'est votre ami anglais, Monsieur le Comte. Milor' Trevingham.*'

'*Merci, Jean, je suis prêt – ou presque.* Come up Justin, I am just finishing my *toilette*.'

'I have done so. Good morning, James. I hope you don't mind me disturbing you at this unpardonably early hour.'

'No, not at all, I'm usually about before noon. Please be seated. I shall be with you in a moment,' replied the Count cheerfully. 'You must excuse me from getting up to greet you but I am at a critical stage as you can see.'

Justin pulled up a chair and, sitting astride it, folded his arms across the back and rested his chin on his hands. Despite the gloom that still depressed his spirits he watched with interest as the Count, who was sitting at his dressing-table, gave all his attention to his cravat.

The valet watched anxiously as his master put the last finishing touches to what could only be described as a work of art. As the Count sat back and admired his handiwork, he held out his hand.

'The emerald pin, Jean, I think,' he said musingly, not taking his eyes from the exquisite folds of crisp, white muslin.

His manservant opened a box bound with Morocco leather and searched among its contents. Then selecting the required ornament, he gave it to the Count. Another long silence ensued as Fabricati's hand wavered an instant before placing the gleaming jewel tenderly amongst the folds of his cravat.

'*Oh, mais c'est parfait!*' cried the little valet enthusiastically.

'Yes, I think that will do,' commented the Count thoughtfully. 'I confess I am not ashamed of my efforts. What say you, Justin?'

'It looks well enough to me. Is it your own creation?'

'I call it the Continental Cascade,' he replied, rising from his chair and allowing his valet to ease him into a square-cut tail-coat of dark-green super-fine. Having ensured by means of a backward glance in the mirror that it set across his shoulders without a crease, he turned to Jean again who quickly fastened all but one of the double row of buttons. Then taking up a nosegay of mignonette, he carefully placed it in his buttonhole.

'Now I am completely at your service,' he said with satisfaction. 'But what is this? Why so down in the mouth? You look as if you have lost a guinea and found a groat.'

'No, it's worse than that, my friend,' he sighed deeply. 'You see before you an object of pity – a star-crossed lover.'

'Wherefore art thou a Romeo?' enquired the Count with sympathetic interest as he reached for his hat.

'I am separated from the woman I adore by her detestable family. That is why I have come to you, James.'

'My sword is at your disposal, naturally,' he offered nobly. 'So lead on, friend Montague.'

This won a weak smile from Trevingham as he rose slowly to his feet. 'Would that I could accept your offer but alas this is London and not Verona. But will you come with me to Angelo's and I shall vent my spleen not with a rapier but with a foil instead?'

The Count gazed at him with a comical expression of dismay on his handsome face.

'What is the matter?' questioned his lordship. 'Can't you come with me?'

'I am entirely at your service, of course, Justin. I just wish you had invited me two hours ago.'

'Why? What difference would that have made?' asked Trevingham looking perplexed.

'The difference between a Continental Cascade and a Belcher neckcloth,' was the succinct reply.

'Count Fabricati, you become more like an Englishman every day you spend in this city!' laughed his lordship, shaken at last from his misery. 'Come then and you shall teach me that trick of the wrist you used against those Captain Sharps when we were in Rome.'

'It will be my pleasure to do so,' smiled the Count, clapping on his curly-brimmed beaver at a rakish angle. 'Let us sally forth.'

The two gentlemen sauntered off towards Bond Street but before they reached number thirteen they were hailed by the Misses Trevingham who happened to be at that moment emerging from Hookham's Library.

'Justin! I thought you intended to call in Grosvenor Square this morning?' said Constance in surprise.

'I did. But I need not have taken the trouble. Now I am going to Angelo's with Fabricati here and he is going to show me some new passes, for I am in a mood to slay a few Capulets.'

'We have been selecting some books,' Sophy explained, paying no attention to her brother but instead fixing her sparkling eyes upon the Count. He looked so handsome this morning, or so she thought, that he outshone every other gentleman of her acquaintance. 'See, I have chosen *Lara*,' she added coyly.

'I have an unforgivable confession to make, Miss Sophia,' replied Fabricati ruefully. 'You will no doubt think me contemptible, but I have to tell you that I have not read any of Lord Byron's poetry. There, now you know the awful truth and I suppose that I am sunk beyond reproach. You may give me the cut-direct from this moment on and who shall blame you?' he mourned dejectedly.

Sophy giggled girlishly. 'You are too absurd, sir. I should never be prevailed upon to do so. How should you have read his works when you have been resident in England so short a while?'

'And I thought that you said the Count was well read, Justin?' Constance remarked shaking her head in seeming disgust.

'Your brother had that not quite right, Miss Trevingham,' the Count interjected apologetically. 'What he meant to say of course, was that I read well.'

Despite herself, for she was determined that she would never succumb to his charm, she could not forbear to smile.

'Why did we not see you at Holland House the other night?' asked Sophy. 'I thought you would have attended with Justin and Dilly. You would have enjoyed it immensely, I am sure. It was a splendid ball.'

'Ah, Miss Sophia, Justin had angled for an invitation for me but alas, being something of a loose fish,' he sighed dolefully, meeting Constance's eye with devilment in his own, 'Lady Holland very naturally cast me off.'

Constance held his gaze without a blush, her blue-grey eyes brimming with amusement. The Count obviously had no illusions about himself and she knew instinctively that he had not been offended by her remark, though she would take Justin to task later for informing him of it.

'Lady Holland is known as a woman of great distinction,' she commented pointedly.

'*Touché*, Miss Trevingham,' he acknowledged admiringly. 'Of course I should have known better than to appear in London in the autumn. One is bound to be taken for a mushroom.'

Constance had to bite her lip to prevent another smile

appearing but her eyes meeting his mock-solemn expression, danced with suppressed merriment which drew an answering gleam from his own dark orbs. Hastily she averted her gaze, her cheeks flushing rosily for some unaccountable reason.

'Well, I think it very unkind of her,' pouted Sophy crossly. 'But you will come to Almack's on Tuesday next, won't you? There is to be a Gala night. Please say you will come?' she implored him earnestly.

'Sophy! Please!' admonished Constance frowning blackly at her sister. 'I am sure the Count has other, more pressing engagements.'

The sharpness in her voice owed more to the anger she felt at herself for allowing a fleeting glance to break through her guard.

'On the contrary, if Miss Sophia insists upon it, I shall of course do my very best to attend,' he replied readily. 'Especially if she promises to save me one of her dances.'

'I'll see that he keeps his promise,' vowed her brother who had already decided to attend himself in the hope that Lady Anne might be there also. They then parted company, the ladies returning home and the gentlemen continuing on their way. As they went up to Angelo's rooms they met Brascombe and two of his cronies who were entering Jackson's for some sparring lessons. Upon learning from Trevingham that the Count was something of an expert in the art of fencing, they expressed an interest in accompanying them in order to view the proceedings. The Count raised no objection and so they all went in together. There were several other gentlemen already engaged in their lessons under the watchful eye of Henry Angelo himself.

When they had prepared themselves, Fabricati and Trevingham took up their foils and fell to with a will but it soon became apparent that the young lord was no match for his gifted opponent. Even Angelo, who had been observing the play of the swords with great interest was drawn to comment on the Count's dexterity.

'It is a joy to watch such virtuosity, sir,' he cried enthusiastically as Trevingham lowered his foil to the floor, quite spent with his exertions. 'Only Italy could produce such a master of the art!'

The Count bowed politely and saluted with his sword. 'Praise from you, sir, is praise indeed.'

'B'gad, sir!' exclaimed a gentleman in a snuff-brown coat who was of Brascombe's company, 'I never saw a man so quick and light on his feet and you take such risks! That last riposte quite took my breath away, you are a consummate artist, sir.'

'Thank you. I admit to being something of a past-master in the art,' he acknowledged much to Trevingham's consternation for he was all too conscious of the innuendo.

'It is quite beyond my poor skills to match you,' he broke in hurriedly, afraid lest his friend say something even more outrageous.

'But not beyond mine, perhaps,' said a voice behind him.

Trevingham spun round, startled. 'Oh, it's you Morton,' he observed with a note of contempt in his voice.

The gentleman inclined his head, disdainfully ignoring the unfriendly remark and turned towards the Count.

'His lordship has not represented us well I fear,' he drawled. 'I have easily mastered him myself on many occasions both with sword and pistol, have I not Trevingham?'

His lordship merely scowled furiously. Morton smirked at his discomfiture and, turning his back on him, continued, 'I should be happy to restore the honour of my country if you would permit me, Count. Allow me to introduce myself. Mr Giles Morton at your service.' He gave a flourishing bow.

The Count responded equally graciously. 'By all means, if that is your desire.' Without further ado they made their dispositions and with a perfunctory 'on guard' took up their stance.

Morton confidently took the initiative and opened the attack with a sudden thrust in tierce as if hoping to goad his opponent into an imprudent reply. Fabricati, however, was on his mettle and parried immediately and perfectly cool-headedly in quarte. They both circled more warily this time until Morton lunged again, trusting that by dint of sheer ferocity he could break through the Count's guard. Fabricati met a series of well-timed thrusts with an apparent ease that made his defence appear almost careless. Then, with a subtle movement of his wrist, he suddenly changed his tactics and replied with a riposte so swift and unexpected that it forced Morton to break ground. He managed to recover his guard at once and delivered another rapid lunge which Fabricati skilfully countered and the blades hissed together. The Count's wrist seemed to be made of steel as he rapidly disengaged and almost without pausing attacked again with such lightning ripostes that he drove Morton back several paces. The sound of clashing metal echoed round the room as the two men fought energetically on. Morton displayed some masterly strokes, he was no mean swordsman but as the minutes went by he began to show signs of weakening. The man's face had lost its sneering look and his expression now was rather grim, the sweat standing in beads across his flushed brow. His breath was labouring under the onslaught of that tireless arm, yet Fabricati seemed hardly winded. His dark eyes were alight with exultation and his lips curved into a smile of sweet pleasure as if he relished the excitement of the combat. He had a panther-like grace and suppleness which, together with his inexhaustible strength, made it appear that he was playing with his opponent as a cat would torment a mouse. Morton was now finding it extremely difficult to maintain his guard and was pressed into retreating again and again. His fury began to mount as he realized he was hopelessly out-matched and when he thought he saw an opening in defence, he lunged with a straight thrust only to meet another clever parry in quinte. He recovered and renewed his attack. The Count seemed to fall back before this determined effort and made a sweeping parade. Seizing his opportunity, Morton slipped under his guard and aiming a deep thrust along the arm, pressed home his foil. The gentlemen gasped in excitement but to their utter amazement the Count, with astonishing speed, evaded the blade and replied with an unexpected riposte followed by a cunning feint which lured Morton's foil into another wild lunge. Their weapons crossed, Fabricati's forte against the other's foible. Morton's arm trembled with fatigue and he gritted his teeth as he strove to master the situation but with a quick, twisting movement, the Count's blade made a glittering arc and his opponent's foil flew out of his hand and spun across the floor.

'Bravo! Bravo!' cried Angelo clapping his hands delightedly. 'I could not have done better myself!'

The Count tucked his sword under his arm and holding out his hand stepped towards Morton. 'My thanks for the exercise, sir. It was most invigorating.'

Without uttering a single word, the man ignored the friendly gesture and turning on his heel strode out of the room.

Everyone else crowded round the victor, shaking his hand and congratulating him on his mastery of the sword.

'I would not have missed that for a hundred guineas,' declared Brascombe joyously. 'I wish you might show me that trick of the wrist you used to disarm your man.'

The gentleman in the brown coat tapped him on the shoulder saying, 'Sir, allow me to thank you. That was an experience, sir, an experience! I hope you will overlook the brutish behaviour of that *gentleman*.' He emphasized the word with a curl of his lip. 'He is a poor loser and disgraces the fair name of England.'

The Count shrugged indifferently. 'He is young and has not yet learned to govern his feelings and therefore I take no offence,' he replied. Then turning to Lord Trevingham who was grinning from ear to ear, he murmured, 'Would that he had been a Capulet.'

'But he was!' laughed Trevingham. 'That's the wonder of it! You don't know how much good you have done my spirits in allowing me to witness such a trouncing! I am greatly in your debt.'

'I am happy to have been of service but if what you say is true it may go ill with your wooing.'

'I do not care, I would not have foregone that pleasure for anything. He has been a source of irritation to me for some time and besides, my courtship could not be in worse case. Now, come, we will go to White's. I can't wait to tell Dilly about this, he will be vexed to have missed Morton's defeat. No one has ever managed to best him before; he is very proud of his reputation as a Corinthian and must be feeling extremely nettled that you ousted him from his pedestal so easily. You will find yourself something of a hero amongst those of us who have suffered the ignominy of defeat at the hands of that braggart.'

'I wonder which wreath I shall be receiving first?' mused the Count as he glanced towards the door through which his vanquished opponent had just passed. The look which had been cast in his direction was deadly indeed.

A little while later they strolled along St James's Street until they came to the imposing building with its famous bow-window facing on to the street, where sat the equally famous members of White's Club. The most illustrious names in the land were entered in the register, mostly of the Tory persuasion and it was considered essential to a gentleman's social standing to be listed in its pages. Entering the historic portals, they were immediately greeted by several of their acquaintances.

Trevingham eagerly began to regale them with the events at Angelo's and the Count, much to his amusement, found himself at the centre of an admiring little crowd.

'I wish I had been there!' announced Lord Dillcott longingly, for he had been one of the hapless gentlemen who had been thoroughly humiliated by Morton's superior skills. It was not so much that he had been fairly beaten, he was too good-natured to bear any malice for that reason, no, it was hearing Morton's derisory remarks about his ineffectual efforts when boasting to his friends how easily he had overcome his young opponent.

'It was about time someone showed that fellow a thing or two. He's such an arrogant prig.'

'Well, he met his match today, Dilly; I don't think he will be so keen to spread this story abroad,' grinned Trevingham who had his own axe to grind with the unpopular Morton.

'Lord, I'd give a monkey to have seen his face when you managed to disarm him so neatly,' enthused Dillcott, a smile lighting his eyes at the mere thought.

'Where did you learn to fence like that, Count Fabricati? In Italy I suppose?' asked Brascombe with interest.

'I have practised in Italy, yes and in Spain,' he answered, pretending not to notice Trevingham's anxious look.

'You must have had some excellent fencing masters,'

Brascombe commented. 'You could teach us all a trick or two I think.'

'Yes, indeed. You've already taught Morton a lesson he won't forget in a hurry,' interspersed another gentleman who had just joined them. 'He has a long memory and a deplorable habit of bearing a grudge when he imagines himself aggrieved. Will you introduce us, Brascombe?' he continued, turning to Sir Francis.

'Of course, my lord. Count Fabricati, this is the Marquis of Fearnley.'

The two men bowed politely to one another and, recognizing the marquis as that same gentleman who had spoken to him at Angelo's, the Count held out his hand. 'I am delighted to make your acquaintance, my lord. I take it that you also are a keen fencer?'

'I have been fortunate to have had the benefit of a good master and fancied myself as something of an exponent of the art. However, having witnessed your performance this noon, I realized at once that I was in the presence of a superior swordsman. I should very much like to have the opportunity to cross foils with you if you would oblige me.'

'I should be honoured. I am entirely at your disposal,' replied the Count with a slight bow.

'Excellent!' smiled the Marquis. 'Now I wonder if you would care to join us in a hand or two of macao? You are familiar with the rules?'

'Thank you, my lord, the answer to both questions is yes,' he agreed willingly.

They moved away to find a table and as the Count made to follow, Lord Trevingham caught his arm and held him back.

'I hope you know what you are about, James. The stakes are always very high at Fearnley's table,' he warned in a whisper.

The Count gave one of his characteristic shrugs saying, 'Then I shall have to see to it that I acquit myself well.'

'Indeed you must,' concurred Trevingham earnestly. 'Your father is not a duke of the realm willing to guarantee your losses.'

'I have no need of a duke, Justin. But I could find a use for a few sovereigns,' he admitted with a wink.

Lord Trevingham gave a sigh of resignation and, having nothing further to say in the matter, let him go and took himself off to order a substantial lunch. When the card table broke up some considerable time later, the Count was able to allay his friend's fears.

'Well, that was quite a profitable afternoon,' he informed his lordship with satisfaction. 'I think it may suit me to remain in London for some time. It seems that the streets are paved with gold, most especially in St James's.'

'I take it that you are not after all being asked to resign?' guessed Lord Trevingham much relieved at the news.

'You really must try for a little more faith in my abilities, you know, Justin,' replied the Count in a rallying tone. 'Did I not promise you that I would never give you cause for embarrassment?'

'I seem to recall your saying something of the sort but you certainly give me some excruciating moments. I nearly expired when you made that remark about being a past-master! If it ever became known that you had....' He paused and looked over his shoulder to reassure himself that they were not in danger of being overheard. 'That you had been a fencing-master,' he went on *sotto voce*, 'then you would be completely ostracized.'

'But I have already been asked to give a few lessons by some of these gentlemen, including the marquis,' he said with a look of innocent enquiry.

'Yes, I am aware of that but you won't be getting paid for them. That's the difference. You won't be a hired instructor,' he explained patiently.

'*"O tempora! O mores!"*. Forgive me, Justin. I spent my earliest youth in Revolutionary France where such niceties ceased to be important for a while.'

'I say, you're not an anti-royalist are you?' Trevingham exclaimed, suddenly struck by a dreadful notion.

'Have I not already told you that I have a great affection for golden crowns and sovereigns?'

'James, please do be serious for a moment and tell me that you are not a revolutionist.'

'I have not come to England to overthrow the monarchy, Justin, you may rest easy on that head. Neither am I about to start a revolution in this sceptred isle,' reassured his friend soothingly.

'Who's going to start a revolution?' enquired Lord Dillcott, interrupting their tête-à-tête.

'No one,' smiled the Count turning to the young gentleman. 'At least, Justin imagined that I might be considering doing so and I was merely impressing upon him that it is not after all the case.'

'Oh, that's all right then,' commented Lord Dillcott brightly. 'Damned inconvenient things revolutions. Makes the hoi-polloi behave very oddly.'

'Yes, my lord, revolutions can cause people to lose their heads completely, can they not?'

'Rather!' agreed his lordship whole-heartedly. 'Devilish unpleasant business. But why should you think that the Count would want a revolution, Trev?'

'Oh, never mind. It's no matter. We were just funning, you know. Come on, let's go and take a stroll in the park.'

'Very well, as you wish,' acquiesced the Count. 'But first, allow me to make my farewells to the marquis. He has been so very obliging,' he confided, patting his pocket significantly.

When eventually they emerged in St James's Street, the Count was able to inform his friends that he had had the felicity of being invited to dine with the marquis the following evening at the Clarendon in Bond Street.

'I have heard that Monsieur Jacquier's establishment is famous for its excellent menu. It is a long while since I enjoyed the delights of some good French cuisine. I shall look forward to it.'

Trevingham gave a low whistle. 'My, my, you are fortunate today. Fearnley is known as a generous host and with good reason. The Clarendon is one of the most expensive hotels in London.'

'Lord, yes! I dined my Aunt Matilda there on her birthday. Do you know that a bottle of claret costs a whole guinea? And unfortunately the old lady is vastly fond of claret wine,' remarked Lord Dillcott reminiscently.

'In that case it is as well that I am to be his guest,' laughed the Count, 'because I also am not averse to a good bottle of claret. However, if Fearnley is such a high-flyer as you suggest, it would perhaps be wise of me to bear in mind the salutary lesson of young Icarus.'

'Drank too much claret, did he?' enquired Dillcott sympathetically.

'Actually, he drank too much water,' explained the Count, ruefully.

'Oh, I don't think you need worry then. I'm certain Fearnley never touches it himself. At least I've never seen him do so. Neither do I as a matter of fact, pretty awful stuff in my opinion. I tried it once at Cheltenham. It was quite revolting. Can't think why this chap you mentioned liked it so much,' he ruminated with a puzzled frown.

'I'm afraid Dilly's mind is something of a labyrinth,' said Trevingham fondly. 'He's apt to wander in it from time to time, often becoming hopelessly lost as you can see.'

'Well let's hope he never finds his way out of it,' grinned the Count as they turned into Piccadilly.

At this hour of the day, the street was full of vehicles and horseriders jostling for position and most of them heading for the park.

There were gigs, curricles, phaetons, tilburys and landaus all threading their way towards Hyde Park Corner for it was the hour of the promenade. Now was the time when members of the *haut ton* converged upon this part of Mayfair to drive in the park, ride in Rotten Row or stroll in the broad walks around the Serpentine.

For the ladies it was the opportunity to display their modish hats, carriage and walking-dresses, riding-habits and various elegant accessories, whilst the gentlemen could show off their newest acquisitions from Tattersall's or arouse the envy of their contemporaries with the latest sporting carriages. It was a time to see and be seen and for both sexes a chance to note the occupants of the passing carriages that they might be the first with the most interesting *on dits*.

The pavements in Piccadilly were always crowded with pedestrians. It was one of the busiest streets in London, for besides the great mansions behind their high brick walls it contained hotels, clubs, grand houses and many coaching offices.

Having given a penny to acquire the services of the little crossing-sweeper, the three gentlemen reached the tollgate and passed the Curds-and-Whey Cottage at the entrance to the park.

As they approached the carriage road intending to stroll in the direction of the lake, they were obliged to wait while a smart barouche drawn by four matched bays bowled past them. A stout, middle-aged woman wearing a richly embroidered mantle and a bonnet adorned with curled ostrich feathers was sitting in the carriage holding on her lap a little Pekinese dog. Just as they were about to continue on again, they heard the woman cry out, a note of panic in her voice. Glancing back, they saw that the dog had jumped out on to the road and was in danger of being run down by a curricle following behind.

The Count, seeing at once that the silly creature was intent upon yapping at the heels of the nearest horses, leapt swiftly after it and seized it by the scruff of the neck, only just managing to avoid the plunging hoofs of a highly-strung pair of greys. He spoke a few calming words to the struggling animal until it lay passive in his grasp, then he walked back to the barouche which had come to a halt several feet away.

The woman had climbed down from the carriage and was turning towards him, her face white with shock.

'You may be easy now, madam,' he said soothingly. 'The dog has taken no hurt I assure you; see, he is perfectly well.' He placed the animal in her outstretched arms and she clutched it immediately to her ample bosom.

'Oh, thank you, sir!' she cried, greatly relieved to find he was speaking the truth. 'It was so brave of you to rescue my poor little Chino. Oh, when I think what might have befallen him!' She shuddered and closed her eyes against the dread thought.

'Well, there's no harm done after all, so please don't alarm yourself any further. Perhaps it would be safer if you kept a tight hold on his collar from now on.'

'Oh, I will! I most certainly will!' she vowed fervently, hugging the dog even tighter and raining kisses on its head. 'I'm so very grateful to you, sir. You reacted so quickly! Such presence of mind! I really cannot thank you enough for saving my darling's life.'

'I am content to have been of service to you, ma'am. Please allow me to help you up into your carriage,' he insisted gallantly and held open the door for her.

'You are very kind, sir. I am most grateful; goodbye,' she said as he handed her into the barouche.

'*Au revoir, madame*,' he replied with a bow and raising his hat, turned away to rejoin his companions.

'Well!' exclaimed Trevingham as the Count came up with them. 'This is quite a day for you, James. First you make an enemy of one Capulet and then an instant friend of another.'

'Oh? Have I managed to do so?' queried the Count, mildly surprised.

'That was none other than the aunt of my sweet Lady Anne,' explained his lordship with a grim smile. 'Would that I had been the recipient of her undying gratitude. Perhaps I might then have had the opportunity to advance my suit a little more successfully. I wish I had your quick wits, James. You always seem so alert to dangers, I remember remarking upon it when we were together in Italy. It's almost as if you are always anticipating the unexpected.'

'Oh, I am usually awake upon any suit, you know,' the Count replied cheerily. 'It probably comes of a misspent youth forever watching for the turn of a card.'

'Well, whatever the reason, you have possibly done me a great good,' he said thoughtfully. 'Yes, indeed, we may be able to turn this piece of luck to our advantage.'

'Forgive me, Justin, but young Dillcott and I are rather in the dark as to why we are suddenly so fortunate,' replied the Count in amusement. 'Perhaps you could enlighten us?'

'Don't you see?' cried Trevingham, his eyes shining with excitement. 'You have rendered her ladyship a great service. She positively dotes on that silly dog and by an act of selfless courage you have just saved it from certain death. Now do you understand?'

'Well, I think we can appreciate the dog's good fortune,' answered the Count exchanging a comical look with Lord Dillcott. 'But we don't seem to find ours quite so obvious, do we, Dilly?'

'Can't yet see what is advantageous about the situation,' grinned Dillcott, hugely entertained.

'Then let me explain matters as simply as I can,' continued Trevingham patiently. 'I am speaking of gratitude.'

'Gratitude?' repeated Dilly, blankly. 'How will that advantage us?'

'Gratitude, my dear Dillcott, will gain us an entry to a certain house in Grosvenor Square. Doors which hitherto were closed to us will now be miraculously opened.'

'I'm sorry, Justin,' apologized the Count, 'but Dilly and I still haven't found the key. You will have to be a little more explicit.'

'I see you are determined to be obtuse. Very well, I shall reveal the trend of my thoughts. That lady to whom you have just given such signal service, is wife to the head of the house of "Capulet". Her gratitude towards you, James, will know no bounds. She is now deeply indebted to you, the heroic saviour of her heart's delight! You will enquire tomorrow morning as to the health of the poor creature and she will invite you in to see for yourself. You and she will become the greatest of friends and she will probably invite you to dine. You will then be introduced to her family and in return you will naturally wish to make your friends known to her, that they also may bask in her favour.'

'Oh, naturally I would!' agreed the Count wholeheartedly, 'if I were in the happy position of being acquainted with her. But unfortunately we did not introduce ourselves.'

'What!' exclaimed Trevingham aghast. 'You did not give her your name?'

'I did not think to inform her of it,' he replied meekly penitent. 'Of course, if I had known the lady's identity, I should have made a push to advance your cause then and there.'

'Never mind. All is not lost. She may well be at Almack's next week and you may have the opportunity to redeem yourself.'

'But, Justin, I cannot force myself upon her notice!' protested the Count laughingly.

'You won't need to. Mama says you are the type of man a woman always notices, even in a crowded room. Sophy told me,' replied Trevingham with a grin. 'Evidently the ladies think you bear a striking resemblance to this Corsair character that Byron has created and consequently you are setting quite a few female hearts a-flutter.'

'I had not realized that Lady Trevingham was romantically inclined, although having listened to her son, I ought to have guessed it!'

'Oh, yes, we are all romantical in our family. All except Connie, of course. She is too much like our father, not at all imaginative, you know.'

'Well, if you imagine I am going to cultivate a closer relationship with that woman in the barouche, you are very much mistaken!' retorted the Count decidedly. 'I'd sooner befriend the dog!'

'Excellent! Anyone who befriends that dog will earn the approbation of the owner.'

'Then I hope *you* are a dog-lover!' declared the Count with alacrity.

Six

It seemed that destiny had determined that the Count was to be thrust upon "Lady Capulet's" notice, for the very next evening whilst dining with the marquis and Sir Francis Brascombe, she crossed his path again.

She arrived at the Clarendon soon after he had sat down to dinner. He recognized her rather large figure immediately but at first she did not see him and he hoped that he would be able to escape her attention altogether. However, it so happened that as he turned to address a remark to the marquis, her eye suddenly fell upon him and he was aware that she was staring intently across at him. He saw her lean towards the man sitting on her right to exchange a few words and then they both gazed in his direction.

The Count pretended not to observe their apparent curiosity and managed to appear oblivious of her presence. It was not until he was leaving the hotel, when he was obliged to pass by her table, that she succeeded in catching his eye but he merely gave a slight bow to acknowledge her.

He decided that he would not mention the coincidence to Lord Trevingham, anticipating the disappointment that would follow, once Justin discovered that his friend had not availed himself of a golden opportunity to further his acquaintance with the lady.

Some days later, he was again reminded of the incident when Trevingham called in Brook Street to reassure himself that the Count had not forgotten his promise to attend the gala night at Almack's.

'I hope you don't mean to cry off, James, because I need you there tonight. All you have to do is make yourself known to the old dragon and then introduce me as your most intimate and respected friend. After that I shall shift for myself.'

'You need not fear, Justin. I shall be there. But only because I promised your beautiful sister. I make no promises to you, however. I am no substitute for St George.'

The Count was as good as his word and made his appearance well before the eleventh hour, the time when the doors would be firmly closed against late-comers, be they the highest in the land.

Sophy was insistent that he dance with her immediately and triumphantly entered the set upon his arm, knowing full well that every female eye was upon them. She was woman enough to rejoice in the knowledge that several of her friends were following their progress down the dance with jealous glances. The Count had excited no little interest since his entrance into their social circles and she realized that she was in an enviable position, thanks to her brother. All the ladies were eager to be introduced to the 'Corsair'; his dark good-looks and buccaneering air had fascinated and intrigued their romantic hearts, already excited by Lord Byron's poetic tales.

Constance alone viewed him with unfriendly suspicion. It troubled her deeply that her family had chosen to introduce such a man into society. What did Justin really know of him? Only such things as this Farenden or Fabricati, as he chose to call himself, had decided to tell him. How could Justin know that even these few details were factual? What sort of man was he in truth? An honest man or a cheat? She rather suspected the latter. It had not escaped her notice that he knew just how to manipulate people to his purposes. He had a way of drawing out confidences that caused his interlocuters to divulge more about themselves than perhaps they were aware. His eyes seemed to miss nothing, although he himself gave little away. She had tried her hardest to elicit information from him but without success; he carefully parried all her direct questions and his guard never wavered, not even for an instant. She could well appreciate how such astonishing reserve could stand a gamester in good stead.

She frowned in annoyance as she observed her sister's rapt expression. What was he saying to make Sophy smile up at him in that moonish way? More ridiculous flattery no doubt, just the kind of compliment he would make to a gullible girl. The man was probably a practised flirt and only too aware of the effect he was having on all these foolish women, whose vain imaginings were fed by the fantasies dished up from the over-flowing cauldron of Byron's egocentric genius.

'I declare, Miss Trevingham, you looked positively thunderous just now,' murmured a voice at her shoulder. 'I wonder what thoughts are passing through your sharp mind?'

Constance turned to Lady Jersey, smiling slightly and saying coolly, 'I daresay I am becoming a crotchety old maid, that would account for my sour expression.'

'Do not say so; I cannot imagine you putting on a lace cap yet awhile. You are far too pretty and I know several gentlemen who would agree with me.'

'Ah but you did not say *young* gentlemen,' replied Constance lightly.

'Well, they were not in their dotage either,' laughed Lady Jersey. 'Colonel Dyson certainly is not,' she added coyly.

'Colonel Dyson is a well-mannered gentleman; I'm sure he would speak graciously of any lady with whom he was acquainted, whatever her age,' she responded smoothly.

'Yes, he is charming, is he not? And so it seems is your sister's partner,' she observed. 'I have never seen her in such a sparkling mood.'

'My sister is always at her happiest when dancing.'

'What an attractive creature this Italian Count is to be sure – and so intriguingly mysterious! Quite fascinating! What a good thing it is that dear George is so occupied at present with his courtship of Miss Milbanke, his nose would be sadly out of joint. I understand that Count Fabricati is a friend of your brother? They met in Rome, I believe? He is perhaps a member of one of the old, established Roman families?'

'I daresay,' replied Constance evincing a sudden interest in her dance card. 'Oh, do excuse me, I see that I promised this next dance to Lord Alvanley,' she explained as she moved hurriedly away.

She bit her lip in annoyance. These were just the questions she had expected but dreaded. People were bound to be curious, the Count must realize that. Did he not care that he had placed Justin's family in an impossible situation? What were they supposed to answer to such enquiries? If it were not for her brother, she would be only too ready to expose the imposter! How dared he embroil them in his dubious games! It really was too bad of Justin to make a friend of this fly-by-night gamester.

When, later that evening, the Count asked her to dance with him, he was summarily refused but the set-down she had given was received with his usual aplomb.

'Is something troubling you, Miss Trevingham?' he prompted gently.

'Why should you suppose that something is troubling me merely because I do not wish to dance?' asked Constance haughtily.

'It is rather obvious that something is affecting your spirits,' he informed her calmly. 'Surely you do not mean to refute it?'

His tone stung her into an immediate retort. 'What leads you to imagine that I should wish to confide in you, Count Fabricati? We are almost strangers.'

'You don't like me very much, do you, Miss Trevingham?' he stated unabashed.

'You are out there, sir, I do not like you at all,' she admitted, equally cool.

'You are very frank!' he answered with a short laugh at her effrontery. 'I wonder exactly how I have contrived to offend you? Am I to be granted an explanation or must I remain in ignorance of the nature of my offence?'

'Can you not guess? Is not that also obvious?' she sneered sarcastically.

'Well, let me see,' he said, regarding her meditatively. 'I read disapproval in those expressive eyes and what else?' He paused and held her gaze. She did not flinch and stared defiantly back at him.

'Ah, yes, distrust,' he went on slowly. 'Undoubtedly you are suspicious, Miss Trevingham and a little afraid of me, I think,' he concluded as if making an interesting discovery.

'Afraid? Of you!?' she cried scornfully.

'Oh but you are,' he insisted with the glimmer of a smile. 'You are afraid that I will bring disgrace and embarrassment to your family. Isn't that why you have been watching me all evening?'

Constance glowered furiously, her temper rising rapidly. So! He had known that she had been keeping a close watch on him and had no doubt found her behaviour very amusing.

'Well, dare you deny it?' he continued smilingly.

'I would dare anything, sir, to protect my family from a ... an ingratiating gull-catcher!' she hissed through clenched teeth.

He received the hurled insult with infuriating calm. 'I see you have formed a very low opinion of me, Miss Trevingham. I do not know what I have said or done, to incur your displeasure.'

'Then allow me to enlighten you. I am not afraid to speak plainly as you must now be aware. My brother has already furnished us with the details of your escapades in Rome and chooses to view them with amusement. It is otherwise with me. I find nothing to admire in deceitful behaviour, especially when it is resorted to for merely mercenary purposes. I mistrust your reasons for insinuating yourself into my family and I dislike the manner in which you have used my brother's friendship to gain your own ends. It is only because he has franked you, that you are now invited everywhere and I think I can guess your purpose in following him so quickly and unexpectedly to London.'

'Oh? And what object do you imagine I had in mind?' he enquired with great interest, not taking his eyes from her face for a moment.

'I am not a fool, Mr Farenden and neither are you, so please do not attempt to humbug me,' she snapped impatiently. 'Your motives are obvious enough. You mean to continue to dupe raw, reckless idiots into parting with their gold. Why else must we address you as *Count Fabricati*? You certainly aren't a nobleman. In fact, I wonder if you are even a gentleman!'

'My silence must answer for me,' he replied evenly but with a flash of fire in his dark eyes. 'Now, having drawn first blood, will you put up your weapon until such time as we can continue this encounter? I see your brother approaching.'

At that very moment Lord Trevingham came excitedly to the Count's side and seizing him by the arm, directed his attention to a group of people standing a few yards away from them.

Constance saw the Count's keen gaze follow in the direction Justin had indicated and, as his glance fell upon the little gathering he stiffened suddenly, his face seeming to pale beneath the sun-browned skin.

'*Conosce chi è quella bruna signorina?*' he murmured in amazement. '*È bellissima! É che begli ochi!*'

'Yes, she is an angel, is she not?' sighed Justin soulfully. 'That, my friend, is the lady of my heart: the Lady Anne Rossmore.'

'*La Signorina Rossmore?*' gasped the Count in stunned accents. '*Dio mio!*'

Constance marvelled at this sudden change in his demeanour. At last he had been shaken out of his hateful complacency. But why?

'*È i due signori che sono con lei?*' he enquired in an undertone, his eyes still fastened on that lovely countenance across the room.

'*Il signore anziano è un zio e quello più giovane è un cugino,*' answered Constance before her brother could form a reply.

The Count turned towards her in some surprise, almost as if he had forgotten her presence.

'You speak Italian, Miss Trevingham – and with a good accent. I wonder that your uncle did not send you to Rome in place of your brother.'

'It is well for you that he did not,' she hissed in his ear. 'For one thing, you would still be lying in prison! My purse strings are not so easily loosened!'

'I would that the same could be said of your tongue, madam!' was his swift retort.

Fortunately, Lord Trevingham dragged him away before Constance could recover her voice. She was left to swallow her anger which irked her grievously. She spent the next few minutes fulminating inwardly, rehearsing in her mind several highly descriptive appellations with which she longed to address that insufferable man – if only she were not such a lady!

Lord Trevingham drew the Count into a quiet corner where they could speak undisturbed. 'I have a favour to ask of you, James,' he said conspiratorially.

'Really?' drawled the Count with a slight lift of his eyebrows. 'I wonder if I might hazard a guess as to what exactly it is you want with me?'

Trevingham grinned. 'I think you know. But now that you have seen her with your own eyes,' he continued eagerly, 'you must understand why it is that I am so desperately trying to gain favour with her family. You said yourself that she is beautiful but it isn't only that which made me fall in love with her. She is such a sweet-natured girl, so vulnerable and innocent, so unworldly and shy. That is why she is entirely at the mercy of her uncle and aunt. She needs someone to protect and take care of her.'

'I see. And you wish to be her knight in shining armour, do you?' enquired the Count in amusement.

'In a manner of speaking, yes, I suppose I do,' confessed his lordship rather bashfully. 'She really does need rescuing from their clutches, otherwise she will be forced to marry for mere considerations of property and position and she will be doomed to unhappiness for the rest of her life,' he added dramatically.

'Are you so certain that she does not wish to ally herself to some great house? The Rossmores are a very wealthy family, are they not? The lady's expectations may be quite different to those you imagine her to have.'

'Oh, so you have heard of the family?' Trevingham said in some surprise.

'Of course. They are mentioned in the same breath as Admiral Hughes.'

'Ay, there's the rub!' groaned Justin dismally. 'Everyone will naturally assume that whoever asks for her hand in marriage will be doing so only because she is an heiress. If only she were not a Rossmore! I should have no qualms in approaching Lord Wyvern and asking his permission to pay my addresses.'

'Ah! Lord Wyvern! Of course, the uncle!' exclaimed the Count. 'But he must know that you are not a gazetted fortune-hunter. Your family connections are far from contemptible and you are in possession of more than a mere competence. Enough to satisfy even the most exacting of in-laws,' he ended encouragingly.

'What you say is true but you don't know how ambitious the Wyverns are for their niece. I don't think my position in life is quite lofty enough for them to smile upon my suit. I shall do all in my power though, to win their approval. But withal "Wishing me like to one more rich in hope".'

As he spoke he looked once more upon the object of his passion who was at that moment dancing with her cousin, the Honourable Frederick Wyvern.

The Count followed his gaze and stood silently watching the couple for some few moments. *'Come balla bene,'* he murmured softly to himself. Then, as if reaching a sudden decision, he said, 'Very well, Justin. Buckle on your armour, we shall try if we can enter the lists.'

'You mean you will help me?' cried Trevingham in astonishment. 'What makes you change your mind?'

'Contrariness, my friend, mere contrariness,' replied the Count slowly and with the ghost of a smile. 'Now come with me.'

He turned and marched resolutely towards the refreshment room where he had earlier seen Lady Wyvern entering on her husband's arm. Noticing exactly where they were sitting, he chose a vacant chair close by and he and Trevingham quietly seated themselves.

'Aren't you going to speak to her?' whispered his lordship impatiently.

The Count held up an imperative hand. 'Watch and learn, my lord, we must play the fox.'

Lord Wyvern had gone to procure some lemonade for his wife and the Count waited a few minutes until he saw him returning with the glass in his hand. Then getting unhurriedly to his feet, he walked casually in Wyvern's direction and brushed past the gentleman who was apparently unaware of his proximity. He seemed to knock against the Count and spilt some of the contents of the glass.

'I beg your pardon, sir!' Wyvern apologized in consternation. 'I did not see you there, I am without my eyeglasses this evening. I hope I have not splashed your coat? Please forgive my clumsiness.'

'Pray do not concern yourself, sir. There is not the least harm done I assure you. I ought to have been more careful. Perhaps you would allow me to fetch another glass?'

'I cannot impose upon you, sir. It was after all, entirely my own doing,' he replied reluctantly.

'Not at all. It will only take me a moment,' and before Wyvern could gainsay him the Count took himself off.

Justin sat watching the proceedings with great interest and saw with growing admiration that his friend was indeed as wily as a fox.

As he came back with another glass, he placed it directly into Lady Wyvern's hand. She looked up at him, her eyes widening in surprised recognition.

'Oh! It's you, sir!' she cried. 'The gentleman I met in the park!' She turned to her husband to explain. 'You remember, Wyvern, I told you what happened to my foolish little Chino last week. It was this brave, young man who saved his life.'

'Of course. I do recall your telling me of it. Well, what a coincidence! You come to our aid again it seems, sir,' he held out his hand. 'Let me introduce myself. I am Lord Wyvern and this is my wife, Lady Augusta Wyvern. May I know your name, sir?'

'Count Fabricati,' he replied with an elegant bow. 'I am indeed honoured to meet you. Alas, being but recently arrived in London I am as yet known to only a few of its inhabitants, so it is always a pleasure to make new acquaintances.' He turned to her ladyship, 'I trust the little dog is quite recovered from his adventure?' he asked with what he hoped was just the right amount of concern in his voice.

'Oh, yes, he is perfectly well, thank you. It is kind of you to enquire. So you are a visitor to England then, Count Fabricati? How long do you make your stay?'

'I am uncertain at the moment. Perhaps another two or three months. Then I must return to Rome.'

'Ah, you are come from Rome? A wonderful city. I visited it in my salad days, you know,' remarked Lord Wyvern with great interest. 'I wonder if it is very much changed since that little Corsican upstart made it a part of his empire?'

'It is not called the Eternal City for nothing,' smiled the Count. 'I think you will find it as beautiful now as it was when you made your grand tour.'

'I hope you may find London at least as interesting, sir,' broke in Lady Wyvern. 'I know you have already tasted some of her delights, for it was you I saw dining at the Clarendon, was it not?'

'You are right, of course. I was a guest of the Marquis of Fearnley. I am indeed fortunate to be able to number him among my few English friends. I hope you will forgive me for not speaking to you that evening, my lady but I did not like to presume upon so slight an acquaintance,' apologized the Count modestly.

'Your scruples do you great credit, sir. I am glad that we have had this opportunty to become properly acquainted. Are you here with the marquis tonight?'

'No, I am with Lord Trevingham. Perhaps you already know him and his delightful family? They are very good friends of mine. Here he is now,' he looked across at Justin who had been hovering anxiously nearby and at a signal from the Count, took the liberty of joining them.

'Good evening, Lady Wyvern, Lord Wyvern,' he said bowing nervously to each in turn. 'This is a pleasant surprise. It seems you are already known to my friend, Count Fabricati?'

'How do you do, Lord Trevingham? And how are your mother and sisters? I suppose they are here with you this evening?' asked Lady Wyvern, acknowledging his greeting with a slight inclination of the head.

'Yes, we are all here. I saw Frederick and Lady Anne a little while ago. Would it be too presumptuous of me to ask your permission to dance with her if she will grant me that happiness?' he rushed on recklessly, risking her displeasure.

She hesitated visibly before saying, albeit rather coldly, 'Very well, you may ask her for one dance. But she does not waltz!' she warned emphatically. Then turning back to the Count and therefore missing the look of sheer joy that lit Trevingham's handsome face, she said, 'As you are quite a stranger to London, sir, I wonder if you might care to come to my niece's birthday ball next month? It is to be one of the great social events of the season. Perhaps the marquis would agree to accompany you, as you are on such intimate terms with him. I know he does not usually like to attend these occasions but I daresay if you were to suggest it to him, he would be only too pleased to oblige you. He is so well acquainted with almost everyone in London society that he would be invaluable to you in performing the necessary introductions.'

She saw him look fleetingly at Lord Trevingham as if in some doubt, so added somewhat belatedly, 'I shall, of course, be sending a card to your family, Lord Trevingham.'

'Then I shall be delighted to accept, Lady Wyvern,' bowed the Count. 'Thank you very much for your thoughtfulness. As for the marquis, I think I may presume upon our friendship enough to elicit his acceptance of your kind invitation. I am sure he will be happy to bear me company.'

He was glad to have discovered the reason for her ladyship's sudden interest in him the other evening. Of course, it was knowing the marquis that had worked so wonderfully well in his favour. It appeared that dining with a duke's son rated even more highly than his daring with a pet dog. She had obviously assumed that he held some sway over the marquis, imagining perhaps that their friendship was of a long duration. Well, he would just have to use his ingenuity to persuade that noble scion of a ducal house that he needs must attend the ball. Having so successfully achieved their object, Trevingham, and the Count took their leave of the Wyverns and returned to the ballroom.

'I say, James!' cried Justin admiringly, 'you certainly arranged matters beautifully! Not only do I have permission to dance with the divine Lady Anne but I also find myself invited to her ball! What amazing luck! You really are the most complete hand!'

'Well, I must confess that though I played the game quite skilfully, the cards fell very much in my favour,' he acknowledged. 'But we were not the only players to walk away from the table with our share of the winnings. Lady Wyvern is by no means a novice and knows how to take a trick or two. Just how difficult is it going to be for me to get Fearnley to this *great social event?*'

Trevingham gave a grimace. 'Devilish difficult! He hates dancing, especially balls. Avoids 'em like the plague. He'd sooner be at Brooks's or White's and prefers watching the fillies over the turf at Newmarket to those showing their paces on a ballroom floor.'

'I guessed as much. I wondered why she bet so heavily on me,' reflected the Count. 'And if I fail to turn up trumps, your suit will be out of luck also.'

'Ah! But you won't fail me, will you, James? I'm beginning to believe in your amazing abilities, did you not insist that I should?'

'Very true. Have I ever told you that one of my family mottos is "I shall contrive"?'

'You would, of course, have more than one,' laughed Trevingham. 'I hope you can live up to it. Now, if you will forgive the weaknesses of we lesser mortals, I am going to claim the hand of my lady fair.'

The Count watched him making his way towards Lady Anne who was just returning to the refreshment room in search of her guardians. He noted how that beautiful countenance grew even lovelier as she listened to Trevingham's request. The cousin relinquished her hand to the eager newcomer and she readily returned to the ballroom with her enraptured partner.

Fabricati remained in silent contemplation of that perfect profile framed in a cluster of dark, shining ringlets. The deep-brown eyes, sparkling with joy, never left Trevingham's face for a moment, so absorbed was she in listening to him speaking and basking in the worship of his every look. Something akin to pain stirred somewhere in the depths of the Count's heart as he observed that sweet smile and traced the delicate beauty of her features. He turned swiftly away, his face hard and set and without a backward glance, hastened from the room already regretting his rash decision to interfere in affairs which were best left alone.

It did not take the Count long to realize the card-room at Almack's was merely for amusement. The stakes were very low and therefore rendered the games unexciting. He was beginning to feel bored, so decided to take his leave of the rest of the party and seek his pleasures elsewhere. He wandered back into the ballroom and began to look about him for Lord Trevingham.

The set had not yet finished but soon Justin would have to return the young lady to her guardians. He might as well get some refreshment while he awaited him.

The Wyverns were still where he had left them, although now they had been joined by their son and another gentleman. The Count recognized the surly young man who had challenged him at Angelo's, Mr Giles Morton. He mulled over the name but it meant nothing to him, although Justin had implied that he was a connection of the Rossmore family.

Where does he fit in? he mused silently. Morton seemed to be rather agitated over something, so the Count drew a little nearer to their table to satisfy his curiosity.

'I must say I am very surprised that you permitted him to dance with her, Lady Wyvern. I thought you had decided to discourage her interest in that gentleman. She is grown too fond of him already and their friendship ought not to be allowed to flourish. She must be made to realize where her duty lies. The Rossmores must look a good deal higher than a mere government official,' he added scathingly.

'There is no need at all for you to point that out to me, Giles. I should, of course, never allow her to stoop so low but I have another scheme in mind. Besides, I have given him permission for only one dance and that will permit small opportunity for any private conversation. I only acceded to his request because I wish to cultivate an acquaintance I have recently made with a friend of his – Count Fabricati.'

'Fabricati! That toady! From what I have learned of him, he is nothing more than a peep-of-day boy. A wastrel who frequents gaming houses. None of these Italian aristocrats have anything to recommend them. They are as plentiful as Russian princes and as worthless!' he exclaimed in disgust.

'I suppose that outburst has nothing to do with his giving you such a public thrashing at Angelo's last week?' enquired Frederick Wyvern, affecting to study the ceiling as he lounged back in his seat.

'It was no such thing!' cried Morton hotly. 'It was a very even match and I would have had him if I had not lost my footing. Besides, that has no bearing on my opinion of him. I was talking to Colonel Dyson the other day, he has some connections in the Bourbon court in Sicily and he has never heard mention of Count Fabricati.'

'That is hardly conclusive evidence against him. Dyson cannot possibly have knowledge of all the Italian nobility,' commented Frederick scornfully.

'It is of no great matter,' interrupted Lady Wyvern impatiently. 'I have not the slightest interest in Count Fabricati. His friends are of far more importance to me. You don't know everything about him, Giles. I happen to have found out something that might prove useful to me. Now be quiet both of you, here is Anne returning to us with Lord Trevingham.'

The young lady, who was indeed not much older than Sophy came up to them, her huge, dark eyes glowing and her creamy complexion prettily flushed.

'Here is your cousin Giles come to join us, Anne. Isn't that a pleasant surprise?' smiled Lady Wyvern as Justin handed her to a seat.

'Yes, of course. Good evening, Giles,' she answered without enthusiasm.

'Good evening, Lady Anne. May I say how very lovely you look in that beautiful gown? But then, just as the glamorous moon diminishes the tender beauty of the stars, so you outshine every other young lady when you appear,' he said silkily and possessing himself of her hand, kissed her fingertips, his lips lingering against her soft skin.

Trevingham stiffened angrily at this flirtatious display of affection, which was exactly the effect that Morton hoped to achieve.

'Will you grant me the pleasure of holding this little,

white hand a while longer and allow me to dance with you?'

'Of course she shall. You will excuse them, won't you, Lord Trevingham? No doubt you have another partner eagerly awaiting you? Do not let us keep you from your friends,' said Lady Wyvern dismissively.

Justin had nothing more to do but take his leave of them, then he turned and walked disconsolately away.

"*El Cabellero de la Triste Figura*," came a voice behind him. 'Take heart. They have only dented your pride and taken a little of the polish off your happiness, not your armour. That shines as brilliantly as ever in the eyes of your lady.'

'Oh, it's you, James. Did you hear then? I am banished from the lists, it seems. For daring to raise my eyes and my hopes too high,' complained Trevingham bitterly.

'Then allow me to share your exile. Let us leave the lists for a while. Anyway, I have a notion that you will do better by engaging in close combat. I shall have to see what I can do to arrange matters for you. Come, what say you to seeking out Fearnley and Brascombe? This is become a tiresomely boring evening. There is no excitement to be found here: everyone is too set on observing the proprieties. Let us see if we can change our luck with the casting of the bones and lift ourselves out of the doldrums by getting pleasantly sprung on a bottle or so of good claret,' suggested the Count encouragingly.

'An excellent idea,' concurred Trevingham willingly. 'There's no sense in moping around here for the rest of the evening. I'll not be permitted to approach Lady Anne again that's certain. I will go and tell Mama that we are leaving.'

Constance observed their departure with mixed emotions. She was glad that the Count had taken himself off but it pleased her not at all that he had taken Justin with him.

Colonel Dyson noted his partner's sombre expression and remarked upon it, saying in his quiet, gentle fashion, 'You know, if there is any way in which I might serve you, you have only to ask. I wish you would trust me with your confidence. I would do anything in my power to restore the gaiety to your smile.'

He spoke with such warmth and sincerity that she felt overwhelmed with gratitude for his kindness towards her. Perhaps she ought to confide her fears to him; she was sure that he was a man of great integrity and would ensure that her confidences were respected. She glanced up at him, reading the genuine sympathy in his eyes.

'It is nothing really, only that provoking man Count Fabricati. His impudence is beyond all bearing. I could wish that Justin did not hold him in such esteem.'

'You don't like him? But he seems pleasant enough, despite his reputation,' he remarked thoughtfully.

'His reputation? What do you know of his reputation?' she questioned a little sharply.

He looked surprised by her sudden interrogation. 'Why, I merely refer to his known preference for the gaming houses,' he explained quietly. 'He has been accepted into Fearnley's circle of friends and the stakes they set are notoriously excessive.'

Her frown deepened at his words and her eyes clouded again.

'Are you concerned for your brother?' he questioned gently. 'You need not fear that he is in the least danger of being lured into that trap. Trevingham is far too sensible. But if it would make you feel any easier in your mind, I am prepared to take it upon myself to keep a friendly eye on him, for his sister's sake.'

'Oh, would you really do that for me?' cried Constance eagerly. 'I should be so relieved if you could watch that he does not fall into harm's way. Not that I think he will, you understand, it is just that it would be reassuring to know that a man of your good sense and discretion were close at hand. To give him wise counsel if he should ever stand in need of it, I mean.'

'You may safely repose your trust in me, Miss Trevingham. I count it a supreme honour that you think me worthy of performing such a service for you,' he replied gallantly. 'But do you truly believe that he would listen to my advice even if I presumed to offer it?'

'I am sure he would; he respects you I know,' she asserted warmly.

'If I am indeed fortunate enough to have been granted

his trust, I know to whom I should look for my recommendation,' he answered softly, looking deep into her eyes.

'It is I who am fortunate, Colonel Dyson. In having found such a kind and considerate friend.'

Seven

It was near four o'clock in the morning when Lord Trevingham and the Count eventually wended their way home. The streets were dark and empty and the air decidedly chilly as they strolled unhurriedly down Oxford Street. A glimmer of light from a single unshuttered window revealed a silver glittering of frost on the paving stones and a keen east wind swept the rustling drifts of sere autumn leaves along the gutter. Justin shivered and turned up the large collar of his redingote. The Count glanced across at him.

'What you need is a warming drink, my friend. And what better way to keep out the cold than a good bottle of French brandy? I happen to have an excellent vintage that I think will impress you. Would you care to sample it with me?'

'Brandy, eh? Then I'm your man! "Lay on Macduff and damn'd be him that first cries, Hold enough!" ' replied Trevingham, full of claret-induced bonhomie.

By the time they reached the Count's house in Brook Street, the voice of the watch was heard announcing the hour. As the dying echoes of his call sank into the silence of the sleeping city, the door was pulled open and Jean the valet appeared holding aloft a branch of brightly burning candles.

'*Bon matin*, Jean. *Il fait très froid, hein? Apportez-moi le cognac. Le meilleur cognac, s'il vous plaît!*'

'*Toute de suite, Monsieur le Comte.*'

Soon they were ensconced in deep armchairs in front of a welcoming fire which Jean had expertly stirred into a cheering blaze. Trevingham, bending towards the warming flames, rolled the glass between his palms watching the reflected light setting the amber liquid aglow. Then lifting it up, he inhaled the delicious fragrance appreciatively before swallowing a mouthful of the fiery nectar. He pronounced it to be superb.

'In fact I have not tasted anything near so good since I sampled the contents of a cask provided by the gentlemen of the Kent coast.'

'Really? It is amazing, is it not, how the quality is improved by removing the excise from the barrel during transportation?' observed the Count knowledgeably, setting himself at ease as he sipped contentedly from his own glass.

'You're a cool one, James, I must say!' said Trevingham with a chuckle as, leaning his elbows on his knees, he gave his companion a long, sideways look. 'You are the most singular fellow I ever met in my life. The more I get to know you, the less I seem to know you at all.'

'Don't tell me,' he answered, putting up a forestalling hand. 'You think I'm a loose fish too. Isn't that what you are trying to say?'

'Actually, I would say you are more like an eel. Just when one thinks one has a grasp on you, you wriggle away again.'

'Oh, a slippery customer, am I? Now, what have I done to give you that impression?' he enquired mockingly.

'Well, for one thing, you had always led me to believe that you were a hardened gamester, intent only on winning. Indeed I thought your very existence depended upon it.'

'My existence, yes. My life, no,' was the lazy response.

'Why did you throw that last game away?' asked Trevingham, intrigued by such unaccountably odd behaviour.

'What makes you think that I did?' replied the Count carelessly.

'I was standing behind your chair. I saw those cards you threw down. That pair of kings easily beat Grayson's hand. Can you afford to throw away eight hundred guineas?'

A strange smile curled the Count's chiselled lips. 'I am in a philanthropic mood tonight,' he murmured, gazing into his glass as he swirled its contents.

'I hope your pockets are as deep as your moods.'

'I can stand the loss. Poor Grayson could hardly stand at all. He drank two bottles of claret during the game, just to find the courage to stay in it until the bitter end. He put every guinea he possessed on to that table in the desperate hope of recouping his losses.'

'He knows the rule. If you can't pay, don't play,' declared Trevingham grimly.

'You would never do so would you, Justin?' stated the Count, quietly reflective.

'Certainly not. That's a fool's game,' replied his lordship with conviction.

'Desperation can make fools of us all, remember that my friend,' advised the Count solemnly, swallowing down the last of his brandy.

'Speaking of desperation, do you think it foolish of me to continue to pursue my dream of winning the hand of Lady Anne Rossmore, James?' asked Lord Trevingham after a thoughtful pause.

'Love, like most dreams, is seen to be the merest nonsense the moment one awakens,' replied the Count derisively, as he refilled their glasses. 'Perhaps that is why a kiss is so much more pleasurable with the eyes closed. You see, I am a devotee of Diogenes not a revolutionist as you supposed. I started in the school of cynicism at a tender age and one seldom forgets the lessons learnt in one's infancy. They are fundamental to one's whole perception of life.' He leaned back luxuriously in the chair and, crossing his ankles, perched his feet on the brass fender. 'However, I am disposed to assist you in your courtship because I perceive that you are in need of a dog of the Diogenes breed to help you face up to these Rossmores.'

'You will have to explain that necessity, James. My powers of recollection are not so acute as yours.'

'Then I shall translate. "I am a dog because I fawn on those who give me anything; I yelp at those who refuse and I set my teeth in rascals". I made a good start tonight with the fawning, did I not? You will require such help, Justin,' he went on, 'because you are at something of a disadvantage, you know. Your visions of life are too much influenced by that method of education advocated by

Monsieur Rousseau and therefore quite impractical. But before I play another hand in this game, I should like to know something more of the Rossmores, beginning with Lady Anne.'

'For me there will be no beginning without her,' sighed Justin soulfully. 'She is all of life to me. Her hair, dark as night, her face as breathtakingly beautiful as the first star of evening, her figure as ...'

'You may spare me the examples of your poetic genius, Justin,' interrupted the Count unsympathetically. 'My eyesight is perfectly good, thank you. All this I saw for myself last night. Tell me something I do not already know.'

'I'm sorry, James. You must make allowance for a man in love,' pointed out his lordship reasonably.

'I have but I warn you, it is almost spent. Now bearing that in mind, would you pray continue without further unnecessary embellishments?'

'What a pity we did not go to the same school,' grinned Trevingham. 'Your imagination would have benefitted from the exercise.'

'Since becoming acquainted with your family, Justin, it has already been stretched almost to the point of exhaustion. But I wonder which of us has taken the better course? Or does a lasting happiness lie balanced precariously somewhere between the two?' he questioned meditatively. Then, as if he suddenly realised his digression, he laughed, saying, 'You see what a simple matter it is to slip from the philanthropic to the philosophic mood? Let us now discuss the subject closest to your heart.'

'By all means. Though there isn't a great deal I can tell you because there are certain gaps in my knowledge that only someone of my uncle's generation can fill.'

'Never mind, just tell me what you do know,' prompted the Count. 'For instance, why does Lady Anne live with her uncle and aunt?'

'Because her late mother willed it so. Lord Wyvern is her mother's brother as you must have guessed. He is her guardian until she reaches her five and twentieth birthday. Although, oddly enough, her father is still living, as far as I know.'

'Then why does she need her uncle as guardian?'

'I am coming to that. But it's a little difficult to explain as I don't know all the facts. It seems that there is bad blood in the Earls of Rossmore. They have always been a ramshackle set of fellows. The present earl is no exception. Before Lady Anne was even born, her father was involved in a duel which resulted in his opponent's death. To make matters worse, the dead man happened to be one of the king's courtiers and Rossmore was forced to flee the country when the king ordered his arrest. He had property and investments abroad and I understand that he chose to go to America until the dust settled. He must have grown to like the life I suppose, for he never did come back, even when the king finally decided to relent. Anyway, having brought such disgrace on the family name which was already somewhat tarnished by his predecessors, his wife left him and went to live with her father. They are both dead now and so Lady Anne was placed in the Wyverns' care. That was about eleven years ago. They have guarded her strictly ever since – for two reasons. Firstly, because of her father's notoriety: they determined to ensure that no breath of scandal attached itself to her fair name. Secondly, they wish to arrange a suitable marriage for her. She will inherit a substantial fortune in four years' time, the late countess left her amply provided for and also she is heiress to such of the Rossmore property as is unentailed, all of which amounts to a considerable sum. The earl suddenly changed his will to include his daughter some months after her mother's demise, presumably to prevent the heir from inheriting more than the title and the entailed property.'

'And who is his heir?' enquired the Count.

'Giles Morton!' announced Trevingham in a voice tinged with disgust. 'It seems he is the only surviving male descendant of the fifth Earl. His branch of the family changed their name to Morton under the terms of a marriage contract two generations ago. The Wyverns brought him out of obscurity at their own expense, they paid for his education in order to prepare him for his new role in life. I first encountered him at Eton. He was a most obnoxious schoolboy, always wanting to rule the roost. The sudden change in his circumstances rather went to his head and he became obsessed with trying to prove to the rest of us just how superior he was in all respects. As you have discovered, he has not altered with the passage of time. You may be wondering why the Wyverns have been so generous to such a distant relative, related only by marriage. Well, they have a daughter of their own. She is only sixteen and is at present attending a ladies' seminary. Unfortunately she is no beauty and I suspect that is why they have planned a betrothal to Morton as soon as she is old enough. He knows that is the reason they have franked him for all these years while he awaits his inheritance. Their fortune has been built on such marriages of convenience. Frederick Wyvern is Wyvern's son from his first marriage. His mother was the daughter of a wealthy merchant and it was her dowry that considerably swelled the family coffers. The present Lady Wyvern brought little more than an impeccable lineage with her but she considers this to be worth more than mere gold. That is why she is so damned top-lofty. She saw to it that poor old Freddy was married off to some ferret-faced female whose ancestors are alleged to have come over with the Conqueror. Probably an attempt to purge his blood-lines of the taint of trade,' he finished contemptuously.

'I think that perhaps Lady Wyvern has similar ideas for her niece, which will not help your case. However, you have two main advantages over your rival,' the Count informed him confidently.

'May I also know what they are?' requested Trevingham, rather puzzled.

'I thought they were obvious,' answered the Count. 'Especially one of them. The lady is in love with you.'

'How can you possibly know that?' gasped his lordship in astonishment. 'You've never spoken to her.'

'No. But she has spoken to me,' he replied mysteriously.

'When? How?' cried Justin utterly bewildered.

' "Sometimes from her eyes I did receive fair speechless messages",' he quoted airily. 'Surely you must have noticed *ces belles yeux brunes*? They are wondrous eloquent! But perhaps you were too occupied thinking of distant Venus to observe the one you held in your arms.'

'I am amazed that a professed cynic is qualified to

translate the language of the heart with any accuracy. And are you aware that you almost waxed poetical just now, my unromantic friend?'

'A cynic like myself, is not blind to love and beauty. I can appreciate them as well as any other man. But I also recognize them for what they are – the implements of the poacher's trade. The net, the snare, the lure laid, to trap, to trip, to entice the unwary soul from out its peaceful shade.'

'If that were so, I would fall a willing victim to my lady's charms. But how could she steal away what is already hers? She has my soul, my heart, my whole life. I give them to her freely if she loves me as much as I love her. Do you really think she cares for me?' he asked anxiously. 'If only it is true, then nothing shall keep us apart, nothing!' he vowed dramatically.

'Would you consider an elopement?' enquired the Count reflectively. 'It might perhaps be the wisest course.'

'Surely you are not seriously suggesting that I should? No, I could not ruin her reputation by exposing her to the censure of those in society who would be only too ready to say that she had inherited more than the Rossmore fortune. Besides, I have no need to behave in such an underhand fashion, it would seem as if I had something to be ashamed of which I certainly have not! And I am not going to insult her by offering a clandestine marriage.'

'Such a pity,' murmured the Count regretfully. 'I could have arranged matters for you so easily.'

'Having learnt something of your methods last night, I don't doubt it for one minute.'

'Which brings you neatly to the second advantage you have – namely Count Fabricati, who is entirely at your service. You may safely leave everything to me. I shall contrive.'

'I admire your confidence!' cried Trevingham.

'Do I detect a note of scepticism?' asked the Count in a wounded voice. 'Well wait and see. Confidence shall be the key that opens up the door to success. You are about to see your standard raised on the field of conflict, so arise, Sir Knight! To arms!'

'I am very sorry to disappoint you, James, but I go abed, good night, to sleep!'

'Perchance to dream?' laughed the Count, helping him on with his coat.

'Doubtless I shall, for waking or sleeping, she is always in my thoughts,' he murmured sighfully.

'Such *stuff* as dreams are made on!' mocked the Count sardonically.

'Farewell, proud Antisthenes!' smiled Trevingham with a wave of his hand as he went out the door.

Despite his dim view of romantic love, the Count for reasons best known to himself, decided to assist the lovers in their wooing. Perhaps it was out of friendship for Trevingham or because he despised the scheming Rossmores. Or possibly it was just the thrill of playing the game, pitting his skill and wits against the world, or in this instance, the worldly!

His opening gambit was made a few days later when he attended a soirée at Lady Sefton's. As luck would have it, Lady Wyvern and Lady Anne were also present and he wasted no time in approaching them. He engaged the aunt in small-talk for several minutes, now and then addressing some remark to Lady Anne in an effort to draw her into the conversation. Then as they both began to relax beneath the spell of his wit and charm, he casually mentioned that he had been invited to a masquerade at the Argyll Rooms.

'Oh, how exciting!' declared Lady Anne, rather wistfully. 'I have never been to a masquerade. How I wish I could go.'

'Certainly not!' snorted Lady Wyvern disapprovingly. 'They are not at all the sort of entertainment that a well-brought up young lady should attend. Such things are considered unseemly, they attract persons of low-breeding and lead to disreputable behaviour.'

'Thankfully, this masquerade is not of that sort,' replied the Count with a seraphic smile. 'It is perfectly respectable, or Lady Trevingham would most certainly not be accompanying us. Nor would she permit her delightful daughters to attend any function which might prove injurious to their spotless reputations. The marquis himself has assured me that it is quite unexceptionable and that I need not have any qualms. You see, as a stranger to

London and unacquainted with its social customs, I have to be a little over-cautious when accepting invitations to events of which I have no real knowledge. One has to be so careful when in a foreign land, not to put oneself beyond the pale. However, I am sure you are the best judge of what is right for your niece, Lady Wyvern, and I know that Lady Trevingham will not be in the least offended by your refusing her invitation to join our party. Perhaps I ought not to have suggested it to her without consulting you first but I wished only to repay your kindness in inviting me to your ball.'

She rose beautifully to the bait as he had gambled that she would and triumphed inwardly. The marquis was proving to be his trump card!

'Well,' she began thoughtfully, 'if Lady Trevingham can assure me that this is to be a genteel affair and as the marquis sees no harm in it, I should of course be prepared to consider the matter very carefully.'

'In that case, might I suggest to Lady Trevingham that she call on you one morning this week to discuss it with you? If it will make you easy in your mind I am sure she will be only too pleased to do so.'

'Very well then. She may call upon us on Wednesday morning,' agreed Lady Wyvern.

'Excellent! But I must not monopolize your company. I see Miss Berry wishes to claim your attention. Good evening, Lady Wyvern, Lady Anne. It has been such a pleasure speaking to you,' he said with an elegant bow and turning away, bestowed a merry smile upon the younger lady who met his mischievous look with a happy face.

All that remained for him to do now was to enlist Lady Trevingham's help but he was sure that she would make no objection, it ought to be a simple matter to persuade her to fall in with his schemes.

His assumption was correct, Lady Trevingham acceded to his request enthusiastically.

'I see your cleverness is more than academic,' she observed, much impressed by his initiative.

Justin, who had been hearkening with rapt attention to the Count's ingenious plot, cried, 'Listening to him is an education, is it not? He has a family motto, Mama, which is indeed apt.'

'And what might that be, pray?' she enquired smilingly.

' "I shall contrive",' the Count informed her grandly but with a twinkle in his eye.

'Well and so you have it seems. Perhaps, Justin, we ought to adopt a similar maxim. What think you of "I shall connive"?'

'It shall be incorporated in our escutcheon forthwith,' laughed her son gaily. 'Now tell me, James, how do you propose to get Fearnley to come with us? That is going to be even more difficult to accomplish.'

'Why should you want the marquis there? Surely he would be *de trop?*' he asked in great surprise.

'But Lady Wyvern will expect to see him there!' exclaimed Trevingham in bewilderment. 'She thinks he is one of our party.'

'Does she?' he said innocently. 'I wonder what put that particular maggot into her head?'

'But I thought you did!?'

'I? Certainly not. I only mentioned that the marquis said there is nothing improper about a masquerade. I happen to have asked him what he thought of them and merely shared his observations with Lady Wyvern. I hope she did not mistake me? I thought my English sufficiently fluent to make myself perfectly understood. If, however, it is not, I am persuaded that she will be most forgiving. I believe her to be *una signora simpatica.*'

'Then I trust she is of the same persuasion, or neither of us will ever again be worthy of her notice,' warned Trevingham.

'You are forgetting we are already invited to her ball.'

'I think you will find that is also dependant upon the appearance of the marquis,' remarked Trevingham a trifle gloomily. 'Even you will be hard put to it to convince him *that* is an occasion not to be missed!'

'Perhaps,' replied the Count unconcernedly. 'We shall see. Meanwhile, you have an enjoyable evening to look forward to, *if* your Mama can persuade Lady Wyvern that angels would not fear to tread a measure in the Argyll Rooms.'

'You may be confident that I shall succeed in so doing,' declared her ladyship decidedly.

'I have not the slightest doubt, dear lady, that you will overcome her reluctance,' smiled the Count, kissing her fingers in courtly fashion. 'Am I not playing my queen?'

'You know, it is true what I have heard of you, Count Fabricati. You are a *very* dangerous man,' she murmured softly and eyed him askance. Then, turning to her son, she said, 'Would you fetch me my shawl, Justin? It is a little cold today. I left it dowstairs, I think. In the blue saloon.'

When he had gone from the room, she glanced up at the Count again. 'I am inquisitive to know how you propose to make the Marquis of Fearnley come with you to Lady Wyvern's ball?'

'I am sure I could not make anyone do anything that they did not wish to do,' he replied, as if amazed at the suggestion.

'But he has agreed to come, has he not? I guessed as much from your evasive remark to Justin a moment ago. How did you do it? Or would it shock me very much to know what underhand methods you used?' she asked playfully. 'I could see that you were not prepared to reveal them to Justin.'

'Very well, I will tell you, since you ask so particularly. I know I shall not have to ask you to remain silent on the subject: you do not want for sense that is plain. The marquis has indeed agreed to accept the invitation.'

'I confess I am fascinated to know how you overcame his avowed dislike of dancing! If he is really intent on going to the ball, it will be quite a feather in her ladyship's cap. She will have succeeded where all other hostesses have failed and you will be a great favourite with her. But you would have calculated for that I suppose? Of course you would! Well, how did you do it?'

'I appealed to his finer nature, that is to say, his sporting instincts. We have that in common, Fearnley and I, the love of the game and the desire to win at all costs, or almost,' he added, remembering Grayson. 'Fortunately, it is well known that the Wyverns keep a careful watch on their niece and she is never permitted to stand up for more than two dances with the same man on one night. Sadly for Justin that is all he will be able to hope for but a marquis? That, if I am not very much mistaken, is an entirely different matter. Fearnley is, naturally, quite in ignorance of her ladyship's designs upon him and so I have managed to present him with something of a challenge, or so he thinks. I have wagered one thousand guineas that he will not be able to dance three times with the young lady on the night of her birthday ball.'

'And he accepted? Well! I must say your methods are very unorthodox. If ever Lady Wyvern should discover the truth, she would be furious!'

'Don't worry, I had the good sense not to enter the wager in the betting-book at White's,' he laughed. 'This is a discreet "gentleman's agreement" with only Sir Francis Brascombe to see us shake hands on it. Now you know why I must keep Justin in the dark about this. He might not appreciate my genius. However, if all goes well, your son's romantic interludes may well develop into a more lasting happiness.'

'But if you are right and Lady Wyvern gives the marquis permission to dance with her niece as often as he wishes, might she not be justified in supposing that he is smitten with her?' asked Lady Trevingham, having mulled it over. 'You see, he seldom ever dances and then only when the duke and duchess hold a ball or when his mama presses him to do so.'

'That is precisely the result I shall hope for,' he answered simply.

'But you will lose a thousand guineas! The whole idea is quite preposterous! You cannot have considered! Justin would not expect you to risk so much! You must have been in your cups to have chanced so large a sum on this mad venture!'

'Only slightly foxed, actually,' he admitted unrepentantly. 'Besides, when I make my bids it is always a rule of mine to keep a clear head. And my judgement was quite unimpaired, I assure you, as I think you will discover in the near future. But we will speak of that another time, I hear Justin returning.'

Lady Trevingham began to think that perhaps Constance was right, Count Fabricati was indeed a reckless gambler! She was amazed and a good deal perturbed by his wild extravagance. Why he should be willing to bear the loss of such a vast amount just so that her son could be in Lady Anne Rossmore's company for a few hours, she could not comprehend. Surely the Count's skill at cards was not sufficient to support this peculiar life-style? Had he perhaps some other, undisclosed source of income? She ought to forbid this madcap escapade. Supposing Lady Wyvern should ask her about the marquis, what should she tell her? If she told the truth, then Lady Anne would never be allowed to attend the masquerade and Justin might not receive a card for the ball. He was so looking forward to both events that she had not the heart to spoil his happiness. She decided to make the visit to Lady Wyvern as arranged and let matters take their course. Judging it best that Constance knew nothing of the Count's plans, she did not confide in her eldest daughter, knowing full well that she would most certainly try to persuade her to have no part in any scheme of his devising. So instead, she took Sophy along with her to Grosvenor Square, adjuring her to dress modishly but primly and to appear as sweet and demure as an innocent babe.

'Then I have only to be myself,' she smiled mischievously. 'Don't worry, Mama, I shall be the very epitome of angelic rectitude.'

She was as good as her word and behaved with the utmost decorum, speaking only when directly addressed and looking as if butter wouldn't melt in her mouth. Fortunately for her mother's peace of mind, Lady Wyvern never once mentioned the marquis by name and merely enquired if they were to be a large party and whether the young ladies would be properly chaperoned. No doubt she wished to conceal her own schemes from Lady Trevingham.

'I shall be present the entire evening and so too will Mrs Chessle. You need have no fears whatsoever on that score. My eldest daughter Constance will also help us to keep a watchful eye on the younger members of our party. She is a mature and sensible young woman with an excellent understanding, as I am sure you know, Lady Wyvern.'

'Indeed I do. Miss Trevingham is held in high esteem. An intelligent girl and very prettily behaved. She must be a source of great comfort to you since the death of your husband and I am sure that when your younger children fly the nest, she will be an ideal companion to you in your declining years. Personally, I do not like to see a girl educated above the usual standards expected of a young lady of gentle birth. Naturally one should see that she is accomplished in all the womanly arts of painting, needlework and music but excessive reading ought never to be permitted. There is a danger in encouraging a girl to form her own opinions. It is a cause of disharmony in the home and gives them unfeminine notions of superiority and they become unbiddable. No wonder then, that gentlemen do not in general, make offers for them.'

'Constance is a most dutiful daughter and I count myself fortunate indeed that she has so many and varied accomplishments. I have every reason to be extremely proud of her, as indeed I am of all my children. And now –' she turned towards Lady Anne forcing a smile to her lips – 'do you think you should like to come with us to the masquerade, my dear?'

'Oh yes!' was the immediate and excited response. 'I should like it above all things! Please may I go, Aunt? I promise I will do nothing that will cause you the slightest concern. I shall be as obedient to Lady Trevingham's strictures as I would to your own and submit to her guidance in everything,' she vowed piously.

'Will you not come with us, Lady Wyvern? Mrs Chessle and I would be glad of your company and of course you would then be able to see for yourself that all is as it should be,' suggested Lady Trevingham, thinking how the Count would smile if he could hear this subtle ploy. 'It will be a lively evening, I think.'

'No, I thank you. I should derive no pleasure from an event of that nature but Mrs Kirby shall go in my stead. I repose the greatest trust in her judgement; she will see to it that Anne comports herself in a proper manner befitting her station.'

'But Aunt! Surely Lady Trevingham ...' began Lady Anne in protest at this unforeseen ruling.

Her aunt frowned at her sudden outburst, her face taking on a disapproving aspect. 'I think I know what is in your best interests, Anne. If you will not accede to my decision on the matter, I cannot possibly permit you to go.'

Lady Trevingham, although just as angry as Lady Anne, could see from Lady Wyvern's uncompromising expression that further argument would be useless and quickly interrupted before the girl could express her obvious disappointment. 'Your aunt is perfectly right, my dear. You would not wish to cause her any anxiety on your behalf, I am sure. You must allow that as your guardian she cannot be too cautious for your welfare. Do I take it that we are all agreed?'

'Yes, certainly. Thank you very much, Lady Trevingham. It is so good of you to invite me,' Lady Anne replied quietly and averted her eyes to her lap but not before Lady Trevingham had seen the glitter of unshed tears of vexation in them.

'We shall see you on Tuesday next, then. Goodbye, my dear.' She shook hands wishing she could say something more to cheer her. Then she and Sophy returned to their carriage and drove home.

When Justin had later been informed of the outcome of this interview, he was as bitterly disappointed as the young lady had been.

'Surely you could have convinced Lady Wyvern that it is unnecessary for her to send a duenna with her niece?' he demanded in dismay.

'I did my best, Justin, but you know Lady Wyvern as well as I do. She will never permit Lady Anne to take one step out of that house without a chaperone of some description,' replied his mother soothingly.

'Well then, the whole evening will be quite spoilt! There is not the least hope that I shall be given any opportunity to be with Lady Anne for a single moment. She will probably be taken home the minute Mrs Kirby realizes that the marquis is not with us. I might have guessed this would come to nothing. She has outwitted us once again!' He flung himself petulantly on to the sofa just as the door opened and Basset announced the arrival of the Count.

'Good evening, Lady Trevingham,' he greeted cheerfully

as he strode briskly forward and kissed her hand, adding in an undertone, 'Do I detect an air of gloom?' He cast a quizzical look in Justin's direction.

She raised her eyes heavenwards saying, 'Perhaps you may try to console him, Count Fabricati; his hopes for the masquerade have taken a set-back. Lady Wyvern is insisting that Mrs Kirby accompanies Lady Anne and now Justin fears that he will not be able to speak with her.'

'Oh, is that all? I thought something really dreadful had occurred to overset our scheme,' replied the Count, unperturbed by the news.

Justin scowled at him. 'I daresay you might not think it dreadful but you don't know Mrs Kirby! I'm afraid you underestimated Lady Wyvern when you hatched this plot, James.'

'On the contrary, Justin, I never underestimate a skilled opponent and I look upon this as a game – a game of chess, I think. Lady Wyvern has moved her piece and now I must reply. If I am to win this battle of wits I must plan ahead and anticipate her moves and that is precisely what I have done. She has played her black rook, *eh bien*, I shall bring forward my white knight, *et voilà!*' he explained simply and seated himself beside Lord Trevingham with an air of complete satisfaction.

'What white knight?' queried Trevingham, suspiciously uneasy.

'Why you, of course,' supplied his friend blandly. 'You are my white knight in this game. Now all you have to do is to put yourself entirely in my hands.'

'I begin to think we are all pawns in your game,' came an angry voice from the doorway. 'For you are prepared to sacrifice any one of us to bring about your success.'

'Miss Trevingham, what a pleasant surprise and may I say how charming you look this evening?' said the Count suavely as he rose politely to his feet.

'You may say so, I suppose. After all, it is a subject you have made a great study of, is it not? I doubt there are many as qualified.' She closed the door behind her and came further into the room. 'I have just heard about this ridiculous masquerade. How could you allow him to draw you into his deception, Mama?'

'Oh yes, I've been meaning to mention it to you, Connie,' began her mother guiltily. 'There is to be a masquerade at the Argyll Rooms on Tuesday and we all thought it would be most amusing if we pretended that ....' Her voice trailed off as she met her daughter's wrathful eye.

'As a matter of fact,' interrupted the Count frankly, 'it is entirely my own idea. We Italians are very fond of masquerades, they are very popular, especially in Venezia.'

'Oh, I doubt not at all that you are a very practised masquerader, *Count* Fabricati,' responded Constance satirically. 'Indeed, I begin to wonder if we will ever see your real face. Tell me, why have you taken such pains to ensure that Lady Anne Rossmore is included in the party?' she challenged him icily, her gaze direct and watchful.

'If you really want to know, he did it for me,' interjected Justin, rising to his friend's defence. 'He knows how deep my feelings are for Lady Anne and has decided to help me.'

'Is it truly for your sake, Justin? Or is he merely helping himself?'

'What do you mean, Connie?!' cried her brother, nettled by her inflammatory remarks.

'Lady Anne is a very beautiful heiress. I could think of a more obvious motive than mere altruism,' she informed him caustically. 'And I saw the way he looked at her the moment he knew who she was!' she added accusingly, her bosom heaving with barely suppressed emotion.

'Constance, please! The Count is our guest!' expostulated her mother in shocked accents.

'Do not distress yourself, Lady Trevingham,' smiled the Count, unshaken by this vehement attack on his integrity. 'I am not offended. Miss Trevingham is naturally protective of her family and I commend her for it. It is, of course, regrettable that I should be the cause of such very ...' – he paused briefly – 'very feminine agitations,' he finished provocatively.

'Feminine agitations?!' exclaimed Constance with indignation.

'Well, I can see that you are upset, Miss Trevingham,' he

amended blithely.

'How very perceptive of you. I ought to have known better than to try to hide my feelings from you,' she said with heavy sarcasm.

'Quite so,' replied the Count, his eyes dancing. 'I suppose this means that you won't be accompanying us next Tuesday?'

'Well you are quite out there, Count Fabricati. I am in fact determined to do so. And I also intend to ensure that you do not continue to manipulate the members of my family!'

Eight

From the carriages that pulled up in Great Windmill Street, there issued forth a stream of strangely garbed characters. Over their costumes they wore gaily coloured dominos and their faces were mysteriously masked.

Inside, the Argyll Rooms were brilliantly lit with sparkling crystal chandeliers that flickered in the glittering, gilded mirrors lining the walls. The atmosphere was heady with excitement, or so thought Lady Anne Rossmore as she entered with the Trevinghams. She was dressed like a shepherdess in a pink-striped dimity gown looped up with cherry-coloured ribbons over white petticoats of starched muslin. Her shining ringlets were clustered beneath a wide-brimmed chip-straw hat tied under her little, pointed chin with broad silk ribbons. In her hand she carried a crook bound at the top with ribbons and silk roses. The upper part of her face was concealed beneath a pink silk mask but Justin, who had been awaiting her arrival with ever growing impatience, recognized her at once. She looked so sweet, fresh and innocent that he felt a sudden rush of love for her. He longed to be able to protect her always, to cherish and care for her but above all, to make her happy.

He watched anxiously as the Count went to greet them, his hopes soaring as he observed that Mrs Kirby was not with them. The Count was speaking to Lady Trevingham and Mrs Chessle and he saw them both glance in his direction. Sophy even went so far as to wave her scarf at him. She was dressed in flowing Grecian draperies and looked every bit as beautiful as the legendary Helen of Troy. Georgiana Chessle was gorgeously arrayed in a heavily embroidered brocade gown worn over an

Elizabethan farthingale. The Count complimented the ladies on their choice of dress.

'But where is your sister, Miss Sophia? Did she not deign to join us after all?'

'Oh yes, she is come,' Sophy replied, her eyes glittering up at him from behind her white velvet mask. 'She is with Mrs Kirby, helping her to pin the flounce on her dress. She tore it a little as she stepped from her carriage. They will be here in a moment, I am sure. Oh! Count Fabricati!' she hurried on excitedly, 'you look magnificent!'

He shook out the Mechlin lace ruffles of his cuffs and made her an elegant leg. 'Thank you, my sweet Helen, I have tried my humble best.'

Sophy giggled deliciously. 'Do you think you will be able to dance in those shoes?'

He glanced down at his silver-buckled shoes with their high, red heels and pointed a toe.

'I shall contrive, no doubt. I am growing accustomed to them already, one only has to perfect a mincing walk, *comme ça.*' He demonstrated a few steps for them, much to Sophy's amusement and she and her companions fell into whoops of laughter.

He turned and surveyed them, affecting a haughty expression, the beringed fingers of his left hand smoothing the curls of the great peruke which fell about his broad shoulders. In his right hand he carried a tall cane, topped with clouded amber and decorated with ribbons of pale-blue silk. His velvet coat was of the same shade of blue, richly embellished with embroideries of silver thread and at his throat was a cravat of antique silver lace. Across his breast he wore a dark-blue sash, pinned at the shoulder with a gold order set with jewels.

'There! You see before you now, the homeless, exiled prince returned from France to reclaim his throne from the usurper and to restore the honour of his house.' He swaggered boldly up to them, leaning foppishly on his cane and struck a regal pose. 'Do you recognize me now, Lady Anne?' he challenged, presenting himself before her and smiling into her eyes.

'Yes indeed, Sire.' She curtsied dutifully. 'You are the Merry Monarch, King Charles, are you not?'

'And no fit company for you, sweet Phyllida,' warned Constance as she came up to join them.

The Count cast her an amused look. "*E cortesia fu in lui esser villano*". Good evening, Miss Trevingham. Will you do me the honour of making me known to your charming companion?'

'This is Mrs Kirby, Lady Anne's kinswoman. May I introduce the Count Fabricati to you, Mrs Kirby?'

'I am delighted to make your acquaintance, ma'am,' he greeted her warmly, bending from his great height to bow over her hand.

'Good evening, sir,' she replied, eyeing him warily, for she thought him rather alarming in the heavy peruke with his face half-hidden by a black mask.

Then her sharp eyes flickered about the room as if in search of something or someone. 'I am happy to meet you at last, Count Fabricati, Lady Wyvern has spoken of you in the kindest of terms,' she continued, twisting her thin lips into the vestige of a smile. 'And of course, Lady Anne and I are very much looking forward to meeting his lordship, we have not before been introduced to him, you know.'

'Have you not? In that case I shall be only too pleased to mend matters for you,' he answered affably. 'Here he comes now,' he announced as he looked over his shoulder.

He stepped back a little to allow her to see my lord approaching and gave a sigh of satisfaction. 'Even in disguise, one cannot mistake him. That proud carriage, that noble brow,' he murmured admiringly. ' "A verray, parfit gentil knyght". Come, my lord,' he called invitingly, 'Mrs Kirby wishes to be made known to you.'

'Good evening, madam,' his lordship said somewhat huskily. 'I hope you will forgive my being out of voice, it is this inclement weather. I have a delicate constitution and my throat is susceptible to changes in the atmosphere.'

'Not at all, my lord,' she replied sympathetically. 'No doubt it is owing to this foggy night air. I also am subject to such chills. I cannot bear to be placed in a draught, for I am certain to contract a feverish cold which invariably results in my being confined to my bed for several days. And whenever the wind is blowing from the east, I have to keep my head swathed in shawls or suffer from the most dreadful earache! But alas, even as a girl I was never very robust and frequently fell prey to every childhood ailment, although I did escape the mumps, though I cannot think how I managed to avoid that. And do you remember when you fell ill with them, Anne, when by the greatest good chance I happened to be visiting my sister in Worcestershire? Thank goodness I was not with you then; I live in dread of taking the infection, it is so very dangerous in persons of my age. I have had the measles three times and each time I endured the severest of symptoms! I cannot tell you what I have suffered!' she shuddered exquisitely.

'I beg you not to try, Mrs Kirby, it would be too painful an experience. None of us, I think I may safely say, would request it of you,' remarked the Count with feeling.

'No, indeed,' interjected Lady Trevingham hurriedly. 'Such recollections are often so distressing.'

'May I introduce Lady Anne Rossmore, my lord?' continued the Count before Mrs Kirby could reply and he drew the young lady forward.

'Oh, but she is charming!' commented his lordship adoringly. 'How do you do, Lady Anne? You cannot know how very much I have been looking forward to this moment. I am so pleased that you could come tonight. The evening would have been quite dull for me if you had not honoured us with your presence. I wonder if I might implore your indulgence, Mrs Kirby? I should dearly like to dance with this beautiful, young lady. And I assure you I shall take the greatest care of her. May I have your permission?'

'Of course, my lord,' she replied instantly, immensely proud that the heir to a dukedom had spoken so civilly to her. Lady Anne handed the crook to her and she watched them as they walked away, anticipating gleefully the delight with which this news would be received by Lady Wyvern. The marquis seemed very taken with Lady Anne. He had ignored all the other ladies present as if he had eyes only for her. Lady Wyvern had warned that it was improbable that he would ask her niece to dance but hoped that she might at least engage him in conversation. Now here he was, having only just met the girl and he had singled her out immediately!

Yes indeed, Lady Wyvern would be more than happy with the result of all her planning. She continued to watch them as they entered the dance; how noble he looked in that long white surcoat emblazoned with a red cross! On his head he wore a steel basinet encircled by a gold coronet but the face beneath was completely hidden behind a full mask.

Lady Anne, a duchess! How splendid that would be and certainly befitting one who bore the name of Rossmore, of which family she herself was a distant relative. Yes, this was an excellent beginning to the evening!

Lady Anne was overjoyed to find herself so soon in the company of her white knight. 'You make a handsome crusader, my lord,' she beamed up at him. 'What a clever idea!'

'I'm glad that you think so,' he answered in a low voice. 'Count Fabricati insisted on the costume; it is an effective disguise, is it not? I am clad from head to foot in chainmail. My own mother would not know me if she had not already seen me earlier this evening. How did you know who I was?'

'Count Fabricati pointed you out to us as we came in,' she laughed. 'But I would have recognized you anyway. You are taller than the marquis and despite your efforts to alter your voice, I have grown too used to listening for the sound of it to be long in doubt.'

'I would be more than flattered if I thought that were true,' he said, wishing that her face were not masked. 'Do you think that Mrs Kirby noticed aught amiss? I confess I was a little apprehensive about the difference in height, I thought she would be certain to remark it. But the Count assured me that having put the notion into her head, it would be a simple matter to convince her that she was meeting the marquis. As for my voice, alas, I never was a clever actor.'

'Never mind. You managed the thing quite splendidly. I know she was not in the least suspicious or she would never have permitted me to dance with you. How subtly the Count misled her. It is so kind of him to arrange everything for us. I still can't quite believe my good fortune. I have a feeling this is going to be the happiest night of my life!' she declared joyfully.

'And mine,' Justin averred fervently and he felt her

return the warm pressure of his fingers as he held her hand.

Unable to see his expression, she had to content herself with the unmistakable note of passion in his voice.

'I'm so glad you can't act,' she whispered softly, looking up at him. 'I don't want you to be anyone but yourself.'

'Then there isn't anyone else I would sooner be tonight. And certainly there is no lady in all the world I would rather be with than you,' he assured her lovingly.

'Truly?' she asked, her voice tremulous and her dark eyes glowing behind the pale-pink mask.

'I swear by this my faithful sword,' he answered earnestly, placing his hand on the hilt of the blade that hung on his hip. 'Will you trust the word of a valiant knight, fair maiden?'

'I would trust you with my life, right noble sire,' she vowed solemnly and then a shy smile slowly curved her rosy mouth.

'If only you would!' he breathed, stepping closer to her and she could see the blaze of his blue eyes bright against the silver mask. 'Oh, Anne! My darling girl!' His words were cut short as he recollected where he was. A crowded ballroom was hardly the place for a lover's declaration. If only he could think of a way to see her alone!

'Shall we go and sit down?' he suggested after a slight pause, during which time he strove to master his emotions. 'I cannot converse properly while we are dancing and I must speak with you.'

'Of course, if that is what you wish. But Mrs Kirby will not permit us to have any private conversation, she is very strict regarding the proprieties.'

'I know but I have thought of a way we might overcome that difficulty,' he explained, drawing her hand through his arm. ' "Bondage is hoarse and may not speak aloud", yet this shall serve our cause, mayhap.'

He led her back to that part of the room where the elder ladies had settled themselves to watch the proceedings. Approaching Mrs Kirby directly, Lord Trevingham addressed her in the rasping voice he had perfected for his disguise.

'I wonder, ma'am, if I might be permitted to sit down

with Lady Anne for a while? I am a poor dancer and I think it must be a punishment for any young lady to be obliged to stand up with me for any length of time. But my tongue trips more nimbly than my feet and thus I hope to redeem myself in her eyes by proving that I can at least converse gracefully.'

'By all means, my lord,' she agreed with alacrity. 'I am sure her ladyship would be proud to bear you company, would you not, my dear?'

'If his lordship so desires,' she complied meekly.

'You are most gracious, my lady,' he bowed and taking her hand, led her to a seat set in a recess of the wall. But first he turned to Mrs Kirby saying, 'Forgive me if I appear to whisper, 'tis this wretched throat of mine, I'm sure you will understand.'

'Oh, indeed, my lord! So distressing for you, I do hope you will be perfectly recovered for the ball next week?'

'Thank you for your kind concern. I am certain I shall be my usual self by then.'

He smiled broadly behind the all-concealing mask, then feeling a tug at his sleeve, turned to see the Count at his side.

'How well you play your hand!' congratulated the Count surreptitiously.

'Thank you, master,' he whispered back. 'I begin to understand your strategies I think.'

Then settling himself beside Lady Anne he prepared to enjoy a quiet tête-à-tête under the benevolent eye of a watchful but triumphant duenna.

'I think Mrs Chessle and I will engage Mrs Kirby in conversation,' Lady Trevingham informed the Count as he came up beside her. 'If I can divert her attention for a while, so much the better for the knight and his lady. Do you go and dance with Georgiana. The poor girl is much hampered by her petticoats and will need a sedate partner who will have a care of her skirts.'

'And as I am a mature, middle-aged gentleman, you very naturally cast me in that role. I am flattered,' he bowed, hand on heart.

'No you aren't! And you know very well that you are a mere boy to me,' she replied airily. 'More ripening than mature! I ask you in consideration of your shoes not your age. You are both handicapped by your choice of costume it seems. Besides, the child dotes on you almost as much as Sophy, I think.'

'Ah, she at least has respect for my years. I shall now go and set a fatherly example. Together we will comport ourselves with such careful grace, our elegance shall render us the envy of all eyes. May I entrust you with my staff of office until I return?' He handed her his cane and with a flourishing bow, sauntered away to do her bidding.

Georgiana, who had watched Sophy disappear into the throng upon the arm of a handsomely dressed officer, was feeling thoroughly miserable. She was almost convinced that she was destined to remain alone all evening. How she wished that she had not worn this silly gown! She had not realized the difficulty it would cause her in a crowded ballroom with everyone jostling around her. The petticoat was so wide that she could not even sit down comfortably. Tears of frustration and self-pity were beginning to gather in her eyes when the Count suddenly appeared before her, bowed gracefully and invited her to dance. Now she was glad that Sophy had already gone off with a partner; this was a happy turn of events. She had often wished that he might ask her to dance but it seemed it was always Sophy who commanded his attention.

The Count took her hand saying with a solemn, courtly air, 'As the sole representatives of two great royal houses, we shall lend dignity to this rumbustious crowd. What say you to a minuet, your majesty?'

'But they are not playing a minuet,' she giggled nervously, somewhat in awe of him. His dark looks and tall figure reminded her very much of the portrait she had seen of the sovereign he was impersonating.

'What matter?' he replied imperturbably. 'I shall count the steps for you and you have only to follow my lead. Come, I will demonstrate.'

He took her aside from the main throng and beginning with a deep, sweeping bow he led her through the graceful movements of a slow minuet. His execution of the dance was so expert that his partner found it a simple matter to follow his direction. Eventually she forgot her self-consciousness, relaxing under the influence of his supreme confidence and indifference to the attention they were attracting. A small crowd of onlookers began to gather around them, highly amused by this odd spectacle of a dance that was more familiar to their grandparents. The Count chose to ignore the laughter on all sides and continued to perform his part with his customary aplomb. Soon, several couples began to try to emulate them, amid much merriment and then more and more people began to participate in the fun. Before long, the musicians, alerted by the sounds of mirth, also took up the triple rhythm until everyone was joining in this stately dance.

Georgiana was now accomplishing the steps with ease and found herself in the happy position of having no lack of partners. The Count relinquished her hand to an eager young man who had been the first to seize the opportunity of dancing with such an elegant young lady.

Well satisfied with the results of his efforts, the Count quietly withdrew to watch the proceedings, a smile of amusement playing on his lips.

'Well, well, Count Fabricati. I see you are making use of your position of royal influence this evening.'

He glanced down to see Constance standing beside him. She was dressed in a spangled gown of silver-grey spider gauze and on her brow was a circlet of diamonds. In the flickering light of the candles in the sconces, she seemed to shimmer from head to foot, reminding him of dewy cobwebs caught in the beams of a September sunrise. His smile grew softer and she saw the look of admiration fire his eyes as they glittered against the black mask.

'So, 'tis Queen Titania fresh from her woodland domains, an I mistake not? What brings you hither on this midwinter's night?'

'I am come to see what mischief you are brewing,' she replied frankly. 'But I think that perhaps this time I have misjudged you. You have puzzled me greatly tonight.'

'How so?'

'It seems that you might, after all, be something of an altruist. Justin has achieved the impossible and has been an hour and more in the company of Lady Anne Rossmore, right under the nose of her duenna. Georgiana is now the belle of the ball when but a short while ago she was like to be without a single partner. There is nothing, it seems, that you cannot do. But what is your purpose in all this? Why are you so concerned for Lady Anne's happiness that you have gone to such extraordinary lengths to help Justin meet with her? You don't even know her.'

'You ask too many questions, young lady. Don't always expect to find answers to life's mysteries, sometimes they are quite beyond our comprehension. "*Le coeur a ses raisons que la raison ne connait point*".'

'Then you do have a heart, Count?' she asked, intrigued by his note of seriousness.

'I have I believe, that which passes for one,' he rejoined lightly. 'It sufficeth me. But don't allow that to disturb you. Pray feel at liberty to continue to berate and abuse me as much as you ever did when you thought I had none.'

'I had seen very little evidence of it,' she retorted defensively. 'A man who follows such a *profession* as yours would have no use for one I should have supposed.'

'You are perfectly right, of course,' he said reasonably. 'A man in my position would certainly find it surplus to requirements. But speaking of matters of the heart, what think you of our pair of lovebirds?' He indicated the place where Justin sat with Lady Anne by his side.

'I think they are besotted with one another,' she smiled affectionately, turning to watch them as they sat deep in conversation.

'Love is a powerful potion, fair Titania,' he continued, pensively gazing at the blissful couple. 'Beware of that philtre or you may awake from your dreaming to find yourself enamoured of an ass.'

'Exactly what am I to infer from that cryptic remark?'

' "*On est aisément dupé par ce qu'on aime*".'

'So you have read Molière, what has that to say to anything?' she snapped a little impatiently.

'No matter, let it pass. "Advice is seldom welcome and those who want it most always like it the least". I quote now my good lord of Chesterfield, a man of great wisdom.'

'Did he not also write "Wear your learning, like a watch, in a private pocket and do not pull it out and strike it merely to show that you have one"?'

'True,' he acknowledged with a grin. 'But he also said "Swallow all your learning in the morning but digest it in company in the evenings".'

'Are you never at a loss for words?' she replied, unable to refrain from smiling in return.

'Hardly ever. I have such a store of them, diligently garnered from the many-flowered fields of literature. Now my head's a honeycomb in which I nurse my thoughts upon the pollen of profundity. 'Tis a sweetness should be shared with those of similar tastes, no matter what the hour. Do you not agree, Miss Trevingham?'

'I can think of nothing more satisfying than the enjoyment of perfect mutual understanding. "Tis a consummation devoutly to be wish'd",' she answered quietly almost wistfully.

He put a finger beneath her chin and made her look up at him, then stared deep into the clear, blue-grey eyes that returned his regard unblinkingly from behind the mask.

'Do you remember what Aristotle said on the same subject? "What is a friend? A single soul dwelling in two bodies". You must never be satisfied with anything less, Miss Trevingham, if you are desirous of finding a lasting happiness. Do you like to read poetry?'

'It is one of my greatest pleasures,' she answered him instantly.

'Then no doubt you are familiar with Donne's *Extasie*, in which he wrote "Loves mysteries in soules doe grow". You have such a soul as that, it shines in your eyes, I perceive it at this very moment,' he ended softly.

Constance gazed into his face as if mesmerized. They were right, Lady Jersey and her mama, there was something fascinating and compelling about this man. Especially tonight, looking every inch a king. He made her feel afraid but it was not fear of him that made her tremble. She was frightened of herself, his eyes saw too much. There was the unnerving intimacy of acute perception in his gaze. She had felt it before when she had spoken with him at Almack's and now again tonight, he seemed to look right into her mind, her heart. She shivered, not cold but strangely exhilarated.

'You seem poised to fly away, sweet Titania,' he

murmured, releasing her chin but not her eyes. 'I hope you will not do so for a while, for there is magic in your presence and your smile. I think I am falling under its spell. Don't break it too soon.'

He stepped closer and took her hand in his warm clasp. Her feet moved of their own volition as he began to lead her into the dance. She knew she ought to protest but this time she didn't want to, self-will for once had deserted her and still his eyes held her captive. The music and the voices around her faded into oblivion and gradually this one man became the whole focus of her attention, all other faculties seemed suspended, all else forgotten. It was the strangest sensation she had ever felt in her life. At once frightening and exciting, to be so out of touch with common sense and reason and so close to rioting emotion. What was happening to her? Had she gone mad? She didn't even like him, certainly didn't trust him! It was no use, she could not arouse animosity. It lay drugged with the opiate he had administered with the touch of his hand, quieted by the sound of his voice.

'I like your hair loose like that, my faery queen,' he said in a low voice, his eyes tracing the fall of her long, flowing tresses. 'How well it becomes you. "From her fayre head her fillet she undight". Yes, that suits you. I'm glad you don't follow the prevailing fashion and wear it cropped.'

'Thank you, sir. But it is my only claim to beauty and I am loathe to part with it,' she confessed honestly.

'You wrong yourself, you have something more than transitory beauty. What was it Pope wrote? "Beauties in vain their pretty eyes may roll, charms strike the sight but merit wins the soul".'

'What merit have I that would win such praise from you?' she asked wonderingly. 'Have I not given you the sharp end of my tongue since first we met?'

'I will not deny it,' he laughed. 'And it sorely pricked my pride. But I am nothing if not a fair-minded man. My infamy had gone before me, the harbinger of my fate. There is naught to say in my defence. Your judgements are just and therefore I accept them. And though your opinions are a little too freely expressed for my comfort, at least they are honest and have their roots in a genuine concern for your family.'

'I had rather you assured me that I was mistaken in you,' she replied in a troubled voice.

'I had rather have done so. But alas, all that you have heard of me is true. I am what I am.'

'I don't yet know what you are. I thought I did but now I am not so sure of my facts.'

'Untie this knot and you will find that you have only an ordinary piece of string,' he replied simply.

'That may be perfectly true. Though the word *ordinary* could never be applied to a man like you in any context whatsoever. However, as to the knot, my nature is such that I cannot but try to unravel it and I am both obstinate and persistent.'

'I had concluded as much,' the Count sighed resignedly. 'Like all women you have an insatiable curiosity, you ought to be careful of it.'

' 'Tis men who continually provoke it. They will never admit us into their confidence.'

'Perhaps that is because it would very soon cease to be one.'

'A woman can be as discreet as any man!' she protested indignantly.

'Indeed? There is an old adage in my country, that roughly translated says, "As a dog with a tail needs must wag it, so a woman with a tale must wag her tongue".'

'You are trying to be humorous, it seems,' she observed with gravity. 'Well, you have succeeded in diverting me. Now will you tell me why, or shall I guess?'

'I thought you might be in need of a little distraction,' he replied innocently.

'To draw me from my other pursuit?'

'Your thoughts do tend to run along one course, do they not? I have already told you that everything your brother said of me is true. What else is there to know? Except that you have nothing to fear from me, of that I can and do assure you.'

'Such reassurance is welcome,' she acknowledged carefully. 'But having witnessed your performance with Mrs Kirby tonight, I am aware that you can appear very plausible when it suits you.'

'Then you will not trust the word of a gentleman? Oh, but of course, I was forgetting. You have your doubts about that too.'

'That was not well done of me,' she replied in a subdued tone, 'and I am very sorry for it. I have a wretched temper and have not yet learned to get the better of it.'

'Well, at least I am enough of a gentleman to accept your apology,' he responded, adding contritely, 'And I see you are too much a lady to mention that I ought not to have forced it on you.'

'I am glad that you have given me the opportunity to do so. I should have found the courage sooner; it was cowardly of me not to have spoken before this. I knew I had overstepped the bounds of civility when I said those things to you.'

'Then I will forgive you if you will pardon me. Shall we cry quits?'

'By all means,' she agreed willingly, happy to have redeemed herself, for she had since regretted that unseemly outburst.

They parted company with cordial feelings on both sides. Constance had not believed it to be possible but tonight she had begun to see him in a new light. She felt easier in her mind, that is until she saw her brother dancing with Sophy later in the evening.

She waited for them to finish the dance and then waylaid them. 'Why aren't you with Lady Anne, Justin? Has Mrs Kirby parted you?'

'Not Mrs Kirby, it was Count Fabricati,' laughed Sophy. 'I was dancing with him a while ago and he persuaded me to ask the *marquis* to dance. He said that my headstrong brother was in danger of arousing Mrs Kirby's suspicions because he was paying Lady Anne too much attention.'

'But where is Lady Anne now? I don't see her with Mrs Kirby?'

'Of course not. She is dancing with the Count,' replied Sophy merrily. 'He stole her from under that woman's nose!'

'The minute my back was turned!' cried Justin mournfully. 'If he wasn't such an excellent shot, I would call him out.'

'Well, he thinks it is time that Lady Anne began to enjoy the dancing. And he is a far better dancer than you, Jus, you must admit. Did you see him with Georgiana dancing the minuet?' she teased playfully. 'Look, there they are! Mrs Kirby will be furious with him for he has taken the liberty of keeping Lady Anne at his side. I must say that they make a very handsome couple, do they not?'

Constance studied them closely for a few moments, her brow furrowed in thought. They were indeed an extremely attractive pair and appeared to be thoroughly at ease with one another. The two dark heads were close together as he addressed some remark to her. He must have said something to amuse her for she began to laugh up at him, her face flushed and animated. Constance had never seen her look so happy and carefree. The question was, which of her partners this evening had made such a change in her? It must surely be Justin's presence that had put her in such an ebullient mood. Of course, how could she doubt it? It was nonsense to suppose that anyone else could replace him in Lady Anne's affections. They had been strongly attracted to one another since the first moment they had met and she was as much in love with him as he was with her. Having reassured herself on this point, Constance ought to have been satisfied. Alas, however, she was not entirely convinced. A little voice somewhere in the back of her mind was reminding her that the Count was very appealing to women. Even she, who had been so determined to set a distance between them, had found herself this very night responding to his manifold charms. There was something almost irresistible about him, or so it seemed. His smile always drew an answering smile, his fearless eyes demanded and won complete attention. He was unconventional, uninhibited and undeniably attractive. Lady Anne was rich, beautiful and very young. She had led such a sheltered and confined life, that a man like the Count would be an exciting diversion. Was not Sophy, who had enjoyed far more freedom, already worshipping at his feet?

She glanced anxiously at Justin, wondering what he thought about this tender, little scene but his face was inscrutable behind that mask.

Lady Trevingham came up to them bringing Mrs Chessle and Mrs Kirby in her wake. 'My dear Sophy, we have been watching your dancing. You really ought to dance more often, my lord, your execution of the steps was a delight, was it not, Mrs Kirby?'

'His lordship is an accomplished dancer,' conceded the lady, deliberately not including any praise for his partner. She had no admiration for that forward young woman, who was far too flirtatious to be thought pleasing in her manners. She had actually had the effrontery to ask the marquis to dance with her! Such an exhibition of impropriety was intolerable. The explanation was probably resentful jealousy because his lordship had plainly preferred Anne's company. No doubt the girl fancied herself capable of engaging his interest. Perhaps she hoped to see herself a duchess one day soon. Well, Lady Wyvern would have something to say to that!

Sophy, who had observed the look of malice cast in her direction, clung more closely to her brother's arm and looking up at him with her sweetest smile said, 'Thank you for the dance, my lord. I really enjoyed it. I don't know why you are so reluctant to dance, you are an excellent partner. You have made this a most pleasurable evening for me.'

Mrs Kirby sniffed audibly, her thin lips tightly compressed into patent disapproval at such odiously encroaching behaviour. At this moment, the Count returned with Lady Anne on his arm and Mrs Kirby glanced at them in some annoyance.

She was not at all pleased that this foreigner had disregarded her strict instructions that he was to dance only once with Lady Anne and then bring her back to her chaperone, instead of which he had kept her in conversation long after the dance had ended.

'Oh, you are come back to us at last, Anne,' she said scoldingly. 'I think perhaps it is time we made our departure. I promised your aunt we would not be late tonight. I wonder if you would oblige me by asking a footman for our cloaks, my lord?' she suggested artfully, hoping to detach him from Sophy's side. 'Anne, do you go with his lordship and order our carriage to be brought round.'

'Oh, must you go?' he asked in tones of disappointment.

'I was hoping that you might stay at least until the unmasking.'

'Alas, my lord, we cannot,' interrupted Mrs Kirby decisively. 'It is late and the fog may be growing worse.'

'In that case, may I offer my services to you and accompany you back to Grosvenor Square?'

'We should be most grateful for your escort, my lord,' she answered promptly and with a look of triumph on her face. Well! This was a fortunate outcome. Sophia Trevingham would find herself with no further opportunities to entice him into her net!

The marquis went away with Lady Anne, leaving Mrs Kirby to await their return. She listened idly to the conversation that ensued between Lady Trevingham and the Count. Her ladyship was speaking of their forthcoming departure for Chailey, Lord Trevingham's country estate in Kent.

'Perhaps you would consider joining us, Count? We shall not be returning to Town until the spring and would be glad to have you with us if you think you can bear to live quietly for a few weeks. London is always very thin of company at this time of year and you might find it rather boring to remain here.'

'Well, I have seen little of your fine English countryside and should like to do so before I return to Italy. I should therefore be most grateful to you if you would allow me the opportunity. Thank you very much for your kind invitation.'

When Lady Anne reappeared with his lordship, the Count turned to him saying, 'I have just been invited down to Chailey for the Christmas festivities. Will you be going also, my lord?'

'Of course. I am quite eager to do so,' he replied, as if surprised at the question. 'I am delighted to hear that you will be accompanying us.'

Mrs Kirby frowned blackly. So that was the way the wind was blowing! The Trevinghams were becoming very great with the marquis it seemed. Well, she would have to pass this piece of information on to Lady Wyvern. They were trying to steal a march on her and she could easily guess their motive. Amelia Trevingham was a scheming woman who had lost no opportunity in trying to secure a coronet for her brazen young daughter. Once they had him under their roof, they would waste no time in forcing him into a declaration. Something would have to be done if it were to be prevented but she could trust Lady Wyvern for that!

'I think we ought to be leaving also,' announced Lady Trevingham suddenly. 'I do not like to be driving in this fog and besides, we can make better use of the carriages if we all depart together.' She turned to Mrs Kirby. 'I am sure you will have no objection to taking Sophy up with you this time, instead of her sister? And as you already have a gentleman to escort you home, perhaps, if the Count does not dislike the notion, he would accompany us on our journey. We shall have to drive to Cavendish Square first to take the Chessles home. You do not mind being obliged to sit on the box until we get there, Count Fabricati? I fear there will be no room for you inside the carriage.'

'That will suit me perfectly,' he assented with a slight bow.

'Then we shall set forth immediately the carriages are brought round. My lord, would you be kind enough to see my daughter safely to her door?'

'Most certainly. I should deem it an honour,' he replied promptly.

'We shall set her down first,' intervened Mrs Kirby assertively. 'And then we three can continue on to Grosvenor Square,' she added with the air of one who had just played a trump card. She was not going to allow the Trevinghams to outwit her!

Nine

After the heat of the ballroom, the night air struck their faces with an icy hand as they waited to step into the carriages. The street was draped with swathes of fog that hung in cobweb-like whorls upon the beams from the lamps, dimming their brightness.

Georgiana was some while settling comfortably, owing to her voluminous skirts but eventually they were arranged to her satisfaction.

The horses, fretted by the delay, stamped their hoofs impatiently, their iron shoes ringing hollowly on the cobblestones. They shook their heads, setting the bridles jingling and blew out great clouds of warm breath from their nostrils in loud, snorting expirations.

Finally, all the ladies were seated and the Count closed the door upon them. Then he climbed nimbly up beside the coachman and the eager horses were at last set in motion. The carriage wended its way slowly through the maze of streets, many of which were as yet unlit. Now and then, patches of thickening fog plunged them into momentary invisibility as they moved phantom-like through the swirling mists.

'I wonder that you can find your way so easily in this dismal weather,' remarked the Count as the coachman turned the horses into another fog-shrouded street.

'Oh, this is nothing much, sir. No more than a misty night to us Londoners. Wait till you're caught in a real fog! You won't see a hand in front of your face! It's a good thing we aren't too near the river though, it's always much worse over there.'

'Have we far to go now? I have completely lost my bearings. Where exactly are we?'

'We're not far from Oxford Street, sir. Just a few minutes more by my reckoning.' He turned his horses yet again and they were enveloped in a damp, grey blanket that muffled the sound of the wheels. Suddenly, from out of the night, they heard a man's voice raised in fear.

'Help! Help! Thieves! Thieves!'

'What was that?' whispered the Count, listening intently.

'Sounds like trouble to me,' muttered the coachman uneasily. 'We'd best keep moving.'

'But someone called for assistance, we can't just ignore it,' he replied, throwing aside the heavy covering from their knees.

'You don't understand, sir. It could be a trap. There are some crafty villains like to be about on a night such as this. Take the advice of a cove as is familiar with this old city and pay no mind.'

'I can't oblige you. I never could mind my own business and I must find out what is happening. Stay here with the ladies or drive on as you think necessary, I can take care of myself. Now pull up your horses, please. I'm getting down.'

'But sir! You must not take such a risk!'

'Do as I say, man!' ordered the Count peremptorily and made to jump down. The coachman shrugged resignedly and reluctantly obeyed. This gentleman was a foreigner and everyone knew they were all excitable and impulsive. Fiery tempers they had too and he had no desire to fan the flames.

The vehicle had hardly drawn to a halt when the Count leapt down and disappeared into the night.

'What's happening? Why have we stopped? Is anything the matter?' enquired Lady Trevingham, letting down the window and putting forth her head.

'The gentleman's run off, your ladyship. Jumped down and run off he has. Shall I drive on?'

'Run off?' she repeated, bemused. 'Why has he done such an odd thing?'

'He's gone to look for trouble, my lady,' he explained, 'And I think he's found it,' he added under his breath as the sounds of an altercation came echoing along the narrow alley on his right.

'What sort of trouble is it?' she asked anxiously. 'What has happened, Thomas?'

'Someone shouted out for help and the foreign gent just up and disappears,' he answered, lugubriously shaking his head. 'Can't see the sense in looking for trouble but foreigners seem keen on it from what I've heard tell.'

'What does he say, Mama?' Constance questioned impatiently.

'The Count has gone to help someone in difficulties, I think. I'm not sure what is happening but that seems to be the reason for our stopping so suddenly.'

'Then I had better go and see what I can do to assist.'

'Oh, do you think that is wise?' cried Mrs Chessle, very much alarmed by this turn of events. 'It might be dangerous.'

'Perhaps we ought to wait here, Connie. I'm sure the Count is quite capable of dealing with this matter, whatever it may be.'

'I daresay he is but someone should go and see what is happening. The coachman can't leave his horses and I am not afraid to go.'

She was already flinging open the door and despite hysterical pleadings from Mrs Chessle and tearful entreaties from Georgiana, she descended precipitately from the carriage.

'Wait, Connie! I'll come with you!' called her mama, who had not the agility of her wilful daughter and could not descend without the steps being let down.

'No, Mama. Do you stay with the Chessles. I shall only be a few moments.' Then, turning to the coachman who was rubbing his chin doubtfully at the young lady's impetuosity, she demanded one of his lanterns. When he had rather reluctantly handed this to her, she said, 'Stay here!' and ran quickly along the dark alleyway, calling out the Count's name.

The haunting cry of a man in pain came to her sharp ears and lifting high the lantern, she strove to see what lay ahead. The light fell upon a ragged curtain of eery mist and she paused hesitantly to peer through the gloom, listening for some sound to guide her.

Was that the sound of stamping feet? A dull, thudding

noise echoed the beating of her pulse. She moved slowly forward, cloaked about by the all-enveloping fog which seemed to both blind and deafen her, bringing a sense of utter loneliness and isolation. The lantern was useless now and she lowered it to her side. Slowly she stretched out her right hand until she touched rough brickwork and then began to feel her way along the alley. How dark it was! Suddenly, a man's figure burst upon her vision and knocked her breathless against the wall. She cried out in alarm, her limbs trembling with the shock but he did not stop and was swallowed up into the darkness. With shaking hands she turned again towards the strange sounds ahead, her heart thumping violently. The fog began to thin again and Constance held the lantern aloft. This time, she could see a small courtyard in front of her and four men, three of whom were fighting fiercely while the fourth lay groaning on the ground.

The Count, in stockinged feet, was holding two men at bay with his walking cane. He had taken up the fencer's stance and was using his stick as if it were the finest Toledo blade. His movements were swift and lithe as he lunged into the attack. The other men were wielding heavy cudgels but to no good effect because he had outmanoeuvred them by forcing them up against the wall where they could not easily swing their arms.

Constance looked wildly about her, not knowing quite what to do to help him. Her eyes alighted upon the fallen man who was beginning to sit up, propping himself on an elbow. Close by him lay the weapon that had fallen from his grasp and she rushed forward to seize it before he could recover his senses. Then setting down the lantern she grasped the cudgel in both hands and ran to the Count's assistance. He had just taken a blow on his right shoulder and was sent reeling. Constance, infuriated by these brutal cowards, leapt to his defence and dealt the nearest villain a resounding blow on the head. He let out a yelp of pain and dropped to his knees.

Exulted by her success in felling her man, she turned back to the Count who was grappling with his assailant in an effort to break his hold on the cudgel. They were partially obscured by wraiths of fog as they twisted and turned in the ensuing struggle. She watched, worriedly biting her lip. The Count's right arm appeared to be useless. He had lost his cane and was holding off the threatening weapon with only one hand. Taking advantage of this, the other man threw his weight against the Count's body, knocking him backwards. Constance sprang towards them just as they disappeared into the fog once again but she felt the blow she had aimed strike its target. There was a sudden groan followed by a fierce invective in terse French. At least, she thought it was French but the words were incomprehensible to her, presumably they were of a selection that lay outside the vocabulary of a gently-born young lady. However, she did recognize that it was the Count's voice that uttered them!

'Hey there! What's going on?' yelled someone behind her. It was the coachman come looking for them. At the sound of his approach, the men seemed to melt into the shadows and vanished from sight.

Constance snatched up the lantern and hastening to the Count, bent anxiously over him. He glanced up at her, half-stunned.

'Ill-met by starlight, proud Titania!' he gasped somewhat painfully.

'Actually it's lamplight,' she corrected, putting it aside.

'I know what I'm seeing!' he laughed shakily. 'I suppose that was your fairy wand you waved over my head just now?'

'Alas, it was no fairy's touch, I fear,' she apologized contritely, kneeling down to look at his face.

'But yes! I fell beneath its spell! One of your "giddy" spells this time, I think,' he added, staggering to his feet with her assistance.

'Are you in much pain?' she asked, deeply concerned for him. 'Oh, I do hope I haven't hurt you!'

'I shall do very well in a moment or two. Fortunately, tonight I have more hair than wit, so there's no harm done.'

'What happened here, sir?' enquired the coachman, scratching his head in puzzlement.

'Footpads. They had set upon a late-night reveller it seems,' he explained, 'I think he left the reception when it became too riotous for his taste.'

'That must have been the man who ran past me in the

alley! What a cowardly act, to leave you at the mercy of those ruthless ruffians!' she declared contemptuously. Then addressing the coachman, she said, 'You had better go quickly and tell the other ladies that all is well. We will be with you in a moment.'

'Yes, miss,' he replied, 'I must get back to my horses; I left her ladyship holding them,' and he sped hastily away.

'Do you think you could help me find my shoes by the light of your lantern, Titania? I kicked them off somewhere hereabouts.'

'Of course,' she answered instantly and cast about the yard until she had found them. As she bent to pick them up, the light from her lantern glittered upon something lying close by. She stretched out her hand towards it and felt a cold, round object. Lifting it into the light she examined it carefully. It was the gold and enamel order that she had noticed pinned to the Count's sash earlier in the evening and must have been loosened in the struggle. She turned it over thoughtfully, noting how heavy it was. This was made of real gold! And if she wasn't very much mistaken, these were real diamonds and rubies, not paste as she had assumed. There were some words painted in enamels around the edge of the ornament, *je vais m'arranger* and in the centre, picked out in precious stones was a gryphon holding a cross and surmounted by a crown.

'Have you found them?' he asked, coming up behind her so softly that she jumped nervously.

'Yes, here they are.'

He bent and put them on his feet and as he straightened up she held out the jewelled ornament to him. 'I think this is yours. You had better put it in your pocket, it looks as if it might be valuable.'

He took it from her without answering and after looking at it for a moment his eyes flicked to her face. 'A pretty thing, is it not? I would have been loath to lose it. Thank you, I am doubly indebted to you tonight it seems.'

'It looks as if it is very old. Is it an heirloom?' she enquired curiously.

He hesitated before replying to her question and then with that familiar shrug of his, he said carelessly, 'You ought never to ask a gamester how he came by his treasures.'

'I see,' she murmured with a slight lift of her arched brows. 'I suppose you acquire many such things from your pathetic victims.'

'I take whatever seems fair. One must always settle one's debts somehow.' He slipped it into his pocket and stepping towards her, took her hands in his and turning them palms up he pressed a soft kiss into each.

'Such little hands, my sweet enchantress,' he mused caressingly, still holding them fast. 'Yet my life, unworthy though it is, could not have been held more safely. I have only once before met such courage in a woman. And only once owed so great a debt.'

'Perhaps that is because you are a very clever gamester, sir,' she responded lightly, suddenly feeling ridiculously shy. No one had ever kissed her hands in that fashion before and she coloured with embarrassment. Thank heavens it was so dark!

'Do you know that for the first time in my life I have lost all interest in the game? Maybe there is something far more worth the winning.' He spoke the words quietly, almost pensively, she thought. 'Why did you come to my rescue, *ma mignonne*? You are not over-fond of my company are you?'

'I may have felt once or twice that I could cheerfully strangle you,' she admitted, 'but I am not so uncharitable as to stand by and watch three men with far less reason than I, foully murder you.'

'You saved my life tonight. You know, in some cultures that means that for the rest of our lives you are now responsible for me. I think that custom is quite appealing. I rather like the idea that my fate is henceforth in your keeping. I hope you mean to take your responsibilities seriously?'

'I do not intend to accept the charge. A man with your propensities would make the task too onerous.'

'Ah! But you have already intervened in my behalf. Perhaps it is too late for you to deny your destiny?' he suggested triumphantly. 'Don't you sense this moment is great with portent, *ma fée*? There is magic all around us.'

His face was very near to hers now and she could feel his warm breath on her cheek. Her hands trembled in his strong clasp and she quickly pulled them free and thrust them behind her back.

'There's nothing in the air but fog,' she retorted soberly and retreated a pace.

'And something of a damper at that,' he sighed regretfully.

'Come, we must get back to the others,' she insisted. 'It is very late and they will be worried.'

'Yes, you are right,' he agreed decidedly. 'Pass me the lantern, please. Thank you. Now hold on to my arm. It's all right, I shan't eat you!' he laughed as she hung back uncertainly.

She slipped her arm through his, out of reason cross that he had not only noticed her nervous reluctance to be so close to him but that he had been amused by it.

He led her straight to the waiting carriage and having reassured the ladies that all was indeed well, he handed Constance up the steps and resumed his place on the box. The rest of the journey was undertaken without further incident.

When the Chessles had been set down in Cavendish Square, Lady Trevingham pressed him to sit inside the carriage for the return to Brook Street.

'First I shall see you safely to your own home, my lady. I can easily walk from there to Brook Street.'

'But you cannot wish to walk alone at this time of night and especially after that dreadful attack on you!' cried Lady Trevingham. 'I will not hear of such a thing.'

'And I will not allow you to continue your journey without a proper escort,' he countered with determination in his voice. 'I fully intend to see you to your door.'

Her ladyship sighed in exasperation. 'It really is quite unnecessary for you to do so.'

'I think not,' he answered emphatically.

'Don't argue with him, Mama, you cannot possibly win. He is used to getting his own way. You ought to know that by now. He listens to no other counsel but his own,' intervened Constance.

'I will not deny it. Though it is not that I am stubborn,

you understand but rather that I have grown accustomed to making my own decisions. It is a difficult habit to break.'

'I think headstrong best describes you,' concluded Constance decidedly. 'At least, I did not manage to break it,' she added wickedly.

'Well it wasn't for the want of trying,' he quipped, gingerly feeling the bruise on his brow. 'But I hope you will be more careful of my heart, Titania.'

She eyed him warily, startled out of her amusement. What did he mean by that remark? He must have been funning. The trouble was, it was always difficult to tell with him. But could he be serious? No, impossible! She tried to see his face but he was sitting too far back from the light, infuriating man! The carriage soon drew up outside the house in Albemarle Street and a footman appeared to let down the steps. The Count alighted first and then helped the ladies out.

'Come inside with us and we shall look to your wounds,' ordered Constance in a voice that brooked no argument.

'There is no need. I am well enough, I assure you,' he replied rebelliously.

'Don't be foolish,' she admonished sweetly and taking a firm grip on his arm she almost dragged him into the house, ignoring his protests.

They found that Sophy had retired to her room but Justin was awaiting them.

'What took you so long?' he demanded as they entered the drawing-room. 'I thought you had gone back to Brook Street, James?'

'Her highness commanded me to come in and I could not gainsay her,' explained the Count, handing her to a seat.

'Oh, Connie rules us all with a sceptre of iron,' grinned her brother, sympathetically.

'Well, she has a divine right, that's certain,' commented his friend, rubbing his head.

Justin looked perplexed for a moment until Constance described their brief adventure.

'Isn't it just like you, James, to take another man's part in a fight? Why must you always take such long odds? And this time you did not have a sword.'

'He managed very well without one,' Constance informed him, throwing aside her domino.

'What happened to your gown?' gasped Justin. 'Isn't that a bloodstain?'

'Is it? No matter,' she said carelessly. 'And you need not worry, it is not my blood.'

'Then whose?'

'Probably mine,' interjected the Count accusingly, seating himself beside the fire. 'Or perhaps that other fellow's whose brains she also tried to dash out.'

'Well he deserved it,' pronounced the unrepentant lady, bending over him. 'And you know very well I did not mean to knock you on the head. Now let me see your hurt.'

He drew away from her saying, 'It is nothing. You need not trouble yourself.'

'Keep still do! I am determined, you know, so there is no help for it; you might as well save your breath to cool your porridge.' And she snatched off his wig before he could prevent her. 'Now you really must be quiet because I am going to have to clean this wound for you and if you keep fidgeting I might hurt you.'

'You had better do as she says, James. Connie's made her mind up to doctor you and there will be no denying her. She is a strong-willed woman.'

'I have reason to believe it,' he replied with an odd little smile which made her catch her breath when she saw the look that accompanied it.

She turned away to hide her discomfiture just as the footman brought in the water she had requested.

'Oh, thank you. Set it down here, will you?' she instructed, pulling forward a tambour-topped table. Then deliberately avoiding the Count's gaze, she concentrated on the cut on his forehead.

She washed away the blood as carefully as she could and parting the crisp, dark curls with gentle fingers, was relieved to find the cut was not deep. It seemed that the peruke and his own thick, cropped hair had saved him from any greater harm.

'There, that's clean now. Shall I bandage it for you?'

'You'll do no such thing, minx!' he warned threateningly, half rising from his chair whilst she tried to restrain him.

'Very well, I shan't insist upon it,' she laughed. 'And I'm sorry to have to tell you that it is unlikely that you will have another interesting scar.'

'Perhaps if I had had you to be my ministering angel when this was done,' he ran his finger lightly over the mark on his face, 'I might still have been the flawless Adonis I once was.'

'Yes, you look as if you have had an encounter with a wild boar. Is that why you are only here for a few months among us?'

'Quite so. I have been restored to Venus for a short time only,' he answered, rather regretfully she thought and gave him a quick, appraising glance. His face as usual, gave nothing away but she remained convinced that there was something more behind his words than mere rhetoric.

Justin brought him a glass of brandy. 'Here, drink this, it will do you good.'

'Thank you, just what I need to calm my nerves.'

'It might if you had any, which I very much doubt, never having seen you display them.'

'Well, as history records, this Merry Monarch, unlike his foolish father, manages to keep his head. And what of you? You acted very coolly yourself, Sir Knight.'

'I did, didn't I? But it is easy to be brave hiding behind another man's back. I just hope Fearnley doesn't find out I impersonated him.'

'What else are masquerades for? In your case, you were doubly disguised, that is all and I thought you carried it off very well.' He lifted his glass in salutation and winced visibly.

'Is anything wrong, James?' asked his lordship with concern.

'It's only my shoulder. I thought at first that the fellow had broken it but it's just bruised, thank God, and will soon mend. No, Miss Trevingham, I do not require you to bandage that either, thank you very much,' he continued hastily as she started up from her chair. He finished his brandy and arose to take his leave of them.

'I wish you had let me bid the coachman wait for you,' said Lady Trevingham as he shook hands with her.

'There really was no need to have kept him any longer

from his bed and I shall enjoy the walk. Don't worry, the odds are very much against my being set upon twice in one night, believe me. And my calculations are usually quite good.'

'You certainly calculated Lady Wyvern's hand accurately,' grinned Justin. 'Tell me, why did you ask about Chailey?'

'I was merely sowing a few seeds in fertile soil to see what might come of them. I just needed you to water them for me.'

'Ah! Another of your plots to be harvested later? I thought as much. You are as devious as my Uncle George.'

They glanced up as Basset entered in answer to the summons of the bell.

'The Count is leaving now, Basset,' said her ladyship. 'Would you show him out, please?'

'Very good, my lady,' he bowed and held open the door as the Count bade farewell to Constance.

' 'Tis time to get you to your flowery bank, Titania,' he said, taking her hand to his lips. ' "Never harm, nor spell, nor charm, come our lovely lady nigh, so good night with lullaby". Sweet dreams.' He kissed her fingers, his eyes meeting hers over them.

'Good night, sir,' she answered, her pulses quickening and that tell-tale blush warming her face.

He smiled and his smile was like a caress. She trembled and he loosed her hand, glancing over his shoulder at the butler.

'My hair and cane, please Basset,' he requested gaily.

Basset raised his brows questioningly, thinking that perhaps his ears deceived him.

'They are here,' intervened Constance, laughing and handing them to the Count.

'We are very much obliged to you, madam,' he replied, clapping the peruke on his head. 'Thank you for an enchanting evening.'

Then taking the tall cane, he made an elegant leg and turned with regal poise to follow Basset from the room.

He strolled homeward through the fog-muffled streets, his thoughts pleasantly occupied with the success of his latest scheming. It was becoming an amusing pastime and at least it was keeping him from growing bored while he waited for events to unfold. Lady Wyvern was an entertaining adversary, a little too predictable to be an exciting opponent but the situation from his own point of view was certainly piquant. Lady Anne was captivating! If all went well, he hoped to get to know her much better. Perhaps, given time, it would be possible to establish a closer relationship? The idea was very appealing. Tonight when he had danced with her, it had been a simple matter to put her at her ease. She had responded to his overtures with an almost child-like trust and warmth. The memory brought a smile to his lips; he might even become fond of her! What an odd experience that would be for him after all these years. Really, it was almost absurd! Well, wasn't life forever proving to be the most fascinating game of all? The rules were constantly changing, making the odds completely incalculable; there was so much to learn and so much that was unpredictable as these recent games of chance had shown. Should he keep the cards fate had dealt to him? Or should he discard them as unplayable? Was he skilful enough to win on all points? Tonight the stakes had been suddenly set even higher, did he dare continue? The thrill of making the attempt was very alluring!

His spirits, ever responsive to new challenges, were soaring high by the time he reached Brook Street and Jean, hearing his merry whistling as he neared the house, already had the door open before his master could knock.

'*Vous êtes très content ce nuit, M'sieur le Comte*,' he grinned amiably.

'*Oui, Jean, tout va bien!*' replied the Count joyfully, handing him his cane and carelessly tossing the peruke at a coat-hook on the far wall where it settled snugly.

'I'm glad to hear it,' came a voice out of the shadows and the Count frowned warily as a man climbed up the stairs that led from the area.

'Oh, it's you, Dupois,' he observed unemotionally. 'I wondered when I would be hearing from you. Have you brought us some news?'

'Would I have come all this way else? But shall we discuss business over a bottle? No doubt you still keep a good cognac in your cellar, even in this barbarous land?'

'Of course. Shall we go up? There is a fire in my sitting-room,' he turned towards the stairs and preceding the visitor, led the way to the first floor.

'Have you been waiting long?' he asked, pulling up a chair to the fireside and indicating that the gentleman be seated.

'A few minutes only. I decided to take advantage of this miserable English weather. No one saw me enter; it is the perfect night for such as we, don't you agree?'

'Fog is rather a furtive element, I suppose,' answered the Count as he poured out the brandy. 'Here, drink this, I think you will find it to your taste.'

Dupois took a mouthful of the warming liquid, rolled it over his tongue and swallowed hard. '*Delicieux!*' he announced. 'French?'

'But naturally. Now tell me, why have you come?'

'I thought it time I paid you a visit.'

'Has Arnaud sent you?'

'As a matter of fact, yes. You did not imagine that I had merely come to enquire after your health?' he asked sarcastically.

'You are not a man to inspire imagination of any kind, Dupois,' rejoined the Count calmly, settling himself in a winged armchair.

A spasm of anger crossed the older man's lean countenance and the fingers of his left hand clenched into a fist but he held his temper in check.

'I see your manners are not improved, Gérard, by your sojourning with these uncouth Englishmen. However, I at least am a gentleman by birth and so shall overlook your discourteous remark.'

If he had hoped to wound the Count's pride with this barbed retort, he was disappointed. Instead of taking offence, he just laughed in sheer amusement and thus it was Dupois who bristled with annoyance.

'What are you laughing for?' he snapped.

'Laughter is the leavening in life's dull dough, Dupois. It would be damned flat without it. And you are so very amusing.'

'What have I said that is so humorous?'

'Well, to tell me that you were born a gentleman,

impresses me as much as if an habitual criminal had reminded his judge that he was born an innocent,' drawled the Count lazily.

'You go too far, Gérard,' snarled the Frenchman furiously.

'You are not come here to exchange civilities,' continued the Count in a bored voice. 'I see no point in pretending that we like one another. The fact is, my fine sir, you are in this for the same reason as myself. We are both being paid for our services. High-born or base-born, we are all now become gentlemen in France, are we not *citoyen*? Let us waste no more time – give me Arnaud's message.'

Dupois shot him a venomous look, his eyes dark with suppressed fury. One day he would wipe the smile off that insolent fellow's face! How he longed for just such an opportunity. But it would come and meanwhile he must learn to bide his time with patient forbearance. He felt in his pocket for the letter which had been entrusted to him in Vienna and without another word, handed it over. The Count broke the seal and unfolded the thick paper, his eyes quickly scanning the closely written lines. Dupois watched him carefully but if he thought to see that devilish face give even one flicker of an eyelash, he was mistaken. His expression revealed nothing that showed whether the news was good or bad.

'Well?' he questioned brusquely, when he saw that the Count had finished his swift perusal of the document.

'Well indeed. If this means war, it could be that our star will rise again. We shall see. You and I must forget our – shall we say differences?' he smiled, remembering Dupois' earlier insult. 'This news makes my business here in London a little more urgent.'

'What progress have you made, if any? I see by your peculiar attire that you are enjoying the pleasures of London society. I trust that in so doing you have not forgotten the purpose of your visit?'

'May I in turn, remind you that I am accountable to no one but Arnaud,' came the immediate reply. 'You may report to him that thanks to my dear friend Trevingham, I am invited almost everywhere. I have even had the good fortune to gain favour with the Countess Lieven; she has been most useful to me, a most knowledgeable woman with many political and influential friends. I have also dined with the Devonshires and their set, where I enjoyed some most interesting conversations. And you would be amazed at how confiding a gentleman becomes when one has persuaded him to imbibe in a few bottles of good wine. *In vino veritas.* Yes, you really would be amazed,' he murmured as he raised his glass, a quizzical smile on his lips. 'I shall, of course, divulge the information I have gleaned thus far, only to Monsieur Arnaud in the usual way. One cannot be too cautious, you understand.'

'Oh, I understand perfectly, Gérard. You choose not to trust me. It is well, for I reciprocate your feelings entirely.'

'Then we may end this meeting in harmony with each other. Goodnight, Dupois. You need not stay, Jean will see you out. I shall send for you when I am ready, just give Jean your direction.'

The Frenchman glowered at this impudent dismissal. That this *salopard* should speak thus to a man of his rank was almost insupportable. But he would not stoop to quarrel openly, there were more important issues at stake. For the present he must follow orders which meant that like it or not, he had to put himself at Gérard's disposal.

When Jean returned, his duty done, he found the Count sitting at his desk pondering over Arnaud's letter.

'Is he gone?' he enquired without looking up.

'Yes, sir. But oh, he does not like you very much, that one!' laughed Jean.

'*Vraiment? Ça ne me fait rien. Je m'en fiche.*'

'*Méfiez-vous de lui, m'sieur.*'

'*Quoi! Tu as peur de lui, Jean?*'

'*Il est un homme dangereux.*'

'*Je pense que tu as raison. Mais ne t'inquiète pas.*'

The Count picked up the letter. 'Monsieur Arnaud writes that there is much dissension in Vienna; in fact it is rumoured that it could even result in a war with Prussia. Now why would he trouble to write and tell me this, Jean?' he muttered thoughtfully, tapping the paper against the palm of his hand. 'He must have known that I would have already heard of this myself.'

He took up the thick sheet and peered at the edges.

Then inserting the fine tip of the pen-knife, he carefully prised them apart revealing a second thin sheet covered with numbers.

'Ah, yes! It is as I suspected. There is more in this letter than meets the eye. This may take me some time to decipher, Jean, so get you to your bed, I shan't need you again tonight.'

'*Merci, m'sieur. Bonne nuit,*' nodded the valet and softly closed the door behind him. This would be another late night for his master, *bien sûr*. Well, he might not need any sleep but here was one who needed no further persuading and smothering a yawn, he took himself off to his room.

It was nearly dawn when the Count finally threw down his pen with a sigh of satisfaction. So! This was why Dupois had been sent post-haste to London. The die might soon be cast! It was not entirely surprising, he had been half expecting it when he had left Rome. How like Napoleon to use this dissension in Vienna to his own advantage. Still, it would take a little while to accomplish, he would have time to finish his business here. Much depended on whether these two influential princes reached an agreement or perhaps a compromise? Meanwhile, he must watch events very carefully. Arnaud expressed confidence in winning the support of the French, but the English? That was quite another matter. From what he had already discovered, opinion was divided on the subject. But conjecture was one thing, a *fait accompli* quite another. His instincts told him that a gamble such as this was foolhardy in the extreme. Positively reckless in fact but it was this aspect of it that appealed to his sense of adventure. It was almost too tempting to resist. Well, no use in deciding yet, he would wait for the other players to declare.

Wearily he arose and taking up the papers, walked over to the fireplace and threw them on to the dying embers. He watched unblinkingly as the edges gradually darkened and shrivelled before suddenly flaring into a bright, orange flame that rose higher and higher. Then slowly the brightness faded into a few winking sparks that one by one were extinguished, until finally all that remained were the frail, disintegrating ashes.

Ten

The following day, Jean was despatched to his master's bootmaker in Grafton Street. As instructed, he asked to see Mr Redman who alone could be entrusted with the task of repairing the Count's elegant footwear. Jean explained to him that the heels required particular attention and Mr Redman assured him that he would deal with the matter personally.

'Count Fabricati is in no great hurry for them,' Jean remarked, handing over a pair of Hessian boots wrapped in thick paper.

'Very good, then I shall have them brought round to Brook Street when they are finished,' replied Mr Redman. 'Please inform the Count that it may take a few days as we are rather busy just now but I shall try to despatch the business as quickly as possible.'

Jean nodded his thanks and departed, leaving Mr Redman with his parcel which he took through to the workroom. Having locked the door behind him, he quickly unwrapped the package and examined the boots thoroughly. Then, taking up an awl from his work-bench, he gently eased the point into a small gap under the heel of one of the pair until he was able to swivel it round. As he had guessed, there was a neatly-folded paper nestled in the hollow beneath the heel and he eagerly removed it from its hiding place. He spread the sheet open, smoothing out the creases and hurriedly glanced down the page. Suddenly there was a tapping at his door and he heard the voice of his young apprentice call his name. Swiftly he tucked the paper into his coat and twisted the heel into its correct position.

'Just a moment,' he answered depositing the boots

beneath the bench and then went to unlock the door.

'Excuse me, Mr Redman, sir. But I f'ought you should know that a gen'leman was 'ere a moment ago. 'E wasn't one of our reg'lar customers and 'e was enquiring as to the Frenchman's business wiv you just now. 'E offered me a shillin' to tell 'im what was in the parcel,' he grinned, showing a somewhat incomplete row of teeth.

'Oh, he did, did he? And what did you say to him?' questioned Mr Redman, eyeing him warily.

'I said, if 'e was so keen to know, why didn't 'e ask the gen'leman 'isself,' retorted the young man, his cheeky grin growing even wider.

'And what did he have to say to that, my lad?'

'Why, only that 'e damned my eyes!' chuckled the apprentice. 'And then 'e went out a-slamming the door arter 'im.'

'Well done, Jos! I shall bless those sharp eyes of yours if you see that man again. Be sure and tell me if you do. I won't have my valued customers being spied upon. This is a reputable establishment and I want to keep it that way, you understand?'

The lad nodded and winked knowingly. 'Trust me for that, sir!'

'Excellent! Oh, and Jos ...' he added as the boy went to the door.

'Yes, sir?'

Mr Redman thrust two fingers into his waistcoat pocket and drew forth a coin. 'This is for your trouble, Jos – and for your discretion.'

The silver was accepted with alacrity and concealed immediately somewhere beneath a decidedly grimy apron.

'There will be another of those for you, if tomorrow you will go to Brook Street and apprise the Count's man of this stranger's interest in his affairs. Will you do that for me, Jos?'

'Wiv pleasure, sir! I'll go now if you want.'

'No, tomorrow will be best. Now run along, I have to go out for an hour or so.'

The young apprentice had dutifully performed his errand early the next day and after a few careful questions, Jean sent him on his way.

The Count was not unduly worried by the news. 'Isn't that just like Dupois? A clumsy amateur! The man has no finesse.'

'But, sir, I think he means you harm. You must have a care. *Il est un diable.*'

'A devil he may be but he doesn't have his luck! Do not fret yourself, Jean. I intend to be very cautious. Have I ever failed to be?'

'*Oui, m'sieur. En Espagne.*' rejoined his valet with a sour grimace.

'Oh but you distress me, Jean,' sighed the Count, affecting to be deeply wounded. '*C'était une mésaventure.* Besides, did I not contrive to turn that unfortunate episode to my advantage?'

'*C'est vrai,*' agreed Jean with undisguised admiration. 'You have the good luck, yes?'

'I hope Madame is still with me, I shall need her company at the ball. There is something more I would do there to arrange matters completely to my own satisfaction.'

Lady Anne Rossmore was equally desirous of having dame fortune attend her birthday celebrations. When at last the day had dawned, she both longed for and dreaded the approach of evening and the anticipation set her nerves on edge. Her maid scolded her several times for fidgeting whilst her hair was being dressed but eventually her *toilette* was completed. The reflection in the glass showed her a young woman who looked outwardly calm and composed but whose inner conflict was revealed in the heightened colour of her complexion and the over-bright eyes. She stared back at the image of a stranger. Or so it seemed. The face, finely dusted with powder, had a peach-like bloom, the lips were a perfect, rosy bow enhanced by the slightest hint of rouge. Her lustrous curls were twisted high on her head to form a coronet intertwined with diamonds and pearls. There were elegant pearl drops in her ears and a magnificent string of pearls about her graceful neck. Snowy-white shoulders, softly rounded, rose from a froth of lace that adorned the bodice of her ivory silk dress and the high-waisted, décolleté fashion of the day revealed a creamy bosom. As she continued to study her appearance, it slowly became clear to her all that it meant to have reached the age of one and twenty. She was a grown woman now. She could order her own life if not her fortune; she could wed the man of her choice and no one could gainsay her. Her guardians could no longer stand in her way. They still had control of the money that her mother had left her but they could not now compel her to marry a man she did not love. This woman in the mirror could stand up to them; she could show them that she was not to be brow-beaten into obedience. She could! She could! Her heart beat fast and she felt breathless with excitement. The Count was right, she must seize hold of her courage and show them that she was taking charge of her own destiny. A woman who had come of age did not need a duenna, Mrs Kirby must be told of this decision at once. It was at this point in her cogitations that Lady Anne suddenly lost her new confidence. How could she find the resolution to rid herself of her kinswoman? She trembled visibly at the thought. Oh, if only the Count were here! Somehow, he had the power to strengthen her resolve. How daring he was and how easily he manipulated her aunt and Mrs Kirby. He wasn't over-awed by Lady Wyvern; he knew just how to outwit her. Even Justin was a little afraid of her; they had hardly spent any time in each other's company until the Count had chosen to assist them. She had actually begun to taste the delights of freedom at the masquerade. It had been so wonderful! He had made that possible. He must come tonight, she needed him to support her in this daring venture. Oh, how marvellous it would be to escape this house and this family, if only for a short while! The Count seemed so certain that he could contrive to free her from all restrictions if only she would do as he directed. She was sure that he could achieve any miracle, he was so very clever. There was something so dependable about him and he had promised to stand her friend. The thought of this warmed her heart. He was a man to keep his promises, he would not fail her, she *felt* he would prove a true friend. Yes, it was so! She did trust him, despite the fact that she had known him for such a brief space of time. He had been so kind to her at the masquerade, he seemed to understand her so completely. He was such a sympathetic listener and felt just as he ought upon every subject that they had discussed. She was comfortable in his company and had found herself confiding all her hopes and fears to him that night. Instead of despairing at her situation, he had actually imbued her with confidence, even made her laugh! He must come to the ball! Her future happiness depended upon it!

Taking a deep breath, she arose from her dressing-table, deliberately selecting Justin's posy from amongst the flowers that had been sent up to her and went in search of her aunt.

The evening seemed interminably long as they received their guests who came in a never-ending stream up the sweeping marble staircase.

All of society appeared to have accepted Lady Wyvern's invitation, perhaps because she was renowned for the richness of her hospitality or perhaps because this would be the last great ball before the *haut ton* went down to their country estates for Christmas. Whatever the reason, this night was going to be remembered and spoken of as a shocking squeeze, a verdict which could only delight a hostess who cared so much for her reputation.

When the Marquis of Fearnley was announced, Lady Wyvern almost fainted with pleasure. This was her crowning glory! She had achieved the impossible! When he expressed the wish that he might dance with her niece, she became bereft of speech. All her greatest hopes seemed about to be realized. With what rapture she received Count Fabricati as he followed close on Fearnley's heels.

'My dear Count! How happy we are to see you here tonight. It is so good of you to have come and I see you did manage to persuade the marquis to join us. Such a pleasurable surprise. I am so very glad to have you both as our guests. I do hope you will enjoy the evening.'

'I am very much looking forward to doing so, especially if you will allow me to ask your beautiful niece to grant me the honour of dancing with her when she is free of her duties?'

'Of course! Of course! I am sure she will be able to find a

dance for you on her card,' averred her ladyship with abounding gratitude.

Lady Anne was also overjoyed to receive the Count. When she saw that he had actually contrived to bring the marquis with him, she felt that surely nothing could be beyond his powers to achieve.

Her welcome was enthusiastic; so delighted was she, that her cousin Giles who was standing beside her, stared at her in astonishment. Why was she behaving in this besotted fashion over a man she scarcely knew? Her face was alight with a genuine pleasure as she smiled up at him and her look was almost adoring. Never had her eyes sparkled like that at sight of him! Nor had he once been granted the warmth of a smile such as she now bestowed upon this interloper! A jealousy which he could not control flared in his brain. What treachery had this foreign upstart been plotting that he had so soon wormed his way into his cousin's affections? How could Lady Wyvern have permitted him to even touch her niece's hand? Who was he anyway? Certainly no one of importance and with the sordid reputation of a gamester. What was Lady Wyvern thinking of to allow such a person into her circle of friends? She who prided herself on the select company she kept, to include a man who was probably nothing more than a sly adventurer. How he had managed to become so great with everyone was beyond comprehension.

He decided that he would watch his cousin very carefully tonight. If her aunt and uncle were not to be relied upon to keep her away from such a fribble, then he would see to it himself.

The Count found the Trevinghams had arrived before him and were already in the ballroom. It was decorated with festoons of hot-house flowers and silk ribbons in shades of pink, looped between the fluted, gilded pillars that edged the dance-floor. Massive chandeliers and ornately carved sconces held hundreds of flickering wax candles. A full orchestra played in a balustraded gallery that overlooked a ballroom filled with men and women dressed in their finest clothes. Silks and satins and splendid jewels of every description denoted the quality of her ladyship's distinguished guests.

'Count Fabricati! How handsome you look,' declared Lady Trevingham, linking her arm through his. 'I see you have followed Mr Brummell's lead.' She eyed the black, ankle-length pantaloons that ended in a strap beneath the shoes. 'I must admit that you appear to advantage in them, although I'm not at all sure I approve of discarding knee-breeches in favour of pantaloons for evening-wear.'

'They originated in my country, you know,' he smiled down at her, 'so I thought it only right that I should encourage the Beau's admirers to follow his example.'

'His admirers need no inducement to ape his fashions. Indeed, they would not dream of doing otherwise. He is acknowledged to be the arbiter of good taste. Not without cause, I think,' she added, glancing appreciatively at the Count's tall person. His spotless white neckcloth was immaculately tied as usual and tonight he wore a plain, white waistcoat beneath a close-fitting, black coat with cut-away tails. His height and athletic build complemented the simple elegance of his attire and lent him an added distinction which set him apart from the more lavishly dressed gentlemen with their satin knee-breeches and extravagantly designed coats.

'I should imagine that a man of your figure would be something of a boon to his tailor,' she remarked teasingly.

'And I should agree with you, my lady,' he replied with equal good humour. 'Indeed, he ought to be able to open new premises, when I settle my bills. They really do amount to a good figure. But I am still a credit to him.'

Lady Trevingham looked startled, not quite sure of his meaning but she had no opportunity to discover it because Justin claimed the Count's attention. 'James! You old fox! How did you do it? Fearnley's here! He's actually here! I've just seen him!' he cried in excited amazement.

'Suffice it to say, Justin, that I contrived,' grinned the Count. 'You have been acquainted with me long enough now to know that I always do so, one way or another.'

He exchanged a comical look with Justin's mama before turning back to Lord Trevingham and saying, 'I hope you have already taken the opportunity to ask Lady Anne for your two dances? Something tells me that she is going to be very much sought-after tonight.'

'The minute we arrived. I was afraid I might be too late else. Doesn't she look ravishing?' he sighed ecstatically.

'Very lovely,' murmured the Count, as the young lady in question appeared with her elder cousin to join in the dancing. 'She is undeniably a diamond of the first water.'

'Tonight, dressed as she is, I would describe her as a pearl without price,' enthused his lordship adoringly.

The Count gave him a swift appraising glance. 'You really do love her, don't you, Justin?' he stated quietly.

'Yes, I really do,' he answered devoutly, not turning his eyes from her direction and therefore omitting to notice the Count's quick frown.

'Excuse me, Justin. Lady Trevingham. I must go. I am promised to Lady Cowper for this next dance.' He bowed and left them abruptly.

They did not see him again until much later in the evening when he had finished dancing with Sophy and brought her back to her mama.

Constance, who was sitting with Colonel Dyson, glanced up at their approach and smiled a greeting. She had not seen a great deal of the Count since the masquerade and actually felt glad that he had come here tonight. Her emotions had undergone something of a change and she now felt more kindly disposed towards him. In fact she had even experienced a sense of disappointment when he had not appeared at any of the social engagements she had attended lately. The warmth of her greeting seemed to take him by surprise and she immediately regretted having revealed her obvious pleasure at seeing him again. She turned quickly away to hide her blush but he came over and stood beside them.

'Good evening, Miss Trevingham, Colonel Dyson,' he bowed to each in turn. 'I wonder if I might take the liberty of stealing this young lady from your side, Colonel Dyson? Will you dance with me, Miss Trevingham?' he begged, holding out his hand.

'I should be delighted. Please do forgive me, Colonel, won't you?'

'Of course,' he replied, politely rising from his chair. 'I think I shall ask Miss Sophia if she would overlook my advancing years and grant me the privilege of partnering her.'

The Count led Constance out on to the floor and took her into his arms to dance a waltz.

'I hope you are quite recovered from the wound that I inflicted, Count Fabricati?' she began conversationally.

'That depends,' he mused thoughtfully. 'To which wound are you referring?' he continued, smiling at her look of confusion.

'Why your head, of course!' she replied wonderingly.

'In that case, you need not trouble yourself to further enquire. It was a mere scratch and is already forgotten,' he assured her lightly.

'I am pleased to know it,' Constance owned courteously.

'Yes, my head is quite whole now,' he went on, 'but my heart, well, that is another matter.' He sighed deeply and she looked up at him accusingly.

'Count Fabricati! I begin to suspect that you are an incorrigible philanderer.'

'Oh! But now you really have wounded me! I have a most sincere regard for you, Miss Trevingham, how could you doubt it?' he protested mournfully.

'Then why have you not so much as paid us a morning visit since the masquerade?' she demanded reproachfully.

'I regret that just lately, my time has been rather taken up with a matter of important business. A circumstance which you cannot deplore more than I since it deprived me of your company. However, I mean to make up for the interruption to our blossoming friendship, or perhaps I ought to say budding?' he added, noting her look of surprised enquiry. 'Well, at least I can hope to improve upon our acquaintance when we are all together at Chailey, can I not?'

She smiled at the note of tender entreaty in his voice. 'We may learn to be a little more agreeable to one another,' she conceded. 'But what important business have you in London? I thought you were here merely to enjoy its pleasures.'

'Ah but you forget that I have made a *profession* of pleasure,' he reminded her, 'and it keeps me much occupied.'

Constance frowned disapprovingly. She did not like to think of that side of his character. Gaming, when carried

The Gamester

to excess, was a deplorable habit. She wished it were not one of his vices. If it were not for that one flaw in him, she was sure that she could like him very well.

'Could you not find a more worthwhile occupation?' she answered seriously.

'Oh but it is very much worth my while, I assure you.'

'Then I suppose you would not consider giving it up?' she suggested tentatively.

'I might, given the right inducements,' he replied with a strange smile. 'But I do not think it at all likely. It is something of a vocation with me.'

'Oh,' she said in a small voice. 'Could no one persuade you?'

'I don't know. Perhaps. No one has ever tried and I am not sure that it would be wise,' he answered quietly and solemnly.

It sounded rather like a rebuff she thought and decided to say no more on the subject. After all, it really was no concern of hers what he did, was it? As the dance ended, she turned and saw Lady Anne had been dancing with her cousin Giles close by. The cousins were a few steps ahead of them as they left the dance floor to return to their friends. Lady Anne addressed the Count as soon as she noticed him behind her.

'Don't forget that you are promised to me for this next dance, Count Fabricati,' she said with a friendly smile.

'I have been looking forward to it too much to be in any danger of forgetting such an honour, my lady,' he assured her with an answering smile.

Giles Morton ceased his conversation with his friends and turned to the Count, a disdainful hauteur in his glance. 'Why, it's our Italian visitor, Count Fabricati,' he drawled with insolence in his tone. 'I did not think to see you here tonight. This must be quite a novel experience for you. Being in such civilized society, I mean. Do you not find it so?'

'Sir, you have sought my opinion on the matter and I cordially give it,' replied the Count unabashed. 'A civilization may best be judged upon the civility of its civilians. I shall allow you to be the best judge of yours.' He bowed graciously and offering his arm to Constance, he moved away without a backward glance.

A murmur of disapproval had arisen from the group about Morton as he had finished addressing the Count and it was he who had been left feeling extremely discomfited.

'I think you came off worst again in that encounter,' murmured Sir Francis Brascombe in his ear. 'Perhaps you ought not to try to cross swords with Fabricati, his ripostes are too quick for you.'

Morton flushed angrily at this pointed reference to his ignominious defeat and the flames of his jealousy began to blaze into an uncontrollable hatred.

Lady Anne's scornful eyes swept him with a look of utter contempt as she deliberately turned her back on him.

So she thought she could treat him like a leper, did she? He who had worshipped her from the first moment he had met her! And yet this insignificant stranger who was nothing more than a common card-sharp, could command her affections, be granted her sunniest smiles and receive the benisons of her brilliant eyes. Even her usually discerning aunt had succumbed to this toad-eating jackanapes. Well, he might be basking in their goodwill for the moment but not for much longer, not if Giles Morton had anything to say in the matter. And as the future Earl of Rossmore he would have a great deal to say!

The Count escorted Miss Trevingham back to her seat and as he handed her into a chair set against the wall, she retained his grasp on her fingers.

'That was very well done of you, Count Fabricati,' she remarked approvingly. 'I applaud your conduct just now. It was quite exemplary. That odious creature Morton meant to offer you an insult. I think you showed great aplomb.'

'Yes, Miss Trevingham, so do I,' he concurred, a smile dancing in his eyes. 'He is an insolent puppy, is he not? But I could not bring myself to whip him as he deserved, he has such doleful eyes, don't you think? Especially when he looks in Lady Anne's direction.'

'What do you mean?' she asked, not quite comprehending his inference.

'Jealousy, my dear Miss Trevingham,' he said, fondly

stressing the term of endearment he had dared to use. ' 'Tis a wicked goad that drives a man to madness.'

'Jealousy? You mean he thinks she is in love with you? She can't be!' she cried incredulously.

'I see you are all amazement. Don't you think me the least bit lovable, Miss Trevingham?' he enquired wistfully.

'You know I don't mean to imply that,' Constance protested. 'I mean, surely Lady Anne is in love with my brother? I am certain she cares for no one else. How could she be in love with you? It's impossible.'

'If you say so,' he sighed meekly. 'It is a sad reflection on my character no doubt but there it is. I am sure you are in the right of it.'

'I would not presume so far as to say *you* are impossible to love,' amended Constance cautiously.

'May I enquire how far you would go in that direction?'

'Only as far as saying you are impossible!' she retorted, trying to smother a laugh. 'Now please go away before you make me say something I might regret.'

'You almost convince me that I should ignore your plea but I must not keep Lady Anne waiting. À bientôt, Miss Trevingham.' He kissed her fingers lightly and left her to meditate upon the odd mixture of emotions that he aroused in her breast.

Colonel Dyson had observed this exchange with interest and came now to sit beside her. 'You appear to have overcome your dislike of Count Fabricati,' he remarked idly. 'Is it because you have discovered that he is not such a threat to your peace of mind after all?'

'Oh, he is still that, Colonel,' she replied thoughtfully, 'but I am not now so certain that he is quite the heartless ogre I once thought him.'

'What has happened to alter your opinion of him?'

'I don't know,' came the hesitant reply. 'I only begin to think that he is more than a mere player of ducks and drakes. No doubt I shall discover soon enough whether I am right or not.'

'Oh? How do you mean to do that?' he questioned in some surprise.

'I shall have ample opportunity to study him while he is at Chailey with us. Mama has invited him.'

'Indeed? Then I also shall have the pleasure of becoming better acquainted with him because Lady Trevingham has included me in her choice of guests. I shall be joining the rest of the party some time in the New Year.'

'Yes, I know. I am very much looking forward to it. I shall take great pleasure in showing you around the park; we have several delightful prospects that I am sure you will enjoy. I just hope that the weather will be kind to us.'

'Well, if you are to be my guide, I shall be doubly blessed,' he said happily, his cool, grey eyes smiling into hers. 'I understand that I shall also have the felicity of meeting the rest of your family. Your uncle may even be able to join us and bring us good news from Vienna, I trust. I suppose his responsibilities are very great. He is one of Castlereagh's chief advisers on the Italian settlement, is he not?'

'How did you know that?' she asked, eyeing him keenly. 'It isn't generally known.'

'One hears many things at the War Office. In fact, the latest news from Vienna has brought a buzz of rumours as you may imagine.'

'I daresay. The news is rather alarming. That is why we are not altogether sure that Uncle George will be able to quit the conference just now. It won't seem like Christmas without him though,' she sighed sadly.

'Are you speaking of George?' interrupted Lady Trevingham, seating herself on Constance's right and rearranging her trailing shawl.

'Yes, Mama. I was just saying that we are in some doubt that he will be able to come to us at Chailey this Christmas.'

'Well, I have but this moment been speaking with Lord Wellesley and he says that the Congress may be brought to an abrupt close if an agreement is not reached soon.'

'According to Justin's news from my uncle, Castlereagh is out of all patience and the discussions are not progressing at all well. But you can be sure that if anyone can prevent it ending disastrously, it is Castlereagh.'

'I admire your confidence, Miss Trevingham. Let us hope it is not misplaced. But if the Foreign Secretary is to try to solve these problems, then you will not be seeing Lord Kemsley at Christmas.'

'Then I think I must postpone the ball. Sophy will be

disappointed I know but I had intended it as a celebration of George's homecoming. We shall wait until January in the hope that all will be well by then,' decided Lady Trevingham.

'We will await the outcome with a keen interest. I am glad that I shall be at Chailey with you because at least you will be kept informed of the true facts. The rumours that circulate in my office are of the unsubstantiated sort. But I am sure you would prefer to be enjoying the dancing, Miss Trevingham. How very remiss of me not to have asked you earlier. Will you be so kind as to oblige me?'

'Of course,' replied Constance with alacrity. 'I thought you would never ask!' She went away on his arm and Lady Trevingham watched them go, a faint smile playing on her lips.

'They make a charming couple, do they not, my lady?' mused the Count, suddenly appearing at her side.

'Is that why you persuaded me I ought to invite him to Chailey?'

He laughed, saying, 'No doubt you see me as a matchmaker? What a romantic family you are!'

'Well, I was hoping that Connie might yet find happiness,' she confessed.

'She will. If she discovers her true self,' answered the Count enigmatically.

'You are very profound!' observed Lady Trevingham, beckoning him to sit down.

'Oh, I am! Very! You see, I have discovered during a lifetime of experience –' he paused to smile at her droll look – 'I am more than ripening, my lady, I am positively mellow with age,' he appended in a confidential tone. 'As I say, experience has taught me that happiness ought not to be sought outside oneself. It is a mistake to suppose that it lies solely in something, some place or someone. Outside influences can add to it, of course but it is essentially an inner attainment.'

'You say that with conviction, Count. I wonder if you are right? But tell me of Lady Anne, is she any happier tonight?'

'I intend to make her so,' he replied with determination. 'My board is set to win. I have my king in place, my knight is already in play and you, my queen, must be prepared to make the next move. Come, let us remove these black adversaries from the game.'

'I am in your capable hands, sir,' she asserted gaily and taking his proffered arm went in search of Lady Wyvern.

Her ladyship was in a state of euphoria. The marquis had begged to be allowed to dance a third time with her lovely niece. He had pleaded so eloquently and so urgently that she could not and would not deny him his request. Her ample bosom swelled with pride as she watched him lead Lady Anne into another set. Nothing could equal her triumph as she saw the effect this had on the astonished matrons. Not only had the marquis attended Lady Wyvern's ball but he had stood up three times with her niece! Surely this could mean only one thing: he must be enamoured of the girl. Well, there was no doubt it would be an excellent match, she was an heiress and very beautiful. She would make a splendid duchess. Lady Wyvern deserved congratulations if she succeeded in bringing him to the altar.

Lady Wyvern thought so too and it was Count Fabricati who was the first to offer them.

'Well, Lady Wyvern,' he confided, as if discovering a remarkable fact, 'I think your niece has captured my friend's heart. I have never seen him so *aux anges* before.'

'Do you really think so, Count?' she whispered eagerly. 'I was beginning to think it might indeed be so myself. But you know him so much better than I.'

'I have never seen a man so smitten,' he said with certainty. 'I daresay we shall be hard put to it to console him over the next few weeks. He is sure to be at something of a loss when this is but a delightful memory.'

'Oh, I am convinced we shall be able to find a suitable diversion for him,' broke in Lady Trevingham cheerfully. 'The company is always very merry at Chailey. My sister and all her family will be there and of course, my girls.'

'Lady Trevingham. I did not notice you there,' acknowledged Lady Wyvern in decidedly unfriendly accents.

'I am come in search of my children,' explained her ladyship, undeterred by the frosty reception. 'Sophy is such a popular girl, I never see her without a partner. Ah! There she is now with Lord Dillcott. And here comes Justin.' She quickly waved him to her side. 'Justin! Where have you been? I have seen nothing of you tonight.'

'I have just been dancing with Lady Anne but alas, I had to relinquish her hand to the marquis. He seemed eager to take my place,' he said in an aggrieved voice. 'I did not even have time to finish our conversation. It would serve him right if I did not ask her after all.'

'Ask her what?' enquired his mother in puzzlement.

'The marquis suggested that Lady Anne would be an enchanting addition to our party at Chailey so I thought that I would invite her, that is if Lady Wyvern does not dislike the scheme, of course,' he added with a deferential bow to her ladyship.

'No, Justin!' cried his mother hastily. 'I mean ... that is ... I am sure Lady Anne has already made arrangements for the Christmas season and we would not wish to interfere with her plans,' she explained, giving him an admonishing frown.

Lady Wyvern glanced from Trevingham's astonished face to his mother's expressive scowls.

'I think a certain young lord, quite close by, would be overjoyed if she were to alter her plans,' remarked the Count, innocently voicing his thoughts.

'I should suppose that it would be too late to do so now, even if she wished it, which I am sure she would not,' interjected Lady Trevingham dismissively.

'I daresay Lady Anne is already engaged, is she not?' enquired Justin tentatively as he calmly met Lady Wyvern's calculating eyes.

Her mind was rapidly considering the proposition. She had learnt from Mrs Kirby that Trevingham had prevailed upon the marquis to accompany them to Chailey. There was no doubt at all that Amelia Trevingham had used her son's friendship with the Count to snare the marquis. It was patently obvious why she had done so. Having failed to find a husband for that elder girl of hers, she was desperate to make a great marriage for her youngest daughter. What a pity that they were already promised to her sister's family in Hampshire this Christmas. But would it really matter if Anne were to cry off? Dare she let her go alone to Chailey? It would mean placing her within Trevingham's reach also. Could she risk that? She glanced across at her niece and saw the marquis at her side. At that precise moment, Sophia Trevingham laid a hand on his arm and smiled coyly up at him in a very coquettish manner. The marquis beamed at her in a friendly fashion as she engaged him in conversation.

That decided her! Anne must go to Chailey if she was to keep the marquis interested in her alone. Mrs Kirby could be sent to watch over her and see that Trevingham was kept at a distance.

'I can tell by your silence, Lady Wyvern, that it is out of the question,' sighed Trevingham dejectedly. 'Lady Anne does have a prior engagement.'

'Yes, she does. But it does not signify. My sister will not take it amiss if Anne does not accompany us this year. I am sure my niece would be only too pleased to accept your invitation, Lord Trevingham. Providing your mama has no objection to it,' she finished, giving her ladyship a challenging look.

'Oh, I am sure Mama has no objections, have you, Mama?' he cried happily. 'We will all be delighted to welcome her.'

Lady Trevingham managed a weak smile. 'Perhaps Lady Anne ought to be consulted first. After all, she might prefer to be with her own family at Christmas.'

'I think I may answer for my niece. I know what would please her best,' retorted Lady Wyvern with a malicious light in her eyes. She had no intention of allowing the marquis to wriggle off her hook. Amelia Trevingham was no match for her wits!

When Lady Anne was informed of the new arrangements made for her, she remembered the Count's instructions and tried her hardest to stifle her joy. It was not easy, her heart was nearly bursting with happiness because his scheme had been so successfully accomplished. Yet she managed to school her features into a calm, dutiful expression and meekly accepted her aunt's will in the matter. She even contrived to thank Lady Trevingham in a cool, steady voice without betraying her emotions.

When the Count whispered 'Bravo' in her ear, she went pink with pleasure. How glad she was that she had not failed his trust in her. She must find the courage to perform the rest of her part and dispose of Mrs Kirby's presence at Chailey. She peeped up at him, her eyes shining like stars. 'Thank you so much, Count Fabricati,' she murmured softly and gave him a smile so full of gratitude that he thought it well worth the thousand guineas it had cost him to promote such feeling.

When the Trevinghams arrived back in Albemarle Street, Justin insisted on drinking a toast to their victory.

Lady Trevingham invited the Count to sit beside her on the sofa. 'You are without equal, Count Fabricati. I now apprehend the reason why you went to such lengths to persuade Fearnley to dance with Lady Anne no less than three times! It was your object from the beginning to make Lady Wyvern believe that he was fallen in love. But it was an expensive way to do it,' she added in an undertone.

'I am a man who loves to speculate, Lady Trevingham,' he whispered back, his eyes twinkling with mischief.

'What have you been up to?' demanded Constance, noting her mother's conspiratorial air.

'We have been playing a game of chess,' explained Justin, taking up the decanter and removing the stopper.

'Is this the game the Count was master-minding a little while ago?' she asked suspiciously. 'The one that began at the masquerade? With all of you acting as his pawns?'

'That's it!' chuckled her brother as he poured out the wine. 'Only we weren't pawns, we were his chief pieces. I was his knight, Sophy the rook, Lady Anne the bishop, Mama, of course, was the queen and Fearnley, being the bearer of a coronet, was naturally the king. It really was an exciting game. James anticipated Lady Wyvern's every move. He knew exactly what she would do before she knew it herself!'

He handed round the glasses and when they all had been served, he lifted his in a toast.

'To the greatest gamester of them all – Count Fabricati!' he announced proudly.

They all raised their glasses in a salute. 'Count Fabricati!' they cried in unison, all except Constance that is. She sipped her wine in silent contemplation of the peculiar powers of this strange, paradoxical creature who had come like a catalyst among them.

Eleven

On 21st December, the Count was preparing to leave London and journey into Kent. He and Trevingham had arranged to drive down together in the Count's carriage the following morning.

As soon as the packing was nearly done, he asked Jean where Dupois might be found. Jean gave him the address and the Count sallied forth to enquire for Mr Johnson at Long's Hotel in New Bond Street.

He was shown up to Mr Johnson's room by a discreet serving man who tapped softly on the door of number eleven and announced the visitor.

'Well, well, my dear Count,' drawled Dupois, feigning astonishment. 'This is indeed an honour. I had expected to have to pay you a visit.'

'I am particular as to the kind of persons seen visiting me,' replied the Count, calmly stripping off his gloves and tossing them into his high-crowned beaver. He placed his hat and cane on a convenient table and sat down in the only comfortable chair in the room.

'Make yourself at ease, won't you?' muttered Dupois sarcastically as he drew up a plain, wooden chair for himself.

'Thank you,' smiled the Count benignly. 'Fortunately, I have the happy knack of being at my ease in any company, even yours. But enough of these pleasantries, let us to our business. I have here a message for Arnaud – coded, of course,' he mentioned deliberately. 'It is urgent so I am afraid you will not be able to spend Christmas in London after all. But I don't suppose you will be called upon to break off any important social engagements, so it matters little.'

Dupois scowled and took the sealed paper from him, almost snatching it out of his hand.

'I have not been invited to a grand house in the country, if that's what you mean. Oh, but I should like to see their faces when they discover what sort of person they have been welcoming into their midst!'

'Now how could you ever hope to have that pleasure, Dupois? Surely you would not betray me, would you?' he questioned silkily, his piercing eyes seeming to penetrate into the other man's mind.

Dupois stared back, rubbing the palms of his hands on his knees as he recalled, rather belatedly, the Count's reputation.

'Of course not!' he blustered angrily. 'I am the Emperor's faithful and loyal servant. And though I feel no obligation to you, Gérard, to betray you would be to betray him and that I could never bring myself to do.'

'How very affecting!' marvelled the Count, as if impressed by this declaration of allegiance. 'I suppose I ought now to feel completely reassured as to the tenderness of your conscience. I say I ought to because, somehow, Dupois, I can't quite believe it. You see, I know you too well. You would sell your soul to the devil if he didn't already own it. And as for your loyalty, we both know what that amounts to, don't we?'

He put his hand inside his coat as he spoke and pulled out a heavy leather pouch which he threw on to the bed.

'That will pay your shot here and cover your travelling expenses. No doubt Arnaud will further reward your *faithfulness* when you arrive in Vienna.'

He got up from the chair and reached for his hat, setting it at a jaunty angle on the side of his head. Then, pulling on his gloves, he said, '*Au revoir, mon cher ami.* Don't delay your departure, will you? I shall feel happier when I know that you are no longer dogging my footsteps. Be sure to guard that paper carefully, it is valuable – to you as well as to me. Tell Arnaud that next time I must have positive proof if I am to convince our man.'

He picked up his cane and opened the door. Then looking back as he went out, he raised his hat, saying mockingly, '*Bon voyage et bon Noël!*'

Dupois stood glaring at the closing door, his seething anger boiling over into a torrent of muttered imprecations. Snatching up the purse, he emptied it on to the bed. Five hundred guineas! And more to come when the message was delivered.

But this was nothing to Gérard. He chanced as much on the turning of a card! That trickster's by-blow enjoyed the life of a lord while a gentleman like himself was treated like a lackey! Well, Gérard's luck would desert him one day and when that moment came, he would make certain that he was there to see it happen. His fist clenched over the money and he scooped it up eagerly. At last he was in funds again! London had proved an expensive place for a man of his tastes. He glanced at the empty brandy bottle on the table by his bed and thrusting some of the coins into his pocket and the bills into the davenport, he hurried downstairs.

As he looked about for the waiter, he spied the Count outside on the pavement. He had been accosted by a young gentleman in a long drab driving coat adorned with several capes. This elegant attire was only of passing interest to Dupois, what stayed his attention was the look on the gentleman's face. It was one of pure hatred. This might be a matter worth investigating.

Dupois slipped unobtrusively towards the street door and pretended to take an interest in a notice pinned to the wall announcing Mr Edmund Keen's forthcoming appearances at Drury Lane.

The gentleman was speaking in a low voice filled with suppressed fury but Dupois was near enough to catch his words.

'I'm warning you, Fabricati. Keep away from her or you'll have me to settle with and this time it will be you who will be taught a lesson. I will not have you jeopardizing her good name. I know what sort of fellow you are. Your name is already a byword in every gaming-hell in the vicinity. My family has had to deal with fortune-hunters before, so don't think you can gull us, do I make myself clear?'

'What is clear, Morton, is that you are making yourself appear ridiculous. It is you who are putting her reputation at risk by discussing this on the streets. As for settling with me, don't you think it would be well to remember that your family name is every bit as infamous as my own? The stain of blood is not easily washed away, as I am sure the Wyverns would agree. If you were to try to shed any of mine, I think you would not find them so generous towards you. Now stand out of my way!'

The young man blanched visibly, trembling with impotent rage. At first, Dupois was sure he was going to strike the Count but alas, he thought better of it and turning on his heel walked quickly away.

Dupois watched as Fabricati strolled idly off in the opposite direction. He wandered out on to the pavement and looked up and down the street. The young gentleman had climbed into a curricle and was jobbing furiously at the horses' mouths as he tried to pull out ahead of a brewer's dray.

The Frenchman called over the waiter. 'Who's the young buck in such a hurry?' he asked casually, pointing across at the curricle as it swept past, sped on its way by some ripe remarks from the drayman.

'Oh, that's 'is nibs, Mr Giles Morton,' sniffed the waiter disgustedly. 'Heir to that old reprobate, the Earl of Rossmore and as full of 'imself as a rooster on a dung 'eap and with as much to say. Still, there's them as will listen when money speaks, so I doubt 'e'll go friendless in the world.'

'Full of juice, is he, eh?'

''E'll bleed freely enough when th' old Earl dies,' predicted the man moving back into the room to answer the summons of a jangling bell.

Dupois chewed his lip thoughtfully before following after him to order his cognac. He would dearly like to know what Gérard was up to now. What had he done to set that young blood at his throat? Who was this lady they were arguing about? One thing was certain, if there was money to be had, Gérard would know how to put his hands on it. He was as cunning as a nest of serpents and as unpredictable. The gentleman had mentioned fortune-hunters, hadn't he? Was that Gérard's game?

He returned to his room to drink the brandy and mull over the events of the morning. As he sat nursing the bottle, he glanced at the paper Gérard had given him to deliver.

'I wonder what this is all about?' he mused turning it over in his hand. 'What could be so urgent that I have to return so suddenly to Vienna?'

It crossed his mind to break the seal and read the letter but he knew it would be a waste of time. Gérard had devised some secret code which only Arnaud knew how to decipher. There would simply be a lot of numbers on the sheet and they would mean nothing to him. Well, there were other ways of finding out, if one kept one's ears and eyes open. When he came back to London he would set about doing just that, starting with this Rossmore family. If he could manage to mark Gérard's cards, he might be able to queer his game once and for all. The thought was exquisite!

As soon as the Count had rid himself of Morton's uninvited company, he walked round to Albemarle Street to enquire if Lady Trevingham was at home. Happily for him, she was and Basset showed him into the morning-room.

'Good day, Lady Trevingham. I am so glad to have found you at home. I have another favour to ask of you.'

'Oh? Another of your games, is it?' she asked, her beautiful blue eyes alight with laughter.

'Well, let us say that I am pleased to see you in a playful mood,' he replied, accepting the seat she offered him.

'What is it this time? What part am I now required to play? I hope it is a leading role?'

'We shall have that advantage when the hand is played. You see, I just happened to meet Lady Anne riding in the park yesterday, with her groom in attendance I might add!'

'Never tell me something just *happened* to you, Count Fabricati! I thought every occurrence in your life was very precisely arranged.'

He grinned delightedly. 'You are quite right as usual. Very well, I received a missive from the young lady. The maid brought it to me on the pretext of having to return a book to the lending library. Lady Anne asked me to meet her to discuss a matter of extreme urgency. How could I refuse such an entreaty?'

'How indeed?' murmured Lady Trevingham in amusement.

'Precisely,' he smiled, meeting her mischievous eyes. 'Unfortunately, her cousin saw us as we were parting and he does not seem to be quite so understanding of my benevolent nature but no matter! The problem lies not with him but with Mrs Kirby. It seems that Lady Anne could not bring herself to part with that lady's company after all.'

'You mean she *will* be accompanying Lady Anne to Chailey?' groaned Lady Trevingham, closing her eyes and shuddering at the dire news.

'Not if we can deter her,' suggested the Count calmly.

Her ladyship's eyes flew suddenly open again and she eyed him cautiously. 'What sort of deterrent did you have in mind?' she enquired, almost afraid to hear what his answer would be.

'Mumps,' said the Count simply and sat back to watch the effect of this announcement on her expressive face.

She stared at him dumbstruck, a look of utter disbelief in her eyes.

'Did I hear that correctly?' she croaked faintly. 'Mumps? You did say mumps, did you not?'

'It is the perfect solution – or should I say infection? Let me explain,' he said, taking pity on her bewilderment. 'You must remember – who could forget? – that Mrs Kirby has a horror of infectious diseases. She mentioned mumps in particular as I recollect. Well, you will call on her today and inform her that you were devastated to receive in this morning's post, a letter from your sister, Lady Mary, who is already resident at Chailey. You will then go on to say that Lady Mary's grand-daughter is showing all the signs of having contracted the mumps from her elder brother and that you are therefore obliged to advise that Lady Anne ought not to put herself at risk of taking the infection from her. At this point in the tale, you must be sure to add that fortunately all your other guests have already had the disease, so that matters are not so awkward as they might otherwise have been.'

'I see,' murmured Lady Trevingham with growing

understanding. 'She must refuse the invitation, of course. But what of Lady Anne? Surely she will not be permitted to go either?'

'That is a risk we shall have to take. But I am willing to wager that Lady Wyvern will bear in mind that her niece had the infection some years ago and that in all probability this is a ploy of yours to prevent the marquis from meeting Lady Anne again. Either way we shall win something, even if it is only the consolation that our little deception will remain undiscovered.'

'Yes, there is a great deal of sense in what you say. Well,' she sighed, 'at least we will have done our best to try to bring Romeo and Juliet together.'

'Then you will do it?'

'Yes, I shall order the carriage immediately.' She arose and went to the bell-rope. 'I just hope we can still make this a happy Christmas for them both.'

She need not have worried, all went exactly as the Count had predicted. Lady Wyvern was not best pleased by the news but she only half-believed it anyway. Mrs Kirby, however, was completely convinced and adamantly refused to be persuaded that she ought to go with Lady Anne. Indeed, the very idea seemed to appal her.

Lady Trevingham helped matters along by saying how sorry she was that they would not now be able to make the visit but that she thought it was perhaps the wisest course.

It was then that Lady Wyvern made her decision. Lady Anne should be allowed to go providing her maid and her groom went with her. Under no circumstances was her niece to be permitted to go out unless accompanied by one or the other.

Lady Trevingham, with a slight hesitation, managed to give a forced smile. 'Well, if you really are quite sure, Lady Wyvern. But I should be mortified if Lady Anne should take any ill while in my care.'

'There is not the least likelihood of Anne succumbing to the infection. She is a strong, healthy girl. Besides, it is highly improbable that a young woman with such a robust constitution should take harm from an illness that did her little hurt when she was hardly more than a child.'

Lady Trevingham, with all the air of a woman defeated,

reluctantly agreed to this piece of wisdom and expressed her happiness at the prospect of having Lady Anne join them at Chailey despite this unfortunate event. They would call in Grosvenor Square tomorrow as previously arranged to take her up with them. Both ladies were left to congratulate themselves on their clever strategy that had won the day.

Lady Anne was in raptures when she knew that everything had been accomplished and that she did not have the terrifying task of facing up to Mrs Kirby. The relief added to her bliss; she had never been so happy in all her life! Now there followed the excitement of the journey, free from the gloomy presence of her dour duenna. She and Sophy chattered like magpies all the way to Sevenoaks, planning and anticipating a hundred different pleasures. Her cup of joy was full and overflowed in gratitude to the Count who had made all this come to pass. His praises were sung at every turn of the conversation until Constance began to wonder just where such adulation might lead. She remembered Mr Morton's odd behaviour at the ball. Was it possible that he had reason to be jealous of Lady Anne's affection for the Count? It might be wise to try to keep the Count out of this young lady's way during the next few days, at least until this ridiculous hero-worship had time to run its course.

They were welcomed to the house by their aunt, Lady Mary Dawlish and her daughter Jane who was clutching the hands of a small boy, some ten years of age and a lively little girl of only six summers. Both were apparently in the rudest of health, judging from their rosy-cheeked smiles and boisterous welcome as they ran to greet the new arrivals.

Lady Mary informed them that the gentlemen were all arrived some time ago and had taken out their guns to try for a few birds in the home wood.

The ladies went up to their rooms to change their travelling clothes and to rest before dinner.

When they came downstairs again later, they found Lord Dawlish with his son Robert and his son-in-law Sir Matthew Wainsford, together with Justin, Lord Dillcott and the Count.

Justin hurried to greet his guest and led her forward to meet his uncle and cousins. The Count watched her face as she curtsied to each of the gentlemen and was satisfied to see her beautiful countenance flushed with happiness. He continued to watch her throughout the evening, amused by her almost child-like pleasure in being free of the constraint imposed upon her by her stern guardians.

Constance could not help noticing the number of times his eyes strayed in the young lady's direction and she pondered over the possible reasons for it. Could it be that he was falling in love with her? She recalled her previous doubts about his motives. What had driven him to expend so much effort on her behalf? Was he merely the good friend he purported to be or was he attracted to her himself? Or worse still, her fortune? No, it was unworthy of her even to think it. He was just being kind, as he had been to Miss Chessle when he had asked her to dance. And what about the concern he had shown for a stranger in trouble that very same night? He had risked his life to help that man. That incident had changed her opinion of him and she was not now so eager to condemn his actions. The truth was that she had begun to like him despite all his undeniable faults and she was reluctant to stand his accuser. She found herself wanting to believe good of him.

Her confidence was somewhat undermined the very next day. She had gone to the stables to take her mare for some much-needed exercise. There was no one about, the stable-lads being occupied, no doubt, with their daily tasks and she slipped into Starbright's stall to give her the apple she had brought as a treat.

As she stood stroking the soft, velvety nose that gently nuzzled her hand, she heard voices outside and glanced enquiringly over the wall, expecting to see the grooms. Instead, just beyond the door to the courtyard, she saw the Count astride a magnificent, black stallion. Constance had not seen him dressed for riding before and cast an appreciative eye over horse and rider. She noted with approval that he had an excellent seat and indeed appeared to great advantage on horseback, so much so that she hoped Sophy would not see him. Poor Dilly was not known for his prowess on the hunting field and would be quite cast in the shade.

The little French valet named Jean was standing beside his master and she heard the Count ask him if he had seen Lady Anne.

'She and the other ladies are driving into the village this morning, sir. I saw them in the hall just now. She looks very happy, *la petite, non?*'

'Yes, I think so too. It was well worth the thousand guineas I had to pay Fearnley to get her away from her family. Now I have every reason to hope that my plans will be successfully concluded. She will make a beautiful bride, will she not?'

'Yes, sir. You are to be congratulated. I have never yet known you not to get your own way, once you've set your mind to it,' grinned Jean, standing back as the Count made to ride off.

Constance drew in her breath sharply. What did he mean? What plans had he in mind for Lady Anne? All the unanswered questions that had so troubled her before, returned to unsettle her tranquillity.

Was he playing some diabolical game with them after all? If only she knew more about him, she might be reassured. As it was, the little she did know could only add to her fears. Why had he paid Fearnley such a large sum of money? 'To get her away from her family', had been his exact words. She suddenly saw Lady Anne's situation in a new light. Hitherto she had been so pleased for Justin that he had the pleasure of the girl's company, free from stifling restrictions, that she had not stopped to consider anything else. But now this seemingly happy circumstance began to take on a sinister meaning. Lady Anne was in a vulnerable position, she had been kept under close supervision all her life. How would she behave having at last escaped her family's vigilance? Might she not be at the mercy of someone who wished her harm? Someone who had placed himself in a position of trust? Someone she had come to idolize?

Constance shivered at the awful implications behind these questions. Should she voice her fears to Justin – or Mama? No, that would be useless. They both thought the Count could do no wrong. Perhaps if she told them about the conversation she had just heard, they would listen to her?

She hastened back to the house. The younger ladies had already driven out in the carriage and Justin and Lord Dillcott had accompanied them on horseback. Lady Trevingham was still in the breakfast-room and Constance went to her at once.

'Oh, there you are, Connie! Everyone has been looking for you. Did you not wish to go into the village with the others?'

'No, Mama. As you see I am about to take Starbright out. But before I go I must speak with you urgently on a very delicate matter.'

'Whatever can you mean?' exclaimed Lady Trevingham, rather taken aback.

'It is about Count Fabricati, Mama,' began Constance hesitantly. She pulled out the chair beside her mother and sat down, nervously playing with her gloves as she tried to decide how best to begin.

'I just heard him, quite by chance, you know, speaking to his manservant. That odd little Frenchman that he has at his beck and call. Well, they were discussing Lady Anne a few moments ago and they did not see me: I was in the stable with Starbright,' she explained hurriedly. 'And I distinctly heard the Count say that he had paid a thousand guineas to steal Lady Anne away from her family. And he said that she was worth it because his plans were now successful and she would make a beautiful bride. Don't you think that sounds very disturbing, Mama? What is he plotting, do you think?'

Lady Trevingham gazed at her daughter in amazement. 'Why, Connie! Whatever are you imagining in that over-enquiring mind of yours? Surely you don't still suspect the Count of having designs upon Lady Anne?'

'Well? And why not? She is an heiress, Mama, and he is a notorious gamester.'

'And so are half the gentlemen in London, I should think. But it doesn't naturally follow that they are all scoundrels. As for the money, the Count is noted for his ... reckless enthusiasms. It is a regrettable fault in him admittedly but it need not concern you, Constance. Now go and enjoy your ride and forget these foolish notions. Lady Anne is in no danger from the Count, I assure you. Good heavens! Is that the time?' she cried, glancing at the clock on the mantelshelf. 'Mary will have been waiting for me this half-hour and more. I must go, my dear. Your aunt and I are expected at the vicarage this morning. The parson and his wife wish to discuss the proposed Christmas supper.'

She quickly arose and went to the door. Then she stopped abruptly, her hand on the door-knob and glanced back at her daughter. 'Constance, you won't say anything of this to Justin, will you? I don't want you to cast any shadows on his happiness. May I have your promise that you will not do so?'

'Very well, Mama, if you insist but I still do not feel easy about this.'

She ought to have known better than to expect her mother to take anything seriously. She was as susceptible as Sophy to a charming man. They were both so gullible. It would not enter their heads that anyone, least of all a man with the Count's genius for deception, could possibly be other than he seemed. What a great pity it was that Uncle George had not been able to come home for Christmas, he was just the person she could have confided in. He would have known exactly what to do. Well, if she must, she would take matters into her own hands. From now on she would keep a strict eye on Lady Anne to ensure that no ill befell her while she was in their care. Lady Wyvern should never be allowed to accuse them of putting her niece in harm's way.

Still reflecting on the possible significance of the conversation on which she had chanced to eavesdrop, she went back to the stables and had Starbright saddled. She had long ago dispensed with the custom of riding out accompanied by a groom and set off alone in the direction of the Long Ride which lay beyond the lake, close by the home wood.

Once there, she gave Starbright her head and the sturdy little mare kicked up her heels joyfully and sped like the wind over the turf, delighting in her freedom.

At the end of the gallop she felt her spirits lifting. They

trotted up the hill overlooking the Weald and Constance reined in the mare so that she might enjoy the magnificent view. This was one of her favourite beauty spots and she determined to bring Colonel Dyson here when he came to visit. She knew he would share her fondness for this place. They had often discussed the things that gave them pleasure and had found a common interest in many of them. It was this that had placed him securely in her affections. She began to wonder if he were missing her presence in London. Would he be thinking of her as she was of him and looking forward to seeing her again?

Her eyes roved over the rolling fields dotted with flocks of sheep and edged with neat hedgerows, to the sweep of the distant downs. A fresh wind was blowing from the north, whipping the colour into her cheeks and tugging at the long veil of her hat. The heavy skirts of her sapphire-blue riding-habit flapped and billowed about her booted ankles and Starbright started nervously.

'Whoa there, girl. Be easy now, there's nothing to be afraid of, it's only the wind,' she murmured soothingly, leaning forward to stroke the glossy neck. As she did so, the strengthening wind caught her veil and it streamed out over the horse's head with a sharp crack. The erratic appearance of a strange object obstructing her vision, caused the mare to take sudden fright and she plunged violently. Constance, leaning precariously in the saddle in an effort to retrieve her veil, was taken completely unawares and found herself tipped incontinently on to the grass. She lay for a moment feeling stunned and winded by the fall and closed her eyes against the pain in her head.

The next thing she knew someone was bending over her and gentle hands lifted her up. She raised her eyelids slowly and gazed up into the Count's dark eyes as he held her cradled in his arms.

'Constance! Are you all right?' he asked quickly and she was struck by the note of deep concern in his voice more than the unexpected use of her name.

'Yes, I think so,' she answered with a weak smile, more to reassure him than to express amusement at her embarrassing predicament. 'I just knocked my head a bit, I think. But it's my dignity that is really suffering!'

' "Pride also goeth after a fall",' he said in sepulchral tones. 'At least you have taken no real hurt. And pride is more frequently bruised than broken.'

'You are probably right. I am fortunate that nothing appears to be damaged, in fact, I think I can stand up now.'

'Don't you think you ought to lie still for a while longer?' he suggested tenderly. 'I am perfectly willing to wait for you to recover from the shock. I am quite prepared to make a morning of it,' he added contentedly, settling her more comfortably in his embrace.

Constance stared up at him in great perplexity. She could make no sense at all of the feelings engendered by this man. One moment he seemed a sinister stranger who aroused her deepest suspicions and the next ... well, it was not suspicion that occupied her thoughts when he looked at her in just that way. It was a distinctly pleasant sensation to be held close in his arms like this and she even felt an odd reluctance to end the moment. But this mood of sweet tranquillity which was stealing over her was abruptly dispelled by the unmistakable sounds of horses approaching. The ignominy of being found in this compromising position brought the colour flooding to her face and she hastily struggled to sit upright before anyone should see her.

The Count gave a low laugh as he helped her to her feet, straightening her hat and offering to assist in pinning up her hair.

'No, thank you. I can manage,' she refused him sharply, blushing even more profusely as he capably tucked her flying tresses under her hat.

He continued to calmly ignore her protests and she glanced fearfully over his shoulder dreading that she should be discovered in this state of wild disorder.

'*Che c'è, cara mia?*,' he said caressingly.

'Please don't. Somebody is coming,' she replied, disconcerted by his lover-like tone.

He put out a hand and gently stroked her flushed cheek with one finger.

' "*Bello è il rossore*",' he murmured softly.

She seized his wrist, her eyes, despite her anxiety, twinkling irrepressibly.

' "*Ma è incomodo qualche volta*",' she replied trying to sound vexed. 'Now will you please behave yourself and stop this idiotish nonsense? Where is my horse? Oh, there she is!'

Constance hurried over to where Starbright stood quietly cropping the grass. 'Help me up, please, Count,' she pleaded, 'and do be quick!'

'Are you going to disappear from sight, Titania? Then you had better take your wand.' He stooped and retrieved her whip from the long grass. '*Arrivederci, dolce mia.*'

He threw her up into the saddle and stepped back to let her pass. Without a backward glance she rode down the hill just as her uncle and cousin were nearing the summit.

'Good morning, Constance,' called out Lord Dawlish cheerily. 'Are you going home again?'

'Yes, Uncle, I am going that way now,' she replied calmly.

'Then we shall accompany you. It is a fine morning for a ride, is it not?'

'Delightful. But a little too boisterous up here for my comfort.'

'I wouldn't be surprised if this were blowing up for some snow,' remarked her cousin Robert as they turned their horses to follow her down the hill. 'It is very cold.'

'Oh, do you think so?' she answered nonchalantly. 'I thought it a little too warm myself,' she added, pressing a hand to her hot face.

'I daresay that is because you have been galloping in your usual madcap fashion,' smiled her cousin. 'I am familiar with your neck-or-nothing style, you were always a fearless rider, even when you were a young 'un.'

'I can take care of myself, Robert, you need not worry I shall break my neck. Come, I'll race you down the Ride!'

A little later, when she had gone to her room to change her riding-dress, she went to the window and stared meditatively out towards the green slopes of the hillside. There was no sign of the Count and she wondered what he was doing now. She pulled off her hat, and her hair, unpinned by the fall, tumbled in a tangled mass about her shoulders. He had done a good job of concealing it from her cousin's inquisitive eyes, thank goodness. She smiled as she threw the hat carelessly on to a chair. He really was a dreadful creature! How dared he say those things to her in that intimate way! His behaviour was quite scandalous. She ought to have shown her outrage at his effrontery. But there had been such gentleness in his voice and his eyes, though wickedly bold, held a warmth ineffably tender.

She remembered with a sense of delight the moment when he had called out her name. He had been concerned in a way which was more than just chivalrous. Surely she had not mistaken that note of sweet solicitude in his voice? A delicious shiver went down her spine as she recalled the ardour in his words. Her hand crept involuntarily to her cheek and she laid her palm against the place where his fingers had touched her skin. She stayed thus for a long moment savouring the memory. Then suddenly, that earlier incident shattered the dream that was lulling her into a besotted stupor. How could a sensible, level-headed, intelligent woman of seven and twenty behave in this ridiculous way? She scolded herself mentally for the turn her thoughts had taken. It was absolute stupidity to believe for one moment that this dark deceiver could possibly be trusted in anything he said or did. What a fool she would make of herself if ever she should begin to place any credence on his displays of affection! She was ashamed to have responded to his devilish charm. How could she so quickly forget all his imperfections? What demoniac power did he possess that could weaken her resolve with just a look or a smile? It frightened her to think how easily he had overcome her determination to resist him at all costs. How was it possible? She did not like him and did not trust him either.

No, that wasn't quite true any more. She had begun to like him, he had the ability to appear pleasing to women and she had not after all, been the exception. But Colonel Dyson was far more agreeable. Didn't she always feel comfortable in his company? He could be relied upon to behave correctly. He never had the impudence to call her by her given name or presumed to use endearments that were acceptable only in an acknowledged lover. He was very properly behaved, dependable, a solid, upright citizen, respectable in every way. While the Count was everything she despised: a gambler, a wastrel, a schemer

The Gamester

and, as she now suspected, a philanderer of the worst kind. Yet when he had held her in his arms, she had completely forgotten Colonel Dyson. With this knowledge came again that strange sensation of fear mingled with excitement that had gripped her when he had danced with her at the masquerade. It seemed that he roused some wild, primitive feeling in her that she had not known existed until he had stirred it into life. She must not give in to it. If she did, she knew that it would sweep away all reason and therein lay the cause of her fear. She must keep a command over her emotions, her peace of mind depended on it.

Later that evening, having engaged to play cards with the Count, she soon discovered the cause of his obsession with gaming. He was really an excellent player. Having lost three rubbers in succession, Constance threw down her cards in exasperation.

'You would have the spade! I ought to have suspected it. You might at least have looked triumphant, I am sure I would have done.'

'I know you would,' he grinned, collecting up the array of court cards in front of him. 'A look at your face is almost as helpful as the sight of your hand. You will never make a skilled player if you give so much away.'

'I suppose you refer to my discards,' she sighed, shaking her head. 'They were ill-judged, were they not?'

'Let us say they were rather daring,' he amended kindly. 'And remember that I do have the advantage of having made a lifetime's study of the art. You are a mere novice in comparison.'

'Why did you decide to make such a study of something that is to most of us, a pleasant pastime?'

'It is a long story, Miss Trevingham, and like most lengthy explanations, would soon grow tedious in the telling.'

'Have you finished your game?' enquired Sophy, looking over her sister's shoulder.

'The game has finished with me,' smiled Constance, pushing back her chair.

'Well, come and join us. We are going to amuse ourselves by making up some acrostics.'

'No, thank you, Sophy, I must go and write some letters, you will have to excuse me,' she replied. 'But I am sure the Count will oblige you. He enjoys playing games of all kinds.'

'I do have an aptitude for them, that is half my pleasure,' he agreed, ignoring the obvious innuendo in her remark.

'Only half the pleasure?' prompted Constance with a lift of her delicate brows.

'Of course. The other half is in the winning.'

'Don't you mean winnings, Count?' she asked pointedly.

'To me it is almost the same thing, Miss Trevingham. I never play unless there is something to be gained.'

'That is what troubles me about you, Count Fabricati,' she answered, turning purposely away from the demons cavorting in the fire of his eyes.

Twelve

Early in the New Year, the snow which had been threatening for the last few days began to fall in earnest. Thick swarms of huge flakes filled the air, swirling in never ceasing flurries that blotted out the landscape. The green lawns disappeared under a white coverlet that shrouded the soft, undulating contours of the parkland. Wood and forest became fantastically transformed overnight, wrapped in deep, muffled silence, motionless and magically mysterious. It was as if the whole countryside had become a vast, marbled mausoleum, deathly still, icy cold and austerely beautiful.

The children pleaded to be allowed out to play and as soon as they were snuggled into warm coats, hats and mufflers, they scampered away like dogs let off the leash. Their elders followed at a more leisurely pace as they all headed for the frozen lake, the gleeful cries of the youngsters pealing out over the snow-bound park.

The gentlemen inspected the ice before pronouncing it safe for skating. Sophy seized the Count's arm excitedly. 'Will you help me put on my skates and then I'll race you across to the bridge?'

'I'll help you, Miss Sophia,' volunteered Dilly eagerly. 'If you will permit me,' he added diffidently.

The Count glanced at him thoughtfully. 'Yes, let Lord Dillcott go with you. I'm afraid I am a very poor skater and will only hinder you.'

'Oh, of course, I suppose you don't have the opportunity to practise your skating in Rome as we do here in England,' replied Sophy understandingly. 'Very well. Dilly shall come with me, he is an excellent skater.'

Lord Dillcott suddenly looked as if he had been awarded

the victor's crown.

'You never play when the odds are against you, do you Count?' murmured Constance, much amused.

'How well you are getting to know me, Miss Trevingham,' he acknowledged, impressed. 'Perhaps you might take pity on my inexpertise, I daresay you are a proficient in this particular sport?'

'My father taught us all to skate on this very lake when we were quite small,' she replied, a fond expression in her eyes.

'You were very close to your father, were you not? I suppose you must miss him still?'

'He was my dearest friend as well as a loving father,' she said quietly.

'Then you were most fortunate, Miss Trevingham.'

Constance looked at him in some surprise, she had never heard him speak so strangely before. His voice sounded cold and distant, his words bitter. He noticed the look of astonishment she gave him and turned away to watch the children with their parents and grandfather out on the ice.

'Love and happiness seem to go hand in hand in this house. I am grateful to have been called to the window. Come, walk with me as far as the woods,' he continued abruptly, 'you can show me the wonders of your fairy kingdom.'

'Gladly, if that is what you would prefer. But let us take our skates.'

They wandered around the edge of the lake and crossed the snow-clad bridge. Sophy and Dilly called up to them from the stretch of ice below.

'Where are you going?'

'To fairyland,' called back Constance laughingly, leaning over the low parapet to wave to them.

Out in the middle of the lake she could see Justin, his arm around Lady Anne's waist as he held her steady. She had never seen her brother look so happy before and she watched them closely for a moment as they gazed into each other's eyes, oblivious of everyone but themselves.

'And what does that smile mean, I wonder?' mused the Count, leaning beside her and studying her sweet expression.

'I was just thinking,' she answered dreamily.

The Gamester

He followed her gaze and saw the two lovers, arms entwined. 'It would not be difficult to divine your thoughts. The course of true love appears to be gliding smoothly. I just hope they are not skating on thin ice.'

'Spare me your platitudes,' grimaced Constance moving on again.

'I beg your pardon, it was irresistible,' he grinned, falling into step beside her.

'Really? I thought you a man of more resolution. But why should you think that their happiness is in any danger?'

'The path of happiness is fraught with dangers but that should not prevent us from pursuing it.'

'They will be safe enough providing they are left in peace by those who would destroy their joy.'

'I hope you don't mean to number me among them?'

'Why should I? You don't wish them any harm, do you?' she enquired with her usual directness.

'Of course not. Have I not done my utmost to bring them to this blissful state?'

'You appear to have done so,' she acceded carefully.

He sighed heavily. 'Was ever a man so misunderstood?'

'Oh, I don't think so, Count. Did you not say a moment since, that I begin to know you very well?'

'As I recall, Miss Trevingham, I said you were getting to know me which is quite a different matter. You still have much to learn.'

'But how can I learn, when you seldom speak about yourself? Other than your interest in gaming, that is, surely there must be more to your life than that? What else is Count Fabricati?'

'I don't think he would interest you greatly,' he replied lightly.

'Oh but he does, I assure you,' she contradicted swiftly.

'Not really. As I said once before, you are merely curious. It has been a part of woman's temperament since Eve first saw the apple and once satisfied may well prove a man's downfall.'

'Now why should you think that?' asked Constance speculatively. 'What harm can come of telling me a little about yourself? It is only natural to wish to know more about a person who comes into one's social sphere, don't you agree?'

He appeared to meditate upon this as they walked towards the woods, for he did not immediately vouchsafe an answer.

Constance did not question him again, she needed all her breath to walk along. The snow was very deep here and so soft that each footstep sank down at least six inches and she had difficulty in lifting her feet. The skirts of her pelisse and the hem of her dress were weighted with snow and slowing her progress. At last she stopped, having grown weary with the effort.

'It's no good,' she panted, 'I can continue no further until I catch my breath.'

He glanced down at her as if surprised. 'I'm so sorry. I should have realized that this is hardly ideal walking weather. I'm afraid I was wool-gathering and did not notice how far we had come. Here, let me help you. There's a fallen tree yonder. Let's sit down while you recover your strength.'

Without further ado he caught her around the waist and swung her easily over the snow, setting her down beside the broken trunk of an ancient elm.

'Wait while I brush away the snow. There, that's better, we can sit down now and admire your domain in comfort.'

'It is like a scene from a fairy-tale, isn't it?' she said, accepting the proffered seat and gazing all around in wonder.

'Like a crystal castle filled with enchantment,' he concurred, smiling at her awed expression.

'Or an Aladdin's cave hung with jewels,' she laughed, twisting her head to admire the tinselled branches above them.

For some while they sat in companionable silence contemplating the majestic beauty of the great fir trees now cloaked in heavy, ermine mantles and the stark elegance of beech and oak dramatically etched in sable and silver. Beside them towered the statuesque grace of the thickly-powdered larch and lower down, the holly and hazel bushes trimmed with crystalline coverings that moulded them into inspiring sculptures marvellous to behold.

'It's so beautiful,' whispered Constance softly, her eyes delighting in such exquisite splendour.

'Sheer perfection,' he murmured feelingly and she turned to look at him, pleased that he was appreciative of all this grandeur.

But he wasn't admiring the scenery now, he was staring at her face and her glance fell to her lap as she detected a certain light in his eyes.

'I never knew roses to bloom so early in the year,' he continued in that same low tone. 'They are quite the loveliest I have ever seen. Have you ever held a rose in your hand, Miss Trevingham, and viewing those perfect, satin-soft petals, felt a desire to press your lips against them and drink in their fragrance? How I wish that I might....' He stopped, leaving the thought unspoken. 'But what is the use in wishing?' he added, turning away.

'Have you forgotten that we are in fairy-land?' she replied, lifting her gaze to the sky, dazzlingly blue above them. 'Here, wishes are granted every day.'

'Only to those who are good and deserving of them, alas,' he sighed melancholically.

'Why do you say that? Is something troubling you?' she prompted gently.

He was silent for a few moments and she realized that he was again preoccupied with his thoughts.

'What is it you keep thinking about? You seem sad.'

'I was remembering an old story. This place is suited to the telling of tales, is it not?'

'What sort of story was it? An unhappy one?' she asked, intrigued by his solemn face.

'It is an allegory, one that will perhaps feed that hungry curiosity of yours. Shall I tell it to you? I wonder?'

'Please do. I should like to listen.'

He studied her face intently, the blue-grey eyes clear and shining, the rosy cheeks and the soft curve of her sensitive mouth. How naively innocent she was!

'Very well,' he agreed, as if making a sudden, rash decision. 'But I doubt that you will understand it. You, my lovely rose, have been cultivated in a walled garden, safe from the chill winds of adversity. And this is a tale of youthful follies, wild and wilful. It concerns a young man whose name was ... well, I shall call him Gérard. He, from infancy's nourishing milk was weaned to feed upon foods gathered from Elysian fields and grew strong and healthy on such a wholesome diet. But his appetite seemed never satisfied, always he wanted something more. Then, poised on the threshold of manhood, he saw life spread before him like a sumptuous feast. A place was set for him at its table, where he found himself seated between two fatherly-seeming companions. When the courses began to be served, the gentleman on his right bid him eat frugally of each dish until he should find something that particularly suited his taste. The gentleman on his left, however, urged him to eat his fill of all that was offered for his delectation, he could have whatever he wished. The platters were piled high with meat of every kind, embellished with sauces, richly spiced and temptingly arrayed with all the art of man's devising. Beholding this mouth-watering abundance, young Gérard dined like a king, partaking generously of everything that was brought before him. Nothing was sent away untried, not even the sweetest dainties, though they soon began to cloy. The gentleman whose prudent advice he had ignored, quietly withdrew. But the other, who had led him unresisting into temptation, encouraged him to even greater excesses until at last, utterly sated, he sickened of it all.

'There remained but one dish untasted. A beautiful bowl of succulent fruit, fresh plucked from the vine, with the dew still glistening upon it. Tender, ripe and sweet, it was as tantalisingly desirable to the eye as Eve's famed apple. No human artistry could better its exquisite perfection. Alas, he knew that his jaded palate would never be able to do it justice and left it lying there. Yet, ever afterwards he would dream of it, oft imagining how delicious it might have tasted.'

'But could he not have taken it with him?' Constance suggested helpfully.

'I fear it would soon have lost its freshness and withered away. It were better left to be enjoyed by a wiser, worthier man. There, the tale is told and now we must go back before you take cold.'

He stood up and handed her down the path they had

trodden on entering the glade. As they made their way along, Constance mulled over all that he had said and after a little while asked him if he would explain exactly what the story had been about.

'I told you that you would not understand,' he smiled. 'How could you? You are a person who has always known contentment; you accept life just as it has been dealt to you.'

'Well, of course I am contented. I have been fortunate enough to have been born into a loving family with everything provided for my comfort and amusement. How should I be otherwise? I lead a very happy life.'

'What you say is true. You are fortunate indeed but not just because you have these things. Your joy lies in being able to know the value of them. There are those who would sneer at such love, seeing it as maudlin weakness and despise your dependency upon it. You really do care about your family, I see that in the way you try to protect them from ... harmful influences,' he smiled. 'And you have compassion. That also is part of your peace, yet compassion is often condemned as mere mawkish sentiment. You have discovered for yourself the true worth of life's gifts and your soul is enriched by these treasures. But for those who aspire to feed their souls upon other of life's abundant and varied pleasures, they can never rest contented because they have chosen the course of endless pursuit.'

'Is that the course you have chosen, Count?' Constance questioned, after some quiet reflection.

'I have done so,' he replied crisply, his gaze fixed ahead.

'But if you do not believe that a lasting joy can be gained in that way, then why must you persist in it?'

'Because having mistaken the way in the beginning, it is too late to start again and besides it is impossible to go back. One cannot change that which is past.'

'I realize that but surely one can begin today to make the necessary alterations for tomorrow and so hope in time, to mend matters and look to a happier future?'

'Alas, my dear Miss Trevingham, some matters are beyond our mending,' he answered as if he had accepted the inevitable.

'You have read a great many books, Count and I have often heard you quote from them, when it amuses you to do so. Let me then do likewise with this ancient wisdom: "Trust the past to God's mercy, the present to His love and the future to His providence".'

He looked down at her and the frown disappeared from his brow. 'What a treasure I have found! Would that I might keep it. Now come, let us go and find the rest of our party. They will be wondering what has become of us.'

The others, however, had gone from the lake and no one was in sight.

'Shall we skate across instead of going over the bridge?' she suggested. 'I'll help you if you like.'

'Why not? I am willing to try if you are. Here, lean on me while I fasten your skates.'

A few minutes later they were on the ice and Constance offered him her hand to steady himself.

'It might be easier if you were to permit me to put my arm about your shoulders. I should feel a lot safer,' he ventured to say.

'Whatever you think best,' she agreed readily.

He hugged her to him as they set off and she guessed that he must be very nervous to hold her so close against him.

A group of small boys came from the cottages nearby to play on the lake. They indulged their high-spirits by throwing snowballs at one another, laughing and shrieking as they ran. The sound of their voices rang on the ice like hammers on an anvil as they chased across the lake, the echoes rebounding from the iron-hard slopes of the hill.

In their joy and enthusiasm, they accidentally bumped into Constance and she and the Count were tumbled into an ungainly heap. Constance, who was well acquainted with each of them, retaliated by throwing a handful of snow at the giggling lads and they gleefully returned her fire.

'Oh! So it's to be a battle, is it?' cried the Count gaily and scrambling unsteadily to his feet, he helped his partner up. 'You prepare the cannon-balls and I shall direct the line of fire,' he instructed, scraping up a mound of snow. 'Stand behind me. We'll give them a broadside.'

The fighting commenced with some heavy exchanges from both sides but owing to the random firing, it was more of a skirmish than a battle-royal. The young gunners did not have quite the range of fire as their larger opponent but what they lacked in strength they more than made up for in number.

At last, exhausted by their efforts, they called a truce and swooped noisily away like a flock of starlings at eventide.

'We were well matched, I think,' declared the Count with satisfaction as he watched the retreat. Then he turned at the sound of Constance's laughter.

'If you could see yourself!' she gurgled. 'You look like a snowman. Come here and I'll help you clean your coat.'

He glanced down at himself and grinned broadly. 'Oh, I've been powdered with shot, that's all but I'll live.'

She skated up to him and began to brush him down vigorously.

'Bend your head a little, you're smothered in snow,' she giggled, ruffling it out of his dark hair as he meekly obeyed. 'There, that's better. Much more respectable. Though I doubt that your valet would approve of my efforts.'

'It would take more than all your efforts to make me respectable, but I wish you might try,' he answered softly.

She paused, the laughter still in her eyes. His words were unmistakably sincere. As she stared at him in puzzled surprise, she had a sudden, almost overwhelming desire to put her arms around him and hold him close. The feelings that had so shaken her serenity at the masquerade, returned to mock the good sense on which she had placed so much confidence. She must not allow herself to fall in love with him! It would be disastrous! He wasn't at all the sort of man she had dreamed of marrying. The very thought that she could possibly consider even for one moment such a foolish thing, was utterly ridiculous. The wisdom that had always stood her in good stead, vied with her rebellious heart. She turned away from him, ostensibly to pick up his fallen hat but it gave her enough time to regain control of herself. He seemed to have sensed her deliberate withdrawal and resumed his usual insouciant manner.

'Come, my little powder-monkey, we had best limp back

to shore for our repairs.'

His light-hearted words did much to restore her equilibrium and she was able to answer him in the same jocular fashion.

'Well, haul away then, messmate,' she laughed.

'Aye, aye, Cap'n,' he grinned, leaning on her shoulders again.

They had scarcely gone more than a few yards when they were brought to a sudden stop by a frightened scream. Startled, Constance turned quickly to discover what was amiss and saw that one of the boys had fallen through the ice on the far side of the lake.

'Oh, hurry! We must help him! Follow me as best you can while I skate across! It will be easier and faster than walking over the snow!' cried Constance, already speeding off toward the reed beds where the accident had occurred. She did not stop to look back to see if the Count could manage alone and so was completely astonished when he skimmed past her with all the fluid grace and perfect balance of an accomplished skater. Swiftly he snaked in and out of the reeds clustered along the edges of the lake and was soon pulling the lad free. He took off his coat and wrapped it around the shivering youngster.

As Constance skated up beside them, he was asking the other children to show him where the boy lived.

'It's Jack, the head-gardener's boy, is he all right?' she asked anxiously, peering at the pathetic bundle in his arms.

'Perfectly but we must get him into the warmth. Where is his house?' he questioned briskly.

'Over there, I'll take you.' She began immediately to untie her skates, then held out her arms for the boy while the Count unfastened his.

Fortunately, the cottage was not far and the frightened lad was soon safely taken into the warm kitchen where the Count handed him over to his capable mother.

'Thank you, sir and Miss Trevingham,' she said gratefully as she set him down in front of the fire. 'Thank God you were both on hand! Here's your coat, sir. Would you care to wait while I dry it for you?'

'No, thank you, ma'am, please don't bother with it. I

shall do very well. We'll be on our way and leave you to take care of your son.'

'Well, if you're quite sure,' she answered doubtfully.

'Of course. There's no need to trouble yourself on my behalf. We'll see ourselves out. Come, Miss Trevingham. The boy is in no danger and will be as right as ninepence in no time.'

'That's right, miss. He's only cold and had a bit of a fright but our Jack's a sturdy lad and will have taken no harm, thanks to the gentleman. Goodbye, sir and God bless you for your kindness.'

They bade her farewell and left her to undress the woebegone Jack.

As they walked out to the pathway, swept clear of snow by the diligent cottager, Constance peeped slyly up at her companion.

'Well, Count Fabricati, you are full of surprises today. What do you mean by gulling us all into thinking you could not skate?' she demanded indignantly.

His eyes twinkled down at her. 'Yes, that was unforgivable of me, wasn't it? But I couldn't miss such an opportunity. You were bound to have left me to my own devices else.'

'You are quite correct. I would have. But I do not think that was your only reason. I think you purposely misled us so that Dilly could outshine you in Sophy's eyes. Am I right?'

'Not at all. My motives were entirely selfish.'

'Why must you persist in making me think so ill of you? Don't you wish to be thought – compassionate?'

'On the contrary. I would always wish you to think well of me,' he replied. 'But better you think ill of me than never think of me at all.'

'I think too much of you already,' she murmured quietly as she went ahead of him through the wicket gate.

It was this last, poignant remark that caused him suddenly to search his conscience. Since she had first thrown down the gauntlet and ranged herself in opposition to him, he had been unable to resist the challenge of winning her over. Now that he had almost achieved his object, he was beginning to realize that he had made an ill-judged move. She wasn't at all the hard-nosed blue-stocking he had taken her for when first they met. He had discovered instead a clever, attractive, sensitive and courageous woman who was as vulnerable to heart-ache as any innocent girl. A lady with her qualities could never be just an idle dalliance as he had very soon learnt for himself. She had real depth of character unlike the frivolous, empty-headed Cyprians he was accustomed to flirt with and now this game he had commenced so capriciously must have bitter consequences.

There was only one thing to be done, he had to throw in this hand even though he held all the winning cards and no matter how great the cost. He still had other hands to play which would require complete concentration and he needed to keep a clear mind if he was to extricate himself from this tangle.

As soon as the weather permitted, he would return to London. Redman should have a message for him by now if the snow had not delayed it.

The continuing freeze proved fortuitous for Lady Anne. She received a letter from her aunt informing her that she must delay her journey into Hampshire. They were all fallen victims to an epidemic influenza which had brought the family very low, most especially Mrs Kirby who had been quite prostrated by the contagion and was confined to her bed. Lady Wyvern advised Anne to remain with the Trevinghams until such time as the danger of further infection was past. She went on to say that as the heavy snowfall had rendered travelling by coach extremely hazardous, she did not look to see her niece for several days to come.

The young lady had been viewing her imminent departure with a growing despondency and this letter sent her into transports! She could scarce believe her good fortune. Perhaps she might even dare to hope to be able to attend the Trevinghams' ball, the date now being set for the end of the month.

Full of eager happiness, she ran to find Justin and showed him the letter. His reception of the news produced an exultation equal to her own and he picked her up and swung her round the room. Then setting her down again, he embraced her warmly. She laughed up at him exclaiming, 'Justin! You are squeezing the breath out of me!'

'I'm sorry, my darling but when a man is as happy as I feel at this moment, he just cannot be expected to behave with decorum.'

'It is wonderful news, isn't it? Not that I wish them to be unwell, of course,' she added guiltily. 'But oh, Justin! I might now be able to dance with you at the ball! And it may be that I shall be able to stay with you until February!'

Lord Trevingham, still with his arms about her and gazing down at her lovely face alight with joy, could contain his feelings no longer. She saw the blaze of passion darken the blue of his eyes and her arms crept up to encircle his neck. For a brief second she returned his ardent look, then suddenly he bent his head and she felt the warmth of his lips against hers as he kissed her, gently and tentatively at first and then with a gathering urgency.

Someone entered the room through the door behind them and they sprang guiltily apart.

'Oh, it's you, James!' gasped Trevingham with a sigh of relief. 'Thank heavens!'

'Oh? Are you in need of rescuing? I had thought for a moment that my appearance might have been inopportune,' replied the Count, looking from one to the other with a quizzical expression.

Lady Anne, crimson-faced, made some unintelligible excuse and fled from the room, head down-bent as she rushed past the Count.

He calmly turned and closed the door after her before speaking again. 'Do I take it that I am to wish you happy?' he enquired casually.

'No, not yet ... that is ... I haven't spoken of marriage,' stammered Trevingham, feeling a little awkward at having allowed his feelings to get the better of him.

'Well, don't you think you ought to have done so?' suggested his friend gently.

'Yes, of course ... I didn't mean to ... I couldn't help ... oh, damn it, James, you must know how it is when you are with a beautiful girl and she looks at you so....' He stopped, noting the raised eyebrows. 'I know, I know, I should have shown a little more restraint but....'

'She is a guest in your house. You must exert a lot more restraint if you wish to avoid a scandal. A lady's reputation is like fine china, of very little value once it is damaged.'

'Don't you think I realize that?' he groaned, desperately running his fingers through his fair hair. 'I have to speak to her uncle. I should have had the courage to do so before and as soon as they are well enough I am resolved to call on him and ask permission to pay my addresses.'

'Are they indisposed?' asked the Count interestedly.

'Apparently they are all stricken with the influenza. Lady Anne had a letter from her aunt this morning and she is to remain with us until all danger of infection is past. It must be of a particularly virulent sort. Mrs Kirby is utterly prostrated. I believe that was the word used to describe her condition.'

'As bad as that is she?' he remarked with rather a wicked smile. 'But I daresay it is a great comfort to her to know that she has taken the infection to an extreme. Anything less was bound to have been a grave disappointment to her. Now, to the purpose of my intrusion. Your uncle has sent me to find you, to remind you that the gentlemen are awaiting you in the courtyard. You promised them a day's shooting, or had you forgotten?'

'The deuce! It had slipped my mind for a moment. Be so good as to tell them I shall join them in a few minutes, will you please, James?'

While the gentlemen occupied themselves with some sport, the young ladies of Chailey spent an enjoyable morning sleigh-riding in the park. Constance particularly relished the opportunity to divert her thoughts away from a certain person who was beginning to appear too regularly in her day-dreams. Since that day at the lake, he had not singled her out for any private conversation, indeed, if anything, he was deliberately avoiding her company. She ought to have felt relief at this fortunate circumstance; the less she saw of him the better for her peace of mind. Common sense could now exercise its calming influence on her judgement. But alas, no sooner had logic reminded her of the Count's utter ineligibility, than sentiment began to argue against reason. That treacherous, inner eye kept his face ever before her, accurately sketching every perfect feature, each speaking look and that teasing, irresistible smile. Constance kept her eyes carefully averted from the far end of the dining-table where he was placed at dinner that night, determined to show him that she was indifferent to him. But when he did not come to the drawing-room with the other gentlemen, she felt vexed and disappointed.

They were discussing their day's sport as they entered the room and she heard her uncle remarking to Justin that he had never seen a finer shot than his friend the Count.

'Never wasted a single shot, you know, Trevingham. Quite exceptional! Is he a military man?'

'No, Uncle, just a keen sportsman. I wish you might see him with the epée. Nerves of steel. You must have noticed yourself that when he takes aim, the barrel never wavers an instant. Steady as a rock. Oh, excuse me ...' he said, suddenly breaking off as Lady Anne approached.

'Did you enjoy the shooting?' she asked a little shyly, her thoughts still dwelling on their last meeting.

'Very much. We were just saying what an excellent eye the Count has.'

'Sophy tells me that you are no novice either,' smiled Lady Anne with a look of adoration.

'Well, I am known at Manton's as something of an expert,' he laughed. 'But alas, I am not near so good as James, or your cousin Giles for that matter.'

She sniffed contemptuously. 'Yes, he is often boasting of his prowess. To hear him speak you would think he is a Nonpareil.'

'He is, or rather he was until James came to London and snatched his laurels.'

'I did hear about his defeat at Angelo's. How I wish I could have seen that! Freddy teased him unmercifully about it, Giles was simply furious! He hates to be beaten at anything!'

'And where is the inestimable Count?' enquired Constance, coming up to them. 'Ought he not to be here to receive these accolades?'

'He is gone to the library, otherwise I should not have dared to sing his praises quite so loudly.'

'Why is that? Do you think his ego inflated enough?'

'Not at all. He is careless of such things. I don't think he gives a fig what people say of him, good or bad. I was merely meaning that he would give me one of his quizzing looks if he could hear me.'

'Where is the Count?' interjected Sophy, setting down her teacup. 'Is he not joining us this evening?'

Justin laughed. 'Not you too! Can't a man have any peace? He has only gone to look at father's collection of old books. We were discussing the subject over dinner and James expressed an interest in viewing them. Now, if that's all you wish to know, I am going to help Mama set up the card table,' and with that he walked away.

'I didn't know that the Count was interested in stuffy old books,' pouted Sophy in disgust. 'How can he bear to spend such a tedious evening?'

'Ah, Sophy,' sighed her sister, shaking her head, 'don't you realize that within those dusty pages repose treasures more precious than any found in the silken recesses of your jewel case?'

'What do you mean? What treasures?' asked Sophy with a frown of puzzlement.

'Thoughts, Sophy. They form in the human mind like pearls growing in an oyster. Most are worthless, without lustre, brittle and flawed. But some develop in unfathomable deeps and when the shell opens – those with eyes to discern the difference see a gem, lustrous, unblemished and with a timeless beauty that is wondrous to behold.'

'Well, I have just had a thought, though I doubt you would consider it a gem, Connie,' she grinned. 'Let's ask Aunt Mary to play for us and we'll practise our waltzing. Come, Anne. Justin shall be your partner and Dilly, mine. Doubtless Connie will wish to go treasure-hunting.'

'Yes, I think I shall. It seems that I am casting my pearls before swine,' she smiled, going to the door.

She found the Count sitting all alone in front of a blazing hearth. He had seemed engrossed in his book but stood up as she entered the library.

'I hope I am not disturbing you?' she apologized. 'I thought I might lose myself in a book for a while. The others are going to dance so it will not be a very peaceful evening.'

He did not speak for a moment or two, just looked at her comptemplatively and she wondered if he were considering immediate flight. Why was he being so elusive lately? Had she unwittingly offended him perhaps?

'Do you object to my joining you? I would not wish to intrude if you prefer to be in private.'

'Not at all, Miss Trevingham. This is your home and you have every right to be here whenever you wish,' he replied. 'It is I who am the intruder.'

'But I have no desire to force my company on you if you would rather be by yourself,' she continued awkwardly and beginning to feel a trifle foolish. Suppose he thought she was trying to put herself forward?

He must have noticed her discomfiture because his face relaxed into a smile and he invited her to be seated beside him on the sofa.

'Well, if you are quite sure,' she murmured hesitantly.

'Perfectly sure, Miss Trevingham. Please, do be seated.'

'Very well, I will if I may. I'll just fetch my book.'

She went to the bookcase and took up the volume she had been reading yesterday. He waited for her to be seated and then resumed his perusal of his own chosen book.

They sat thus, side by side without speaking for about half an hour. Try as she might she could not immerse herself in the book she had selected. Her attention was constantly wandering and she was distracted by their very silence. The fire crackling in the grate, the clock stolidly ticking on the mantelshelf, the wind rattling the shutters and even the sputtering of the candles on the table beside her, all combined to distract her thoughts. But most of all, she was aware of the man sitting next to her, so close that she could reach out and touch him if she dared.

She stole a surreptitious peep at his face; his head resting on his hand as he leaned his elbow on the arm of the sofa and the dark curve of his thick lashes as he looked fixedly down at the book in his right hand.

How she wished he would look at her with half as much interest! Then, before she could avert her eyes, he suddenly slid his gaze away from the page and gave her a long, sideways glance from beneath lowered eyelids. The colour rushed to her cheeks as she tore her eyes quickly away, feeling mortified at being caught staring at him so.

'I ... I was just wondering what it is that you are reading with such avid attention,' she stammered hastily, pretending to examine the page he had been studying. 'Oh, it's the Michelangelo sonnets, is it not? The language is so beautiful it lends itself to poetry, don't you agree? I love to hear them read aloud, it's such a very musical tongue.' She stopped suddenly, realizing how ridiculously she was babbling on. But his smile was not mocking as she had feared it would be, instead he was watching her with a tender light in his eyes.

Then, without looking down at the open page, he gazed into her eyes and spoke the lines of the poem written there. The warm, fluid tone of his voice enraptured her and the sound of the Italian words was like water flowing over pebbles in a brook. It made her feel deliciously languid, as if he were making love to her.

When he had finished, she sat silent and still, not wanting to break from this sweet reverie, her eyes unable and unwilling to part from his.

'Will you translate it for me?' she asked softly. 'You are far more skilful than I and I should like to hear your rendering of its meaning.'

'Very well. It reads something like this:

'I have no need to gaze on outward forms
Of loveliness which fade, your inspiration
Has made me seek inside, a peace that warms
Me with a love so purified, you purge away tempta-
    tion.
Even if this woman God designed
Should show imperfect to the eye, I would not mind,
For though some her beauty may deny
To me she far outshines all other of her kind.
He who is obsessed by worldly lust
Will never cease to yearn, his passions burn
As if forever, yet all must fall to dust.
These sensuous desires are not even
Born of love, they are the soul's destruction,
But tenderness is blessed on earth, still more in
    heav'n'.'

There was such feeling in his voice as he uttered the words, it seemed to her that he meant her to believe they came straight from his heart.

She waited with baited breath hoping to hear him say something more, this time in his own words, that would tell her what he really felt.

He closed the book and set it aside, saying as he did so, 'Language in its artform is the perfect medium for the revelation of our deepest thoughts. It is the distillation of the human spirit poured from the pen. A sweet anointing, is it not?'

'Certainly. We each have a need of self-expression and poetry is one way in which we can meet with another soul at a point beyond and above our physical senses. It is a fine thing to be able to share our thoughts and feelings. To understand that we are not alone but an integral part of eternity through this same golden thread of life which links us together.'

' "No man is an island, entire of itself". Is that what you mean?'

'Yes, exactly. You know the truth of that, don't you?'

He looked at her intently before answering. 'Once, like Pilate, I would have replied with scorn, "What is truth?" But I have now discovered for myself the simple fact that truth is that which is. Unquestionable, unanswerable, unalterable and eternal. A very rock indeed. An old friend of mine tried to explain it to me years ago. Father Benedict is his name, the wisest man I know; only it took me a long time to learn the lessons he tried so patiently to teach me.'

Then with an abrupt laugh, he got to his feet and going to the fireplace, kicked the smouldering logs into flame.

'Why do you laugh?' questioned Constance wonderingly, realizing that the mood was broken.

'If you had known me before I came to London you would not need to ask,' he replied, folding his arms and leaning his shoulders carelessly back against the high, marble mantel.

'But I didn't know you then,' she murmured quietly.

'Alas no, more's the pity. Well, let me tell you that there are those among my acquaintances who would be amazed to learn that I have spent almost an hour alone with a lovely woman and progressed no further than broaching spiritual matters and discussing poetry. What is it about you, Miss Trevingham, that makes me question my motives at every turn?'

'I wasn't aware that I was having that particular effect, Count Fabricati,' she said, rather disconcerted.

'No? In that case you will also be in ignorance of the fact that you are entirely responsible for resurrecting my conscience from its peaceful resting place. I have as yet to consider whether this is a matter for rejoicing or a most regrettable misfortune.'

'Conscience is the means by which a man may be lifted high in the estimation of his friends but more importantly gives rise to his own self-respect. Cause enough for gladness, wouldn't you agree?' she suggested thoughtfully.

'Regarded in that light, I must concur,' he smiled. 'And yet it may also be a burden that weighs one down as heavily as responsibility.'

'Yes indeed. But it is in learning to carry it daily with dignity and perseverance that strengthens the character,' concluded Constance decidedly. 'And conscience, if heeded, must always stand a faithful guide in the wilderness of this world.'

'Is it even to be followed at the expense of happiness, Miss Trevingham?'

'Such obedience, I believe, could never be at odds with happiness. Doing what we feel in our hearts to be just and right, brings its own contentment.'

'Provided we have the wisdom to discern the difference between conscience and self-righteous bigotry,' he intervened carefully.

'Yes; there lies the danger that could lead one astray,' she admitted. 'Yet it can be avoided if conscience walks hand in hand with humility.'

'And if we remember to place another's good above our own. Alas, my memory has hardly been troubled with that particular piece of wisdom but I may begin to remedy the lapse. Now, if you will excuse me, I have to make arrangements for my journey tomorrow.'

'Your journey? I don't understand. Where are you going?' cried Constance in surprise.

'I am returning to London. Didn't your brother mention it?'

'No ... no ... he did not,' she faltered dazedly. 'I had no idea you meant to return quite so soon. Must you go?'

'Yes, Miss Trevingham, I rather think I must,' he replied in a quiet but decisive tone.

'But you are coming back, are you not?'

'I am not entirely certain of my plans, although I shall try to attend your Mama's ball, if I can.'

'I see,' murmured Constance, swallowing her disappointment. Pride came to her rescue and she forced a smile to her lips. 'Well, I wish you a safe journey, Count Fabricati,' she said brightly. 'And as I may not have the opportunity tomorrow, I shall also say goodbye.'

She held out her hand and he pressed it to his lips. Then with a brief bow he said, almost in a whisper, '*Au revoir, ma chère mademoiselle*,' and without another word, left her alone.

Constance waited until the door clicked shut behind him and the sound of his footsteps had died away. Now she picked up the book he had placed on the arm of the chair and opened it at the page he had been reading. Silently she studied the sonnet again and when she had done, she slowly closed the book, muttering beneath her breath, 'Fool! Fool!'. Then her chin sank to her breast and she gave way to hot tears of anger and a strange, inexplicable grief.

Thirteen

Mr Giles Morton drove up to his lodgings in Jermyn Street, unaware that his arrival was noted with keen interest by a gentleman lounging against a gas lamp a few yards from his door. 'Mr Johnson' had been watching for him ever since his own return to the capital several days earlier.

From the moment Dupois discovered that Mr Morton had 'expectations', he had determined to make himself conversant with that gentleman's affairs.

Discreet enquiries made immediately upon his arrival in London, had revealed that the Rossmore estates were extensive and that the young heir and heiress would one day inherit a sizeable fortune.

Dupois congratulated himself. It had not taken him long to guess the reason for that quarrel between Morton and Gérard. Gérard had a nose for a plump pigeon and this bird had particularly pretty feathers it seemed! No doubt he had her already in his sights. Perhaps this Morton fellow would be extremely grateful to learn all there was to know about Count Fabricati! But was the young man of a generous disposition? That would, of course, have to be ascertained.

Dupois knew that he would gain great satisfaction from spoiling Gérard's plans but even more would he triumph if he could turn the situation to his own advantage. He decided to keep a very close eye on Giles Morton until he was a little more sure of his man. The letter Arnaud had entrusted to him could wait a day or two; he hadn't yet decided what he was going to do about that highly dangerous piece of information. This time he had opened the document. He knew that he could reseal it, he had done it before quite successfully. From the moment Arnaud had given it to him with such strict instructions to deliver it only into Gérard's own hand, he had realized that this was something very special. Arnaud had insisted that he must keep it safely hidden every moment of the day or night. He had warned him that he must be extremely vigilant while it remained in his possession. Also, he remembered Gérard's emphatic words, 'Next time I must have positive proof'. He had noted them most particularly.

Well, this package certainly contained that! He had found the letter, written in Arnaud's distinctive script, urging Gérard to act immediately. The Emperor was returning to France! If all went according to their carefully laid plans, he would be back on French soil by the end of February. Folded inside Arnaud's letter was another, this time signed by the Emperor himself! Dupois recognized the signature immediately. His hands shaking with anticipation and excitement, he read the Emperor's words:

My dear Friend and Brother, King of Naples.
 When you receive this letter I shall be on my way home to my beloved France. My soldiers have not forgotten their Emperor and my trusted friends bring me news that my people are eager for my return. This Bourbon could never hope to deserve their love and loyalty, that still belongs to me alone. I shall be honoured to have you join us, to be there at my side when I enter the Tuileries! March with us! Remember Marengo, Ulm, Austerlitz, Jena, Friedland and Wagram! Come, Joachim, mon brave chevalier, let us rejoice together again in victory! With you and your cavalry to aid me, all Europe shall kneel before us. Austria shall bow to you and you shall place your heel upon her proud neck! Come, let us be brothers-in arms once more. The whole world will wonder at our daring and courage as we march victoriously shoulder to shoulder! Nothing shall stand in our way, our armies shall triumph over all our enemies! Your fearless heart will not hesitate, I know. I shall see your glittering standards arise with the glory of a spring sunrise.

Italy and France shall be mighty conquerors! Sound your trumpets! I shall be listening for their rallying call!'

The letter ended with one word *Napoleon*.
This letter was possibly the most valuable piece of paper he had ever held in his hand! What to do with it? That question would take a great deal of pondering. He must consider his options very carefully. This might be just what he had been waiting for – a chance to destroy Gérard, to see his arrogant pride humbled and wreak revenge for all his slights and insults. But he would have to think of a way of achieving all this without harming himself as well. And most importantly, he must seize this moment to make himself a rich man.

Thus it was that Dupois set himself to learn something of Mr Morton's character before he made his next move.

Giles had been staying with friends in Derbyshire and on his way back to the metropolis had called upon the Wyverns in the hope of seeing Lady Anne. He was astounded to be told that not only had she spent Christmas with Lord Trevingham and Count Fabricati but she had already been several weeks in their company without the protection of her duenna! The additional news that Fearnley was also included in their party, astonished him beyond belief. It was well known that the marquis always went to his hunting-lodge at Christmas and it was impossible to imagine that he had chosen to attend a family gathering at Chailey instead. As to Lady Wyvern's explanation that his love for Anne had wrought this change in him, that too would take some swallowing! Fearnley had been at great pains to keep his head out of the matrimonial noose and apart from dancing once or twice with Lady Anne at her birthday ball, had never shown the slightest interest in her. He suspected a conspiracy. Had he not seen his cousin speaking to that profligate Fabricati in the park, the day before he himself had left for Derbyshire?

His lips compressed tightly and a muscle worked at the corner of his mouth as he considered these events. When his manservant timidly greeted him and held out the salver on which lay a sealed letter, the poor fellow shrank back instinctively against the wall. The look on his master's face boded ill for anyone crossing his path today. However, once the closely written sheet had been read, the young gentleman's face broke into a broad smile and he even clapped his hand on the valet's shoulder, this time a friendly blow.

'Is it good news, sir?' he enquired nervously.

'The best possible news, man! My day is about to dawn! That old reprobate Rossmore is on his death-bed! Quickly! Have my curricle sent round. I'm off to see my lawyers!'

When Dupois saw this equipage approaching the door, he summoned a nearby hackney and ordered the jarvey to follow close behind it.

The Frenchman, watching for his man, saw how excited he appeared to be as he stepped hurriedly into the curricle and whipped up his horses in eager haste to be on his way. Something interesting must have happened to make him suddenly smile and leave the house again so soon after entering.

The curricle was driven at a spanking pace towards the Strand and eventually drew up outside a building which bore a brass nameplate beside the door. Once Morton had entered this elegant portal, Dupois took the opportunity to acquaint himself with the information inscribed upon the plaque. It seemed that Mr Morton was calling upon a firm of solicitors.

He emerged again some good few minutes later and looking a little more subdued. The scowl was back again on his face.

His next destination was Cribb's Parlour where Dupois eventually espied him drinking with one of his intimates.

It was during this convivial meeting that Dupois, seated in a booth behind them, was privy to a most interesting conversation which convinced him that his luck was undeniably taking a turn for the better.

The first thing that made him prick up his ears was the mention of that call Morton had just made in the Strand. Dupois detected a note of uncontrollable excitement in the man's voice as he began to boast of the many changes he would make now that the old earl was about to breathe his last.

So that plum is soon to fall into his lap, is it? thought the Frenchman, a calculating gleam in his eye. In that case the new earl will be in a position to be extremely free with his largesse.

'That idle fellow Jessup wasn't in his office when I called, neither was his partner,' Morton complained bitterly. 'I was fobbed off by that sallow-faced clerk of his. Says his master had urgent business in some provincial backwater. What is the point of having a London lawyer if the damned fool spends all his time dashing off to rural parts without so much as a by your leave? Just when I need his services, he disappears. Well, let me tell you, Jerry, they'll get none of my business once I'm the Earl of Rossmore. I shall give my preference to others more reliable. When I think of the money he makes out of my family! And what is there to show for it? He can't even manage to grant me an interview. Doesn't he realize what an important client I am going to be?'

His tirade was suddenly interrupted by a group of slightly elevated young bucks who stopped at their table to exchange greetings and to invite the two gentlemen to accompany them to Brooks's.

"Course it won't be the shame without Fearnley to hold the bank,' slurred a gangling young sprig in a tight green coat that sported an enormous nosegay in the top buttonhole. 'He's shtill in Leishter ... (hic) ... Leishtershire.'

'But I thought Fearnley was staying with Trevingham in Kent?' ejaculated Morton, his attention suddenly arrested.

'No, 's defin'tely not in Kent, is he Dris?' hiccupped the skinny gentleman, turning to his companion for corroboration of his statement and consequently staggering to one side like a man in a strong gale.

'You're quite right, Tommy. Fearnley's gone to his box as always, saw him off myself. Brascombe too. They left before Christmas and don't intend to return until next month. Can't think why you should imagine him to have gone with Trevingham, Morton. You must know he hates family occasions.'

'Yes, of course. I must have been misinformed,' muttered Mr Morton, his expression beginning to grow thunderous. 'You'll excuse us if we don't join you, Driscoll, we've another engagement this evening.'

'Very well. Goodbye to you then,' he replied cheerily and they all lurched off into the street.

'Did you hear that, Jerry?' hissed Morton in a voice of pent-up fury. 'I've been duped by that scheming blackguard Trevingham and his toad-eating accomplice Count Fabricati!' He almost spat the name as he realized how cleverly they had misled Lady Wyvern and lured Lady Anne into their net. Or was she a party to the deceit?

'I say, Giles, old fellow. What on earth is the matter? You look as queer as Dick's hatband.'

'There's a great deal the matter,' snarled Morton grimly. 'I have to go into Kent immediately. Will you come with me, Jerry? I may need your services. The honour of my family is at stake. Will you lend me your support?'

'Why, yes, naturally I will,' responded Mr Symes, feeling utterly bewildered by this peculiar change in his friend's demeanour.

'Good. Then meet me tomorrow morning at nine o'clock sharp. Just pack a portmanteau. I do not intend to be long about settling this business,' he declared through clenched teeth.

'Nine o'clock? In the morning?' echoed Mr Symes faintly and blanched visibly.

'Yes, I shall be outside your lodgings on the hour. Don't keep me waiting. I shall be in a great hurry. Now I must go. I have several important matters that must be dealt with before morning. Good night, Jerry and don't fail me!' he warned, striding to the door.

Mr Symes took a fortifying swig of Blue Ruin and tottered after him. The last time he had been up before nine in the morning, he had been going to bed!

Nevertheless, being the obliging fellow he was, Mr Symes was ready at the appointed hour, albeit feeling rather fragile. His eyelids grazed his eyeballs every time he tried to lift them, his head felt so heavy that his neck seemed inadequate for its continued support and his stomach, which he had recently appeased with a slice or two of sirloin immediately followed by a pint of very strong ale, was apparently still undecided as to whether or not it wished to retain them.

The speed at which Mr Morton turned out of Cork Street and hurtled towards Bond Street, almost settled the issue then and there. Mr Symes, whose interesting pallor was becoming an even more curious shade of green, was on the verge of casting up his accounts. His dignity was spared when the press of traffic down towards Piccadilly persuaded his companion to pull in his leaders.

To Mr Morton, eager to be on his way, this enforced delay seemed nothing short of an act of deliberate provocation. He became loudly vociferous on the subject of intellectual meanness as displayed by the travelling public and even managed to win the hearty approval of a couple of shopkeeper's apprentices who happened to form part of an audience gathering on the pavement. They gave enthusiastic encouragement as he roundly berated an unfortunate farmer driving a cart loaded with cabbages, which had become wedged up against the wheels of Mr Morton's smart equipage. Poor Mr Symes, who had never in his whole life been subjected to such a display of ill-manners, began wishing himself back in his bed, snug and at peace with the world.

This was what came of arising at an ungodly hour. No wonder then, that a gentleman kept his bed until noon! Never would he allow himself to be persuaded into such folly again. How Morton could stoop to bandying words with these uncouth plebeians was beyond his comprehension.

'Giles, please be quiet! The road is clear now, let's be on our way,' he pleaded urgently. 'We are becoming a spectacle for every tradesman in London!'

'Yes, yes! I have managed to free the wheel,' he muttered irritably. 'But if that damned idiot has scraped the paint ...! Hey there! Out of my way, you numbskull!'

A young lad in a long canvas apron had come to the farmer's assistance and was helping him back the cart to the side of the road. He glanced up with a broad grin. 'Where's the 'urry, yer 'igh an' mightiness? Late for yer coronation are yer?' he yelled after the irate gentleman and a guffaw of raucous laughter echoed in their wake.

Hardly had the carriage disappeared from sight, when a

post-chaise pulled up beside the cart. A man's head was thrust out of the window and the occupant called out to the apprentices, 'Which way did that yellow-bodied phaeton take?'

Having ascertained its direction, the gentleman drew in his head and the chaise continued down the street. The young man in the apron gazed wonderingly after it. The last time he had seen that face it had earned him a shilling or two. It might be worth his while to mention its reappearance again. In fact he would call in Brook Street this very morning.

His information was received by Jean with great interest and he was requested to repeat it once more in the presence of the Frenchman's master.

The Count questioned him very precisely. Was he absolutely sure it was the same man who had called at Mr Redman's establishment?

'Yes, sir, there's no mistaking 'is ugly mug. It was 'im right an' tight. I took pertic'lar obserwation,' he answered, nodding his head vigorously.

'And the gentleman he was following? What was he like?'

'Oh, a reg'lar fire-eater! Temper as 'ot as the coals in a forge furnace! Dark 'air, small, dark peepers, bit close togevver – an' a beak yer could 'ave tripped over! 'Is pal wot was wiv 'im called 'im Giles, 'e did. Yes, that's it. Giles was 'is 'andle.'

'Well done, Jos. You've a keen pair of eyes it seems. I am most grateful to you.' The Count held out his hand and Jos put his own rather grubby paw in it and they shook hands heartily.

'Thank you, sir,' he said happily, accepting the coin pressed into his palm, his eyes lighting up at the sight of gold. 'I 'ope I see 'im again – often!' he grinned.

When Jean had shown him out, he returned to find the Count in pensive mood but already planning his next move.

'Jean, we must pack a few things as quickly as possible. This matter may have some connection with the news we received from Mr Redman. There's trouble brewing, I can feel it in my bones!'

'*Oui, m'sieur, moi aussi!*' replied Jean gloomily. 'But where are we going?'

'Back to Chailey, I think. *Allons-y! Dépêchez-vous!*'

Within the hour they were on the road. The Count, who could drive to an inch, skilfully avoiding the mishaps that had beset Morton's hasty exit from the city.

Fortunately, the snow had almost vanished but the roads remained slippery and slushy as the ground began to thaw. It was now late February and the Count had been unable to return for Lady Trevingham's ball. He had been kicking his heels in London waiting for Dupois and the important news he would be bringing. The discovery today that he had been in town without informing either Jean or himself of his arrival, put a martial light in the Count's dark eyes that would have terrified Dupois if he could have seen it. What game was he playing? One of his own choosing, it seemed. It wasn't the weather that had delayed matters after all. How long had he been in London and what had he been up to since his return? Well, he would find the answers to these and other questions when he caught up with him, even if he had to choke it out of him with his bare hands!

By the greatest good fortune, the Count managed to overtake Morton on the road, thanks to the Dover to London mailcoach and Morton's own carelessness. He sped past the phaeton without being recognized by the irate owner of the vehicle, who was wholly occupied with the exertions required to extract its rear wheels from a deep ditch.

There had been no sign as yet of the chaise in which Dupois was reported to be travelling but no doubt he also had overtaken the phaeton and was waiting somewhere up ahead ready to resume his pursuit.

By the time the Count pulled into the courtyard of The Lamb Inn just a few minutes later, he was fairly certain of the reason for Morton's angry haste. He had been correct in his surmise that Chailey was his objective, the house was but a mile or so further along the road.

As he descended from his carriage, leaving Jean to issue orders to the ostler, he entered the inn hoping to come to grips with Dupois in a very short space of time!

He called out for the landlord, intending to learn from him whether Dupois had stopped here earlier. There were two inns in this village and the Count was certain that Dupois must be at one of them.

At the sound of his voice, one of the inner doors opened and a shapely figure robed in an elegant riding-habit, suddenly emerged into the passage.

'Count Fabricati! I thought I heard your voice! How wonderful that you have come back to us!'

'Lady Anne! I did not look to see you here!' he exclaimed in great surprise.

Then recalling Morton's imminent arrival, he added hastily, 'May I speak with you a moment, my lady? In private? There is something I must say to you.'

'Of course,' she replied at once, noting the urgency of his tone. 'There is a private parlour just here. I have exclusive use of it at the moment while I await Constance. She has gone to the smithy. Starbright cast a shoe as we rode along the lane.'

She passed into the room ahead of him, glancing over her shoulder as she did so and smiling happily. 'I'm so glad to have this opportunity to speak to you alone, there is something I have been longing to tell you. But I had begun to fear that you would never come back.'

'Would that have made you unhappy?' he asked, softly closing the door and drawing closer to her.

She looked up into the dark eyes, wonder in her own. 'Yes,' she answered simply, 'I rather think it would.'

When Constance led Starbright into the inn yard and gave him into the care of Lady Anne's groom, she was startled by the unexpected appearance of Giles Morton who was at that very moment coming from the direction of the stables in the company of a young gentleman of fashion.

Quickly gathering her scattered wits, she hastened into the inn to warn Lady Anne of his arrival but alas, he had seen her sudden flight and leapt rapidly after her.

Lifting up the sweeping train of her riding-dress, she rushed down the passage and threw open the parlour door.

'Anne! We must hurry! Your cousin Giles....' Her voice

trailed away and she stood transfixed in the doorway, staring as if seeing a ghost.

Mr Morton almost blundered into her, so abruptly had she halted. The occupants of the landlord's best parlour sprang apart but not before the newcomers had seen their tender embrace.

The Count, seeing Miss Trevingham's stricken expression, swore softly beneath his breath. Matters were about to go from bad to worse!

'I guessed as much!' cried Morton hotly, his already exacerbated temper now reaching fever pitch as he pushed roughly past Constance who still stood as if turned to stone. 'You damned scoundrel! I'll have your blood for this!' he blustered, almost beside himself with jealous rage.

He strode jerkily across the room, his face as red as a turkey-cock and made to strike out at the Count's impassive features. The blow fell on empty space as Fabricati took a pace backwards and then Morton felt his wrist taken in an iron grasp.

'Where are your manners, Morton? Or must I teach them to you? There are ladies present, had you forgotten? Please at least try to behave like a gentleman.'

Morton gasped like a goldfish as he struggled to overcome his spleen. At last he recovered his speech enough to say in strangled accents, 'I demand satisfaction for this outrage upon my cousin! Name your friends, sir! Symes!' he choked, turning to his bewildered companion. 'You'll second me, will you not?'

'Er ... yes ... yes, of course,' assented the embarrassed gentleman awkwardly. 'Be happy to oblige you in any way that I can, Giles old fellow.'

Lady Anne, who had hitherto been watching the proceedings as one struck dumb, suddenly seized her cousin by the coat-sleeve.

'Giles! Please! Don't be so ridiculous! Are you gone mad? The Count has done nothing improper, I assure you. Only think of the scandal if you two should fight over me! Please listen to reason. I tell you we have done nothing wrong! You are under a misapprehension, the Count and I met merely by chance. Tell him that is so, Constance,' she urged, her face as white as the lace cravat at her throat.

But Miss Trevingham had vanished as suddenly as she had earlier appeared.

'Well, sir?' demanded Morton savagely, shaking himself free of Lady Anne's grip.

The Count sighed resignedly, time was wasting. 'If you will have it so. But remember – you forced the quarrel on me and must suffer the consequences. Now, I have important business to attend to,' he continued with careless indifference to his predicament. 'Lord Dillcott will represent me, I am sure. He will call on your man when we return to Town.'

'No! That will not do! I will have satisfaction and have it now! Symes and I shall put up here for the night and our meeting can take place tomorrow at first light.'

'Pistols at dawn, is it?' laughed the Count taking up his hat from the table. 'Well, I've no objection to such theatricals. I'll ask Dillcott to meet you here this evening to make the arrangements. Come, my lady. Do you have your groom with you? Then I will take you to him. Á bientôt, Morton,' he called gaily as he donned his curly-brimmed beaver. 'I shall leave your friend Mr Symes to arrange for the saw-bones to attend you. Though there will be precious little for him to do, I've no doubt.'

With this Parthian shot, the Count departed leaving Mr Morton to chafe, his choler bubbling over a fire of fierce, yellow flames.

Outside in the courtyard, the Count did his best to stem Lady Anne's tears, wiping her eyes with his handkerchief and assuring her that there was nothing to fear.

'I want you to promise me you will say nothing of this to anyone,' he said solemnly. 'I shall deal with it in my own way. Just trust me, that's all I ask. Have I ever failed you yet?'

She shook her lovely head, looking up at him with great, tragic eyes. 'You will be careful, won't you? I should never be able to forgive myself if anything happened to you because of my foolishness.'

'Nothing is going to happen to me. Stop worrying. There is no need, truly.'

'But what about Constance? You saw her face! Oh! This is all so perfectly dreadful!' she wailed miserably.

'Leave Miss Trevingham to me. I shall be coming up to the house shortly and I will smooth matters over, never fear. Now you must be on your way, it is getting late.'

When she had gone, the Count went in search of his valet. He found him in the stables talking to the ostler.

'Come here, Jean, I must speak to you at once.'

The valet hastened to his side.

'Well, Jean?' he asked quietly.

'*Très bien, m'sieur le Comte*,' grinned Jean looking decidedly pleased with himself. 'It was as you guessed. He appeared a moment after that angry gentleman.'

'You mean Mr Morton, I think,' smiled the Count grimly. 'He was angry, very angry. So angry in fact that I am now challenged to a duel.'

'A duel? *Mon Dieu!*' exclaimed Jean aghast.

'Don't worry, I have no intention of meeting him. I cannot spare the time just now. He will have to live with unsatisfied honour. You see, Jean, there are certain advantages attached to being not quite a gentleman,' smiled Monsieur Gérard. 'But I must prevent him from coming up to the house, so I needs must engage Lord Dillcott's help. Now, on with your story.'

'Ah, *oui!*' replied Jean readily. '*Eh bien*, Monsieur Morton arrives with his friend and they follow Mam'selle Trevingham into the inn. They all go to the parlour and then – *quelle horreur!*'

'Yes, thank you, Jean. Pray confine yourself to your observations of what took place outside that room.'

'*Pardon, m'sieur. Je continue.* I see Dupois hiding over there. He sees M'sieur Morton enter behind mam'selle and he follows. Oh, he is crafty, that one! He hears the big voice of this Morton and he creeps to the door. I think he hears everything. When you and milady appear, he goes *sur le pointe des pieds*, quickly, *comme un souris*.'

'Well done, Jean! Now you must be extremely careful. I want you to watch him everywhere he goes. You will need to disguise yourself. *Un payson*, as you did in Spain, remember? I must go to Chailey, I shall need to speak to Lord Dillcott on a matter of some delicacy!'

Fourteen

Lord Dillcott, having been reluctantly persuaded to call on Mr Symes before the dinner hour, returned to Chailey to inform the Count that the meeting was to take place in the home wood. The Count thanked him for his help and discretion, contented that Giles would now be prepared to leave them all in peace at least for the time being. That part had been easy to accomplish. His attempt to speak with Miss Trevingham had not fared so well. She had refused his request to see her privately and had made it perfectly plain that she had nothing at all to say to him. She told him in no uncertain terms that she wished him at the devil!

Justin, however, was delighted to have his friend's company again and eagerly introduced him to his uncle.

'Uncle George, this is Count Fabricati of whom you have heard me speak. James, this is my uncle, Lord Kemsley.'

'I am honoured to meet you, Lord Kemsley,' bowed the Count. 'Justin has told me a great deal about you and I have been looking forward to making your acquaintance.'

'Count Fabricati, is it? Well, how do you do, sir? I too am happy to meet you at last. Justin has told me something of your exploits in Italy. I am particularly interested in that part of the world and would be glad to hear the opinions of one of its natives. Do you concern yourself at all with politics, Count?'

'I confess I find them somewhat intriguing,' admitted the Count with a tiny smile hovering on his lips. 'As you must be aware, our political climate is rather unsettled at the moment.'

'I presume you mean Naples?' interposed Colonel Dyson who had lately joined the party at Chailey. 'But surely our old adversary Murat, is firmly in control? I understand that he has a formidable force at his disposal and therefore will continue to maintain a foothold in that kingdom.'

'It would certainly seem so,' agreed Lord Kemsley carefully. 'But let us pursue this discussion later. The ladies are awaiting us. Ah, Sophy, my dear!' he cried cheerily as she entered the drawing-room. 'How lovely you look this evening. As sweet and fresh as a rose, is she not, Lord Dillcott? But where is your sister?'

'Constance isn't coming down tonight, Uncle. She is having a tray sent up to her room. I think she might have contracted a chill while out riding today. She came home looking quite flushed and her eyes seem almost feverish. I hope she is not going to be ill.'

'I'm sorry to hear it,' he replied looking concerned, 'It is very unlike Connie to be unwell, she is usually so robust.'

'It has seemed to me,' observed Colonel Dyson, 'that Miss Trevingham has not been at all in spirits just lately. She is lacking her natural vivacity, at least, I thought so.'

'I daresay she is just a trifle pulled by all the gaiety we have had of late,' concluded Sophy. 'I shall look in on her after dinner.'

The Colonel had indeed noticed a change in the lady he had intended to woo. She had become rather withdrawn in her manner, as if her thoughts were fully occupied with some weighty matter. She seldom smiled now and he had made no progress at all in his courtship. It really was most perplexing. He had been so sure of her in London. What had happened to overset all his hopes? Had his journey here been wasted, or could he yet succeed in the object of his visit?

Meanwhile, Mr Morton was also plagued by doubts. He had dined early this evening and was now considering, over a bottle of port, the possible consequences of his impetuosity. Suppose, just suppose, Fabricati were to kill him tomorrow? The Count would then be free to wed the Lady Anne and win for himself her entire fortune. And what of the scandal? A man like Fabricati would not care about that but if it was the Count who should die? Wouldn't he, Morton, be arrested? Fabricati had managed to make himself very popular with some influential people and duelling was frowned upon these days. This might mean that he would suffer the same fate as the fifth Earl and be forever exiled leaving behind all his properties and the chance of a profitable marriage. Whichever way he viewed it, this sordid affair could well ruin his dreams. If only he hadn't lost his temper! This matter could have been dealt with some other way. The Count, with his propensity for gaming, could easily have been offered a sum of money to persuade him to relinquish his hold upon the lady's affections. His interest lay entirely in her fortune that was certain, only she was too besotted with that wretched man to see it! Perhaps it might not be too late to solve the problem with bribery? But it might seem that he was afraid to face the Count in a duel. He couldn't bear it if Fabricati spread that rumour about the town! What was he to do?

Mr Symes, watching his friend as he brooded darkly over his half-empty glass, correctly surmised that Giles was regretting his rash actions. That vile temper of his had finally got him into a very awkward situation. Mr Symes had always known that it would. A man could not continually abuse his fellow creatures in the offensive way that Giles did, without eventually incurring someone's wrath. Now there would be the devil to pay. 'I say, Giles, couldn't you bring yourself to offer an apology? I'm sure that Lord Dillcott and I could arrange a reconciliation if only you will see reason.'

'Don't be such an ass, Jerry! A blow has been struck. There can be no reconciliation between us,' snapped Morton moodily.

'But I am sure Count Fabricati might overlook that. After all, you did not manage to land the blow and....'

'Damn Fabricati!' shouted Morton in exasperation, irritated by this untimely reminder of his foiled attempt to punish that guttersnipe for daring to lay his hands upon the woman he loved. 'Damn him, I say! I shall see him in hell first!' and he banged his fist down so hard that his glass tipped over, spilling the wine across the dark wood of the table. In his morbid imagination it seemed like his own blood, spreading out over the cold earth as he lay wounded and dying.

'Allow me to refill your glass, sir,' came a softly spoken voice at his elbow. He started from his reverie to glance at the figure that had so silently appeared beside him. It was a fellow-traveller, a gentleman who had arrived at the inn earlier in the afternoon.

'Thank you, sir. How very civil of you, to be sure,' responded Mr Symes, embarrassed by his companion's morose silence. 'Won't you join us? One ought never to drink alone and we should be glad of your company. My friend is a little melancholy this evening. I hope you will overlook his odd behaviour, he is not at all himself.'

'I can make my own apologies,' growled Morton churlishly, scowling across at his long-suffering friend.

'No need, sir, no need,' murmured the stranger placidly, setting down the bottle between them. 'I shan't intrude upon you. Help yourself to the wine, I have already sent for some more.'

He made to move away again but Morton called him back. 'You might as well sit down if you are going to leave your bottle.'

'Yes, please do,' insisted Mr Symes, hoping to end the day in a more civilized manner than it had begun.

'Thank you,' bowed the gentleman, pulling out a chair and seating himself at their table.

'Forgive me if I seem inquisitive but did I not hear you mention the name Fabricati just now?' he enquired politely. 'I'm sorry but you did speak out loud; I was not eavesdropping, I hasten to assure you.'

'And what is that to you?' answered Morton curtly.

'Well, it just so happens that I have been looking for a man of that name. By the way, my name is Johnson, Mr William Johnson. May I have the honour of knowing yours, gentlemen?'

Mr Symes obliged him.

'What is your interest in Fabricati?' questioned Morton sharply, fixing Mr Johnson with a somewhat belligerent glare.

'It is no coincidence that I am here,' began Mr Johnson in a confidential tone. 'I have followed this so-called *Count Fabricati* all the way through France and Italy. Now I have traced him here but I lost his trail somewhere along the road this morning.'

'What do you mean to imply?' demanded Morton, suddenly interested in his new acquaintance.

'I happen to have been introduced to him while I was travelling abroad last year, only then he was using the name Monsieur Gérard,' he disclosed mysteriously.

'Gérard? His real name is Gérard?' reiterated Morton in astonishment. 'Are you saying that he is not an Italian Count?'

'He most definitely is not. He is a Frenchman of no importance and a notorious gamester!'

Mr Symes gasped in shocked horror. 'An imposter! But Morton here is engaged to meet him in a duel. This is most irregular!'

'Hold your tongue, Jerry, damn you! Do you want everyone to know my business?' hissed Morton crossly.

'A duel, you say?' murmured Johnson quietly and eyeing Morton warily. 'Well, it's no concern of mine, of course, but I would not care to be in your place. He is known as a deadly marksman. He has been out several times in France and there's not many men would care to face him at twenty-five yards distance,' he warned, sounding extremely worried.

Mr Morton had begun to suspect as much and felt a little sick.

'Have you already made your arrangements?' asked Mr Johnson.

'Yes, this evening,' admitted Mr Symes dismally.

'Then you were best advised to offer an apology, if he can be persuaded to accept it,' he added doubtfully.

'Never! I shall never apologize to that lying, deceitful, conniving trickster! Whatever his name may be!' vowed Morton passionately.

'I see,' muttered the newcomer, rubbing his chin thoughtfully. 'You seem to dislike the man almost as much as I do.'

'Oh? What has he done to you?' questioned Morton, finding himself warming to this sympathetic gentleman. 'Will you tell us why you have been searching for him?'

'Very well. You have confided in me, so I will return the compliment. The man has cheated me of a very large sum of money and I am determined to recover it if I can.'

'How do you propose to do that? He doesn't seem the sort of man who would respond to persuasion,' observed Mr Symes despondently.

'Quite so,' agreed the gentleman with a deep sigh. 'And yet I have discovered in the course of my pursuit of him, certain information: information that, were it made public knowledge, would send him to the gallows.'

A sudden hush fell upon his auditors at these solemn and awesome words.

'The only trouble is,' continued Mr Johnson carefully, 'if I denounce him to the authorities, I shall have my revenge but I shall never see my money again. It has been at a substantial cost to myself that I have followed him thus far and I need to recoup my losses or face a life almost of penury. I had planned to threaten him with the exposure of his villainy unless he returned every penny of my money to me but such is his vicious nature that I fear for my life if he should learn all that I know of his treachery. So you see my dilemma, gentlemen?'

'Yes, yes, it is a dreadful predicament,' concurred Morton, pouring out the wine the while his brain feverishly considered this extraordinary tale.

He pushed the brimming glasses towards his companions. 'Let us drink a toast, gentlemen,' he smiled with an air of satisfaction and lifted his glass.

'What shall we drink to?' enquired Mr Symes, noting his friend's suddenly smug expression and wondering what had brought about this puzzling alteration.

'To Count Fabricati's demise! I have a proposition to put to you, Mr Johnson. I am about to become a very wealthy man. If you will share your information with me, I will share my new prosperity with you. If you can help me get rid of this rogue once and for all, you will not find me ungenerous. We can come to some mutually satisfying agreement this very evening. What do you say to that, sir?'

'I say let's drink to it, sirs!' cried Mr Johnson willingly. 'Here's to Count Fabricati's demise, may the devil take him indeed!'

The clinking of their glasses echoed in the silence of the dining-parlour, empty save for these exultant gentlemen and one ancient yokel tucked out of sight behind a high-backed settle apparently sound asleep.

'Now here's how I propose we set about the business ...' began Mr Johnson leaning closer across the table.

Jean waited until all three gentlemen had left the room before he arose from his place of concealment beside the inglenook. He grinned delightedly to himself, anticipating his master's pleasure when he told him everything that he had seen and heard.

While the gentlemen had been at their early dinner, Jean had awaited his moment and slipped softly upstairs to Mr Johnson's chamber. It had not taken him long to find where Arnaud's letter was hid. Did not Monsieur Gérard comprehend Dupois, oh, so perfectly? And now Jean also knew just what Dupois was scheming. Soon he would be able to acquaint Gérard with all that he had discovered. Then would not Monsieur take sublime revenge!

Within the hour, he had reached Chailey and gained an interview with Count Fabricati while the other gentlemen sat over their port.

'So the Emperor has already made his move!' muttered the Count pensively. He took a few, quick strides about the room, his hand to his brow.

'We may yet turn even this act of perfidy to some advantage,' he said, at last ceasing his perambulations. 'You have done excellent well, Jean.'

A knock sounded at the door and Jean opened it to reveal the under-footman bringing a note for the Count. He dismissed the man and handed the note to his master.

'Well, let's see what that Judas has to say,' he said, smiling grimly at the expected missive. He read it quickly and gave a mirthless laugh.

'He explains that he was delayed by the treacherous weather! Ha! does he think us still spoon fed? There's treachery involved here sure enough but it has more to do with man's foul nature.'

'What will you do, *m'sieur*?' asked Jean anxiously.

'I shall let him set his puny trap and then spring one of my own devising! I shall go now to Dillcott and inform him that Morton has tendered me an apology which I have decided to accept. Here's what you must do, Jean. But we must make our moves quickly.'

It was just after midnight that the Count finally slipped out of the house. Everyone was abed save for himself and Lord Kemsley who was known to keep late hours.

Constance, too miserable to sleep, sat in the window embrasure in her room looking out over the moonlit garden, her chin propped dolefully in her hand. Below her she could see candlelight spilling out on to the stone paving of the terrace. Her uncle must still be in the library.

She lifted her gaze again to the brilliance of the full moon, its huge, silver disc mottled with strange shadows. How beautiful it was and how lonely it looked tonight, suspended high above her in that great, glittering void. The tears formed almost unbidden in her eyes as she thought again of that tender little scene at the inn. He had kissed Lady Anne! How could she have allowed him to do such a thing? Had she forgotten Justin so easily? Could it be that her adulation for the Count had turned to love? Was Giles Morton right to be so suspicious after all? Had his jealousy been justified? Had Lady Anne really succumbed to the 'Corsair's' charm? But why should that be so difficult to believe? Had not the sophisticated Miss Trevingham, so wise and discerning as she imagined herself to be, surrendered to the might of a smile that delighted, the strength of an intellect that fascinated, the power of eyes that burned into her very soul and left her thrilled and breathless?

She dashed a hand across her own sparkling orbs. How she hated these tears! Lachrymose women were only objects of pity! She despised this weakness. And a man such as he was not worth her tender emotions. To think how eagerly she had watched for his return and longed for his presence. That they should meet again like this! Something very like a sob broke from her trembling lips and she swallowed hard. No! She would not cry! She lifted her head proudly erect and stared defiantly at her reflection in the window glass.

As she did so, her eye was caught and held by a dark shape moving down the line of laurels that edged the lawns. She peered into the gloom, screwing up her eyes in an attempt to discern whose figure it might be flitting among the shadows of the hedge. Surely there was no mistaking that tall, broad-shouldered silhouette? It must be Count Fabricati! What was he doing out in the garden so late? Constance drew in her breath sharply. Perhaps he was going to meet Giles Morton? The duel! But it must be too dark for that? Unless they had chosen rapiers? There was moonlight enough for swordplay and she knew the Count was a gifted fencer. Someone ought to prevent them. Oh, the scandal if it should become known what part the Trevinghams had played in this ridiculous game! Why had they allowed themselves to become entangled in the Count's reprehensible scheming? Suppose one of these fools were killed? What then? And even if the result were not fatal, someone might come upon them. There would be an arrest and the whole silly escapade would be revealed. It might damage Justin's political career for ever. She decided then and there to try if she could bring them to their senses without waking the household or bringing her uncle into this tangle. Perhaps if she appeared on the scene they would have the grace to settle their differences in a more civilized manner. Snatching up her cloak, she slipped down the back stairs and let herself out of the side door. Without pausing for further reflection, she hastened down the shallow, stone steps and on to the lawn. The ground was cold and hard beneath her thin shoes and the grass was very wet, soon soaking her feet. Ignoring the discomfort, she hurried on towards the shrubbery where she had last seen the Count heading.

Once she had reached its shelter, she was able to walk along the flagged pathways, edged with clipped yew hedges. The line of hedge was broken every few feet where the main walkway was intersected by other, narrower walks running east and west. It was dark and silent save only for the scrape of a few of last autumn's leaves on the stone paving, as gusts of wind sent them skittering past her floating skirts.

Where should she begin to look? There were so many paths that he could have taken, it was going to be very difficult to find the right one. Not a woman to give up easily, she continued in a southerly direction, stopping at each turning to peer right and left, listening intently for any sound which would lead her to her quarry. Eventually she came to the end of the walk, beyond which lay the ha-ha and the open pastures of the park.

There was still no sign of life; all was peaceful and serene, the landscape undisturbed by any human presence. Slowly she turned and retraced her steps, checking each avenue once again as she made her way back towards the house.

Halfway along the path she bethought her of the summer-house set in a secluded square of garden and decided to look there. Quickening her pace, for she was beginning to feel very cold, she headed westwards and came at last in sight of a little stone structure tucked away in the corner of a rose garden.

The moon obligingly lit the scene and unmistakably this time, she saw two men clad in long, dark cloaks, deep in converse at the entrance of the summer-house.

Fortunately, they were so engrossed they did not notice her appearance and she was able to creep forwards, hidden by the thick shadows cast by tree and shrub. Forsaking the relative convenience of the flagstones, she trod across the flower-beds so that she could come right up to the steps of the building. Taking care to remain concealed in the bushes that grew against the garden wall, she crouched down and listened for the sound of their voices. There was no doubt in her mind now; she knew that one of them was indeed Count Fabricati!

It was not Morton though but a stranger who stood beside him. The man started nervously as a branch scratched eerily against the stonework.

'*Qui est là?*' he whispered hoarsely, glancing anxiously all about him.

The Count sat himself down on a small bench just inside the entrance.

'*Il n'y a personne. Asseyez-vous, Dupois. Il y a du vent ce soir, c'est tout. Écoutez-moi! Où est la lettre? Je dois la voir immédiatement!*'

'*C'est dans ma poche. La voici.*'

Dupois handed him the letter and the Count took it from him, eyeing him suspiciously. '*Qu'avez-vous, Dupois? Il me semble que vous êtes très agité.*'

'*Rien de tout. Je vous assure. Mais je dois partir bientôt.*'

The Count caught him by the sleeve, pulling him down beside him. '*Pas si vite! Réstez-ici!*' he commanded imperiously.

'*Mais pourquoi? Vous-avez la lettre,*' protested Dupois, growing fractious.

'*Tais-toi! Vous parlez trop!*' snapped Fabricati rising to his feet and moving out on to the steps. There was a glimmer of light and then Constance heard the crackling of paper as he spread open the letter and studied it closely. He was standing so near to her hiding place that she thought he must hear her teeth chattering with cold.

When he had finished reading, she heard the sharp intake of his breath. '*Zut! L'aigle s'envole!*' He spun round to face Dupois. '*Vous êtes un imbécile!*' he exclaimed furiously.

'*Parlez moins fort, Gérard. Quelqu'un vous entendra,*' hissed Dupois, sounding rather frightened.

'You are coming back to the house with me, Dupois. And we will have to speak only in English from now on.'

'But I tell you I must go! It is very dangerous for me to remain here. Someone might see us together. You know very well that Arnaud does not like us to take such risks.'

'No one will see us if we are vigilant. You must come with me now. Because you have taken so long to bring this news, you will have to return to France again immediately. I have some information that must reach Arnaud without delay. It is imperative that you deliver it within the next few days. If you knew what this letter contained you would realize the need for urgency.'

'Then I will arrange to meet you first thing in the morning. I cannot leave tonight, it is very late and I am exhausted from my harrowing journey,' he ended feebly.

'You wring my heart, Dupois,' retorted the Count in a voice dripping with sarcasm. 'But you will have plenty of time to rest when you are aboard ship. If you drive down to Folkestone tonight, Captain Prentice will take you across on the first tide. Now hurry! We are wasting precious time with useless argument.'

Dupois still hesitated, unwilling to go with him. This was not at all as he had planned it! He had only wanted to give Gérard the letter to make sure he had it on him when

Morton arrived. If Morton knew he had given the letter to Gérard, he would be suspicious. No one must ever know that it had been in his possession in the first place. If Gérard were to be handed over to the authorities, there must be no evidence to connect 'Mr Johnson' with this plot. He had already explained to Morton that he had stumbled upon the truth about Gérard merely by chance, having been keeping a close watch on him for the last few weeks. Morton was at this moment awaiting him at the main gates, expecting to ride up to the house with him. He was only supposed to have gone on ahead to make sure that Gérard was caught in their trap. Morton had been led to believe that Johnson had sent a note to Gérard, luring him into keeping the traitorous evidence about his person. Dupois gnawed his bottom lip worriedly. If he didn't go to Morton at once, everything would go awry. Unfortunately he couldn't think of a reasonable excuse, not one that would sound at all plausible to a man as astute as Gérard.

Annoyed at Dupois' obvious reluctance, Gérard suddenly seized him by the arm and began to propel him along the path to the house.

'Come along, man! This is no time for a debate!' he muttered impatiently.

Dupois was forced to accompany him. He was afraid of Gérard, sensing that he was in a dangerous mood and knowing that he was not a man to be crossed. Perhaps there would be an opportunity to escape his clutches before they reached the house.

As they neared the terrace, Gérard whispered sibilantly in his ear, 'Ssh! Not a single sound now! They are not all gone to their beds yet.'

He still had tight hold of Dupois' arm as he almost dragged him towards the house. A stealthy figure detached itself from the shadows lurking beneath the covered terrace and slowly crept to meet them.

'It is well, Jean,' murmured the Count in a hushed voice. 'I have the letter. Wait here with Dupois while I check that there is no one about.'

Soundlessly he slipped through the French windows and disappeared inside the curtained room.

Fifteen

Now is my chance! thought Dupois. He was not afraid of Jean, so small and insignificant as he was.

'I'll take a look in the garden, Jean. Just to make absolutely certain there is no risk of our being discovered.'

He made to slip away but before he had taken two steps, Jean had leapt in front of him and was barring his escape. In his hand he held a small pistol which was pointed directly at Dupois' heart.

'M'sieur le Comte does not like his orders disobeyed,' warned Jean, his voice soft but threatening. 'M'sieur says wait, *donc*, we wait.'

Constance had followed them all the way back to the house and had seen the Count enter through an unlocked window, leaving the two men out on the terrace. If she returned through the side door again, she would be able to warn her uncle without setting up an outcry that might alert these conspirators to the fact that they had been overheard. She had no idea what this was all about but whatever it was, it was something that needed investigating. What did that letter contain, that it had to be delivered at dead of night? Why had the Count arranged to meet this Frenchman out of sight of the house? Thank heavens that Uncle George was not yet gone to his bed, he was just the person to deal with this extraordinary situation.

Keeping her head low, she ran to the corner of the house and pausing only briefly to ensure that she was undetected, she picked up her skirts and dashed up the steps, unaware of the little drama being enacted on the terrace.

The light still showed beneath the library door and Constance hastened in without pausing to knock. To her astonishment, Lord Kemsley was not alone. The Count was standing with his back to her, while her uncle sat facing him across the large, walnut desk set a few feet away from the French windows that opened onto the terrace.

'Uncle George! Beware! There are two men hiding out in the garden! I saw the Count meet with them ...'

'Connie! Good God! What are you doing here?' interrupted Kemsley looking astounded.

'Your niece has a *penchant* for *les grandes entrées*,' murmured the Count with a wry smile. 'However, I wish that this time she had missed her cue.'

While he yet spoke, Jean and Dupois appeared at the window directly behind Lord Kemsley and the Count, with a slight movement of his head, indicated that they should enter.

Lord Kemsley spun round at the sound of their approach and as they stepped across the door sill, the Count moved forward and quietly closed the window after them. Jean's pistol had mysteriously disappeared from sight.

'Allow me to introduce a friend of mine,' began the Count cordially. 'This is Mr Johnson, my lord. I must apologize for the unconscionably late hour at which he has called but he is such an impulsive fellow, there is no gainsaying him.'

Constance stared at his imperturbable features in wonder. Surely he must have guessed that she had discovered his secret assignation in the summer-house? Why wasn't he disturbed by that knowledge?

Suddenly there came the sounds of an altercation in the hall and voices were heard outside the door. Then two men burst in upon them unannounced and came to a halt in the middle of the room. There was a short silence as they all gazed at one another.

'What a charming tableau we all present,' observed the Count dryly. 'Good evening, Mr Morton. What an unexpected pleasure.'

'I regret this unseemly intrusion, Lord Kemsley,' intervened Colonel Dyson hurriedly, 'but I was waiting for Count Fabricati, having something particular to say to him, when this gentleman knocked at the door. As there seemed to be no one about to perform the office, I took the liberty of answering it myself; I did ask him to wait while I informed you of his arrival but as you see he is most impatient.'

Mr Morton brushed him aside and strode forward to face the Count. 'I see you have detained Mr Johnson against his will! No doubt you thought you could threaten him into keeping silent about your evil treachery! Well, I am not afraid of you! And I mean to expose you for the villain you are! We have witnesses enough. Mr Johnson and Colonel Dyson will ensure that justice is seen to be done!'

'I don't understand you, Mr Morton,' said the Colonel, seemingly confused by the strangeness of this unconventional visit and the oddness of Mr Morton's behaviour.

'I am afraid we are all very much in the dark,' agreed Lord Kemsley. 'Sir,' he continued, addressing Mr Morton, 'I hope you can provide me with an explanation as to why you have forced yourself into my nephew's house?'

'Most certainly I can, my lord!' declared Morton, gloating at the Count, his eyes glittering with unholy glee. He pointed an accusing finger at Fabricati. 'That man is an imposter! His real name is Gérard and he is one of Bonaparte's agents!'

Constance gasped in horror, leaning against the desk for support as her knees trembled violently.

'Good grief, man!' cried the Colonel aghast. 'I hope you know what you are saying! You will have to prove your words, you realize that?'

'Of course,' replied Morton confidently, rejoicing in his hour of glory. 'I don't precisely know what he is plotting but I do know that he has in his possession some secret papers that will assuredly condemn him as a cowardly spy! If we cannot discover them about his person, they will undoubtedly be concealed somewhere amongst his belongings. I demand that he be searched at once!'

'Really, Morton! This is perfectly ridiculous!' scoffed the Count dismissively. 'You are talking utter fustian! Surely you don't believe such absurd nonsense, my lord? I think our friend here has had a glass too many with his dinner tonight.'

'Don't think you can gammon me, Fabricati!' snarled Morton. 'You won't be able to lie your way out of this!' Then, turning to Lord Kemsley, he said, 'You don't know what has been going on here while you have been abroad. Your sister and her family have been foisting this bogus *Count Fabricati* upon society and conniving with him to lure my cousin Lady Anne Rossmore away from her guardians. Ask your niece if it is not true!'

'What do you know of all this, Constance?' questioned Lord Kemsley, frowning heavily.

Constance did not know how to answer. Her head ached abominably and her legs felt so weak, she wondered that she could still stand upright. Morton's denunciation had shocked her to the core of her being. From all that she had just witnessed in the garden, it seemed that his accusations were justified. The Count was indeed a French spy! Despite her growing conviction that he had been using her family to cover his nefarious deeds, she yet clung to the dwindling hope that this was all a terrible misunderstanding. How could she have fallen in love with a man so completely without scruples? It wasn't possible! She would have known, have sensed if he were such an evil deceiver. This couldn't be right; there must be an explanation for his apparent duplicity.

'Constance, I asked you a question,' repeated her uncle harshly.

She started nervously, her eyes flying involuntarily to the Count's face. He was regarding her quite calmly. Even now, standing before a man who was accusing him of a terrible crime, he maintained a stoic expression, undisturbed by the jeopardy in which he stood. Could he be guilty and still look at her with such tender sympathy in his gaze?

'I ... I ... don't know what Mr Morton is talking about,' she replied in an agonized whisper, her face as white as chalk.

'She's lying!' sneered Morton, looking from one to the other. 'She's trying to protect him! No doubt he has inveigled her into believing herself in love with him, just as he did with my cousin!'

Colonel Dyson eyed Miss Trevingham disdainfully. So

that was the way of it! He had failed in his pursuit of her because she had fallen in love with Fabricati! The silly, little chit! She had wasted too much of his time and all for nothing!

Lord Kemsley considered his niece thoughtfully. 'Very well. There is only one thing to be done. Count Fabricati, much as it pains me, you being a guest in this house, I must ask you to allow me to search your pockets. If you are innocent, there is nothing to be afraid of and I shall see that this gentleman offers you an immediate apology. But I cannot let such a serious accusation pass without some investigation. Permit me, sir, if you will.'

'There is no need to put yourself to the trouble,' answered the Count evenly. 'This time you hold the highest cards. Here, I think this is what Mr Morton is looking for.' He put his hand inside his coat and took out the papers Dupois had given him in the garden. Kemsley accepted them in silence while Morton watched in heady triumph.

Not a sound echoed in the room as everyone waited with baited breath for his lordship to finish conning the documents. When at last he glanced up, Colonel Dyson drew nearer, alerted by the stunned expression on Kemsley's face.

'May I see that?' he asked quietly, plucking the papers from Kemsley's lax hold.

'What have you to say now, Count Fabricati?' demanded Lord Kemsley. 'These letters prove your guilt beyond all doubt. You are an enemy of peace and would betray us all, yes, even your friends!' he added bitterly, putting a comforting arm about Constance's shoulders. 'Mr Morton, you are in the right of it, it seems. This man must be placed in custody immediately. Colonel Dyson, you and Mr Morton can guard him while I go to inform the authorities.'

'I'm sorry, gentlemen,' apologized the Count ruefully, 'but I am afraid I cannot oblige you by remaining here any longer. Entertaining though your company has been, I regret that our ways must now part.'

'What the devil do you mean?' cried Kemsley, bristling angrily.

The Count regarded him with some amusement. 'You surely didn't expect me to stand meekly by and allow you to outwit me at the very last? I mean to serve my Emperor better than that! Is it possible that Mr Johnson forgot to warn you what a dangerous fellow I am to cross, Morton? You might otherwise have been better prepared.'

Mr Morton was suddenly seized in a painful grip, his arm twisted behind his back. He was powerless to move and his terror increased when he felt the pressure of cold metal against his neck.

'If anyone moves even one step, this man dies,' stated the Count in murderous accents.

Constance clung to her uncle as waves of nausea swept over her. This must be a nightmare! She must surely awaken from it soon!

'Jean! There is another pistol in the right-hand drawer of this desk. I took the precaution of placing it there earlier this evening. Get it will you?'

Jean quickly obeyed.

'Excellent, *mon ami*! Colonel Dyson! Bind Morton's hands!'

The Colonel caught the cords that Fabricati snatched from the curtains and threw hastily to him. Then the Count pushed Dupois to stand beside Constance and her uncle while Jean kept them still and helpless before the threatening pistol.

'You'll pay for this!' ground out Morton, almost choking on his fury as Dyson tied his arms and legs. 'I'll see to it that you are hunted down wherever you try to hide! I'll see you hanged yet, see if I don't!'

'Empty threats carry no weight, Morton,' grinned the Count serenely. 'And I must tell you that I think it most dishonourable of you to go to such lengths to avoid our meeting. I had not thought you so craven-hearted!'

Morton's impotent rage burst forth in a torrent of vile curses and the Count shook his head reproachfully. 'Must I remind you yet again of your manners, Mr Morton? I do apologize for his regrettable lack of them, Miss Trevingham but I shall see to it that he causes you no further offence.'

Morton found himself roughly gagged by a large

handkerchief before he could further express his indignation. Next he was bundled out of sight of the door and unceremoniously wedged behind the heavy sofa.

Constance watched these proceedings as one in a dream. Why couldn't Colonel Dyson do something? Or was he afraid for their safety if he tried to overpower the Count? It was at this point in her deliberations that she received another jolt to her self-assurance. The Colonel strode up to Jean and relieved him of his pistol without a struggle or a word being spoken! Then Dyson held the muzzle against Lord Kemsley's head.

'You and your niece will do exactly as I tell you,' he instructed coldly. 'I think you both know what will happen if you do not. Quickly now, our horses are waiting. I have hidden them in the water meadow. You two must accompany us to guarantee our safe passage.'

'That shouldn't be necessary,' argued the Count. 'There will be no one about outside at this time of night. And the smaller our numbers, the more chance we have of escaping undetected.'

'I tell you we may have need of them. This way we will be sure of a safe conduct. Miss Trevingham, take your uncle's arm and walk ahead of me. Jean, you bring Dupois and be sure to watch him closely.'

They herded their captives out on to the terrace and silently crossed the garden, heading towards the river that fed the lake.

Constance clung to her uncle, her heart in her mouth. This was too dreadful to comprehend. None of this made any sense to her. The Count, Colonel Dyson, the letter that this Mr Johnson had brought. Or was his name Dupois? What did it all mean? What had this to do with Bonaparte? He was a captive on Elba, wasn't he? Surely he was no longer a threat to England's security? What was happening here tonight? And what of Colonel Dyson's sinister part in all this? She had never heard his voice sound so hard and vicious. The friendly, grey eyes had lost their warmth and when she had seen his grim, unsmiling face she had felt suddenly terrified.

Her uncle walked stiffly at her side, his lips firmly compressed, his expression unreadable but she could sense his tightly controlled anger as he gripped her arm.

As they came at last into the meadow, the Colonel pointed towards a clump of willows and ordered them to hurry into the shelter of the trees. There were four horses saddled and bridled, tied to a branch where they could remain hidden from view.

'Jean and I had not expected our party to be quite so large,' admitted Dyson as they untied their mounts. 'However, Miss Trevingham shall ride up before me and Jean, being the lightest, can take Kemsley with him.'

'There is no necessity to take them with us any further, Dyson. We are safe enough now and they will only slow us down,' protested the Count reasonably.

'We are still too near the house for my comfort. I have no wish to give them an opportunity to raise the alarm. They must act as our hostages until we are safely away,' insisted the Colonel implacably.

A few moments later they were trotting out across the open meadow, travelling in the direction of the woods that stretched in a great, dark mass along the perimeters of the estate.

Constance had been seized roughly by Colonel Dyson and dragged up before him, his arm tight about her. She struggled violently at this cavalier treatment but when he hissed in her ear, 'Have a care of your uncle!' she lay passive in his hateful embrace, desperately afraid of what he might do.

The wind whipped her hair about her face as they rode down through the long grass and turned the horses towards the trees. She could not help thinking of the last time she had come into these woodlands when they had been a wonderland of beauty and the Count had seemed so very different to the man she had seen tonight. The pain caused by his shameless deceit was worse than any she had yet endured. Worse even than the knowledge that he did not love her. She still felt numb with the shock of discovering the truth of his mendacity and her thoughts were in such chaos that she was unable to gather her wits.

Colonel Dyson's complicity in all this was as nothing compared to the Count's insidious guile. But he wasn't an Italian nobleman, was he? He was a French spy! How could Giles Morton have known that? What had brought him to the house at so late an hour? How had he known that the Count had the letter on him? It had only been in his possession a short while before Morton's unexpected arrival. Perhaps this man Johnson was the key to that? Morton had appeared to be already acquainted with him. What did the letter contain that had brought them all to this mad flight at dead of night? The ache in her head, combined with the pain in her heart, made her feel faint and tired. She longed for this horror to end. She hated being in this odious proximity to Dyson; his touch disgusted her. How could she ever have thought him kind and considerate! He was despicable and she wished she had the strength to kill him!

How strange to feel blood-thirsty towards him and yet this man Gérard, who even more than Dyson deserved her deepest loathing, remained a source of emotion that was far removed from hatred. Why should that be so? Surely love must die in the face of so many betrayals of trust? What was left to give it life?

They had by now penetrated the dense woodland and were in sight of the boundary wall. The brightness of a full moon, well past its zenith, shone on an old gate set in the wall and which gave on to the lane beyond.

Dyson told Jean to open it and then ordered Kemsley to dismount.

'This is where we must part company, my lord,' he announced ominously and swung Constance down to the ground, quickly dismounting himself to maintain his grip on her.

'What are you going to do?' cried Constance, an icy shiver passing down her spine.

'Alas, your uncle is privy to some information which I cannot allow him to share with anyone else,' replied Dyson, coldly matter-of-fact. 'It is a pity that you read the letter, my lord, this would not otherwise have been necessary, perhaps.'

He raised the pistol and levelled it at Kemsley's chest. Constance screamed and tried to knock the gun from his hand but he pushed her aside with a vicious blow.

'Just a moment, Dyson!' intervened Gérard, stepping

between him and Kemsley.

'Not squeamish, surely, Gérard? I had thought that one of the Emperor's most notable agents would be quite accustomed to such exigencies.'

'But naturally. That is why I merely wish to suggest that you leave this to me. This is the Emperor's business and I am prepared to deal with it myself. The Emperor would hold it to be my responsibility to see the job done properly.'

So saying, he pulled his own pistol from his coat.

'No, James! I beg of you! Please don't harm him!' sobbed Constance, struggling to her feet. 'If you have any regard for me at all, please spare his life!'

Dyson glanced keenly at Gérard's face, then at Constance's anguished countenance, so pale in the moonlight. He reached out suddenly and pulled her back into his grasp, clapping his hand over her mouth, almost stifling her.

His eyes narrowed evilly as he looked down at her, struggling like a wild thing in his arms. So she had rejected his advances for those of a handsome rogue? What better punishment then, than that she should see her lover shoot down in cold blood the uncle she adored? Oh, but this was too delightful to miss!

'Very well, Gérard. I have heard tell of your remarkable skills. You will make quite sure of him, I know. Do it quickly, man and let us be gone!'

'Keep her quiet then,' warned the Count without turning his head to see it was done. 'Step a little further into the moonlight, my lord. I don't want to have to shoot twice. One shot must be sufficient or we will have the whole neighbourhood down on us.' He raised his arm, his eye and hand perfectly steady as he took careful aim. 'Alas, all great men must fall to earth, never to rise again, my lord. *Au revoir*.'

There was a loud report followed by the acrid smell of burning powder and Kemsley dropped like a stone to lie still and lifeless in the shifting shadows of the writhing, leafless trees.

'She's fainted, sir!' cried Jean as he saw Constance fall limp in Dyson's arms.

'We will leave her here,' said Dyson indifferently, letting her slump slowly to the ground. He walked over to Kemsley's body and stood staring down at it. Then he lifted the man's head with the toe of his boot and saw the blood seeping into the sward. Satisfied, he let it fall again and it lolled heavily to one side.

'You are every bit as good as your reputation, Gérard,' he congratulated. 'Not a man to have as one's enemy, is that not so, Dupois?'

'*M'sieur! M'sieur!*' shouted Jean excitedly, 'Dupois! He is gone!'

'*Malédictions!*' swore the Count, spinning round to find the gate swinging open and one of the horses missing. 'No matter though, he will not get far.'

He too walked over to inspect his handiwork, kneeling beside Kemsley's motionless form and examining the wound.

'Ah, yes, that is neat work,' he remarked unhurriedly. 'It pleases me well.'

'Be quick, Gérard. Someone may have heard the shot, we must be on our way. And if your friend Dupois has betrayed you once, he may do so again. You ought to choose your companions a little more wisely.'

'He was not my choice, unfortunately, Colonel,' he muttered dryly. 'I prefer to work alone, save for Jean here, who has proved his mettle a hundred times over.'

He straightened and went to Jean's side. The little man was bending anxiously over Miss Trevingham.

'Come, Jean, get to your horse,' he commanded softly. Jean mutely obeyed.

Gérard loosed his cloak and spread it over Constance's huddled form. Then, crouching down beside her, he smoothed the tumbled hair back from her alabaster brow that felt so cold to his warm touch and stroking the petal-soft cheek with gentle fingers, he whispered, ' "Never harm, nor spell, nor charm, come my lovely lady nigh". Fare thee well, sweet Titania.'

Jean brought him his horse and he swung easily into the saddle. Casting one final glance down at her face as she lay like one sleeping, he turned resolutely away. Then kicking his heels sharply to set the horse into a trot, he ducked his head as he passed under the arch of the gateway and cantered off along the lane.

Sixteen

As Gérard came up with the Colonel, he reined in alongside him.

'I have arranged for a carriage to meet us at the crossroads,' he explained. 'Our horses we will leave at the posting-house and we will then be able to make all speed to the coast. There is a Captain Prentice in Folkestone who will take us across the Channel, without troubling us for explanations.'

'Dupois also knows that route of escape,' muttered Jean sourly. 'Suppose he means to put them on our trail?'

'Dupois will not betray us again,' Gérard replied with conviction.

'I must congratulate you, Gérard,' remarked the Colonel approvingly. 'I am all admiration for the way you handled this affair tonight. You have the commendable ability to keep your head in a crisis. No wonder that the Emperor reposes such trust in you. I have to admit that I thought all our plans would come to nothing when Morton burst into the house and denounced you. Things looked very unpleasant for us, did they not? It was not quite what I had been expecting. I wish I had known before today that you were one of Bonaparte's men. Although I always thought there was more to you than a mere gamester. But you play your part as well as I play mine.'

'I could not confide in you until this evening, Colonel, because I did not have the Emperor's letter. I was under orders not to approach you with our proposition until the plans for his escape were completed. Unfortunately, Dupois chose to keep the information to himself and that is why I have had to act with such speed today. I have lost too much time as it is. Dupois had opened the letter, of course. He has done that before, believing I would not know of it. The fool! As if I could not detect when a seal had been tampered with! But at least it taught me to be wary of his loyalty. It is a pity the Emperor was not able to use our code! Dupois knows everything now. He must have plotted to betray me to the British authorities, damn him! Morton has his own reasons for wishing me out of the way. I can only guess that Dupois also knew of them and hatched this scheme to destroy me and make himself a large profit into the bargain! But there it is, one cannot be in this business and remain without enemies.'

'True enough,' concurred Dyson. 'It is well that you are aware of such dangers. Is that what caused you to take the precaution of placing a pistol in Kemsley's desk?'

'One must be prepared for any eventuality, Colonel. As I had instructed you to meet me there at such an unsociable hour, I did not like to chance that we might be interrupted when I handed you the Emperor's letter. It would have been difficult to explain our business there in the small hours of the morning. But a pistol always precludes the demand for explanations, don't you agree?'

The Colonel laughed softly. 'You and I are very much alike, Gérard. We are both professionals and it is only through our cunning and enterprise that these great men we serve can carve their destinies. All the same, it must have taken a good deal of courage to maintain such presence of mind in the face of betrayal and the shock of finding Kemsley in the library. And then, of course, you had the added intrusion of Miss Trevingham to contend with, did you not? Yes, Monsieur Gérard, you are indeed worthy of your hire. I hope the Emperor is duly grateful to you.'

'I am depending on it,' grinned Gérard. 'Look! There is the chaise ahead of us. Quickly, we shall pursue the course of destiny when we are safe inside.'

It was only minutes later that they were travelling with all haste along the Dover road. The Colonel took the Emperor's letter from his coat pocket and read it through again. Then he glanced across at Gérard sitting opposite and observing him in silence.

'Do you believe that the Emperor has already escaped from Elba?' he asked pointedly.

'I think it certain. His plans have been carefully laid these many months. He will seize the crown of France from King Louis, never doubt it. But if he has the support of the man you serve, namely King Joachim Murat of Naples, he will be able to keep a permanent grip on it. Murat has a sizeable army at his command and the Emperor will need the aid of these men if he is to retain his foothold in France.'

'But why should Murat risk his throne, merely to secure one for Bonaparte?'

'King Joachim might care to remind himself that it was the Emperor who gave it to him in the first place,' answered Gérard stiffly. 'But let us not argue over that. Let us look at matters as they stand today with the Emperor unwilling to remain in exile on Elba. He was forced into abdication last spring and terms were agreed. But they have since been broken and the Emperor therefore considers himself no longer bound by them. The soldiers of France are discontented under King Louis' rule and will welcome their Emperor back with open arms. Your king, Joachim, still has his crown of Naples but only because the Austrians allow him to keep it. We know that he abandoned the Emperor's cause before the abdication and sided with the Austrians against us. It was the Austrian Foreign Secretary, Prince Metternich who persuaded him to sign that alliance in January last year. He pledged to support Murat's claim to the throne of Naples in return for Murat's assistance in expelling the Empress Josephine's son, Eugène de Beauharnais, from Lombardy. That has given the Austrians a strong footing in the north. But you and I know that Metternich is not to be trusted to abide by that alliance. That is why Murat has asked you to try to find out exactly what they are planning at this Congress of Vienna.'

'You are very well informed, my friend,' observed the Colonel, impressed. 'You are right, of course. Murat trusts my judgement implicitly. I have served him well over the years. A colonel in the British Army is above suspicion you see, and privy to all kinds of useful information. I discovered that Kemsley had been appointed chief adviser to Castlereagh on all matters pertaining to the Italian settlement under discussion in Vienna. Murat's own emissary was barred from the Congress and so it became of paramount importance that I do my best to learn all I could of Kemsley's opinions on the subject of Naples. We know that Talleyrand is pressing for the restoration of the Bourbon King Ferdinand to the throne of Naples. Naturally, Murat is anxious that Austria continues to support his claim to that throne and is concerned lest Metternich succumbs to Talleyrand's over-persuasive tongue. He knows that Metternich is his only ally at the Congress and is entirely dependent upon his faithful adherence to their alliance.

'I was fortunate enough to strike up a friendship last summer with Kemsley's niece, Miss Trevingham. I found her to be well informed on the political situation in Italy and hoped to be able to discover through her, something of her uncle's opinions. When I was invited to Chailey, knowing that they expected Kemsley to join them direct from Vienna, I saw it as an invaluable opportunity to gain his confidence through my close acquaintance with his niece. I have been under a great deal of pressure from Naples to send them news of the Congress. Ever since the Triple Alliance was signed last month, Murat has been fearful that Metternich would eventually abandon him. Now that France, Austria and Britain are bound together by that alliance, it does seem more likely that Austria will be tempted to forsake Murat.'

'Did Miss Trevingham prove as helpful as you had hoped?' enquired Gérard with great interest.

'No, she did not! She was extremely reticent for a woman. I got very little out of her that was of any assistance to me, especially after you came to London,' he added wryly.

'My only object has been to allay her suspicions of me,' explained Gérard. 'She is a very astute young woman and I could not afford to have her against me.'

'Did you not return her affection at all, Gérard?' murmured the Colonel with idle curiosity.

'You must know as well as I that there is no room for sentiment in our profession. I have had to nurture a friendship with her brother in order to carry out my instructions. The Emperor was eager to know why Kemsley had sent Trevingham to Rome. He feared that the British might be planning to intervene in Naples. It was very much in the Emperor's interest that Murat remain in power there. I was so successful in winning Trevingham's trust that I was further instructed to follow him back to London. Firstly, I had to gauge the mood of both political parties towards the events unfolding in Vienna. The Emperor wanted to choose the right moment to effect his escape. There are those in influential positions in this country who would be prepared to accept Bonaparte if he manages to depose Louis. Secondly and most importantly, I was to make contact with you as soon as the escape from Elba was prepared. The Emperor knew that Murat had placed all reliance on your keeping him informed of what is happening in Vienna. If you persuade him that it is in his own interest to join forces with us, the Emperor will guarantee him his crown and ensure that the Bourbons are kept in exile.'

'But supposing Bonaparte fails? He was ousted before. If Murat's army marches with him and he falls again, the crown of Naples will fall with him. At least Metternich appears to be abiding by the alliance. Murat will not wish to risk setting that alliance in jeopardy for a precarious enterprise.'

'He has no choice,' replied Gérard succinctly.

'What do you mean?' questioned Dyson sharply, his eyes narrowing suspiciously.

'I mean that Metternich is secretly plotting with Castlereagh to overthrow him,' Gérard answered with certainty.

'How can you possibly know that?' gasped the Colonel disbelievingly.

Gérard lifted his right foot up across his left knee and taking hold of the heel of his boot, twisted it to one side and pulled out a piece of paper concealed in the cavity.

'Look at this,' he instructed, handing it over to Dyson.

The Colonel took it from him and leaning towards the carriage light, unfolded it and scanned it hurriedly.

'Good God! How did you come by this?' he exclaimed incredulously.

'We have contacts in high places also, Colonel Dyson,' smiled Gérard urbanely. 'Do you recognize those signatures?'

'Of course! You are right then! Britain and Austria do mean to remove Murat. This changes everything!'

'I thought it must,' observed Gérard in amusement. 'I only received that information recently. It cost us dear, I can tell you, but it is worth it if it will convince the King of Naples to accept the Emperor's invitation.'

'There can no longer be any doubt of that,' replied Dyson grimly. 'He will almost certainly begin by thrashing these contemptible Austrians!'

While the chaise continued on its journey southwards, Dupois had fled back to the inn and slipping quickly and silently up to his room, began packing a bag.

Kemsley's death had terrified him. He knew Gérard would have guessed at once that he had been deceived the moment Morton had unwittingly given him away. There was no doubt in Dupois' mind that the same fate which had befallen Kemsley now awaited him. For the first time in his life, he had lost all interest in making money. All he could think of at the moment was how to save his own skin. He dared not waste time in rousing the landlord to ask for a conveyance because Gérard might not be far behind him. The horse would have to suffice until he could reach a posting-house where he would be able to hire a chaise. Having thrust a few essentials into his valise, he abandoned the rest of his luggage and crept back downstairs. All remained quiet and undisturbed as he let himself out into the yard and flung his bag up across the saddlebow. He glanced nervously about him as he set his foot in the stirrup. The yard was pitch dark and deserted, the only sounds that came to his straining ears were the creaking of the old signboard as it swung on its rusty chains and the sudden jingling of the bridle as the horse shook its mane. Giving a shuddering sigh of relief, he threw himself up into the saddle and turned his mount towards the road. Once out on the highway, he dug in his heels and galloped away as if the devil was on his tail.

At the very moment that Dupois had seized his chance to flee from the woods, Lord Trevingham was pacing up and down his dressing-room. He had been expecting his uncle to send for him and wondered what was causing the delay. Lord Kemsley had given him strict instructions not to come down until he should receive word that it was safe to do so.

As the minutes ticked by and still no word came, he began to feel uneasy. Surely this business should have been concluded by now? He was on the point of disobeying his uncle's instructions and going downstairs anyway, when he heard a distant echo as of a gunshot. He stood stock-still, listening intently. The sound had fallen into a silence made deeper by the sudden, shattering explosion. Had he imagined it, or had that indeed been the report of a firearm? A gamekeeper shooting at poachers perhaps? He went to the window and peered out over the gardens. There was a full moon just dipping above the dim line of the horizon and by its pale light he could see that all was peaceful and nothing moved outside save for the shifting shadows across the lawns.

Nevertheless, a niggling doubt began to unsettle his mind. Supposing something had gone awry? He wished now that he had remained within the vicinity of the library. If anything was amiss he would have known of it straight away.

It was no use, he could not hesitate any longer, he must go down if only to put his mind at rest.

He cautiously peeped into the library, taking care to make no noise. The room was completely unoccupied and the whole house was ominously silent. What had gone wrong? Where was Uncle George? Growing increasingly anxious, he crossed the room and glanced out of the window. As he did so he thought he heard a muffled sound which seemed to come from behind the sofa. He gave a quick frown and strode over to investigate. Dragging it away from the wall, he started in shocked surprise as he discovered Giles Morton trussed up like a chicken, gagged and unable to move a muscle.

'Good grief! Morton! What's happened here?' he exclaimed, hastily bending to push the sofa aside and untie the handkerchief that covered the man's mouth.

'You'll ... you'll all pay for this!' croaked Morton

painfully. 'Untie me, damn you, I am nigh paralysed!'

Trevingham went to the table and snatched up a paper-knife. Swiftly he cut through Morton's bonds, firing rapid questions at him as he did so.

Morton rubbed his numbed wrists as soon as his hands were free.

'Give me time to breathe, man! I've been half suffocated!'

'I don't care! Just tell me what happened! Where is my Uncle Kemsley?' demanded his lordship in desperation. He was in an agony of fear for him and Morton's sluggish responses were infuriating.

'All right! All right! I'll tell you! But first get me to a chair – and then get me a drink!' snapped Morton peevishly.

Trevingham hauled him none too gently to his feet and pushed him down on the sofa; then he splashed some brandy into a glass and thrust it at him.

'Here drink this! And then for God's sake explain what has taken place here tonight!'

As the brandy began to revive him, Morton launched into his tale of woe. It took some time to tell because he interspersed his sentences with all manner of dire threats against Trevingham and his entire household. When he reached the part where the Colonel had insisted on taking the others with him, Justin groaned aloud.

'Where has he taken them? Do you know?'

'I heard him say that he had hidden the horses in the water meadow. This is all your doing, Trevingham! You introduced that confounded spy among us! I hope you are prepared to suffer the consequences!' snarled Morton viciously, taking another large swig of brandy.

Trevingham was already halfway to the door and never paused to reply.

He ran up to his cousin's chamber and roused him from his bed.

'What on earth is the matter?' murmured Robert Dawlish in sleepy confusion.

'I've no time to explain everything now, Bob! Constance and Uncle Kemsley are in grave danger. Get dressed quickly and come to the stables!' ordered Trevingham. 'I'll meet you in ten minutes. But for heaven's sake, don't wake a soul!'

Soon they were riding out of the courtyard and spurring off towards the carriage drive. After crossing the bridge over the lake, Trevingham turned sharply to the right, set his horse plunging down the steep bank and sped onwards toward the river and the water meadow.

If Dyson had hidden horses here, there was only one obvious place of concealment; that clump of willows on the far side.

When they reached the spot, he reined in and leapt down from his horse.

'Wait just a moment, Bob!' he called over his shoulder as his cousin galloped up behind him.

Trevingham went down on his haunches and studied the ground. The grass was well trampled here, there was no doubt that they had come this way. He frowned thoughtfully. It was unlikely that they would have left by the main gate for fear of rousing the gatekeeper's suspicions. No, he did not think that would have been their choice. But there was another way they could have got through the boundary wall and that was much nearer than the lodge-house.

'Come, Bob!' cried Trevingham, swinging back into the saddle, 'we're heading for the woods and the old keeper's gate!'

Soon they were careering madly across the grassy tracts that lay before them, plunging in and out of pale pools of moonlight as they hurtled at break-neck speed towards the deep woodlands.

Lord Trevingham knew every path in these woods and weaving quickly and skilfully between the trees, he led his cousin on through the seemingly impenetrable shadows. At last he came in sight of the gate and saw also the unmistakable figure of his sister running towards him.

'Justin! Justin! Oh, thank God you are come! They have killed Uncle George!' she sobbed brokenly, hurling herself into her brother's arms as he hurriedly dismounted and turned to meet her.

'Hush now, Connie,' he murmured soothingly, cradling her gently against his chest. 'Be brave, my dear. Show me where he is.'

'He is lying there,' she said, trying to speak calmly and pointed to a huddled shape wrapped in a cloak, hideously still.

'Let me take a look. Stay here with Robert if you wish.'

He loosed her and went hastily to his uncle's side. He knelt down by his body and leaned over to examine his wound. Then he undid Kemsley's neckcloth and felt for a pulse before bending his head to listen for a heartbeat.

Constance and Robert stood anxiously looking down at him.

'Is he gone, Jus?' whispered Constance, her voice trembling with sorrow.

'No, he isn't dead yet. But we must get him back to the house at once. Bob, help me lift him on to my horse.'

'Are you sure he is still alive? They both said he was dead! And that awful wound in his head! I thought it must be fatal,' she shuddered.

'It looks much worse than it is, I assure you. The bullet appears to have merely grazed him; a fraction closer and he would most certainly have been killed outright. As it is, he has lost a little blood but I am confident he will recover. He is a tough old bird, Connie, never fear!' he added heartily. 'I suppose this is Dyson's doing?'

'No. He wanted to do it but the Count insisted that he be the one to pull the trigger! Oh, Jus! He really is quite ruthless! I was never so mistaken in anyone in all my life!' she murmured dully.

'James did this?' gasped Trevingham incredulously. 'You saw him?'

'With my own eyes, I swear. It was horrible! Cold-blooded murder! Or at least it was meant to be. When I heard him say *au revoir* in that cold, deliberate way and then the shot! ... well, I must have fainted and when I came to my senses, I was all alone except for Uncle lying there so dreadfully silent! And I thought ... I thought....'

'You were mistaken, Connie, thank God. It's all right I tell you. You'll soon see that there is nothing to be afraid of — just try to calm yourself. Now, Bob, help me move him. Gently. I'll get in the saddle first and then you can hold him steady while we lift him up.'

Once this had been accomplished, Constance climbed

on to her cousin's horse and he swung up behind her. As quickly as they could they made their way back to the house. To Constance's relief, by the time they reached the door, her uncle had recovered enough to enter unaided.

He insisted on seeing Morton at once but as that ill-used young gentleman had by now had a little too much recourse to the brandy bottle, he was in no fit state to enter into any discussions. As silently as they could, Justin and Robert carried Morton upstairs and laid him upon the Count's bed to sleep off the effects of his palliative.

When they returned to the library, they found Constance engaged in binding up her uncle's wound. It seemed that the bullet had only grazed his temple after all and it had merely been the fall that had stunned him so badly. He must have struck his head on a stone as he dropped.

'Justin, I am going to London tonight,' he announced briskly. 'It is imperative that I see Harrowby at once. Rouse my valet and have him pack a bag. Robert! Go to the stables and tell them to prepare my carriage, if you please!'

'But Uncle!' protested Constance in horror. 'You must rest! Your poor head!'

'Pooh! That's nothing. Besides, I have urgent matters to attend to and must brook no delay. Justin, hold! You are to follow me first thing tomorrow morning – or rather, later this morning. I would take you with me now but I need you to speak to Morton as soon as he arises. He must be made to understand that what happened here tonight must not be spread abroad. I shall meet you at the office as soon as you are able. Understood?'

'Yes, sir, of course. I'll see to it,' promised his nephew, hurrying from the room.

Lord Kemsley turned to Constance. 'There's no time for explanations, Connie. I'm sorry, I know you must have so many questions buzzing in that pretty head of yours but you will have to wait for a more convenient moment. That letter Dyson took from me contained important information that must be relayed to my people in London immediately. But one day soon, you shall know all. Now, I must leave you. There is much to do. Get you to bed and try to sleep. God knows you must be in need of it after this night's doings!'

But sleep that night was impossible. So many thoughts

whirled around inside her brain that she could find no peace. The Count was a Bonapartist agent! A wretched, murderous spy! No! It could not be! It was too horrible to contemplate! Yet she had seen him shoot her uncle down in cold blood! How could all this be possible? Could she really have been so utterly taken in by mere charm? Was love indeed so blind?

When morning finally came and she wearily arose from her crumpled bed, she dressed and went down to the breakfast-room. She found Justin about to embark upon his journey. Lady Anne was with him looking pale and anxious. Justin had charged her with the task of securing her cousin's silence, as he could wait no longer for Morton to appear. Lady Anne had no idea what this was all about; Justin was unable to tell her exactly what had occurred during the night. How Giles came to be sleeping upstairs in the Count's room, she did not understand. All she knew was that Giles had discovered something about Count Fabricati that must not be revealed to anyone else. Her cousin must be made to keep silent about everything that had happened here last night. If he should speak, the entire Trevingham family would be involved in a dreadful scandal!

'I wish I knew what I am supposed to say to Giles,' she said to Constance after Lord Trevingham had driven away. 'Do you know what happened last night, Connie? I have never seen Justin look so worried.'

'Why should you care how Justin feels?' replied Constance cuttingly.

'Because I love him,' the girl answered, quietly dignified. 'And because we are soon to become man and wife.'

It was Constance's turn to look bewildered. 'But I saw you only yesterday with Count Fabricati! He kissed you!'

'It was the kiss of a very dear friend, not a lover,' she replied, looking Constance straight in the eye. 'I had just informed him of my betrothal to your brother. His salute was merely one of congratulation. It meant no more than that. I owe my chance of happiness to Count Fabricati and I wanted him to know how grateful we both are, Justin and I.'

'I see. Then I owe you an abject apology for leaving you so abruptly yesterday. May I now offer my best wishes for your happiness and ask your forgiveness?' she begged contritely.

Lady Anne smiled. 'Of course and thank you. We have told no one else because Justin thinks it proper to speak to my uncle first. So please keep this to yourself for a little while.'

'Very well. But you may be sure that everyone in this house will be delighted with Justin's choice of wife.'

'Not everyone,' grimaced Lady Anne as she heard the sound of Giles's irritable voice in the hall outside.

The door was flung open and he appeared in the room looking pale and dishevelled, having slept in his clothes all night.

'Where is Trevingham?' he demanded petulantly. 'I have several words I wish to say to him. I see you are returned to us unharmed Miss Trevingham. But had you suffered any hurt it would have been entirely due to your own reprehensible conduct in foisting that obnoxious gallowsbait upon us!'

His complaint was halted by a sudden, loud ringing of the doorbell, soon followed by the sound of Mr Symes's excited enquiries.

Giles put his head around the door and called him into the room.

'Giles! Thank God! How glad I am to see you alive and well!' he cried, hasting towards him. 'When I discovered that you had not returned to the inn, I was seriously alarmed. But when the news of Mr Johnson's murder came to us a short while ago, I was positively terrified!'

'Johnson has been murdered?' Giles gaped, momentarily forgetting his grievances.

'Yes! Is it not dreadful? They found his body on the Dover road. Only a short distance from the safety of a posting-house. He had been shot clean through the heart! It must have been thieves I suppose, for he had nothing of value left on him, only his passport in his pocket. When the coachman brought the tidings early this morning, the landlord felt obliged to go and view the corpse. He had already discovered that our friend Mr Johnson had disappeared during the night, leaving his luggage behind at the inn.'

Mr Morton looked thunderstruck. 'Well, well! This is a fine imbroglio!' he exclaimed, eyeing Miss Trevingham balefully. 'Your family has a great deal to answer for!' he added accusingly.

'Mr Morton, please calm yourself. My Uncle Kemsley is already setting matters in hand. I am sure he will be able to deal with all of this entirely to your satisfaction. If you will only keep silent on this subject, just for a short while, I promise that everything will be set to rights and ... and explanations provided,' she finished lamely.

'Oh, yes!' he snorted derisively. 'I am quite sure all of you will try to prevent me from speaking! A fine broth of scandal you Trevinghams have brewed for yourselves! Well! You need not think I shall lift a finger to help you escape the consequences of your ill-judged behaviour!'

'Giles! Please do as Miss Trevingham asks!' pleaded Lady Anne, turning large, beseeching eyes upon him. She wrung her hands pitifully, remembering Justin's face and his earnest request that she swear her cousin to silence. 'I will do anything if you will but promise to say nothing of what occurred here last night. I don't understand any of this but surely it cannot be so terrible that you will refuse to grant her this one favour?'

Giles was about to make another scornful retort, when he suddenly paused and gave her anxious face a quick scrutiny. 'I wish to speak to my cousin privately,' he insisted crisply. 'Where may we converse undisturbed?'

'There is no one in my brother's study. You may go there,' answered Constance stiffly and wondering all the while what he meant to do.

As soon as he had her to himself, he faced Lady Anne, his eyes glittering strangely. 'So you would do anything to keep the Trevinghams from this calamitous scandal, would you? Very well, I will give you my promise if you will give me yours.'

'I don't understand you, Giles. What do you mean? What promise do you require of me?' she questioned, her dainty brows drawing together in puzzlement.

'I require your solemn promise to be my wife,' he

announced triumphantly. 'That is the price of my silence. And quite a fair one, considering you are asking me to protect a murderer by holding my tongue.'

Lady Anne's eyes opened wide, a mixture of shock and horror reflected in them. 'Murder? You mean that the Trevinghams are somehow involved in that poor man's death last night? No! I will not believe it!'

'It is quite true, I assure you. Why do you suppose that Miss Trevingham is so desperately trying to persuade me to help them by remaining silent? You see, I am the only witness against them. I saw everything that happened here last night and I know who murdered Mr Johnson. If I speak, the Trevinghams will find themselves in the midst of a scandal that will ruin them completely! Now do I have your promise?'

'No! No! I cannot! You do not know what you ask of me!' she whispered brokenly, her eyes full of fear and dread.

'Then there is nothing further to discuss,' he replied in a clipped voice and moved towards the door.

'No, wait! Let me think! Give me time to consider!' she cried in great agitation, her arm flung out to him as if she would detain him.

'I must have your answer now!' Giles insisted, gloating over her predicament. Now he would have his revenge on them all! The Count, the Trevinghams and the Wyverns who thought they could force him into wedlock with their whey-faced daughter! He was soon to become the new Earl of Rossmore and he would see to it that he not only had a beautiful countess but the entire Rossmore fortune!

Lady Anne knew it would be useless to appeal to him again. She recognized in his stubborn look that her pleas would not be heeded. He would not hesitate to ruin Justin and that she could never permit him to do. How in heaven's name had the Trevinghams become embroiled in the murder Mr Symes had spoken of just now? But it seemed certain that they were, Giles spoke of being a witness to it!

'I see I must give you my word. You leave me no choice,' she responded bitterly, her hand dropping to her side as she turned deliberately away from his exultant face.

'Excellent! I see we have come to an understanding at last. We shall keep this to ourselves for a while, I think. I yet have need of Wyvern's pecuniary assistance, alas. But I am confident we shall not have to delay our nuptials for very much longer! We but await your father's blessing! Goodbye for the moment, dear coz. No doubt you will be returning to the fold now that your erring lover has abandoned you?'

He laughed mockingly as the proud head drooped and she sank heavily into a chair. The door opened and closed again as he rejoined his friend Mr Symes. She heard him call out that they were leaving and then the sound of their footsteps receded along the hall. It was only now that she allowed herself the consolation of anguished tears.

Seventeen

The next few weeks saw many worrying events unfold. The news of the Emperor's escape and successful return to France, caused shock, fear and much speculation as to the possible results of this catastrophe.

Lord Kemsley was now fixed in Brussels and Justin had gone dashing off to Vienna in complete ignorance of Lady Anne's predicament.

Constance alone knew the truth. Lady Anne had confided in her immediately after Morton's departure from Chailey. Only Justin's return could save this unhappy situation. As Wellington gathered his polyglot army in Belgium, she could not help wondering if all this was somehow connected with Count Fabricati and that mysterious meeting in the summer-house. She had told no one of the peculiar events of that fateful night. Her uncle had obviously wanted it so but how she wished she knew what it was all about!

Lady Trevingham and Sophy had been astonished at the sudden departure of nearly all the gentlemen and often discussed the possible cause of it but without ever finding a plausible explanation. Constance hesitated to enlighten them, it would only add to their anxiety. To know that they had been harbouring a Bonapartist agent in their midst must surely terrify them. They had thought the Count so very charming. Well, and so he was! Just how charming she hoped they would never know. They had all been enslaved beneath his despicable spell!

And yet ... his dark face swam now before her like a vision of the angelic Lucifer. His smile so ineffably tender, just as she had seen it that night in the library when he had met her stricken eyes with such sweet concern in his own steady gaze. Then too, there was the matter of his cloak. She had awoken from her swoon to find it wrapped snugly about her, knowing instinctively that his had been the hand to lay it there.

Her memory brought afresh the moment when, having inexplicably taken that same cloak up to her room, she had held it to her breast and nestled her cheek against the thick folds.

That was when she had discovered the letter. A small package had been concealed in a deep pocket of the cloak, her name written upon it in an elegant hand.

The remembrance led her now to arise almost involuntarily and cross to the dressing-table. Opening a drawer, she took out that same package and mechanically unfolded it to remove the object it contained – a golden jewel set with precious stones in the form of a gryphon. She laid it in her open palm, gazing down at it as if mesmerized. Then she read again the lines penned in the same hand that had inscribed her name on the other side of the folded paper:

'*As the heavenly bodies move, In their set courses high above,*
So daily, nightly, thou shalt prove, As Constant Constance in
  thy love'.

Thus began the strange missive. She read on: *You refuse my plea. I have no more time. And yet I find I cannot leave you as I ought, with only silence between us and so....*

Here followed a few verses which she had long since committed to memory.

Must we then part, our thoughts unspoken?
No vows exchanged nor lover's token?
What says your heart?
Am I not to know the reason why
A glist'ning tear bedews your eye?
Say 'tis not so!
Shall love so rare, like sunken treasure,
Lie fathoms deep, perhaps forever?
Do you not care?
Or has a bitter fate decreed that we

*Henceforth must live quite separately?
Is it too late?
How pale your cheek, the roses fled,
Your silence fills my soul with dread,
Oh! Won't you speak?
And thus go I? No hand to hold,
Nor kiss to keep me from this cold
Goodbye?*

The letter ended with the words: *Keep the trinket, I should like to hope that some day you might wear it over your heart. Forgive me. James.*

What could it mean? Dared she console herself with the thought that he had cared for her as much as she had cared for him? For she had fallen in love with him at last and against all her better inclinations. Oh, why must she choose to love a man like this one, when far better men had courted her? It was all so useless! Fate had mocked her cruelly indeed! The clever, discriminating Miss Trevingham had fallen hopelessly in love with a common spy! And a cold-blooded murderer, it seemed. How very amusing!

She began to laugh silently, replacing the letter in the drawer and tossing the ornament in her jewel case. Her shoulders began to shake and she sat down in front of the looking-glass, covering her face with her hands as the tears began to stream down her cheeks.

In April the Trevingham ladies had returned to Albemarle Street. The golden trumpets of the daffodils thronging along the park railings, heralded their arrival. By mid May they were reading of Murat's defeat at the hands of the Austrians. His army had been halted as he tried to cross the river Po and now Napoleon had no hope of support outside of France, for King Joachim had been forced to flee Italy.

At the end of the month all kinds of rumours came rumbling over the Channel like ominous claps of thunder. The storm was not far away and was soon to break loose over Belgium. A little village called Waterloo was about to take its place in the annals of history.

In the clubs of St James's, the betting was leaning heavily in Bonaparte's favour, fluctuating only slightly whenever a fresh piece of news was passed among the gentlemen gathered in these hallowed precincts. An air of excitement and anticipation hung over them all as information filtered through the courier services that a great battle was about to take place upon the hitherto peaceful Flemish farmlands.

The first tidings that set the City astir was the report of Wellington's defeat. It was said that the allied armies were completely routed and were pouring into Brussels in fearful disarray. People gathered in hushed groups to discuss the outcome and the newspapers were seized upon the moment they came into print. Rumours ran rife, until one warm June evening when the Prime Minister, Lord Liverpool and his cabinet were dining with Lord Harrowby in Grosvenor Square.

Harrowby was seated near the open windows when suddenly the sound of loud, cheering voices drifted up to them. He glanced over his shoulder, a puzzled frown on his brow.

'What the devil is happening now?' he muttered, rising quickly to his feet and going to the window to look down into the square below.

'Good God!' he gasped incredulously. 'Gentlemen! Come and see this!'

They all crowded to the windows and gazed out of the open casements, leaning excitedly on one another's shoulders to gain a better view.

A chaise and four was being driven at a furious pace along the road, having just turned into the square. It was covered all over with French flags, regimental banners and the Emperor's eagle insignia. As the horses plunged to a standstill at number forty-four, they saw Wellington's aide-de-camp Major Percy, leap out without waiting for the steps and run with long strides up to the front door. Seconds later he burst in upon them and announced the tremendous victory at Waterloo. Wellington and his glorious armies had crushed the French in a decisive battle on 18th June and Napoleon Bonaparte had fled with the remnants of his Old Guard. Percy handed the Iron Duke's dispatch to Lord Bathurst, the Secretary for War and that gentleman proceeded to read out the official announcement of the momentous event.

It was as Lady Trevingham and Constance were reading an account of these joyful tidings in the *Morning Post*, that they were interrupted by Basset bearing a salver which he proffered to her ladyship. She took up the card that reposed upon it and frowned in puzzlement.

'The gentleman had hoped to speak with Lord Trevingham, my lady. But when I gave him to understand that his lordship was still from home, he desired to be brought before you.'

'Then show him up,' she replied.

A moment later a soberly clad, elderly gentleman was ushered in. His hair was quite white, his face unusually gaunt as if he had been in ill-health and he walked with a slight stoop. He bowed courteously to Lady Trevingham and her daughter.

'Forgive this intrusion, Lady Trevingham. But I am most anxious to speak to your son. Your butler has informed me of his absence and I have therefore taken the liberty of bringing my business before you. I would ask you if you know when he will be returning to London?'

'We expect him any day now, sir,' she answered, looking mildly surprised at the urgency of his tone.

'Then will you oblige me by giving him my card as soon as he arrives? I would not presume so much but there is a matter of extreme importance I must discuss with him,' he explained hurriedly.

'Are you then acquainted with my son?' enquired her ladyship.

'Our acquaintance is slight, I must confess, but Lord Trevingham once did me a kindness and came to my aid when I was *in extremis* and I am hoping he may do so again. May I make so bold as to ask for your assurance that my message will be conveyed to him immediately upon his return?'

'Yes, you may have that assurance, sir. I only wish I could be a little more certain as to the precise time of his arrival. But I am confident that it is imminent.'

'Then I shall hope to see him hourly. Thank you for

your kind indulgence. Good day, my lady.'

'Good day, Mr Colton; Basset will show you out.'

She rang the bell as she spoke but it was Sophy who first appeared at the door.

Lady Trevingham briefly introduced her to the visitor, explaining that he was just leaving. As Mr Colton passed her, he stopped abruptly.

'That is a very pretty jewel you are wearing, young lady,' he commented with apparent interest. 'A most singular design, is it not?'

'Yes, I suppose so,' answered Sophy, glancing down at the gold brooch pinned to her bodice. 'It belonged to my brother's friend, Count Fabricati, but I do not think it is of any great value. It is merely a costume piece. I found it in your jewel case, Connie, while I was looking for the ear-rings you said I might borrow. I had no notion that the Count had given it to you. I hope you don't mind my borrowing this also? I will take the greatest care of it, I promise.'

'I hope you will,' murmured the old gentleman. 'It is of more value than you know, I think. Good day ladies.' He bowed again and withdrew.

'Well! I wonder what mystery is here?' mused Lady Trevingham thoughtfully. 'What do you think, Connie?' She turned to her eldest daughter who was sitting staring at the door as if her thoughts were far away. 'Connie? What is the matter? Did you not hear what I said?'

'I'm sorry, Mama, I was day-dreaming. But to answer your question, didn't Justin tell us that he rescued another man from that horrid prison in Rome? His name was Colton, I am sure. Could that have been the same person perhaps?'

'I really don't remember his name. But I daresay you are right. Your memory is usually excellent. No doubt Justin will confirm it. Now where are you going?' she asked in surprise as Constance hurriedly left the table.

'I must speak with Sophy before she goes out. Excuse me, Mama!' With that she sped away, leaving Lady Trevingham shaking her head in bewilderment.

The mysterious gentleman had not been gone above an hour or two when another caller arrived, this time to speak with Miss Trevingham.

Constance was furbishing up one of her last season's bonnets when the visitor was announced and she glanced up in surprise as the lady entered the room. She was dressed all in black and wore a lace veil over her face. When Basset had closed the door, she threw back the veil to reveal a beautiful but pallid countenance.

'Lady Anne!' cried Constance as she recognized the newcomer. 'I did not know you had returned to Town. We thought you remained at Hartsmere. But I see that condolences are due to you?'

'My father died some weeks ago. The news only reached us recently. That is why I am come to see you, Connie. Now that Giles and I are to come into our inheritance, he is insisting on an immediate wedding. I told him I could not possibly marry for at least six months, not now that I am in mourning for my father but he says we can have a quiet ceremony by special licence. Oh, Connie! What am I to do? I must speak to Justin at once! Is he home yet? I am sure he will be able to make Giles see reason! He still means to carry out his threat to involve you all in scandal. I know from experience what havoc such things can wreak in a family and I mean to do all I can to save Justin from that danger.'

'Come and sit down while I think what is to be done,' invited Constance calmly, patting the seat beside her. 'Don't worry, my dear, there's no need to cry. This marriage cannot possibly take place. Justin would never allow you to make such a sacrifice on his behalf.'

'But Giles is gone this morning to see the lawyers about the marriage contracts!' she wailed miserably.

Constance frowned blackly, wishing she could have the opportunity to give Giles Morton some excellent and precisely worded advice.

'Then I must see what can be done to put an end to this nonsense,' she replied determinedly. 'I think my Uncle Kemsley is the best person to aid us. We had word last night that he is home again and Mama has gone this very morning to see him. He may well know when Justin will reach London. I shall go to his house at once.'

'Do you think you can ask him to come to Berkeley

Square this afternoon? That is when the lawyers mean to bring the papers for me to sign.'

'This afternoon?' Constance gasped, somewhat taken aback. 'Well! Giles does not waste time now that he is the new earl, does he? But why Berkeley Square? Are you not with your aunt and uncle in Grosvenor Square?'

'Yes, I drove down with them yesterday. They know nothing of Giles's scheming. I have not the courage to tell them yet, they are so set on his marrying Agnes. But Giles is to take possession of Rossmore House as soon as the legalities are over. We are all to meet there to hear the reading of my father's will. No one has set foot in that house since my mother ordered it to be closed up. She hated the place because it was there that Papa fought that infamous duel. Yes, it is shocking, is it not?' she added, noticing Constance's wide-eyed surprise. 'But my papa cared nothing for honour. My mama said he was a vicious brute and cursed him with her dying breath for the misery he brought upon us.'

'How perfectly dreadful all this must have been for you,' murmured Constance pityingly. 'You have had your share of the miseries of scandal and I shall do all in my power to keep you from being harmed by the indiscretions of our family. Now wait a moment while I fetch my bonnet and shawl and then you may take me up in your carriage. I shall go to my uncle at once.'

As soon as Lady Anne had set her down outside Lord Kemsley's house, Constance lost no time in seeking an audience with him. Lady Trevingham was still there when Constance was shown into the morning-room and she listened with growing indignation to the recital of Giles Morton's despicable actions.

'We shall soon put an end to his ambitions!' she declared irately. 'How dare he bully that poor innocent! His conduct is utterly deplorable! Come, George! We are all going to Rossmore House,' she announced briskly, the light of battle in her fine eyes. 'I need to give Giles Morton a piece of my mind!'

When they arrived in Berkeley Square, Lord Kemsley beat a loud tattoo upon the door of Rossmore House, a grandiose mansion with a magnificent Ionic portico.

The Gamester

After the space of two or three minutes and several peals of the bell, the door opened to reveal a tired-looking manservant with a perpetual frown between his eyes. Lord Kemsley stated their business and without waiting to hear the man's reply, strode briskly into the hall closely followed by his two staunch supporters.

'But sir!' protested the valet. 'My master is not at home and he has left me with orders to admit only members of his family today.'

'No doubt that is so,' smiled Lord Kemsley affably, 'but I think we will wait anyway. Our business with Mr Morton is of the utmost importance.'

'But sir, the house is not ready for the reception of visitors. The furniture is all in holland covers and there are no staff employed here yet.'

'We shan't mind that, shall we ladies?' he interrupted brusquely. 'You must have some chairs in one of these rooms if you are expecting the family. We shall wait there for Mr Morton's return.'

Still protesting faintly, the man led them into a nearby saloon and left them to their own devices.

Constance looked about her with keen interest. The room was of magnificent proportions with vast walls covered in huge, faded tapestries. Overhead was a lofty ceiling in high relief which drew the eye inexorably upward. The furnishings and pictures were draped in dust sheets giving the room a ghostly appearance. On the far side were three long, rectangular windows that rose from floor to ceiling and faced on to the square. They were hung with deep-red damask curtains that fell to the thickly-carpeted floor in heavy, dusty folds. It was gloomy in here, the shutters had not yet been unlocked and only the candles in the wall sconces were lit, leaving the corners of the room hidden in deep shadows.

Constance could not help thinking of Lady Anne's words concerning the duel in this house and a chill tremor ran through her as she wondered if this might be the very room where the grim deed was perpetrated.

Just then they heard the sound of a carriage outside and within moments of this, Morton's voice raised in anger in the hall.

He burst in upon them, his face red with fury. 'What business have you in my house?' he cried vehemently. 'I left strict instructions that none but members of my family were to be admitted. What do you mean by forcing yourselves upon my servant?'

'Good afternoon, Mr Morton,' greeted Lord Kemsley pleasantly, as if this tirade had never been uttered. 'I am glad to see you in such rude health. You were half-seas over when last I saw you. Drank a whole bottle of my nevvy's best brandy and had to be carried up to your bed like a baby! Well, I daresay your nerves were shot to pieces that night. I know mine were,' he chuckled. 'Thanks to that scapegrace, Gérard.'

'Oh, is that why you are here?' sneered Giles, thinking that he had Lord Kemsley's measure. 'Now that you're back in England and Bonaparte is safe in British custody, I suppose you think all danger is past! Well, I think not! There is Mr Johnson's murder to account for to the authorities. And your nephew's part in bringing that French spy among us!'

'Yes! You thought you could use that against us and so bend poor Lady Anne to your will!' cried Lady Trevingham, bosom heaving with righteous indignation. 'But you were very much mistaken if you thought we would let you get away with that piece of villainy!'

'Oh? What will you do to prevent it? You know you dare not move against me for fear of all that I could reveal about your family! It was thanks to you Trevinghams that cursed Frenchman managed to escape with a secret document and so endangered this country of ours! You will not wish that to be generally known, an I mistake not the matter!'

'But it is you who are under a misapprehension, Mr Morton,' replied Lord Kemsley gently. 'You see, although Monsieur Gérard is undoubtedly a Frenchman, he is also a British agent. In fact he is a member of my staff and acts under my instructions.'

Lady Trevingham looked triumphant as she met Morton's startled eyes. Constance merely looked quite as stunned as Mr Morton.

'You're lying!' blustered Giles unbelievingly. 'This is just one of your ploys to wriggle off my hook! Well, it won't do! Mr Johnson knew him for a French spy, he had been following him closely for some time and knew his every movement. He knew Gérard had that letter on him, it was he who told me of it. Alas, he paid for his loyalty to England – Gérard killed him because of it!'

Lord Kemsley sighed and shook his head sadly. 'How easily you are duped, Mr Morton. Don't you realize even yet that *Mr Johnson* was the real Bonapartist agent? He merely told you that tale because he saw his way clear to making a profit out of his extraordinary situation. Don't speak of Dupois and loyalty, I pray! And don't tell me that he had asked for no remuneration for his information, because I won't believe it!'

Mr Morton reddened suddenly, a guilty flush colouring his face as he remembered the bargain that had been struck that night at the inn.

'I thought so,' continued Kemsley, a note of disgust in his voice. 'I think your part in this, unlike Monsieur Gérard's, will not stand close scrutiny.'

'But Uncle George! Why did this Gérard shoot you, if he was your own agent?' questioned Constance, unable to contain herself any longer.

'Come, let us sit down and I will explain everything. We still have plenty of time before the others arrive. You too, Mr Morton, I am sure you would like to hear a few more details, wouldn't you? I see you are as yet unconvinced.'

Morton scowled and flung himself into a chair, sudden doubts beginning to trouble his mind.

'Monsieur Gérard and I met several years ago, when I was at the French court during the months following the Amiens peace treaty. He was a great favourite of the Empress Josephine. She was forever calling him to her side to seek his help in understanding some point of language, when listening to the political discussions which took place at her receptions.'

'Ah, yes! I remember now!' intervened Lady Trevingham delightedly. 'No wonder he looked at me so slyly when first he came to me in London! But he had not that scar in those days, of course! He was such a handsome boy! We all wondered if the Empress ...'

'Please allow me to continue, Amelia,' broke in her brother quellingly. 'He was also a very skilful gamester even then. His father had taught him all his tricks and the boy had soon mastered the art. They made a good living between them. It was by the merest chance that I discovered more of his artfulness. He often assumed a grand title in order to gain an invitation to sit at the tables which offered the highest stakes. I did not seek to expose his fraud, because I began to see how such a man might prove useful to me. Gérard was extremely convincing as a grand gentleman, despite his less exalted origins. It was soon after this that he did me a very great service, in gratitude for my silence about his somewhat unscrupulous activities. He warned me of Napoleon's intention to imprison every Englishman found on French soil. All those aged between eighteen and sixty years of age, that is. But thanks to Gérard's daring and courage I managed to evade capture and he got me safely away to England.

'Now that war had been declared again, I lost no time in recruiting Gérard to our cause. A man who could speak several languages and assume any character he chose, was invaluable to me in my work for our national security. Gérard confessed to no particular allegiance and liked the challenge with which I had presented him. And I was proved to be right about my judgement of his character. He has served us faithfully and well over the years, especially since the French captured him in Spain.'

Constance had been listening in awed silence but at this she gasped saying, 'He was captured? But surely they would have shot a spy?'

'Indeed they would and nearly did! But by the merest chance, one of the French officers was a captain in their secret service. Believing that Gérard was nothing more than an idle gamester, who had fought alongside the Spanish peasants for sheer devilment, he offered him his life if he would work for them. This gave us the most wonderful opportunities to keep one step ahead of them when they hatched their plots. All we had to do was to provide Gérard with seemingly important information, in order to safeguard his position as one of their valued agents. They came to trust him so completely that he was used as a messenger by Bonaparte himself during his exile on Elba. We arranged for him to strike up an apparently chance acquaintance with Sir Neil Campbell, the English commissioner on Elba. Naturally the French thought this all a part of Gérard's skill as an accomplished agent. It was because he was working in Italy that I arranged for him to keep a friendly eye on Justin, although my nephew never knew it! It would have wounded his pride if he had thought I had not trusted him to take care of himself. Again the French thought this another of Gérard's schemes to learn of our secrets and were quite happy for him to appear friendly with an Englishman. It has been so simple to manipulate them! They even believed that he had been risking his life on their behalf in London.'

'What was he doing in London, George? You never explained that to me when you asked me to see that he met all the right people,' enquired Lady Trevingham, much intrigued by all that she had heard.

'Ah, yes! You were invaluable to me, my dear Amelia,' smiled her brother gratefully. 'Between you and Justin, Gérard was able to keep his French masters satisfied that he was doing everything they had asked of him and at the same time perform an important task for us.'

'Mama! Did you know all along that the Count was one of Uncle's agents?' cried Constance, regarding her mother with unfeigned surprise.

'Of course I knew,' laughed Lady Trevingham, giving her a hug. 'You don't think that I would otherwise have let a man of such doubtful character and so wickedly handsome into the bargain, near my precious innocents?'

'But why did you not tell me? You knew how worried I was when he came among us?' she demanded, a little annoyed at being kept out of the secret.

'That was my doing, I'm afraid,' apologized Lord Kemsley contritely. 'I made your mama promise to say nothing. I will now explain to you both why that was necessary. We had suspected for some time that someone with military knowledge had supplied the French with valuable information during the Peninsular campaign. The source of this information remained a complete mystery to us until recently. You asked me a moment ago,

Amelia, just what Gérard had been doing in London. Well, the Bonapartists had asked him to make contact with a man who would be instrumental in helping them achieve their greatest ambition. This man they desperately needed to assist them was none other than Colonel Dyson! It was thanks to Gérard that we discovered our informant. Colonel Dyson was in Joachim Murat's employ and had been for several years. I'm sorry to tell you Connie, that he had chosen you as the means of interfering in my affairs. He hoped to learn through you everything that we were doing in Vienna concerning Naples. I did not confide in you because I wanted him to believe that he was under no suspicion. He was a very devious and clever man and if you had known our secret, you would undoubtedly have been unable to appear natural in his company and he might have escaped the net. As it was, you unknowingly lured him deeper into it. He was sure that he had won your trust and affection, that is why he came so willingly to Chailey when Gérard persuaded your mama to invite him.'

'So that's it!' cried Lady Trevingham. 'I thought he wanted Colonel Dyson there for Constance's sake. I assumed he was match-making again!'

'Yes, he has been dabbling in that lately, it seems. I shall have a few words to say to him when I catch up with him! It was because he couldn't resist that particular challenge that he brought you down on us, Morton, and nearly ruined everything! I don't know what got into Gérard; he has never behaved so irresponsibly before, not in the middle of such serious business anyway. But as to Dyson's visit, that was arranged because I wanted him at Chailey. The time was fast approaching when we would land our fish. Gérard and I had been in contact through an intermediary in London while I was away. This man has a seemingly innocuous trade in footwear. It was a most convenient method of communication between us, providing an excellent courier service that kept us one step ahead of our enemies. I only wish the Bonapartists had such worthy employees. Unhappily for us, they had chosen a man who put his own business ahead of theirs and tried to line his pockets at their expense. That was

Johnson; you saw him in the summer-house that night, Connie. The letter you saw him give to Gérard was for Dyson to deliver to Murat. It contained vital news concerning Bonaparte's plans. Alas, he had kept the letter for his own purposes, eh, Morton? This delay unfortunately made it impossible for us to prevent the Emperor's escape. But we did prevent Murat from joining forces with him.'

'But how?' asked Constance, totally intrigued by her uncle's narration.

'We plotted all along that Dyson should take that letter to Murat. By stealing it from me he revealed his true identity and would never be able to return to England to cause us any more harm. That was my main objective in having him with me at Chailey. I wanted to trick him into showing his hand. We had no positive proof against him otherwise. Gérard sent his valet to the inn to find out exactly what the letter contained. We had a good idea, of course but needed to know the exact date of the planned escape. As we discovered that the eagle had already flown, I decided that we could not only trap Dyson but use him to be the means of settling a problem which had caused Castlereagh great difficulty at the Congress. Talleyrand had been pressing for the return of the Bourbon king to the throne of Naples. Castlereagh agreed that it was the best course but Metternich, although he had no real objection to it, had been postponing a formal agreement. This indecision on his part had caused Castlereagh to grow impatient, he wanted the matter settled finally. Metternich had been evading the issue merely because he signed an alliance with Murat, promising to support his claim to the crown. The answer was quite simple. If Metternich did not care to break the alliance, perhaps Murat could be persuaded to do so! That way, Austria would no longer feel obligated towards him and could happily side with her partners, France and Britain.

'I had provided Gérard with the means to convince Dyson and therefore, Murat, that he should support Bonaparte. I had only to alert Castlereagh and Metternich to that certainty and as soon as Murat decided to make his move, the Austrians would be ready to bar his path.

'Now as to Gérard's attempting to murder me, Connie, it was no such thing. He had to pretend to do so in order to prove to Dyson that he was the ruthless French spy he purported to be. Also, he had to stop Dyson from firing the shot himself because that snake would not have hesitated to put an end to my existence. Gérard only shaved me with his shot, he had no wish to do me any permanent damage. I thank God for his timely intervention and his cool-headed skill. Do you recall him saying, "All great men must fall to earth never to rise again"?' he asked. Constance nodded.

'Well, that was his warning to me to drop like a stone as soon as the gun went off. If you knew Gérard as well as Justin does, Connie, you would have been saved a great deal of anxiety. You see, Gérard said *Au revoir* before he fired the pistol! You told Justin that yourself, when he came to your aid in the wood. He realized immediately that Gérard would have said 'goodbye' if he had really intended to kill me. He is always so particular in his use of those words. I must admit that I found the distinction very reassuring under the circumstances! The only trouble was that when I played my part and fell to earth, I couldn't rise again because I knocked my head on a stone as I fell and rendered myself unconscious.

'Well, that is the truth in its entirety. So you see, Mr Morton, to expose *Count Fabricati* would be to advance his popularity even further. He has been doing heroic work for us in France and Belgium these last few months. Ah, I think I hear your other guests arriving.'

Eighteen

To Constance's astonishment, it was Justin who entered, brushing past the bewildered valet who seemed at a loss to know what his master now expected of him.

Lord Trevingham halted on the threshold as his eye fell upon the occupants of the room.

'Good Lord! What are you all doing here?' he exclaimed, looking startled.

'Good afternoon, Justin. I wondered when you would put in an appearance,' grinned Lord Kemsley. 'You went dashing off in such haste this morning, I had no time to speak to you.'

'Did you see the old gentleman, Justin?' interposed his mother, consumed with curiosity.

It was Lord Trevingham's turn to smile broadly. 'Yes, I did! I cannot thank you enough for persuading me to go to him, Mama. When I heard what this limb of Satan meant to do,' he glowered at Morton, 'my first instinct was to come and break his scrawny neck!'

'I should like to see you try!' cried Morton hotly, rising from his seat.

The quarrel which now threatened to ensue was interrupted by the arrival of Mr Morton's expected visitors. Now their numbers were swelled by Lord and Lady Wyvern, Lady Anne and an unknown gentleman who was suited all in black and carried a document case beneath his arm.

'I did not know you were entertaining guests today, Giles,' remarked Lady Wyvern, somewhat taken aback by the sight of the unexpected assembly, seated in these rather sombre surroundings.

'Nor am I!' snapped Giles waspishly. 'Guests usually wait

to be invited: these people are neither invited nor welcome!'

'Er ... shall we get on with the proceedings, sir?' interceded the gentleman in black, spreading his papers upon the great mahogany table which dominated the centre of the room. 'I have the marriage contracts here as you requested and the late earl's last will and testament.'

'Marriage contracts?' reiterated Lady Wyvern in puzzlement. 'What marriage contracts?'

Lord Trevingham was already at Lady Anne's side, smiling down at her with glowing eyes.

'Giles meant to force my poor darling to accept him as her husband but I have every intention of performing that role, by your leave, Lord Wyvern.' He kissed his lady's fingers reverently. 'It was a noble gesture, Anne my sweeting, but I would never have allowed you to immolate yourself on any altar – least of all one of Giles Morton's making.'

'Giles! Is this true?' demanded Lady Wyvern angrily. 'You meant to jilt my dear little Agnes? After all we've done for you?'

'I am perfectly able to choose my own countess, thank you, Lady Wyvern. The Earl of Rossmore may look to the highest in the land for his bride,' retorted Giles loftily.

'But you are as good as betrothed to Agnes, as you well know!' cried Lord Wyvern heatedly. 'Why else do you suppose I've been franking you for all these years? And as to you Lord Trevingham, I shall never give my consent to your proposal! I am still my niece's guardian until she is five and twenty and you'll not see a penny of her money, if that's what you think to gain!'

'You are insulting, my lord!' replied Trevingham through gritted teeth. 'Anne and I love each other. Her money means nothing to me, I would to God she were penniless and I should not then have to listen to such vile imputations!'

'Gentlemen, gentlemen!' interrupted the lawyer. 'If the marriage contracts are not after all to be signed, shall we move on to the other business? I think my colleague has just arrived, so we may begin the reading of the will. Perhaps your private discussions could continue afterwards?' he suggested mildly.

'Very well, let's get on with it,' agreed Morton testily. 'The sooner the better as far as I am concerned and then I shall have every right to throw you all out of my house!'

The door was opened yet again by the over-worked manservant and another caller announced. 'Mr Colton to see you, sir,' said the valet wearily and tottered from the room.

'Good afternoon, ladies and gentlemen,' he murmured with a low bow and then approached the table. 'We may as well all be seated. There are any number of chairs set at this table,' he went on, setting down his leather case and unfastening it. 'It is a little unorthodox to have so many persons gathered who are unconnected with this business. Do you have any objection to their presence?' he enquired.

'I suppose not,' replied Mr Morton carelessly. 'It looks as if Trevingham will get his own way eventually and become one of the family, so pray continue, Mr Colton. I am beginning to find all this rather tedious.'

Mr Colton nodded at his partner. 'Please begin, Mr Jessup.'

The reading began and the hostilities were suspended, though tempers were still simmering on both sides of the table.

Mr Jessup cleared his throat and picked up a sheaf of papers. Perching his pince-nez more comfortably on the bridge of his nose, he commenced the reading of the last will and testament of the late Lord Edward Felix John Anthony, fifth Earl of Rossmore.

Morton yawned ostentatiously, apparently bored by all this hocus-pocus and only sat up and took notice when Mr Jessup started to list the late earl's properties. Finally he reached the part – ' "Hartsmere and all its demesnes, together with all other properties hereinbefore listed, all investments in the Funds and all monies deposited in my accounts in England, America and India, or such as may remain after my death, I do hereby will and bequeath to my only son and heir, James Edward Farenden Anthony, Viscount Deverell." '

There was the sound of sudden, sharply-intaken breath as those words rang out loud and clear in Mr Jessup's finely modulated tones, followed by a few seconds of stunned silence. It was Mr Morton who broke it, shrieking,

'What game are you playing with me, you scoundrels? You know very well that Deverell died years ago! How could he be the sole beneficiary? What of my claims and those of Lady Anne? She is Rossmore's daughter!'

'I am sorry to have to tell you that the fifth earl changed his will almost six years ago,' explained Mr Colton quietly. 'It was I who drew it up for him. Unfortunately, I have only recently returned to England to inform anyone of it. These documents only came to my hand this very morning.'

'But the viscount is dead, I tell you! He died in France during the Revolution! How can a dead man inherit anything?' protested Morton, growing red in the face with fury. 'You all know that he is dead!'

'I'm sorry to disappoint you, cousin but as you see I am very much alive!' came an amused voice from the doorway. 'I have been winged but not in the sense that you had hoped, or had you thought father and son now united in a warm embrace?'

'Count Fabricati!' cried his relatives in unison.

His tall, elegant figure framed in the dark doorway made him look larger than life. Poised only briefly on the threshold, he stepped further into the room, his handsome countenance alight with laughter at the look of shock and surprise on all their faces.

Lady Anne, as speechless as the rest of them, gazed on him with wonder and a gathering excitement that shook every fibre of her being. Avidly she drank in each detail of his face, recognizing now the similarity between the shape and colour of their eyes, the thick, dark hair with its tendency to curl and the straight Grecian nose.

He was exquisitely dressed as always, his long legs encased in immaculate pantaloons and glossy hessians with their elegant, gold tassels. A diamond pin glittered in the folds of his cravat and his coat was worn negligently about his shoulders, one sleeve hanging empty because his right arm was held across his broad chest in a black sling.

'Well, little sister? Have you no kiss for your long-lost brother?' he said with a tender, wistful smile.

'Brother?' whispered Lady Anne, her lips trembling with unimaginable joy. 'You are my brother? Oh dear God, I must be dreaming!'

Constance also was gazing at him in awed fascination, her heart thumping violently with the shock of his sudden and astonishing appearance in this house. She felt strangely light-headed as the thrill of his presence surged through her whole body. She, like Anne, felt a peculiar dream-like state numbing her faculties. She remembered her uncle's saying that Gérard adopted titles that were not his by right and wondered if perhaps this was another of his tricks.

Lady Anne rose from her chair and flew to his side. As he bent his dark head to kiss her, their resemblance seemed so striking that it was a matter for wonder that no one had remarked it before.

'You scheming, lying, conniving trickster!' exploded Morton, his temper almost at fever pitch. 'I don't know how you've managed to convince these poltroons that you are Deverell but you will not find it an easy matter to fool me! Fortunately, I am familiar with your deceitful methods of gulling poor simpletons! Kemsley here has described them to us quite openly. You are an imposter, sir and I shall see to it that you are brought to justice!'

'Calm yourself, Mr Morton. This will do no good. This gentleman's history has been thoroughly investigated, I assure you and it is quite certain that he is the sixth Earl of Rossmore,' said Mr Jessup, trying to pacify the irate young man.

Mr Morton, on hearing Mr Jessup use his newly acquired title in reference to this despicable usurper, turned on him venomously.

'He is not the earl, I tell you! I am! How dare you address him as such? I'll throttle anyone who calls him by that name!'

Lord and Lady Wyvern had been listening in wordless amazement to these exchanges, quite unable to believe their ears but at last they found their tongues.

'Can this possibly be true? Are you indeed my nephew?' cried Lord Wyvern, fumbling for his spectacles.

'You are Charlotte's son?' exclaimed his wife, astounded.

Wyvern put on his eyeglasses with shaking hands and stared intensely at the viscount's face.

' 'Pon my soul! I do believe it is Rossmore's whelp! I've never taken heed of you before, nor seen you clearly because I generally dislike to wear my spectacles in company. And that scar, of course, is very disfiguring but I can see now that you are the image of your grandfather. It's quite extraordinary!'

'I shall have to take your word for it, Wyvern; I've never had the dubious pleasure of knowing him. My grandmother was forever telling me how closely I resembled him in looks but she always assured me that there the resemblance ended, I thank God!'

'But we were informed of your demise years ago. Your father himself told us of it. He said you were killed the night the mob stormed your grandmother's house in Paris. It broke your poor mother's heart; she never quite recovered from the shock. I've often thought it was that terrible blow that hastened her end.'

'Happily, my time had not come to die. I was rescued from the chaos by my tutor, Father Benedict. He was my grandmother's family priest. The earl was informed of my survival, naturally; he even visited me once but he chose to conceal the truth for his own diabolical reasons.'

Mr Morton, listening unwillingly to this conversation began to feel a flicker of doubt and with it a gnawing fear.

'Don't listen to him! This is a grotesque invention of his! He is a plausible liar! Did he not lie to you about Fearnley? The marquis was never at Chailey in his life! This is a plot hatched between him and these avaricious lawyers. They are trying to trick me out of my inheritance! If this ridiculous tale were true, don't you think he would have spoken before today?'

'I had no desire to inform anyone of my true identity,' replied Deverell coldly. 'It is twenty years and more since ever I named that evil reptile "father". I would not acknowledge the relationship now, save for Mr Colton and Trevingham. They gave me two excellent reasons why I should set aside my vow and take the name of Rossmore once again.' He looked at Constance and his sister as he spoke.

'It has yet to be proved to my satisfaction that you are entitled to bear that name!' scoffed Morton.

'We have all the necessary documents and other evidence to substantiate this gentleman's claim. And I too, remarked upon the indisputable likeness to the fourth earl when first I set eyes on *Mr Farenden* as he was then known to me. He is almost the twin of his grandfather when he was the same age. There was once a portrait hanging in this very room, which would have proved my point. He is most certainly of the Rossmore blood.' He turned to Deverell. 'You remember how startled I was when I first saw you clearly at your lodgings in Rome? My eyesight had suffered somewhat in that prison and I, like Lord Wyvern, am at something of a loss without my eyeglasses. But as soon as you stepped into the sunlight, I felt an old, distant memory stir somewhere in my enfeebled brain. However, it was not until young Trevingham united Mr Farenden with Count Fabricati that I was absolutely certain that I had at last found the man I had been seeking all these long months.'

'Yes! I remember that portrait!' intervened Lord Wyvern excitedly. 'My sister had it removed to the attics along with several other family likenesses. She couldn't stand the sight of any of 'em after that dreadful scandal and the news of your death, Deverell.'

'Well, don't bother to have them resurrected on my account, I beg of you,' replied his nephew with a comical look of dismay. 'Dust to dust, you know.'

Morton grew afraid. Wyvern was already convinced! He could suddenly feel his new-found wealth slipping from his grasp.

'But he killed a man!' he shouted accusingly. 'He's a murderer!'

'I confess to having been responsible for Dupois' death,' replied Deverell coolly. 'But I think you are a little harsh to call it murder, Mr Morton. You see, I prefer to look upon it as an execution. *Necessitas non habet legum.* My French blood demanded that. However, Monsieur Dupois thought himself a gentleman and so I gave him the opportunity to die like one. My English blood demanded that.'

Morton fell into silence, his thoughts darting hither and thither like a shoal of fishes as he strove to find a way to rid himself of this hated opponent.

'Am I to understand that I have been employing the son

and heir of the Earl of Rossmore, as one of my secret agents?' laughed Lord Kemsley delightedly. 'Well! You certainly pulled the wool over my eyes, young man and there's not many have done that successfully, I can tell you!'

'Yes, Uncle,' interposed Justin, hugely amused by Lord Kemsley's astonishment. 'I only knew of it myself this morning when Mr Colton revealed the secret. I have been longing since then for this moment, when I could see the looks on all your faces!'

'So you were a secret agent, were you, my lord?' remarked Lady Wyvern, her eyes narrowing thoughtfully. 'No wonder then, that you were an adept at deceiving everyone in that deplorable way. You must be perfectly accustomed to using such underhand methods to gain your own ends.'

'It is second nature to me,' he admitted unashamedly. 'And when we are angling after a large fish, sometimes it requires a deal of cunning to land him in our net, as I am sure you will agree, my lady.'

She bristled visibly at this retort, eyeing him suspiciously. Then seeing how his eyes danced impishly, her face relaxed into a sudden, unexpected smile.

'Do you know, nephew, you and I might deal very well together, I begin to think.'

He bowed. 'Indeed I hope we may.'

'I suppose that business with Fearnley was of your arranging? Though I am still not quite certain how you contrived the whole,' she remarked with a puzzled frown. 'How did you manage to outwit me?'

'Madam, you made it irresistible to me,' he answered frankly. 'And I think I may say that my moves were just a trifle more judicious than yours.'

'My lord,' intervened Mr Colton in his usual quiet manner, 'perhaps I may be permitted to explain this rather peculiar situation to everyone?'

'Very well, Mr Colton, I suppose you must. I shall be only too relieved to leave the telling of this Gothic tale to you.'

The newly proclaimed earl seated himself between his sister and Miss Trevingham. He met Constance's shining eyes with such glad warmth in his own that her heart leapt wildly.

Mr Colton took up a stance in front of the empty hearth and commenced his recital.

'Six years ago, I was summoned to India by the late Earl of Rossmore. He had written to me on a matter of urgent business, which necessitated my travelling immediately to his house in Calcutta. When I arrived there, he invited me to dine with him and during the course of the meal, he asked me what I knew of the circumstances surrounding the loss of his only son. I admitted I had heard that he had died in Paris, along with his paternal grandmother, when her house was attacked by the rioting mobs that once rampaged through that unfortunate city. "Yes," he said, "that is the accepted story. I left him with my mother because his own was not fitted to the task of bringing up a Rossmore. She was an over-fond parent and would have turned him into a milksop with her constant mollycoddling! I wanted my son to be a man to be reckoned with, a man like his father! Well now, Colton," he went on, "I shall let you into my little secret. The viscount is still very much alive, or at least he was a few months ago. I see you are all amazement, I thought you would be. The boy was rescued from the débâcle by my mother's priest, one Father Benedict. The good father's own life was also in great jeopardy at that time and so he took the child to an old acquaintance of mine – a Monsieur Gérard. He and I were wont to enjoy the many and varied delights of Paris together. Gérard had a son, born on the wrong side of the blanket. He was about the same age as my own whelp but had succumbed to a fatal illness. The priest thought it would be a simple matter for Gérard to exchange the boys' identities and using the dead child's papers, take young Deverell into Spain. Gérard was easily persuaded, doubtless he thought I would pay him handsomely for his trouble, he could usually turn any situation to his advantage. But to continue. Gérard succeeded in bringing my brat safely to the abbey at Toledo, where the priest eventually managed to join them. It was Gérard who informed me of the happy news of their arrival but I was not so foolish as to believe anything he chose to tell me. I came to Toledo to see if for once in his life he spoke the truth. Imagine my surprise when I found that it was indeed so!

' "Now, to explain the rest I shall have to take you further into my confidence, Colton, but it cannot be avoided. Besides, it matters nothing to me to have your good opinion. I had suspected for some time, despite her denials, that my dear wife was enjoying an *affaire de coeur*. Chancing one day to come upon her with her inamorato – and in my own house, mark you! – I taught the impudent dog a lesson! Unhappily for me, the king took my justifiable zeal in aversion and I was forced to cool my heels as far from England as possible. I went to America where I own several hundred acres of Virginia. It was here that Gérard finally tracked me down. Now to my exquisite revenge! I chose to tell my wife and the world in general, that the viscount was indeed dead. It was the perfect way to punish her for all the trouble she had brought upon me. As I mentioned earlier in this narrative, she doted on the child.

' "I also told Deverell that his dear mama was dead and that I had no desire to saddle myself with an unfledged halfling. I gave the priest some money for the boy's upkeep and placed him in the care of the brothers at the abbey, until such time as I decided to send for him. The years passed and I put him from my mind. I had a daughter also, or so I heard, enough of a Rossmore to support my wife's claim that I had sired the girl. So I suppose she had some consolation for her loss after all.

' "One day, a visitor was announced – Viscount Deverell, no less! By now he had reached his majority and had escaped the confines in which I had placed him. I immediately guessed his reason for coming to see me. Undoubtedly he had come to claim his inheritance. However, it transpired that Gérard had revealed my little deception concerning my wife's demise. The blackguard had applied to me for funds and as I had not seen fit to oblige him, he had acted against me. I was therefore put to the inconvenience of dealing with an incensed youth, determined to bring me to account. I argued that there was little point in quarrelling over something that was past helping and besides, the woman was by now beyond all earthly cares so what did it matter? Alas, he refused to see my point of view and I was obliged to defend myself.

' "Being of like temper, we fought then and there. But my years were against me and I found myself in the singular position of suing for mercy! The young devil had his sword at my throat, damn his impudence! Happily for me he had not the backbone to press home his advantage. Instead he informed me in no uncertain terms, that he never wanted to set eyes on me again. He cursed me foully to my face – called me an abomination! – and then swore that he meant to sever our connection completely. He repudiated my name, he said, then dared to tell me that I had stained it to such a degree that he would find it a burden and an embarrassment to bear it any longer. Then he made the mistake of turning his back on me. He really thought he could speak to me – to me! – as if I were a common lackey! I gave him good reason to remember whose blood flowed in his veins! The devil marks his own, Mr Colton!

' "Now to conclude, for I grow weary of all this. After our quarrel, I decided to have a will drawn up that would enable me to leave such of my estate as was unentailed, to my daughter. The rest would go to some obscure relative of mine. However, it came to my ears that my wife's relatives were planning to lay their hands on my property, by arranging a marriage between their daughter and my unknown kinsman.

' "I mean to put a stop to such pretensions by altering my will again. I want you to draw up the necessary papers for me to sign. My sole beneficiary is to be my son Viscount Deverell. He thinks he can go his own way, does he? I'll show him who has the last word! I shall force my name down his throat! I shall die happy knowing that it will be like to choke him!"

'I did as he instructed me and prepared the papers for his signature. When all was done he took them into his own keeping and gave me leave to return home, further charging me with the unenviable task of trying to trace his son.

'I left immediately he had freed me from my

obligations, having no desire to remain a moment longer in his vicinity and wishing that I might never set eyes on him again. He had given me to understand that Father Benedict would give me any assistance I might need in my search for the viscount, so I proposed to take ship for England and begin my investigation.

'Unfortunately for me, the ship on which I was voyaging was wrecked in the Bay of Naples but being, by the grace of God, brought safely to shore I found myself taken prisoner by the French. It was as I languished in that miserable condition, that heaven sent a friend to succour me. The gentleman who rescued me from that hell into which I had fallen, was named Farenden. I did not know it then but I had met the very man I sought. I had been informed by the earl that his son was using the name of the Frenchman who was assumed to be his real father, Monsieur Gérard. And so I remained in ignorance of my saviour's true identity until a few days ago.

'After Mr Farenden had returned me to my family and as soon as I was well enough, I wrote to Father Benedict at Toledo, explaining my purpose and requesting him to furnish me with any information he might have as to the viscount's whereabouts. It was he who gave me the incredible news that Deverell was now living in Italy under the name Farenden! He told me I would know him by the scar on his left cheek which was a permanent and unmistakable means of identification. Furthermore, he had in his possession an ancient and valuable gold ornament which had belonged to his grandmother's family, the Beaurois. That same jewel which had been described to me in great detail, I saw this very morning and was told that it belonged to a *Count Fabricati*. This additional mystery was solved only a few hours ago, when I finally obtained an interview with Lord Trevingham whom I knew to be Mr Farenden's intimate. It was he who brought me to meet Viscount Deverell at long last! Between us we persuaded him to forget his vow and return with us to lay claim to his rightful inheritance.'

'And the devil of a time we had of it too!' exclaimed Trevingham. 'I never knew a man could be so reluctant to lay his hands on a fortune!'

'If my sister had not been in such extremes, I would never have allowed myself to be persuaded,' retorted the new earl. 'But when Mr Colton pointed out that I would be her legal guardian, it seemed that I could not refuse that title.' He smiled fondly at his sister. 'I never even knew of your existence until I came to London. I was never so amazed in all my life as when you appeared at Almack's with your uncle and aunt. Your resemblance to our dear mama, as I remember her, was quite a shock to me. I dared not make myself known to you as I had to retain my identity as Count Fabricati until our work was completed. But I was eager to know everything about you. I soon discovered that you were as much in love with Justin as he was with you and when it seemed that you might be forced to marry against your natural inclinations, I decided to intervene. I could not stand by and see you enter a marriage that would have made you as unhappy as our mother. Despite my fears that my uncle might recognize me, I did all I could to encourage this very proper English gentleman to carry you off as his bride. But he needs must insist on considering the proprieties! Now I am obliged to intervene yet again. I'm sorry, Uncle but I intend to overset all your schemes for acquiring a coronet for Anne. As her guardian I shall see that she weds the man who has won her heart. Yes, Justin, you have my blessing. You may place your banns when you will.'

Lady Anne gave a cry of delight and hugged her brother joyfully before running into her lover's eager embrace.

Lady Trevingham sighed happily and surreptitiously wiped a tear from her affectionate eye.

'As to you, Morton,' continued the earl, turning from this scene of tender emotion, 'you deserve that I should call you out! But you might evade me again,' he said with a wicked grin. Morton opened his mouth to express his indignation at this calumny but Rossmore held up a quelling hand. 'No, don't keep rising to my lures, Giles. I mean to forget our differences. I have decided to give you the East India property. You will be able to live like a rajah there, which will suit your temperament admirably. We are distant cousins, after all and I intend to keep us that way!'

'That is very generous, Rossmore,' muttered Giles, swallowing his pride. He had expected to come out of this with nothing and he could not afford to reject this offer out of hand. Besides, such a life might indeed suit him very well. He might even become something of a nabob and that thought was very pleasant to contemplate.

Mr Jessup gave a discreet cough. 'Ahem! My lord, I wonder if you would be willing to sign these papers and then Mr Colton and I can leave you in peace?'

'Very well, Jessup,' smiled the earl, accepting the quill pen he was proffered, 'you have my full attention.'

When the business had finally been transacted, Lady Trevingham invited them all to return with her to Albemarle Street to drink a toast to the newly engaged couple.

Mr Morton very naturally refused and took his leave of them. Lord Rossmore addressed his uncle and aunt. 'I would like it very much if you would accompany us, Uncle. There have been enough quarrels in my family and I mean to pursue a different course, if possible.' He held out his hand and Lord Wyvern unhesitatingly placed his own in it.

'I am of the same mind, Rossmore. I will come and make my peace with Lord Trevingham too.'

'Yes, indeed,' agreed his wife, taking the earl's arm as he offered to escort her to her carriage. 'You have yet to meet your cousins, Rossmore. Agnes in particular will be so excited! Such a dear, sweet-natured girl. I'm sure you two will get on famously!' she enthused.

'I daresay we shall, Aunt,' he smiled disarmingly. 'I was thinking I might introduce her to a friend of mine, the Marquis of Fearnley. What do you say to that?'

She met his eye with an answering twinkle in her own. 'Checkmate?' she suggested, finally conceding the game.

As they all returned to their carriages, the earl waited by the door to see them off. When Constance made to take her leave, he held her back. 'I shall be driving you home,' he said authoritatively. She opened her mouth to protest at such overbearing manners but catching his eye, suddenly decided not to pursue the matter.

Having watched them all depart, he closed the door at last and led her back into the now empty room.

'Come here, Constance,' he said, leading her towards the great fireplace. She did not rebuke him for making free with her name but meekly obeyed and stood looking up at him questioningly.

He reached up and removed the dust sheet from the huge picture hanging above the mantel.

Constance gasped in surprise as she saw the portrait of a beautiful woman dressed in a magnificent brocade gown embroidered all over with pearls. She had the earl's lustrous, dark eyes and they seemed to look down upon her, as if amused by her wonderment. Then her eye fell on the gold order fastened to the lady's bosom. The artist had painted it in minute detail and it seemed to glow against the blue sash that crossed her breast.

'That is the Countess Hélène, my grandmother. She was a great lady of a noble and ancient French family. That jewel she wears so proudly was part of her family's history. The rest of the collection she hid in the cellars of her house in Paris. Father Benedict retrieved them and they are now in his keeping until I choose to send for them. But this one she gave me with her own hand, taking it from her gown on the night that the mob invaded our home. She pinned it inside my shirt. She refused to leave the house. "We Beaurois always stand our ground", she said. "I shall contrive." Then she bid me go with Father Benedict and I never saw her again. How much more gracious her gift of remembrance, than this.' He briefly touched his face, his eyes still fixed on the beautiful countenance above him. 'I'm glad the portrait still hangs in this house.'

Constance stared at him in horror. She lifted her hand to his cheek and laid it gently against the vicious scar.

'This is your father's doing,' she said softly, her voice a mixture of anger and pity.

He smiled caressingly down at her. 'This is the Earl of Rossmore, his mark,' he murmured, placing his slender fingers over her own small hand. Then turning his head towards it, he pressed a tender kiss in her palm.

'Have you forgiven me enough to wear the keepsake I gave you?' he asked in a low voice.

She withdrew her hand from his warm clasp and slipped her shawl off her shoulders. Glittering against the delicate muslin of her dress was the gift he had given her at their parting.

'Sophy was wearing it this morning. She found it in my jewel case. I was consumed with the most ardent and dreadful jealousy when I saw that she had taken it. The violence of my feelings was such that I knew I still loved you, despite all that had happened. I could no longer pretend that it was otherwise. Having once given my heart, I found it impossible to retrieve it. It was lost to you forever. That is why I wear this gift you gave me over the place where once it beat in lonely solitude.'

'Perhaps I ought to tell you that, according to the traditions of my noble French ancestors, this jewel passes at death to the heir's chosen bride. My choice has fallen on a lady as brave as the one who last wore it. Constance, my darling, I had meant to be noble and allow you to find a husband more worthy of you. Monsieur Gérard has a somewhat tarnished reputation, alas. That is why I left you so abruptly after Christmas. But when I met you again and saw how you tried to save me from Morton's spite, despite all the evidence against me, I could not bear to let you disappear from my life. Can you still be so forgiving and overlook my past faults? Will you do me the very great honour of becoming the next Countess of Rossmore?'

'I would have been just as happy to become the next Mrs Gérard,' she answered lovingly.

'Ah, yes,' he laughed wickedly, 'except there never was a previous Mrs Gérard, the lady having settled for the *carte blanche*.'

'I suppose I must hope that you do not adhere so tenaciously to the family traditions of your ignoble French ancestors,' she smiled saucily.

'Then you will settle for being a countess?' he prompted hopefully. 'Even though you must become a Rossmore?'

'My darling James, I will settle for just being your wife. I leave the choice of name entirely to you.'

'I shall only require you to change yours once,' he grinned. Then pressing her close to his heart, he murmured tenderly, 'So this is not goodbye?'

'Not if you love me too, James,' she replied coyly, laying her head against his shoulder and peeping up at his face.

'*Si cara, t'amo moltissimo. E per sempre. Je t'aime avec tout mon coeur.* Yes, I love you, my dear one, heart, soul and body,' he assured her passionately.

Her eyes, reflecting the depth of her feelings, shone more brightly than any jewel and seeing that look, his arm tightened about her. Slowly he bent his head until his lips met hers, in a kiss that expressed far more than any words could ever tell.